COAL

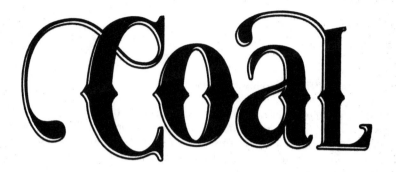

COAL

**J. JASON
GRANT**

Kensington Publishing Corp.
kensingtonbooks.com

HOLLOWAY HOUSE CLASSICS are published by

Kensington Publishing Corp.
900 Third Avenue
New York, NY 10022

All Kensington titles, imprints, and distributed lines are available at special quantity discounts for bulk purchases for sales promotion, premiums, fund-raising, educational, or institutional use.

Special book excerpts or customized printings can also be created to fit specific needs. For details, write or phone the office of the Kensington Sales Manager: Kensington Publishing Corp., 900 Third Avenue, New York, NY 10022. Attn. Sales Department. Phone: 1-800-221-2647.

HOLLOWAY HOUSE CLASSICS is a trademark of Kensington Publishing Corp.

KENSINGTON and the K with book logo Reg. US Pat. & TM Off.

ISBN: 978-1-4967-5528-5
ISBN: 978-1-4967-5529-2 (ebook)

First Kensington Trade Paperback Printing: May 2025

10 9 8 7 6 5 4 3 2 1

Printed in the United States of America

The authorized representative in the EU for product safety and compliance is eucomply OU, Parnu mnt 139b-14, Apt 123
Tallinn, Berlin 11317, hello@eucompliancepartner.com

I dedicate this novel to:
My daughters Kathy, Delani, and Donna.
Then last but not least, and most especially, to a dynamic
Grecian lady, Vasiliki.

Foreword

While the Black presence in the Old West has been well documented, that presence is still largely unknown to the average American. From *The Lone Ranger* and *Gunsmoke* of early TV fame to enduringly popular music like Bon Jovi's "Wanted Dead or Alive," the images, themes, and storytellers have been predominantly white. So few and far between have been the commercially and culturally significant works portraying people of color in Western-inspired, mainstream roles that not even Beyoncé could ascend country music's mountain after introducing her alter ego "Cowboy Carter."

Perhaps it shouldn't surprise us then that the most prominently showcased concept of white masculinity in America's history would be the least accepting of outsiders. Cowboys carried pistols. Cowboys roamed the land without restriction. Cowboys had sex with white women. Those three traditions remain among this nation's least-endorsed privileges for men of color, even when practiced lawfully. Well into the third decade of a no-longer-new millennium, there is still fear of what Tzvetan Todorov labeled "the Other." It is the same unfounded fear that Indigenous, Latino, and Black lives stirred in early white settlers who deemed darkness and difference a double threat. The very icon of the Western film genre, an unrepentant racist born to the name of

Marion, but better known as actor John Wayne, even spoke openly of his real-life bigotry off-screen. While acting, his characters juxtaposed the savage, criminal imagery of darker people. One can surmise that he supported the message.

Yet, despite the utter ignorance of Wayne, many of his generation—and sadly, many in their collective lineage living today, righteous frontiersmen in the United States—weren't all of European descent. In fact, historians have estimated that a full quarter of the cowboy population was Black. Whether author J. Jason Grant knew this is uncertain. What is certain, though, is that his Western tale of the character whose name is inspired by his skin helps reclaim frontier-inspired literature for a broader audience: *Coal* makes a compelling contribution to the true Americana from which the popularity of cowboys originates.

Written along the country's timeline and within the context of major historic events, Grant's plot emerges at the devastating moment of an enslaved child's separation from his family. What Grant creates from there is a masterful road-to-revenge fantasy Western-style, filling pages with powerful irony as Coal's hateful owner becomes his most crucial mentor. Grant's visual description, symbolism, and careful sensibility to assign characters of all races a sense of humanity give the novel a soul that adds layers to the horse-riding and trigger-filled action. The author even pays tribute to the original American cowboys, the Spanish-descended vaqueros—who, like Coal, were darker than John Wayne. As a result of so much texture, Grant's story, originally published in 1978, feels more elegant than the average Western, but lacks not an ounce of grit.

Ultimately, Coal himself is revealed as a classically fearless cowboy with honor, pride, determination, and all the traits of a traditional hero. His blackness is both feared—like that of death—and admired, like that of a clear midnight sky. Through not only his outward appearance, but his inner complexities,

Grant's title character embodies the larger intrigue of Old West legend. It was a land where both ex-slaves and the Indigenous helped make history, a place to which they can lay claim.

—Eddie B. Allen, Jr.,
author of *Low Road: The Life and Legacy of Donald Goines*

Coal

Chapter 1

Countless minuscule particles of dust performed a dreamlike dance in thin rays of sunlight that filtered through the dilapidated structure of a southeast Texas barn, in the year 1836. Two sweating and bearded men stood transacting the sale of human beings.

"Ah guess that does it, Solomon Pinkney. You sure you don't want to sell that thar boy along with them two breedin' females? Ah'll pay you a handsome price for him, like say another thousand added to the fifteen hundred Ah jes' handed you."

"No sale, Mr. Lassiter, 'cause Ah'll be needin' him. But if'n ya still are of a mind to, Ah will join ya in that drink ya suggested a while back."

"Sure enough, Solomon, Ah'll be glad to. Kin we leave'm here till we git back?"

"Ah don't see why not. Ain't but so far they kin go with them chains on 'em. Come on."

They left the barn, carefully locking the exit on the two chained females and the small lad whose smoldering eyes belied his six years of age. Immediately after hearing the lock click into place, the shackled black woman beckoned with outstretched arms to the boy, who raced to her. Speaking very softly to him, she placed one hand over his eyes to block out the blatant hate revealed there in the eyes of a mere child.

"Coal baby," she whispered, "please, son, listen to yo' momma. Don't ya nevah, evah, let Mistuh Pinkney ketch ya lookin' and showin' wit' ya eyes what Momma knows is in ya heart. He'll whip ya to death if'n he evah sees dat!"

"Shit on Mistuh Pinkney, Momma!" he cursed. "If'n Ah was a man growed, Ah'd kill his no-good ass fo' sellin' you'n Becky."

"Hush, baby, please," she pleaded, frightened with motherly concern for her offspring. "Coal, you is only a baby, and them ain't no fit feelin's ta have in yo head."

"Momma, Ah ain't no baby no mo'. And even if Ah'm li'l right now, Ah ain't gonna stay li'l. Momma," he began to cry, "when Ah's growed, Ah's gonna sho-nuff kill his stinkin' ass fo' sellin' you'n Becky away from me," he vowed. "Momma, ain't Ah evah gonna see y'all no mo'?"

"If'n God be willin', Coal son," she murmured in utter despair.

"Oh Momma, Ah's gonna miss y'all so much, 'cause Ah loves ya and Becky too," he cried, as his ten-year-old sister moved closer to hug him for the last time.

"We knows dat, son, and we loves ya back jes' as much, li'l Coal. We's gon' think of ya foevah, ain't we, Becky child?"

"Yes, Momma," a tearful Becky concurred. "But li'l Coal, you do what ya jes' promised. When you's a man growed, you make'm pay fo' doin' dis, li'l Coal. You make'm pay fo' splittin' us up!"

"You hush yo mouth, Becky. Son, promise yo Momma dat ya won't do nuthin' dat'll make Mistuh Pinkney flog ya, and dat ya won't evah forgit yo Momma and Becky."

"Ah promise, Ah promise, Momma. And Ah promise somethin' else, too. Afta' Ah kills 'em, Ah's gonna find y'all and make ya free. Ah promise ya dat, Momma."

"And we'll be waitin', son Coal. Wherevah we be at, son, we'll be waitin'. Hush now, Momma hears dem comin' back," she cautioned.

When Solomon Pinkney reentered, they found the tear-stained

trio clinging together. He and Lassiter then had to forcibly pry the man-child away from the arms of his mother and sister. As Lassiter herded the wailing duo out to his wagon, Coal cried out in heartbroken agony. "Bye, Momma! Bye, Becky! Bye, Momma, bye! Momma!!!" he howled, as Pinkney held him fast.

The black-bearded Pinkney did not release his grip on Coal until long after Lassiter and the boy's family were far out of sight. When he did so, the frantic youngster wheeled on him with fury in those big black eyes. "Why fo' you sell my momma and sister?!" he demanded, unafraid, as tears rolled down his soft ebony cheeks. "Why fo', ya sonofabi—"

He never completed his statement as the big callused left hand of Pinkney struck the side of his skull. For long seconds, objects inside the barn moved crazily about, as young Coal's senses went lopsided.

"For as long as you live, little nigger, don't ya ever speak to this white man in that tone of voice. Ah don't ever have to explain shit to you. Not ever. Ya understand that?!"

Coal shakily rose to his feet, but he did not reply. Solomon stared at him hard, before climbing up into his wagon bunk to take a nap.

Hours later, when he awakened, a cold chill swept the course of his spine. Perched atop the driver's seat and staring at him with unblinking eyes was the lad Coal. Solomon had seen that particular expression before, but never in the eyes of a boy. This was what unnerved him. Getting up, he left the wagon to relieve himself out back. When he returned, there was Coal exactly where Solomon had left him, staring.

Casually strolling to the front of the wagon, he suddenly reached up and collared Coal, snatching him from the wagon seat. Kneeling, he pulled the boy up close to his face, and Coal smelled his breath of whisky and stale tobacco.

"Now Ah'm gonna say this jes' once, Coal. If'n ya was a man, and I caught ya lookin' at me that way, Ah'd kill ya quick. Now listen good. You're six now, but if'n ya wants to git to be seven, boy, Ah'd better not ever see that look again. Ah knows that ya don't like what Ah did this mornin', but that's the way it is. Your momma and sister was costin' me more'n they was worth, so Ah sold 'em, and that's that. I'm a gunsmith, and in my trade, your momma and Becky was useless. I kin teach it to you, and in time you'll be of some help. There ain't no point in frettin' about them goin', they're gone. You understand?"

"They ain't nevah comin' back?" Coal asked.

"Never!" came the reply, as he released Coal's shirt and stood up. "Now help me git them horses hitched, Ah've had enough of this town."

In the turmoil-filled history of early Texas, no single year held more violence, bloodshed, racial hatred, and chaos than did Coal's sixth year upon this earth. Texans were arrogantly persistent in their demands for annexation from the Republic of Mexico, which the Mexican government and Congress adamantly refused. Thirteen years prior—through diligent perseverance and tact—Stephen F. Austin persuaded the Mexican Congress to grant his entreaties to form an American settlement in Texas. They rendered him an enormous land grant in east Texas, with the understanding that Austin would settle three hundred pioneer American families there. The Americans were subsequently to become Mexican citizens and Roman Catholics. This was to officially begin its implementation in 1823.

By 1836, upward of thirty thousand Anglo-Americans had flooded into Texas. Many of them were farmers and settlers, but others were rabble, outlaws and other assorted mercenaries seeking fortune, causing the Republic of Mexico no little consternation. Forays by armed bands of Texas raiders and Mexican bandoleros were alternately conducted with bloodcurdling continuity, outraging the Officer Corps of the Mexican Army. General Antonio López de Santa Ana Pérez de Lebrón's subsequent annihilation of the Alamo and all of its 183 defenders was a direct ramification of those deadly forays.

Terrible, bloody clashes ensued as the Texas-Mexico war raged on, and in September of 1836, Texans voted for independence from Mexico with hopes of joining the United States of America. Ninety days afterward, the arrogant Texas Congress served notice to Mexico that the Rio Grande was forevermore the boundary line marking the Texas-Mexico border. This bold declaration by the lawmakers of Texas was then compounded by them. They openly encouraged the merciless acts of piracy perpetrated upon Mexican shipping by unrestrained American sea captains, and national animosity toward the United States rapidly soared throughout Mexico.

On top of that, Texans also found themselves entrenched in other fierce battles away from the Mexican border. These savage confrontations were of another sort, with a different, bold, dangerous, and courageous enemy. The Naconas, Yampiraka, Kotsotekas, and Kwahadi Comanches, comprising the Comanche Nation, and their allies the Kiowas. Most of the settlements then existing inside Texas were manned by civilians, and they were no match for the disciplined, swift-moving Comanche warriors. This, then, was one of the major reasons why all of Texas was so hell-fired anxious to become a part of the United States, assuming that once they fell under the protection of the big guys in Washington, Cavalry troops would then be dispatched to help combat the Indian nemesis. Racial hatred soared during this period.

Texas newspapers did nothing to diminish the fervor of racism against non-whites. In fact, they encouraged it. One chronicle referred to Mexicans as "those abject genetic bastards of an imbecilic nation whom, like the mosquito, it is easier to kill than to tolerate its annoying buzzing." Indians and blacks suffered no less in the journals of that period; subsequently, prejudice and violent atrocities became an everyday mode of life. It was this atmosphere in which young Coal grew up under the domineering guidance and tutoring of the infamous gunsmith-gunfighter, Solomon Pinkney.

On Coal's thirteenth birthday, the gunsmith, who was also a much feared gunman, presented him with an unprecedented gift from a white man to a slave. The completely surprised Coal simply stared.

"Coal, young'n, Ah want ya should have this here six-gun. Ah mean for ya to wear it night and day. Sleep with it! Eat with it! Even shit with it on ya! Ah don't even wanna see ya take it off to wash your black ass. 'Cause you'll nevah learn to use it kerrectly until it becomes like an extra limb to ya. Now ordinarily, I would nevah even think of doin' somethin' like this. But you'n me, we be travelin' through them mean and wicked badlands, and hostile Injun territory. So in the future, if them blood-suckin' bandits or redskins come swoopin' down on me, it'll be a damn sight better to have two guns blazin' away at 'em than one. Ya git my meanin'?"

"Yessuh, Mr. Pinkney," he replied, still unable to remove his eyes from his gift.

"Alright. Now, Ah'm gonna learn ya how to git to it and git to it quick-like. And Ah don't mean to be repeatin' myself either, so when I tells ya somethin' about your six-gun, you'd better not forgit! In these here parts, a body ain't likely to git no second chance. Now listen to this, boy. Gittin' it is one thing, but hittin' what ya be shootin' at is another."

"Yessuh."

"Ya ain't too big, Coal, but Ah been noticin' that ya got unnatural large hands for a young'n your age, so ya should be able to handle it. It'll seem a mite heavy to ya at first, but that'll soon pass. Think ya kin handle it?"

"Yessuh, Ah kin handle it," he answered, giving one of the rare smiles he ever gave to Solomon, and experiencing a brand-new feeling that encompassed his entire young body.

Holding the newly made weapon in his hands, young Coal made himself a silent promise. *Ah'm gonna handle it alright, Solomon Pinkney, and when Ah'm sure that Ah'm as good as anybody evah was, Ah'm gonna give you a present. From Momma and Becky!*

In the summer of 1830, a terrible, bloody slave uprising took place in South Carolina. Many white slaveowners died before it was quelled, and their demands for guns were enormous. This was how Solomon Pinkney happened to be that far east and south of Texas. He traded his guns for the comely, young, black slave woman with the four-year-old girl and her newborn boy child she held in her arms. Never did he dream that one day he would place a gun in that child's hands, but he did, and that was the beginning of the end for Solomon Pinkney.

Chapter 2

Those next few weeks while on their way to Stirrup, Texas, old Solomon commenced with Coal's introduction to the six-gun. Strapped to his left thigh was a splendid handmade pistol, designed and perfected by Solomon himself, the exact mate of the one presented to Coal. Where weapons for killing were involved, the bearded gunsmith was a highly expert and talented man. Nothing in the multifaceted spectrum of firearms escaped his vast knowledge. Compounding this fact was his legendary reputation for using them without the slightest hesitation. This maker of death tools was a man of many moods, a man without family ties or roots. He gave less than a damn about anyone or anything, with the doubtful exception of the young black then seated beside him. Solomon's only joys were cards, guns, and bawdy women.

While selling his wares throughout the South and Southwest, Pinkney acquired the infamous reputation as a man who one walked around, a man who one did not rankle unless one was prepared to kill him. During the course of his travels, he encountered many gunslingers who thought him easy prey and subsequently stood over their graves while they got buried.

Having fashioned a gun belt to accommodate young Coal's slender waistline, Solomon decided to give Coal his first lesson in what was to become a daily ritual. Reining his animals to a halt, Solomon stepped down and called to the youngster. "You ready to learn how to handle that piece of yours?" he asked, and observed a light go on in those enormous black eyes.

"Yessuh, Ah'm ready," Coal eagerly replied.

"Then git down here, and let's git at it."

Coal leaped from the front seat to stand at the gunsmith's side. Solomon studied him for a prolonged moment, measuring the location of Coal's gun handle in connection with the lad's elbow and wrist. Adjusting Coal's gun belt, he stepped back.

"Now, how's that feel, better?"

"Yessuh," he answered, instinctively sensing that the way his gun handle was resting against the inside of his right wrist was the correct way.

"Now, young'n, don't concern yourself with speed right now. What ya have to concern yourself with is gittin' it out and pointed in one easy motion. Now try it."

With the six-gun appearing incongruous in comparison to his small body, young Coal did as Solomon requested, and the gunsmith's eyes caught something. "Do it again, Coal."

The lad braced himself and again pulled iron for the man who owned him. What Solomon's eyes detected was speed, a natural kind of speed, the kind which could never be taught.

"You been practicin' since the other day when I give you that gun?"

"Yessuh."

"How come, without me tellin' ya to?"

"Ya said it was mine, so Ah was foolin' 'round whilst ya was asleep sometimes."

"Hummph!" Solomon grunted, thinking about that. "Alright, let's see ya git it. Keep on gittin' it and puttin' it back into ya holster until Ah tells ya to stop."

For several minutes, the old gunfighter observed Coal slapping leather.

"Ah thought Ah told ya to forget about speed?"

"Ah did forget about dat. Ah can't help it."

"Ya can't, huh? Okay, now let's see what'cha do when ya tries to git it in a hurry."

Again the boy braced himself and drew. Solomon saw it, but he didn't believe it. "Coal, all them times when we be in them different towns, like Stirrup for instance, you been askin' Sheriff Tucker or somebody how to draw a six-gun?"

"No suh," Coal softly told him.

"Then how come ya kin git to it like that?"

"Ah dunno. First time Ah did it, it jes' happen."

Ah ain't gonna throw no praise at 'm, thought Solomon, 'cause Ah don't want him gittin' no wrong ideas. But as sure as cathouse pussy smells foul, that there boy is a natural-born gunslinger. For a split second there, old Solomon entertained the thought of taking Coal's six-gun and never giving it back to him again. He grudgingly reached into his vest pocket and withdrew six .44 shells. Handing them to Coal, he watched as Coal deftly inserted them into the pistol.

"How come ya knows how to do that so easy-like?"

"From watchin' you."

"Hummph! Think ya kin hit somethin' if Ah lets ya shoot a few?"

"Dunno, nevah tried."

"See that ol' tree stump over there?" he pointed. "Kin ya hit that?"

Up until then, Solomon had only worked with Coal on his draw, without any other instructions. Young Coal stepped away from his tutor, his eyes trained on that tree stump. Like a veteran gunhawk, Coal pulled iron and fired, missing the stump by a foot or more, frowning.

"Coal, young'n, ya wanna know what'cha done wrong?"

"Yessuh."

"Ya aimed after ya pulled."

"Dat's wrong?"

"For you it is. Ya see, for some men, that way is fine. But for one with unnatural fast hands like yours, it's all wrong. Ah knows, 'cause Ah had the same problem when Ah was a young'n. Coal, with hands like yours, ya aim before ya shoot, 'cause in your case, the hand is faster than the eye. Go ahead, try aimin' before ya shoot this time."

Doing as he was told, the lad grabbed his iron, instinctively crouching and then fanning the hammer with his left hand, sending four out of five bullets directly into the stump. *Ah'll be damned!* Solomon secretly marveled at the exhibition. Coal turned to face him, those eyes of his literally sparkling. "Dat better, Mistuh Pinkney?"

"For a tree stump, but don't go thinkin' you're up to takin' on a sho-nuff gunfighter, 'cause all that'll git'cha is killed."

A few days later found them in Stirrup, a town where Solomon had grown up as a boy. Coal was always glad whenever they stopped there, because Stirrup was also where Mr. and Mrs. Lars Munsen lived. Lars Munsen was the town blacksmith who had settled there some 30 years prior, fresh from Sweden with his wife. From the age of six, Coal had been befriended by the foreign couple. During those prolonged nights and days while Solomon was doing his gambling and whoring, he would leave his wagon in the Munsen livery stable with Coal in it. The blacksmith and his gentle woman never failed to take the lad into their own home, where they would bathe him, feed him, give him a warm bed to sleep in, and the only genuine affection he had ever received from anyone other than his mother. In no time at all, they grew to love him, and he them.

One afternoon while Solomon Pinkney was still away on his binge, young Coal encountered his first taste of violence born of prejudice. He was in the process of doing a few chores in the stable for Lars when a tall man halted near Solomon's wagon. He glanced inside, then looked around as if in quest of someone.

With him were three teenage boys, of which two were about Coal's age, and one appearing to be around sixteen or so. All three looked just like the tall man.

"Kin Ah help ya, mistuh?" asked Coal. He received a blatantly derisive appraisal, but no reply.

The boys began to laugh. Being a kid and wanting to be friendly with other kids, Coal smiled also. To his surprise, their mirth instantly ceased. He immediately sensed something awry but was too naïve to define it.

"Nigger, where's Solomon Pinkney, the white man who owns this gunware wagon?" the man snapped.

"He somewhere 'round town here," Coal replied, no longer smiling. "He left me here to take care o' his wares."

Coal was completely surprised to see the man's face grow red with fury. Coal's mind raced to his pistol inside the wagon, which Solomon had forbidden him to wear in town. The aroused anger he was then witnessing was simply there because Coal had omitted a "sir" in his reply.

"You belong to Mr. Pinkney, nigger?" the thin man wanted to know. Coal nodded, and the man collared him with excessive roughness.

Although Coal was only thirteen and indoctrinated into subservience from birth, the only man for which he held any degree of fear was Solomon Pinkney. He stared hard at the man.

"Ain't Pinkney ever taught you to say *sir* when you talk to a white man?!" He shook Coal, then raised his hand to strike him.

His wrist became suddenly locked from behind in a viselike grip, and the pain was real.

"Mister, you would not strike a mere child, would you?" It was Lars. For a long moment, Lars continued to squeeze the emaciated wrist before releasing him.

"Where the hell you get off helpin' a goddamn slave nigger?!" the man raged.

"He is not that to me, sir, merely a child," stated a simmering

Lars. "And, in my establishment, you will not use such language!"

"If I was a gunman, I would kill you for what you just did, Swede," he glowered.

"If. But since you are not, my advice is that you simply leave my place of business."

As the man and his sons headed for the door, the oldest boy turned a menacing glare on Coal. "We'll git you for this, nigger," he threatened. Coal just returned the glare.

Later that evening, Lars strolled across the unpaved street to have his customary evening's drink at Stirrup's main saloon. While there, he saw Solomon and told him of the earlier incident. Meanwhile, Coal was still at the livery feeding Lars's horses. He was almost through with his volunteered chores for Lars when he heard someone behind him. Turning, he was met by a clenched fist banging against his right eye, which evoked a burst of multicolored stars inside his head.

In pain, he covered his eye as he fell against the side of the stall. Out of his good eye, he saw the thin man's oldest boy prancing and taunting him. "Get up, li'l black sonofabitch, 'cause Ah'm gonna sho-nuff whup your ass!"

Coal charged at him, driving his throbbing head into the pit of the other's gut. They wrestled in the sawdust for a second before getting to their feet. Once upright, they tore into each other, with Coal getting the worst of it from the taller lad. He would swing and miss in anger, only to be punished with lefts and rights each time. Still he came on, backing Junior out into the street. Onlookers on foot and horseback halted to observe. If Coal had been grown, he would have been attacked or killed, but enjoying the excitement and witnessing the shellacking Coal was taking, the townsfolk rooted and laughed. By then Coal was bleeding from his nose and a busted lip.

Someone ran into the saloon just as old Solomon was raking in his winnings.

"Solomon Pinkney! If'n ya wants to save any parts of your nigger, you'd best git at it, 'cause he's gittin' the pure piss whupped outta his black ass!"

"Who's doin' the whuppin'?" Solomon asked, standing up.

"That oldest Wiggins boy, and he's sure puttin' somethin' on 'm."

Solomon broke through the crowd of cheering Texans, all of whom were rooting for Wiggins Jr. Lars went to intervene, but Solomon held him back. Coal was landing on his ass for the umpteenth time.

"And Ah'm gonna keep dustin' ya 'til ya says ya quit!" Junior boasted.

Enraged and bleeding, Coal went at him again, swinging and missing and getting hit unmercifully. Solomon stoically observed the one-sided affair and suddenly stepped in between them. "Time!" he said, smiling, bringing the cheering to a halt. "Shit folks, a fight as good as this one is, seems only right that we should git a li'l bettin' goin' on here."

His suggestion brought forth cheering agreement from the throng. "Y'all sees what's happenin' to my li'l nigger, but Ah wants to bet on him anyhow. Now who's gonna lay me two . . . maybe three-to-one?"

He received all the bets he could take on, and pulled a bloodied Coal off to the side. "Now listen Coal, forgit about Junior's head. Ya been tryin' to hit it, but bein' that he's a full head taller than you, he jes' keeps pullin' back, and you keep on missin' like a damn fool and damn near gittin' your head torn off."

"Dat's alright, Ah'll git his ass," Coal vowed.

"Sure ya will young'n, if ya does what Ah'm gonna tell ya. Forgit about his head, Coal, git into his middle and try to punch his guts out. Hit what'cha kin reach, boy. Git down low and put it to him," he advised, and then shoved Coal back toward Junior. "Time in!" yelled Solomon.

The boys began circling. Junior swung with encouragement

from his father, and Coal ducked down low, cutting loose with a punishing left to Junior's stomach. Totally surprised, Coal watched him fall to his knees. Straining, Junior regained his feet and charged Coal. Again Coal shot a fist into his stomach, making his face blanch, but he remained upright. One, two, three, four more punches landed, making Junior upchuck. Solomon and Lars had all they could do, tearing Coal off Junior. By now the crowd had become surly. Solomon collected his bets as Coal wiped his bloodied nose with his shirtsleeve.

"Now if there's anybody here who wants further satisfaction," stated an unsmiling Solomon, "take it up directly with me." His eyes roamed the crowd. Silence.

The old gunman remained in poised challenge until everyone dispersed. "Coal, young'n, seems like your six-gun ain't all Ah'll have to teach ya." Solomon looked down at him; counting his money, he headed for the cathouse without so much as examining Coal to see the extent of damage done.

Filled with moral indignation, a silently infuriated Lars watched the gunsmith stroll away. Reaching to his left, he placed one huge hand upon Coal's shoulder and gently pulled him to his side.

My Lord, thought Lars. *Why, he cares no more for the lad than he does for the animals that pull his wagon. Not even the human decency to inquire as to his welfare. No, he simply walked away and left him here bleeding. I must try to get Coal away from him, I must.*

"Come Coal, get your other trousers and shirt from the wagon, then I shall take you home and see what we can do about patching you up."

Without a word, Coal climbed up and gathered his belongings. While inside, he opened a trunk and grabbed his pistol and gun belt, folding his fresh clothing around it. When he was done, Lars locked up for the night, and they walked the short distance to his home. One glance at Coal and Benta Munsen went livid.

"God in heaven! Lars, who did this terrible thing to Coal?"

"Now settle down, Mother, it's not quite as bad as it appears. He'll look a lot better after we've cleaned him up a bit."

Mrs. Munsen was unaccustomed to anger, but she experienced it as she hugged Coal to her bosom. "Coal, son, was it Solomon who whipped you?"

"No ma'am. Ah was fightin'."

"With whom?"

"It was the oldest Wiggins boy, Mother," Lars answered.

"Ah whupped his butt, too," Coal added, just above a whisper.

Her eyes shot up at Lars, wondering how Coal's statement could possibly be true.

"That's right, Mother. We had to pull him off."

"Well, if he looks any worse than our Coal, he must be near dead."

Leaving them, she went to get medication for Coal's minor wounds. Lars placed water upon the stove to heat. Not long afterward, they had him cleaned and at the dinner table. During the course of dinner, Lars informed her of Solomon's act of indifference toward Coal.

"But how could he do such a thing? A cold and heartless man is that Solomon Pinkney. Coal, doesn't he ever show you tenderness?"

"No ma'am, and Ah don't want none from 'm," Coal told her, wincing as his fork touched that split lip. "Ah hates Solomon Pinkney for what he done long time ago. All the tenderness in the world ain't gonna change dat."

"Long time ago?" she questioned.

"Dat man," he continued, and his eyes began to fill, "h-h-he sold my momma!" Coal suddenly yelled. Then, "Mrs. Munsen, ma'am, Ah ain't hungry no mo'. Kin Ah go up to my room now please?" Tears of longing fell down his cheeks.

"Of course, son," she said, wiping at her eyes with her apron.

"Coal," Lars called just before he turned away, "wait just a second. Mother, I've been thinking . . ."

"Yes, Lars," she smiled, reading his mind. "There's a little over three thousand in our life's savings. Use it all, Lars, if you have to. See if we can get him for ourselves and raise him. Coal, son, if Lars can buy you from Solomon, would you want to stay with us . . . like our own?"

"Yes ma'am." He wiped at his eyes. "D-dat would be the bes' thing dat evah happen to me. B-b-but he won't sell me to Lars, Ah knows he won't."

"But how can you be so sure, son?"

"'Cause Ah knows him. If'n he was ta sell me to Lars, den he wouldn't have nobody to boss ovah," he enlightened them.

The boy's astute insight into the character of the slaveowner made them grow silent as they examined his statement.

"Still and all," Lars persisted, "I would not be able to live with myself if I did not try! Mother, Coal, I'll be back as soon as I have a talk with Solomon." Taking his hat from a living room peg, he left.

When the door closed behind him, Mrs. Munsen walked with Coal to the foot of the stairs.

"Coal, it's true, Solomon committed a truly devilish act by selling your mother and sister. But son, it ain't Christian-like to harbor such a fierce hate for anyone. Couldn't you find it in your heart to forgive him?"

"Not as long as Ah breathe."

"But Coal, if you were to grow to manhood with this hate eating at you, you'd wind up hating all whites, and all white folks ain't Godless like Solomon."

"Ah could nevah hate you and Lars, Mrs. Munsen, 'cause y'all ain't like real white folks. No disrespect, Mrs. Munsen, but if you was my real momma, could you forgive a man dat used ya and den put ya in chains and sold ya and then stole your baby?"

His eyes held her transfixed by what she saw there in them.

* * *

Those eyes filled with pain are no eyes for a child. Oh God, she silently prayed, make Solomon say yes. As for Coal's question, she could not honestly render a positive reply.

Coal received a gentle kiss upon his swollen cheek from her, and slowly climbed up to his bedroom. After closing the door behind him, he strapped on his six-gun. Standing in front of a full-length mirror with his knees slightly bent, he pulled iron. Turning his back after holstering his weapon, he took three steps only to suddenly turn and draw again. Gazing into the mirror, his bruised face broke into a wide grin. *It ain't so much as a body would notice, but Ah'm faster than Ah was last week.*

Lars Munsen searched high and low for Solomon Pinkney, finally catching up with him as he stood against the rear end of the bar in Stirrup's Take A Chance saloon. Solomon was laughing with a fairly young whore whose powdered face and painted lips starkly advertised her profession. The place stank of sour sweat and alcohol. Lars strode up to him and tipped his hat to the whore.

"Excuse me, ma'am. Solomon, if I may, I'd like to have a serious talk with you."

Old Solomon eyed the blacksmith, wondering what was on his mind.

"Sure, Munsen. Tillie, excuse us for a few minutes, huh?" The whore walked away, and Lars ordered drinks for himself and Solomon. "What's on your mind, Munsen?"

"Coal."

"What about 'm?"

"Well, my wife and me, we'd like to buy the youngster from you. You see, we are childless and getting on in years. Coal, well, he is loved by us, and we would purely consider it a blessing if you'd consent."

Solomon's eyes narrowed somewhat as he looked at Lars. "Munsen, Ah don't understand you or your wife. Love, ya say? You and your wife purely loves a nigger. Ya both must be crazy. Hold on, wait, before ya say anything more, 'cause Ah'm truly tryin' to hold on to my temper. Now Ah've been toleratin' him stayin' at your house and all, but makin' such a fuss over a nigger, any nigger, is wrong. Sure, Coal is brighter than any nigger Ah've seen, he kin read'n write'n count. All them things Ah taught 'm, but Ah didn't teach him so that he could live or be on a equal standin' with white folks. Ah did it so he could be of a help to me! Now if ya and your wife want to keep on playin' house with Coal whenever he's in town, that's alright, but don't ever approach me again wantin' to make a white man out of him. If he was white, Ah would have adopted him long ago. But he ain't. The answer is no, Munsen."

"Not even for three thousand?" Lars kept at him.

"Not for any price, now let's not talk about it anymore." The conversation was ended.

Wanting to strike him but well knowing that he would die for it, Lars turned on his heel and stalked away. Solomon watched him all the way through the door.

The instant Lars walked into his home, his wife read Solomon's decision upon his face.

"He is a despicable man," Lars told her, "and one day he shall meet a terrible end. Where's Coal?"

"He's been up in his room ever since you left. I don't think he's in bed yet."

Slowly trudging upstairs, Lars knocked and then entered. He found Coal holstered and standing in front of the mirror. Alarm consumed him as he misinterpreted Coal's intention. "Now son, that gun won't solve anything," he cautioned, making Coal smile at him.

"Not now it won't, but it'll be another story when Ah's a growed man."

"Explain what you mean, Coal?"

"Ol' Solomon give me this here six-gun, Lars. Dat same man dat wants ta keep me a slave forevah. Well, he don't know it yet, but he done give me my freedom ticket. When Ah'm sure dat Ah'm ready, my six-gun is gonna set me free forevah and evah."

The blacksmith observed as Coal continued to practice at the mirror, thoroughly awed by what he witnessed. Just into his teens, Coal handled his six-gun with fluid dexterity. Lars's eyes noticeably saddened as he silently prayed for Coal's well-being and ultimate freedom. Little did he or Coal know that before another day passed, young Coal would kill his first man.

Chapter 3

Early the next morning, when Coal and Lars arrived at the livery stable, they found Solomon already hitching up his wagon's team of horses.

"Mornin' Munsen, what do Ah owe ya?"

"Nothing," came Lars's curt reply.

Coal, realizing that they would be hitting the trail again, gritted his teeth in sad resignation.

"How come?" asked Solomon.

"The chores Coal has done for me has more than compensated for your team's board. Has he time to bid farewell to Mrs. Munsen, Solomon?"

"Sure, Munsen."

Reversing their tracks, they were soon back at the house. Mrs. Munsen was busy in her kitchen. Coal approached her with Lars at his back. "Mrs. Munsen, ma'am, Ah thanks ya for everything. Ah has to be goin' now."

She looked from one to the other, her eyes questioning.

"Yes, Mother," Lars concurred. "Solomon has his team about hitched. He's leaving town and taking Coal with him again."

"Did he say where he was going to or when he's coming back?" she asked, going to Coal and hugging him to her.

"No, Mother, he didn't say, and I didn't ask. I found it difficult to even speak to the bas . . . man," Lars caught himself before swearing.

"Coal," she murmured, stroking his back, "don't you fret none, son. We'll be right here always, and this is your home, too. Don't fret, little Coal, we love you. Will you remember that?"

"Yes'm."

"Coal, is there anything you'll need, son?" Lars queried.

"No suh. All Ah need is to get older to man-size," he said, making Lars recall what Coal had told him the night before, up in his room.

"Then you take care, son, and don't do anything foolish. Will you promise us that, Coal?"

"Ah promise. Gotta go now."

They watched him leave with tears in their eyes. "H-he'll be alright, Mother." Lars patted her. "Already he's more man than most I've known," he reassured her.

Stirrup was located between what was to become Fort Worth and Fort Richardson. Leaving town by the north road, Solomon aimed his horses northwest toward Kwahadi Comanche country. All day they rode in the summer heat with hardly any wind at all. Just around dusk, when Solomon's eyes were searching for a place to camp down, Coal spied three rugged and filthy riders off to his right.

"Three men comin', Mistuh Pinkney," he said, making Solomon's head swivel into the opposite direction.

"Shit!" Solomon cursed, sensing trouble. Coal's young body began to tingle as his baptism became imminent.

Solomon halted the heavily laden wagon some twenty feet from the riders. They observed the trio as their greedy eyes roamed over the wagon and their persons. Pulling the brakes into place, Solomon stepped down with Coal following him.

"What'cha got in that there wagon, Pilgrim? You're leavin' mighty deep tracks."

The gunsmith, with gunfighter's instinct, measured the two he sensed to be most dangerous of the three.

"What Ah got in my wagon ain't rightly none of your god-damn business!"

"Well, lookie there! Damn if his little nigger ain't wearin' a pistol! Y'all see that?"

They began to laugh, seemingly ignoring Solomon and his statement. The spokesman for the rabble called out to Coal. "Nigger, bring that there six-gun over here to me! Be quick about it! Pretty as it is, Ah'm sho-nuff gon' keep it for myself."

Coal never moved, his large eyes watching the man's hands. What he did do surprised the hell out of Solomon.

"Mistuh!" Coal yelled. "Kiss my ass!"

Without hesitation, they grabbed iron. The boy never appeared to move as his right hand magically filled and fired twice, sending two bullets into the robber's hairy chest. In that same instant, Solomon emptied two saddles with two head shots. Looking to his left at Coal, Solomon found him staring at the dead man he had just killed.

Solomon went to put a hand on Coal's shoulder and was shrugged off. Coal was desperately fighting the urge to vomit. In a trance-like state, he walked to stand above the corpse, and Solomon followed. The dead man's eyes were open. Coal gazed into them, only to turn and retch violently, again and again.

When he fully recovered, he discovered Solomon back up in the driver's seat. The three horses were then tied to the rear of the wagon.

"Kin Ah ride his horse?" he asked, and Solomon searched his eyes, wondering.

"Ain't them stirrups too long for ya, Coal?"

"It's easy enough to shorten dem up."

"Well, git at it, it's damn near dark. When you're done, ride up in front of the team where Ah kin see ya."

Shortly Coal was up in the saddle, and he rode where Solomon could see him. Later after pitching camp, they sat eating beef jerky and beans. In retrospect, old Solomon went over that day's events. *Ah was twenty at least before Ah was as good as that boy showed me today. Hot damn! Them two shots of his was no more'n one inch apart. Solomon ol' boy,* he mused, *ya might have to face that six-gun of his one of these days or nights. What then? Ah'll handle it, that's what Ah'll do,* he concluded.

"Coal."

"Yes suh."

"Tell me, jes' what was ya feelin' before we had to fire on them som'bitches?"

Coal thought about that for a moment or two. "Excited. Light-headed like."

"Ya wasn't scared at all?"

"Ah was only thinkin' dat dat man was gonna take my six-gun."

"Ya won't allow that, huh?"

"No suh, not 'less Ah be dead." Solomon's booming guffaw filled the night. Soon they were asleep.

Northwest from Stirrup lay the Staked Plains, smack in the heart of Comanche country, and that was precisely where Solomon Pinkney was headed with his heavy load. Many years before Coal was born, Solomon had taken a wife. No white person ever knew of his nuptial endeavor, and with good reason. She was a Comanche. One day at the age of twenty-three, Solomon had fearlessly gone hunting buffalo meat in Indian territory. He was immediately set upon by five young warrior Comanches. Although wounded in eight different places, he killed all five, then lapsed in unconsciousness.

Other braves arriving on the scene surveyed the evidence, concluding the unconscious Solomon had indeed fought bravely. Too bravely, in fact, for them to subsequently take his life. So, they spared it and carted him off to their nearby village. To the Comanche, a man who would not fight was in truth not a man to them. While recovering, he fell in love with the maiden who had nursed him back to health. Her name was Riva, and they were married for three years until she died in childbirth. The boy child died with her. Solomon made intermittent trips back to the Kwahadi stronghold, but he never stayed among them too long. After a while, he stayed away altogether. This trip would mark his first in thirty-one years. He did not doubt his safety, for he spoke their language fluently.

During an especially hot day on the way to Indian country, Coal spoke suddenly, giving the thinking Solomon a startle. "Mistuh Pinkney, when ya told me how to whup dat Wiggins boy, how come ya know'd dat?"

"Used ta be a prizefighter, Coal."

"Ya mean for money?"

"That's right, young'n. Was pretty good, too, 'til Ah got my nose ruined. Couldn't breathe too good after that, so Ah had to quit."

"How many men ya whupped?" Coal wanted to know, driving at something.

"Sixty-one."

"How many whupped you?"

"Ten."

"Hmmm," Coal pondered. "Will ya teach me, suh?"

"How many damn things ya want to learn at one time? Ya ain't nearly mastered your six-gun, ya know, whether you think so or not!"

"Will ya teach me, suh?"

Solomon eyed him. Coal was sure anxious enough. "Ya really want to learn how ta fight, do ya?"

"Yessuh. Ah'm strong even if Ah ain't too big. Dat Wiggins boy hit me more times, but Ah damn sho' hit him harder."

"Ah'll admit that, young'n," he agreed, remembering. Yes, Coal indeed could thump for his weight.

"Alright young'n, but Ah wants to get somethin' straight. Fistfightin' is somethin' jes' as serious as gunfightin', and damn near as fatal. While we're with the Comanches, there'll be plenty of time for ya to learn. If'n Ah don't miss my bet, you'll git plenty of fistfightin' time," he laughed, making Coal wonder at his meaning.

"We's goin' where the Comanches is?" he asked, wide-eyed.

"That's right."

"Why fo'?"

"None of your business. And, if'n ya gets into any fracases with them Indian young'ns as Ah knows ya will, ya are not to ever use your six-gun."

"Why not?"

Solomon frowned at him. "You're up to your ass in questions this mornin', ain't ya? Well, Ah'll tell ya why not. Indian boys your age ain't quite ready to become warriors yet, goddamnit, and if ya was ta shoot one of 'em, they'd fry your ass blacker than it is now!"

"Dat's why, huh?"

"Ain't that enough?"

"Ah reckon. So if one prods me, ah should jes' bang him one in da mouth, right?"

"Ah guess. Only make sure he ain't playin' before ya bang him one. Ya finished with your questionin'?"

"Yessuh."

"We'll be seein' 'em soon," said Solomon. "When we do, jes' act natural-like."

"What if dey ain't friendly no mo' to ya?"

"Then my ass most likely will end up jes' as black as yours!"

To gain a more lucid perspective into the area into which Coal and Solomon Pinkney were then venturing, one must first appreciate the power possessed by the five bands comprising the proud Comanche Nation.

Approximately 1700 A.D., all of the Comanche tribes migrated down from what is now Wyoming into the southwestern region of North America, annihilating any and all opposing Indians who sought to block their path. From the middle of the eighteenth century, they were the undisputed, undefeated, equestrian reigning rulers of the southwestern plains. As warriors, the mere name of *Comanche* was enough to send settlements into a state of frantic panic.

These equestrian masters were peerless horse warriors, autonomous unto themselves and with total freedom to wage war wherever they chose, but not against brother Comanche tribesmen. Whereas other tribes would ride into combat and dismount, the Comanches did their fighting from horseback, and none could match their equestrian mobility.

At the time of Coal, these undaunted horsemen ruled an open range of more than 240,000 square miles, numbering approximately 25,000 strong of which more than 9,000 were skilled, disciplined horse warriors. Most of them inhabited Texas, but their domain included sections of what is now Oklahoma, Colorado, New Mexico, and Kansas.

Of all the Comanches, the Kwahadi and the Kotsotekas were the largest bands. They roamed the Texas plains. Although all Comanches were warlike, the fiercest of them were the Kwahadies. These were the mounted men whom the eyes of young Coal spotted on the morning after his request to learn how to fight.

Silently riding up on the front seat with Solomon, the lad was reaching behind them for the canteen when through the rear opening of the canvas-topped wagon, he spied twenty or more mounted Indians. A raiding party, and they were sporting war paint on face and body. They remained some fifty yards behind them, moving their mounts at a walk.

"Mistuh Pinkney, there's a whole lot of Indians behind us."

"Ah know, Coal, they been there for more'n a mile now."

"How come they's jes' ridin' back there and ain't sayin' nuthin'?"

"Be quiet, Coal. One of them up front of us is gonna do the talkin'."

Coal's head shot around and his eyeballs almost popped. Just ahead of them was another group larger than the one in the rear. Unlike many other North American Indians, the Comanches were big men with strong torsos and fierce in appearance. Solomon reined the team to a halt and waited. Encircling the wagon, they drew near enough to touch. Most of them were young men. Solomon could not detect a familiar face behind all of that war paint. Shaking them up, the gunsmith raised the palm of his right hand and spoke in the Comanche tongue: "Brother Comanches, we come in peace. I am Solomon, who once lived among you. Solomon the son-in-law of Running Wolf and the husband of his dead daughter Tonacey. The boy beside me is called Coal."

An excited murmur ran through the band of warriors, with some of them suddenly smiling. They had heard of the white eye whose life had been spared due to his display of courage and prowess in battle. The leader of the party guided his horse close to the side, where Solomon sat smiling and looked up at him. Coal stretched his neck to get a better look. What he envisioned was a man about six feet with raven black braids that hung down to his stomach, with the lower half of those braids wrapped in beaver fur. The surface of his upper body was covered with a thin coating of buffalo grease. Slashes of red, yellow, and black paint donned his forehead, cheeks, forearms, and chest. Under ordinary circumstances, he would have indeed been absolutely frightening.

"I am Bull Bear, and I bid you welcome, brother Solomon. I was only a boy when the death of Tonacey drove you away, but I remember you, Solomon. The years have grown much hair upon your face," he cracked, creating laughter among the band.

Ignoring the comment about his beard, Solomon asked, "My father-in-law, he still lives?"

"He still lives, but he no longer wages battle. He is one of the esteemed members of the Council of Wise Ones, a lawmaker of the Comanches," Bull Bear explained.

"I am anxious to see him," said Solomon.

"And you shall, brother Solomon. But first, tell us. Is the black one with the owl's eyes truly a warrior?" Bull Bear laughed. "His gun seems almost as big as he is!"

While they all enjoyed his little joke, Coal simply stared, not understanding what the Indian said but sensing it was in reference to him.

"No," said Solomon, "he is not yet the warrior that we are, but he has already killed."

This brought admiring *ahh*s from them. One Indian, simply to see what Coal's reaction would be, reached toward the boy's six-gun as if to admire it. Young Coal immediately slapped his hand away, unsmiling. They roared with laughter at his action.

"Brother Solomon," said Bull Bear, "this man little Owl Eyes has killed. He was a Comanche?"

"No, my brother," answered Solomon. "He was one of three white robbers seeking to kill us."

"I hear your words," Bull Bear said and smiled, "but it is hard to believe of one as small as he."

"Coal," Solomon suddenly addressed him, "show them."

"Show them what?"

"How good ya kin shoot."

"But ya said Ah must nevah shoot one o' them?"

"Not one of them, stupid. Pick out a target and hit it."

"What?"

"See that warrior over there, the one with the red lance, Coal."

"Yessuh."

"Hit the lance."

"He ain't gonna like it."

"Do what Ah said, dammit!"

Coal stood up on the driver's seat, his eyes trained on that lance. In a blur, he drew and fired, severing the lance only inches above the hand that held it. Instantly angered at first by the destruction of his lance, the brave glared at Coal prior to showing a wide smile of approval. More than a few of them proceeded to pound Coal's back.

"What will he be able to do once he becomes a full warrior?" asked an impressed Bull Bear. "Brother Solomon, the black one is a man in a child's body!" He praised Coal.

"You could say that," Solomon grudgingly admitted, and they proceeded to journey to the Comanche camp not far away.

Almost two hours later, they arrived at the encampment, which consisted of more than a hundred Indian lodges. Coal's eyes never missed a thing as they entered into that totally new environment. He saw many children and women with scores of mounted men moving about. Comanche men, unless they were sitting down or sleeping, never walked anywhere unless their horse happened to suddenly drop dead.

Coal also witnessed the warm welcome Solomon received from many there in the camp, causing him to ponder, silently. *Ah wonder if they would be so damn glad to see his stinkin' ass if they know'd what a no-good sonofabitch he really is?*

Soon after the greetings were done, Coal was introduced to Solomon's ex-father-in-law, and they headed for Running Wolf's lodge. Just before entering, Solomon whispered to Coal. "Once we're inside, don't ya speak a word unless you're spoken to."

Comanches and all other Indians had their own strict codes of etiquette, behavior that was governed by rules. Coal got his first taste of it right then. Upon entering the teepee, he followed Solomon to the right and waited for Running Wolf to invite them to sit in the area reserved for guests on the left of Running Wolf, at the rear.

"Many moons have passed, Solomon Pinkney," said the gray-haired warrior, smiling. "I thought these old eyes would never see you again. You have fared well?"

"Yes, Running Wolf. And it gives me much pleasure to see my old friend again."

"Solomon," he said, firing up his pipe. "You have remarried?"

"No, my friend, I have not."

"A man your age, Solomon, should not be without one, perhaps two or three wives to bring you comfort during the waning years."

"Perhaps I shall do just that. I intend to remain amongst my Comanche brothers for some time."

"That pleases me, Solomon, and we shall have much time to recall the glory days of our youth."

"That we shall. Running Wolf, I have brought you something you once loved as a young man. Coal, go to the wagon and get one of those cases."

While Coal was outside, the old Indian studied the countenance of Solomon. The Comanches knew of the black man's plight, having been enlightened by many escaped slaves. Running Wolf did not at all like the picture that Coal being with Solomon presented to him.

"Solomon, you have grown soft in your old age and adopted yourself a son?"

"Coal? No, he is not my son," he answered, making Running Wolf frown.

"Then he is your slave?"

"Yes."

"He will not be your slave here, Solomon. Do you understand?"

"I understand, my friend, and I shall abide by Comanche law while here amongst my brothers."

To the Comanches, a man who was not free to embrace life and all of its wonders autonomously was a man dead.

The Indian's eyes lit up when Coal reentered, licking his lips at the sight of the whisky case. "This all for me?"

"You and all you choose to share it with." Solomon smiled.

They shared the bottle, passing it back and forth. The old Indian's eyes settled upon Coal, and he shocked the boy by suddenly speaking to him in English. "How old are you?"

"Thirteen, suh."

"Where are your parents?"

"Ah dunno, suh."

"You have no family?"

"Not anymo', suh."

He eyed Coal for a prolonged moment, then he smiled. "Solomon, the young one there beside you. He has the eyes of a fearless warrior. Do I read them correctly? Is his heart big and full of challenge?"

"Yes," Solomon answered in Comanche. "Although he never challenges me. But I've never seen him show fear to anyone since he was born."

"Ah! It is as I thought," he replied in kind. "But one day, Solomon, this one will challenge you. His eyes say so."

Chapter 4

In the life of any young boy on the way up, those early teenage years are most vitally important, and for Coal, it was no different. Although Solomon never told him why he was suddenly free to move about as he pleased, this atmosphere of freedom and being in the company of other boys his age was exactly what a lad of Coal's temperament needed.

After a few months there, Solomon took himself another Indian wife. She was the esteemed widow of a warrior who had died as bravely as he had lived. Her name was Una. Coal lived with them in a big lodge, where he and Solomon were expertly cared for by the quiet, pleasant Una. There were no chores for Coal to do for the first time in his life, for in the world of the Comanche warrior, men were born and groomed to fight. The women performed all the work, which had to be done, from the building of the teepee to making the clothing, cooking, having babies, etc. The men hunted to provide the food and fought to protect them all. And young Comanche boys lived a life of fun and games.

For the only period of his existence, young Coal consistently ate hot meals through the day, prepared by Una. The food and the way it was prepared was all new to him, but his palate quickly adapted to Comanche cooking. The buffalo meat and foods such as corn, wild peas, prairie turnip, were all a part of his new diet, and his young body made good use of it. Deer, elk, mountain sheep, pheasant, and wild rabbits were in such abundance that meat was always plentiful.

To the surprise of Solomon and Coal himself, the lad began to sprout up, growing taller and fuller of body. As he had agreed to, Solomon daily schooled Coal in the fine art of fisticuffs. He painstakingly showed him the vital points on head and body where a man was most vulnerable. But regardless of what other happenings were in progress, young Coal religiously practiced his six-gun anywhere from two to four hours a day.

The seasons came and went, with Solomon dubiously carrying on his trade and living with the Indians. All of that period was not totally blissful for the young Coal. Often during those years, when Coal and Pinkney were on the road to somewhere, they would encounter mean men, both red and white. While traveling through those badlands and occasionally having to fight for his life at the side of old Solomon, Coal had to kill eleven men by the time he reached eighteen years of age.

As Solomon had told him how it should be from the moment he presented Coal with that walnut-handled six-gun, it indeed became as another limb to the jet-black youngster. At eighteen, Coal could get to his six-gun and fire within the bat of an eyelash and hit a barn fly dead in the ass from fifty feet away. All totaled, Coal had fired only eleven shots in his life at fellow human beings, with eleven kills. Coal was deadly, gifted, accurate, and snake-quick.

Some six months after his eighteenth birthday, Solomon informed Una that he felt the urge to visit his home town of Stirrup, informing her that he would return within the year. As was the way of Comanche women, she merely nodded, void of expression.

Later that same night, while Solomon was alone with his wife, Coal sat alone with Running Wolf. Since that first meeting between them, the old chief had taken a liking to the one the Comanches called Owl Eyes. They conversed in Comanche. "Owl Eyes," he said softly, "you shall return with Solomon when he comes back?"

"No, Running Wolf, I will not."

"In the five years you have lived amongst us, Owl Eyes, you have not been happy?"

"Yes sir, I have been happier with your people than ever before."

"Then why shall you not return with Solomon?"

"Because, Running Wolf, either him or me won't be alive too much longer. Once we're alone on the prairie on the way to Stirrup, I'm going to demand my freedom. If he refuses, which I'm certain he shall, then one of us will most surely die."

"Your words stir my memory, Owl Eyes. That first day you entered my tent, when you went to get the whisky, I predicted to Solomon what you have just said to me. I am fond of you both, but in a matter such as this, the warrior in me must side with you, Owl Eyes. It is a crime against the gods for one man to enslave another."

Coal remained silent, and Running Wolf continued. "If you survive, my son, will you come to live with us?"

"I cannot promise you that, my friend, because there is something I must do, and I don't know how long it shall take."

"What is this that you must do?"

"Find my mother and sister."

"Do you know where they are?"

"No sir, but I will find them."

"I shall pray to all the gods on your behalf, young Coal," he said, switching to English.

"Thank ya, suh," Coal replied, and they spoke no more of it.

That next morning at sunup, they departed from the Comanche stronghold. Coal bade goodbye to the many friends he had made while there, most of whom had become young warriors. The trip to Stirrup was hot and dusty and slow.

All during their journey, Solomon noticed that Coal was even more closemouthed than usual. Accustomed to the fact that Coal was never one to talk much, Solomon did not bother to inquire what was on his mind, figuring that whenever he got around to it, Coal would say what was churning inside his head. Secretly, Solomon was proud of this black, whom he had owned for all of his life. Glancing sideways at Coal, he silently recalled how eager the youngster had been to learn. The more Pinkney taught him in the intricacies of gunmanship, all the more Coal inquired about it, absorbing it all. *They say niggers are dumb.*

Removing his hat, Solomon reached behind their seat for a sweat-soaked rag, with which he mopped his head and neck. Ironically enough at that time, Coal was thinking about his mother and Becky when he heard Solomon address him. "Coal, give me them reins and climb on in back there and git that canteen we been savin' from the sun. Ah think we kin both use a cold drink right about now. Goddam if it ain't hotter'n a whore's pussy with the pox! Texas must sure as shit be hell's own corridor!"

Listening to him bitch about the heat, Coal rose easily from his sitting position and got the canteen. Returning to his seat, Coal resumed his driving while Solomon drank. When the canteen was offered to him, he refused. Solomon eyed him but said nothing as Coal sat with large eyes scanning the terrain in front of them.

"Coal, it'll be sundown 'fore too long. Head for that thick green over yonder. More'n likely we'll find fresh water there."

Presently they came upon a water hole filled to the brim with cold, clear, nature's gin. Making camp, Solomon watered down the horses while Coal prepared their dinner of beef jerky and beans. All through dinner, they ate in silence. Coal was thinking that then was a good time as any to assert himself, for tomorrow they would be in Stirrup.

Just after dark, they stretched out on blankets on opposite sides of the fire, each with his own thoughts. Slowly raising up on one elbow, Coal remained in that position for a minute or more, staring at Solomon Pinkney. The wizened old gunfighter observed Coal from under his hat brim, silent, waiting.

"Ah wants to go on my own way, Mistuh Pinkney."

Solomon raised his brim, momentarily confused by that sudden statement from the face across the fire. "Go? Go where, boy?"

"On my own. Away from here, away from you!" Firelight danced in those unblinking black eyes.

Aware that something had been biting at Coal's ass, he had no idea it was this. He could well understand any young man wanting to be on his own, but to his way of thinking, Coal's request was completely out of the question. Could it be that those years with the Comanches had made Coal forget his place? Forgetting that he was still Solomon's legal property? Besides, he was accustomed to his assistance, the constant company during those lonely prairie days and nights.

Shit, he must be crazy, Solomon angrily thought. *I own his black ass, body and soul.* Putting a halter on his flaring temper, Solomon sat up straight. "How come, Coal? Why do ya wanna leave me? Ain't Ah been good to ya, huh? Ain't Ah seen to it that ya been fed and clothed and had shoes on your feet? Shit, that's more'n a lot of white men in these here parts kin lay claim to. Ah ain't laid a hand on ya since ya was twelve. Is it that Ah don't pay ya for your labor? Is that it?"

His eyes then moved from Coal to thoughtfully peer into the fire, rubbing hard at his bearded chin. "Alright Coal, tell ya what Ah'm gonna do. Ah'll give ya, startin' right now, ten whole dollars a week! How's that?"

"Ah don't want no money, Mistuh Pinkney. Ah jes' wanna go and be on my own, my own man. My freedom is what Ah wants," he said, his voice low but firm.

"Goddamnit, boy! Ah'm offer'n ya forty a month and sometimes more. Damnit to hell, Coal, what the fuck's done gone wrong inside your head anyhow?"

"Ain't nuthin' wrong with me that bein' free won't fix," Coal persisted.

Solomon quickly decided to switch tactics and his manner. "Coal, young'n, come over here. I wanna show ya somethin'," he beckoned, reaching for his saddlebags.

From it, he withdrew a cloth package wrapped in rawhide. After untying it, he handed some papers to Coal. "Read these, damnit, then maybe y'all get them damn crazy ideas outta your head."

"Ain't nuthin' gonna change my mind, Mistuh Pinkney."

"Read 'em, goddamnit, and stop givin' me your sass!" Solomon roared.

Coal read those sheets of paper, which declared Solomon's sole ownership of his person for life, and stipulating that in the event of the death of one Solomon Pinkney, Coal would inherit the wagon, horses, and all other worldly goods and possessions of the deceased. Whereupon, Coal would then immediately become a free man. Free to go anywhere he so chose.

"Now, don't that make ya feel a whole lot better?"

"No, it don't. What Ah read it to mean is that if you outlives me, Ah'll be a slave 'til Ah die."

Solomon's face reddened then, and he rose to his full height. "Piss on all this goddamn bullshit and backtalk! Now you listen, young'n and listen real good, goddamnit! Ah don't wanna hear no more shit about you goin' a goddamn place! Ya belongs to me, for as long as Ah sees fit. And if ya runs off, Ah'll have a posse or the Rangers drag your ass back to me in irons! Is that clear enough for ya?"

"Ya would sho-nuff do that to me, Mistuh Pinkney?"

"Ya kin bet your black ass Ah would! Now git some sleep, so's we kin git a early start come mornin'. Ah don't wanna hear another goddamn word about it."

Coal's first inclination was to push it, but he decided against that. He knew Solomon well enough to know that the old gunman meant exactly what he said. Instead, Coal pulled the blankets up over his shoulders. He would need his rest for tomorrow. Prior to drifting off to sleep, Coal swore a silent vow. *If Ah don't leave here alone in the mornin', Ah'll be in this goddamn ground too dead to know the difference.*

As the stars began to dim with the coming dawn, an unmoving Coal lay watching them disappear. Rising from his blankets, he went to the cold stream to wash his face and mouth. While waiting for Solomon to awaken, it occurred to him that to simply plant a slug right into the back of Solomon's skull would drastically simplify things. But the fire of challenge then running rampant through his veins was too immense to cast aside.

Since his seventeenth year, Coal began to wonder if indeed he could best his teacher if push came to shove. Either way, he would damn sure know the answer to that this morning. Long ago, Solomon had taught him that if a man was dangerous enough to shoot, he was dangerous enough to kill. Coal fully realized that if he ever drew on the gunmaster, he would have to kill with his first shot. There would be no seconds.

Flexing his fingers, Coal dropped his arms to full length. Then with a mercurial flick of his wrist, his hand magically filled with iron. Time and time again, there by the stream, he repeated the exercise. Tenderly settling his six-gun into place, he turned away. He was as ready as he would ever be.

Now, you no-good bastard, thought Coal, *Ah'm gonna give ya the present Ah promised myself five years ago—from Momma and Becky.*

Silently walking over to a nearby tree, he leaned against it with his eyes riveted to Pinkney's sleeping form. The old gunhawk awakened without opening his eyelids, sensing danger.

By coincidence, he had just then been dreaming about himself and Coal, and the first time they rode into Comanche country, when Coal was a little boy. Slowly parting his lids, he sighted Coal casually leaning against the tree. Only this was the present-day Coal. Five feet ten inches tall, and 175 pounds, hard of muscle and bone. For long seconds, he studied Coal.

"So it's come to this, huh Coal?" he asked, getting to his feet.

"It don't have to be nuthin', if ya jes' let me go my own way," Coal softly stated, intensely watching that man who had more tricks than a cornered Apache.

"Coal, Ah feels death all 'round us, and I surely knows that one of us is gonna die this mornin'. But before ya makes me lay ya to rest, tell me what suddenly brings on this feelin' inside ya for me? Ah kin feel it and see pure hate in them black eyes of yours."

The youngster's mind warned him not to be swayed by Solomon's talk and get caught off guard. *Watch the man's eyes*, his brain cautioned him, *the way you were taught. Solomon's eyes will let you know.*

"It ain't sudden, this feelin' Ah got for ya, and Ah'll tell ya why, ya sonofabitch! My Momma and Becky who ya sold, is why ya kin see my hate! And Ah'm gonna send ya to hell for that!" Coal promised.

In that split second, the veteran gunfighter experienced doubt, as his mind ran instant reruns of all those times when he saw Coal grabbing iron, and the cagey Solomon attempted to trick the younger man.

"Coal, before we slap leather, maybe Ah kin prevent havin' to kill ya. Young'n, if Ah told ya where they was and gave ya the money to git 'em back, would that make ya forgit your hate?"

Solomon's sudden revelation that they were still alive was just shocking enough for the gunsmith to assume the advantage. His grizzled hand came up filled with instant six-gun, and the second before he fired, Coal's six-gun barked, and a button midway up Solomon's shirtfront was driven deep into his chest with brutal impact. Bullet force sent him sprawling onto his back, with thick blood gushing from his chest and mouth.

Dying eyes focused upon Coal looking down on him with the smoking pistol in his right fist. Kneeling, Coal raised the huge limp head.

"Befo' ya die, Mistuh, tell me where they be!"

For an answer, he received a bloodied wad of spittle spat into his face. "Find 'em yourself, nigger, you're free! G-go t-t-to that nigger graveyard in Amarillo and dig 'em up, 'cause they been there since that Amarillo flood got 'em eight years ago," he gasped, and died.

So, thought Coal, *they ain't alive no more. Ah don't have to keep on hopin' to see them again, 'cause they gone.*

Raising from the dead Solomon's side, Coal got a shovel from the wagon. After digging a grave, he shoved the ex-slave owner into it with his booted foot. Retracing his steps, he replaced the shovel and extracted a captured old Arapaho arrow pouch and bow. Quickly making a fire, Coal lit three arrows and deliberately shot them into the outer frame of the wagon. As the flames began to build, he went to the stream and filled a large bucket. He then doused the flames, after which he fired Solomon's rifle and his own until both were empty before reloading his own. When he was done with hitching up the team and covering Solomon, Coal slowly drew his six-gun and shot himself in the left shoulder. The searing pain dropped him to one knee. Minutes later, he managed to get up onto the seat and start the horses toward Stirrup, which was half a day's ride away. Clumsily bandaging his shoulder, he attempted to stem the flow of blood.

Having grown up around Texans, Coal knew they wouldn't swallow any story about his master getting killed and Coal surviving without a scratch. He chose Stirrup mainly because he and Solomon were on friendly terms with Sheriff Pace Tucker. Also, there was Mr. and Mrs. Munsen. The no-nonsense sheriff would most certainly keep the curious townsfolk in line. He was known to kill for less than the questioning of his authority. Old Pace Tucker was a lawman in every sense of the word, and the law was all that really mattered to him.

Along about four that afternoon, pedestrians observed the wagon slowly entering town, with the bloodied black slumped in the driver's seat. Coal was not totally unconscious, but he made them think so. One of Pace's deputies caught hold of the lead horse's reins, guiding the wagon to a halt in front of the sheriff's office, and raced inside. Pace Tucker was outside in a flash, his eyes taking in the scorched wagon and the burnt arrows still imbedded in the wooden frame. One glance at Coal told him that the fellow was in dire need of a doctor. Dispatching a deputy to find the doctor, Pace and another man lifted Coal's limp form into the office. When they laid him on the cot, he moaned.

"Easy there, easy young'n, the doc's on his way. No now, don't try to talk, jes' rest easy, Coal."

Heavy footsteps resounded behind him, and Pace turned to find Lars Munsen filling the office's doorway. "Where's Coal? Someone said he's hurt real bad."

"He's right here, Mr. Munsen. Your boy's gonna be okay, Ah reckon, although he ain't exactly a boy no longer." Pace pointed at the cot.

Lars approached the cot with worry and amazement clouding his features. "I-I see the face. It is Coal for sure. Will you take a look at that?" Lars began to smile with pride. "Why he's filled out just fine, almost as tall as me."

A vibrant roll of thunder rumbled in the background as the sky darkened. Pace Tucker addressed the crowd hovering around the door. "Ah want a dozen of you men to ride out aways and see if'n there's any sign of Solomon Pinkney. Go as far as that comin' storm will allow ya to and take them extra rifles, too, 'cause it looks like Arapaho trouble to me. Ah'm gonna stay here, 'cause Ah wanna be around when Coal wakes up."

Dispersing the other onlookers, he called to one of his men. "Clem, Ah wants ya to watch over this here wagon. If anybody tries to go into it, arrest 'em. If they won't stand for that, shoot 'em! Ah don't want nothin' in it to be handled."

The sedulous old doctor arrived, and the sheriff guided him inside. Observing doctor and patient from a distance, Pace Tucker quietly studied Coal, while Doc Simpson probed deep for the bullet. For several minutes, he probed. "There's the little bugger," the doc sighed. "I'd best clean out this wound before infection sets in. Pace, ya should be able to talk to him sometime later tonight. But for right now, I advise that ya let'm rest. He's lost a great deal of blood."

"Will he be alright, Doctor Simpson?" inquired an anxious Lars.

"He's strong as a young bull, Mr. Munsen. He'll be okay in a few days at the most."

"Gentlemen, excuse me, I've got to run and tell Mother that Coal's come home a man grown." He smiled and hurried off.

"Doc," said Pace. "Ah'll do jes' what ya suggested and let 'm rest. If Ah'm not mistaken, Ah think them Injuns done caught up with ol' Pinkney. 'Cause if he was still alive, he woulda been in that there wagon. Ah'm sure gonna miss that ol' gunhawk, even though he was a ornery ol' cuss. And Ah'll bet he took a few of 'em with 'm, 'cause Ah ain't never seen a man who was better with a six-gun than ol' Solomon was."

Bursting into their kitchen where his wife stood preparing dinner, Lars walked up to her, grinning. "Mother, guess what?" he asked, and she took in his flushed appearance.

"From your face, it must be something special."

"Mother, Coal is home, and he's come back full-grown. He's a man."

"C-C-Coal?!! Where, Lars?"

"Now Mother, you mustn't get yourself upset. He's been shot . . ."

"Shot? Oh my God!"

"No, Mother, it's only a shoulder wound. He's still unconscious, but the doctor says he'll be up and around in a few days. Good as new. Mother, you should see our Coal."

"That's exactly what I intend to do," she said, reaching for her shawl.

"Not now, my love," Lars held her. "He's unconscious and wouldn't know you were there anyway. But if you were to fix some of your Swedish soup for him that he likes so much, Mother, I'm sure he'll be glad to have it when he wakes up."

"Y-yes, I'll get it ready for him right away. Landsakes! Our Coal is home." She smiled, wiping at her eyes.

Not long afterward, the sky opened up, and an incessant downpour fell on Stirrup on into late evening. Around midnight, Coal stirred. His eyes found Sheriff Tucker and four deputies in attendance, and he could hear the sound of raindrops against the rooftop.

"Howdy, son." Pace smiled. "You and ol' Solomon's been away for a long time. How do ya feel, Coal?"

"A might shaky, kind o' lightheaded."

"That's only natural. After losin' all the blood ya did. Ah felt exactly like that after each of the eight times Ah stumbled into a bullet. Ya feel like answerin' a few questions, young'n? Tell ya what, suppose ya drink some o' this here hot soup Mrs. Munsen brung over for ya. Git some o' that in your belly first, then we'll talk a bit."

Hot, rich, Swedish soup burned the pit of his stomach, but it tasted awfully good. While eating, Coal could feel their eyes watching him. After two bowls of soup, he smacked his lips and gently eased his aching body against a wall behind the cot. Sheriff Tucker then pulled a chair over to sit closer to Coal. Just as he was about to speak, Lars Munsen entered the office. "Just waiting to take him home with me, Sheriff," he said, and leaned against the wall.

"Now, suppose ya tell me jes' what happened out there, Coal?"

"Ain't much to tell, Sheriff Tucker. Jes' after wakin' up this mornin', Mistuh Pinkney tells me to walk slow'n natural-like over to the wagon. From the way he was actin', Ah knowed he was smellin' trouble. So Ah does what he says, and then all hell breaks loose. There was five or six of 'em, firin' and shootin' them damn arrows. Mistuh Pinkney kilt two of 'em befo' he was hit in the chest. Ah kilt the one who kilt him, befo' Ah got hit, suh."

"Hmmmm, seems likely that it coulda happened that way, Coal, but one thing about this bothers me. How do ya account for them there powder burns on your shirt?"

The office grew silent as a tomb while they awaited his reply. Without batting an eyelash, Coal peered straight into the eyes of the old lawman.

"Like Ah said, Sheriff Tucker, all hell was breakin' loose. Befo' Ah knows anythin', they was right on top o' us. Ah was fightin' with the one that shot me, befo' Ah kilt him."

Rumblings of distant thunder rolled, disrupting the enraptured silence inside that brick enclosure. Crackling flashes of lightning eerily penetrated inside there.

"Well, as far as Ah kin see, ol' Solomon jes' had some plumb bad luck. But Coal, young'n, yours been pow'ful good. Not only did ya save your own skin, but from these here papers Ah found inside your wagon whilst ya was asleep, it appears that you are now a free man, Coal." Coal's eyes moved to find an elated Lars, beaming.

"Ah don't understand what ya mean, Sheriff Tucker," Coal faked, his ebony face void of expression.

"What Ah mean, Coal, is that these here papers say you are now absolutely free, since the second ol' Solomon kicked the bucket. Not only that, young'n, but the wagon and all his worldly possessions is yours. Now what do ya say to that, young feller?"

"Ya mean I don't have to do nothin' for 'em at all? All belongs to me outright?" Coal inquired, feigning astonishment.

"That's correct, young'n, and it ain't no more'n right, from the way Ah sees it," Tucker declared, grinning at Coal's wide-eyed state. "Ever since ya was no more'n a pup, Ah seen ya doin' exactly like Solomon dictated. And as Ah kin recall, ya ain't never caused him a bit o' trouble. As Ah sees it, Coal, you're jes' gittin' what ya deserve. Now if ya jes' sign these here legal papers of release from bondage, Ah'll jes' turn everything over to ya."

Coal eased up from the cot, his left shoulder burning like hell. As he walked over to the sheriff's desk to sign, Coal spied his six-gun and holster hanging from a peg on the wall. Following the line of his gaze, the sheriff motioned that it was okay for him to retrieve his sidearm. First Deputy Colter grew red-faced at the action of his boss.

"Ya don't mean you're gonna let him wear that six-gun of his, jes' like he was a white man?" an aghast Colter queried.

"Don't see as to how Ah kin legally stop 'im from doin' so, seein' as how he's now a free man'n all," Pace patiently explained.

"Well Ah'll be dipped in shit!!" Colter fumed, turning a pale blue glare on Coal. "Ya better damn well wear it quiet-like, or Ah'll sho-nuff take it from ya, nigger, and that's fo' damn sure!"

Coal rendered him a cursory glance without bothering to reply. "Ah wants to thank ya, Sheriff Tucker, for gittin' me the doctor 'n all. Ah'll be leavin' now, suh, and Ah'm much obliged."

"Ya mean you're leavin' town so soon, Coal?"

"No suh, not tonight, anyhow. Ah'm goin' over to Lars's livery stable and bed down me and the horses. If ya wants me, Ah'll be there in the wagon."

"Good thinkin', young'n, 'cause the best thing for a gunshot wound is rest. Sleep easy, young feller, you're now a man of property. Goodnight, Coal."

"Goodnight Sheriff," he said, and walked out with a smiling Lars behind him.

When the door closed behind them, Coal halted and turned to face Lars, his eyes full of feelings for his friend. "Hello Lars," he said softly, "damn but Ah'm glad to see ya."

"Hello son, welcome home," Lars choked, grasping and shaking the strong right hand of Coal. "Come, Coal, I'll help you with your horses."

Inside the sheriff's office, a racist, ignorant deputy was bigotedly enraged. "Well, Ah'll be a cunt-suckin' mongrel dog!" Colter snarled, his face beet-red. "Ya treated that there nigger jes' like he was white! That smart-assed black sonofabitch! W-why he kin even write like a white man, goddamn him!"

"Colter, ya kin credit Solomon Pinkney with that. He taught Coal jes' about everythin', jes' like Coal was his own boy. And here's some advice to ya, Colter, even though Ah knows you're too ornery to take heed. One night a while back, when me and ol' Pinkney was in our cups, he told me about Coal and that six-gun of his. Now them what knowed Solomon also knowed that he wasn't one to praise nobody! But he told me that Coal's as natural pure-fast with that six shooter of his as a rattler in the bushes what's jes' been pissed on," the sheriff warned.

"Oh yeah? Bullshit! Ain't no nigger ever lived seen the day he could outgun me! Ah knows Ah'm good, and sho-nuff fast!"

Sheriff Tucker didn't bother to pursue the subject any further, diverting his attention to the WANTED posters lying scattered atop his desk.

Chapter 5

"How's the shoulder feel?" Lars asked, as they entered the livery.

"Like Ah could do without it."

"That's to be expected, I guess. I can't say that I'm pleased about Solomon, but I'm overjoyed at your good fortune." He smiled.

"Lars, how is Mrs. Munsen? Ah've missed her."

"Ask her yourself, Coal, she's right behind you."

He turned to find her eyes beaming as she motherly appraised the sight of him. Crying, she hugged him as he embraced her with his good arm. "You're not my little Coal anymore, are you? Why, I have to stand on tiptoe to kiss your cheek . . . after you bend down, that is." She laughed.

"Yes ma'am," he said, grinning. "But Ah'm still your Coal jes' the same."

The cherubic little Mrs. Munsen immediately took over. "Coal, now you get your belongings out of that wagon right now, and come to the house where you belong."

"Mrs. Munsen, would ya be mad if Ah waited 'til tomorrow befo' Ah come? This is the first night in my life that Ah've been free, and Ah want to git it straight in my head first," he explained.

"Well, I don't too much like it, son, but I think I understand. Coal, son,"—she placed her chubby hands at both sides of his face—"welcome home. We still love you, you know that, don't you?"

"Yes ma'am," he answered in his quiet way.

"You hungry, Coal?"

"No ma'am. Your soup filled the hole."

"Then I'll see you tomorrow when you come, and I'll change that bandage on your shoulder."

She kissed them both, and as she left: "Lars, don't you stay up too late, it's way past your bedtime."

"Lars," said Coal, "is it alright if Ah keep the horses and wagon here 'til Ah gits ready to leave?"

"Need you ask? Keep 'em here for as long as you wish. Coal, I have a favor to ask of you."

"Ask ahead, Lars."

"As a favor to me, if my wife tries to mother you a little, let an old woman have her few moments of pleasure, will you?"

"Ah'll be with Mrs. Munsen like Ah've always been. That good enough, Lars?"

"Perfect, Coal. Now, is there anything you need at the moment?"

"Rest, Lars. This shoulder is pitchin' a bitch!"

"Then you'd best rest yourself and it. I'll see you in the morning."

"'Night, Lars."

Coal's reason for not going to the Munsen home immediately was not exactly candid. Once inside the wagon and away from inquisitive eyes, he went to what Solomon thought was his secret hiding place, which was situated under the floorboards. As he lifted the middle slab, Coal's breath caught inside his chest. There at his feet lay a wealth of cash money. He proceeded to count for just less than an hour, and his tally amounted to $11,000 in paper and $880 in twenty-dollar gold pieces. Long afterward, he remained there staring at it before replacing it into the stash. Then for the first time, the full impact of being free began to penetrate his awareness.

Upon acquiring such a sudden bonanza, most young men undoubtedly would have commenced making fabulous plans. This was not the case with Coal. Such a reaction would have been contrary to his nature.

Gritting his teeth against the burning pain in his shoulder, Coal climbed into his sack and went to sleep. In fitful dreams that night, Solomon's bloodied, laughing mouth taunted Coal. Telling him that he would never be able to make it in the white man's world, despite his gifted command of his six-gun. Saying to Coal that for all of his prior life, he had been guided by the white man in the white man's domain.

Coal awakened, screaming his defiance with his six-gun tightly gripped in his right mitt, not knowing how he managed to get to it in his sleep but welcoming the cold steel confidence it instilled within himself. Almost lovingly, he eased it back into his holster.

"Shit! Ah wish this goddamn shoulder would quit throbbin'," he bitched.

Lifting himself from the wagon bunk, he climbed out in search of water to quench his thirst. No sooner had he filled his thirst did hunger pangs begin to gnaw at his belly. Going back to the wagon, he gathered some food and prepared it over the blacksmith's furnace. After getting the wrinkles out from under his belt, Coal discovered his shoulder even felt somewhat better. Sounds of a horse's hoof stomping and snorting caught his attention, making him stroll out into the corral. In the early morning's light, Coal's eyes beheld something so magnificently compelling, he blinked twice before believing it.

Running and rearing up on its hind legs was a big blue-black stallion. A powerful Morgan thoroughbred. In an instant, Coal became obsessed with that creature. If it killed him, thought he, he had to own that animal, have him for his very own. Coal had no idea whether the current owner would sell it or not, but by hook or crook, he intended to get him. For long moments, Coal remained frozen in his tracks, watching the stallion romp.

Swiftly returning to his wagon, Coal collected three lumps of sugar and then slowly moved toward the fence of the corral. When he reached the perimeter, he stood still, waiting for the animal to become curious. Certain that it had, he began to speak softly to it. "Hello, black-as-me." He grinned. "Pretty soon you gonna belong to me alone and nobody else. Ah promise."

From behind, the voice of Lars startled him. "I'm afraid you won't be able to keep that promise, Coal."

"Mornin', Lars. Why not?"

"He belongs to Jake Whitlock, the gambler. I suppose I felt the same as you when I first saw him. There ain't a finer piece of horse flesh in this world, I don't believe. I offered Whitlock one thousand for that animal, and he told me that he wouldn't give it up for twice that much. I've been standin' over there watching you fall in love with this critter, but it ain't no use, Coal. He's not for sale. I can purely understand your pinin' for him, but you'd best forget it, son."

Coal stared hard at the ground for many seconds before raising his eyes. "Lars, Ah'm gonna have this beauty. As sho' as the sun shines, Ah'm gonna have him," Coal vowed, and slowly walked away. Halfway across the space between the corral and the livery, Coal turned to find the eyes of the stallion upon him.

"Don't worry, Big Black, Ah'll be back for ya. Next time Ah lays eyes on ya, y'all be mine." Instantly the animal whinnied again, prompting Coal to sense that it understood.

Coal climbed back into the wagon to sleep and regain his strength. He slept throughout the day. When he awoke, it was near dark, and the clang of Lars's hammer no longer resounded. After washing and eating, Coal strapped on his six-gun, tied it down, and made a beeline straight to Stirrup's largest saloon.

None of the blacks of that town ever frequented the place, a fact Coal well knew. Their patronage was not missed by those who were in daily attendance. What with having been reassured by Sheriff Tucker that he was a totally free man, and his un-flinching confidence in his ability to protect himself, Coal strode a straight path up to the swinging doors. Momentarily hesitating at the entrance, young Coal slid his handgun up and down in the holster for good measure; then he walked inside.

An instant hush fell inside the smoke-filled saloon, abruptly halting all activity as the eyes of whores and patrons alike turned his way. Gunmen professionally observed the style in which Coal sported his tie-down six-gun, as if he knew what it was all about. Big black eyes passed over everyone as he walked to the far end of the brass bar rail to stand alone, for Solomon once stressed that when at all possible, it was best to keep one's back free of any and all bystanders. Seeing Coal enter, Lars threw in his poker hand and strolled over to him.

"Hi Coal, I see you've taken off that sling. How does it feel?"

"Evenin', friend Lars. Still hurts a mite, but not as much hangin' as it did in the sling," he pleasantly replied.

"Coal, you know how my wife and me feels about you, don't you?" Coal nodded yes.

"Then permit me to ask you a question. Do you think it wise for you to be in here, knowing how these people feel about blacks?"

Coal studied the eyes of his friend the giant, and a faint smile passed over his lips. "Lars, Ah'm a free man now," he softly de-clared, "and ain't a livin' ass gonna ever again tell Coal where he kin plant his feet at. Ah'm much obliged to ya for worryin' 'bout me, 'n Ah appreciate it, Lars. But rest easy, Ah kin handle it."

Lars knew that any further discussion on the topic was point-less. A man had to do whatever his destiny dictated, come what may. "Would you like to have a drink, Coal?" Lars smiled.

"Lars, you know they say we gits crazy when we drinks. Ah

ain't never had a drink of lightnin' water in my life," Coal confessed, using the Comanche terminology for whisky.

"Be that as it may, and in case you don't know it, Coal, it ain't customary to do what you're doing at the moment."

"What? All Ah'm doin' is standin' here."

"Exactly. You're suppos'd to have a drink of some kind in front of you," Lars explained, making Coal half-smile at him.

"Well then, if that be the case, Ah'll have some suds water if y'all join me. Ah'm buyin'," Coal told him.

Lars beckoned the bartender, who hesitantly came over, as if uncertain how to react to the duo. "Two beers, nice and cold if you will," Lars pleasantly requested.

The barkeep threw a furtive glance at the other patrons intently watching him. Confusion clouded his demeanor, then his eyes caught those of Coal's. Whatever he saw there prompted him to grab two mugs and fill them. The entire saloon was hushed in deadly silence, and a voice boomed forth from across the saloon with meanness coating its words.

"Drink jes' one more drop, niggah, and Ah'll kill yore black ass, real quick-like!!"

Coal's eyes instantly found the owner of that snarl and clung to him. An indignant Lars faced the antagonist. "The lad is doing no harm to anyone at all. It is wrong that you should wish to harm him," Lars smoldered, feeling unaccustomed anger building inside himself.

"Swede, be damned glad that you ain't wearin' a six-gun like yore burr-headed niggah friend, 'cause Ah don't like yore kinda white man any more'n Ah does him! Now mind yore own goddamn business a'fore ya wind up dyin' for a niggah!" Bad Frank warned.

Very slowly, his eyes never once leaving the gunman who wanted to die, Coal laid his mug gently atop the bar. "Move away, friend Lars," Coal softly said.

"B-but Coal, that man is known for killing other gunmen! He

is cowardly seeking to take advantage of you. Come Coal, come with me, let us leave this place," Lars implored.

"Ah said move, Lars."

His voice, still soft, sent chills racing up Lars's spine. With a gesture of futility, Lars turned his palms upward and moved away, shaking his head. Coal, his eyes still glued to the gunfighter, stepped away from the bar to fully face that fool who badgered him.

"Kiss my black ass, mean man!" Coal barked for all to hear, at the man some fifty feet across the room.

Enraged, Stitch's left hand streaked for his pistol, and Coal was the last person he ever saw in this life. With a visual blur of movement, Coal's right hand found his six-gun and fired twice—sounding more like once—sending one bullet into each of Bad Frank Stitch's eyes. Blood gushed from those vacant holes all over everything near to the figure, which was a corpse before it crashed to the filthy floor of the saloon.

An oldtimer, who was standing at the middle of the bar, began to do a jig in one spot, unable to restrain his awed excitement.

"WHOOooeeee!! WHOOooee, goddamn! Did y'all see that there nig . . . young feller git to his iron?! Did ya see?! Goddamn!" he exclaimed.

"Ah'd be a liar if Ah said Ah seen 'm git to it," another voice joined. "And Ah was sho-nuff watchin'! Fast ain't even the word for what that young'n jes' done."

Coal, moving easy, walked over to where the ex-gunman lay sprawled in a pool of blood, spit, and sawdust. Pausing over Stitch, Coal noisily spat into the two empty sockets. Whereupon his eyes slowly lifted to observe all who had witnessed the violent decimation, sending a silent, blatant challenge. He received no takers.

Chapter 6

Footsteps echoed from the outside boardwalk. Deputy Colter barged in just as Coal was returning to his place at the bar. Colter scanned from the customers then frozen against the walls, to the carcass on the floor, to Coal. Again his eyes went to the mess that was still oozing blood from its head. Colter was well-acquainted with the man whose name used to be Bad Frank Stitch, and he had also seen that infamous gunman in action. His mind warned him that if Coal had done that to Stitch, then he himself had better be very, very careful. But his bigotry and his badge overruled his better judgment.

"Ah told ya what Ah'd do if ya caused any trouble, nigger. Didn't Ah? Now hand over that gun of yours, you're under arrest!" Colter ordered.

"If Ah am, then ya better find another way to git my six-gun besides askin' for it, 'cause Ah don't give up my gun to nobody!"

"Then Ah'll jes' have to take it from ya, nigger!" Colter threatened, advancing.

"That's jes what y'all hafta do, bad-ass redneck," Coal urged him on.

Only the hurried entrance of Sheriff Tucker prevented another sure killing. Quickly sizing up the situation, he stepped in between the two adversaries. "Now jes' hold on there, and Ah mean hold on! Ah wants somebody here to tell me jes' what in tarnation has all this goddamn shootin' been about. And who the hell was it who done shot that man's eyes outta his head? Who is that sprawled out there anyhow?"

The little Oldtimer, who had witnessed countless gunfights in his time and who was still amazed at Coal's lightning draw, shuffled up to Pace, pointing. "That was Bad Frank Stitch, Sheriff. He drawed on that young'n standin' over there. And Sheriff, ya wouldn' believe it even if we was to tell ya. Ya jes' wouldn' believe what we jes' seen!"

Pace Tucker walked closer to examine the cadaver, thinking, *Ol' Solomon wasn't lyin' none about Coal's six-gun, 'cause it seems like he hit'm directly into both eyeballs.* He then picked up Stitch's gun, sniffing the barrel. Standing over the remains, he mentally measured the distance between himself and Coal. *And he ain't jes' accurate,* the sheriff mused. *He had to be faster'n hell to kill Stitch before he could even get off a shot. That Oldtimer said Stitch drew first on Coal.*

Returning to stand at the side of Coal, the sheriff leaned his back against the bar rail. "Suppose you tell me about it, Coal. Since it seems that you're the one who done him in."

"Sheriff," Colter interrupted, "to hell with all this bullshit talkin'. Ah'll jes' haul his ass in for murder!"

"Be still, Colter, and damn glad that Ah walked in here when Ah did," Pace halted him, his eyes returning to Coal. "Well, how's about it, Coal? Ya wanna tell me what went on in here?"

Only because the man had always treated him decently did Coal bother to tell him anything at all.

"Dat bad man layin' on the floor over there tol' me if Ah was to drink any more of my beer, he would kill me for it."

"And???" Tucker prompted.

"And, he must o' bit off a bigger chunk than he could swallow, from the looks of 'm."

"Hmmmm. And where was ya standin' at when ya put out his lamp?"

Coal didn't understand the purpose behind that particular question, but he softly answered, "Right where Ah'm standin' now."

"From all the way over here, huh? Hmmmm."

"And that's the gospel truth, Sheriff," the gnarled little Old-timer backed Coal up. "Yessiree, from exactly where he's standin' he shot out both his eyes, by crackey!"

Sheriff Tucker appeared to be deep in thought. "Seems to be a straight-up case of self-defense to me. Somebody git this here mess cleaned up!"

Lars was just in the act of placing a huge hand on Coal's right shoulder, and the saloon was buzzing over the shoot-out. Full of curiosity, Deputy Colter shinnied up next to his boss at the bar.

"Coal, young'n," said the sheriff, "Ah'm powerful sorry for havin' to do this, but Ah'm gonna have to ask ya to leave town by sundown tomorrow."

Coal merely stared at him, saying nothing. It was Lars again who spoke.

"Somehow that doesn't seem quite fair, Sheriff. Coal was only defending himself. You didn't expect him to stand there and let Stitch kill him, did you?"

"No, Mr. Munsen, but there's another reason why Ah'm askin' Coal to go. Coal, Stitch was a gunman who enjoyed his trade, which was killin'." He laid Stitch's pistol on the bar's surface next to Coal. "See here, take a look at his gun handle and count the notches whittled into it. Fourteen! Now, there's gonna be lots of men jes' like Stitch who, when they hears word of this, will jes' be itchin' to have a go at the man who done Stitch in. Ah don't want more 'n my share of gunfighters traipsin' through Stirrup. Understand, Coal, it ain't nothin' personal. Ah jes' don't want this town turned into a ghost town like a lotta others round about."

Still, Coal gave him no response. "Well, Coal, how about it?" Silence. "Now Coal, Ah done seen what ya kin do with that there six-gun of yours, son, and Ah ain't about to fight ya fair if Ah have to. If it gits to that, Ah'm gonna have to come for ya with three other men sportin' shotguns, if Ah have to. Coal, Ah'd rather not have to."

He patiently waited for Coal to answer him, but instead, Coal ordered another beer. After draining half of it, he gazed straight into the eyes of the old lawman.

"Sheriff Tucker, Ah gots somethin' to take care of first. Ah'll need two more days in town, then Ah'll leave."

Their eyes held fast for seconds or more; then Sheriff Tucker nodded. "Alright, Coal, ya got it. Two more days," he agreed, and departed with Colter.

The Oldtimer who had backed up Coal's story immediately sidled into the space vacated by the sheriff.

"Young'n, if ya don't mind, Ah'd jes' like to shake that right hand of yorn. That's if ya don't mind," he cackled, showing a line of empty gums. "Yessiree! Ah done seen 'm all, by crackey! Deacon Crenshaw, Buck Talbot, Monte Clay, Tom Fitzgerald, Amos Ringo, and yeah, by crackey, Bad Frank Stitch, too, who ya jes' sent to hell where he belongs. Ah seen every last one of 'em, but ain't none Ah jes' mentioned or ever heard of ever seen the day they could take you, young'n. Now maybe, jes' maybe, Monte Clay might'a matched yore speed. But fer speed and accuracy, Ah ain't never seen the likes o' what you showed us this day. Ah heard the sheriff call ya Coal. Jes' call me Oldtimer, young'n, everyone else does." He cackled again, shaking the left hand that Coal extended to him. "By crackey, if ya don't git shot in the back, ya jes' might live forever! Ah'm real pleased to meet'cha, young'n, and a long life to ya," he gummed, releasing Coal's hand.

In wonder, Coal watched him shuffle away. Lars then confidentially inquired, "Coal, why did you just now shake with your left hand?"

"Solomon Pinkney once told me the story 'bout a right-handed gunfighter who shook hands with a left-handed gunfighter and got shot to death for it. Ah ain't never gonna forget that story," Coal said, and Lars nodded his head in understanding.

"He taught you well, that swine who had the gall to own another human being."

Yeah, thought Coal, *so well it got'm kilt.* "Lars, which man in here is Jake Whitlock?"

"Th-the one over there dressed in black, with his back against the wall," Lars said, and pointed. "But Coal, I . . ."

Coal was already heading for the gambler's table. When he reached the wooden circle surrounded by five poker players, Coal stood facing the pale, handsome Whitlock. The other players, unaware of Coal's intention, quickly dropped their cards and moved away, giving him room. Whitlock's countenance grew even paler as he, too, mistook Coal's true purpose, for he was not a gunfighter.

"Jake Whitlock?" Coal softly inquired.

"Y-yes, I'm Jake Whitlock," he stammered.

"Ah'm here to buy that black stallion of yours. How much do ya want for 'm?"

"I'm afraid he's not for sale, Mr. Coal. Only yesterday I was offered one thousand for him, which I turned down," he stated, his blue eyes scornfully appraising Coal's shabby attire, silently inferring that amount was way over Coal's head.

"Ah'll give ya two thousand," said Coal, his face expressionless.

"I'm sorry, Mr. Coal, but . . ."

"Three."

"Not for any pri—"

"Four."

"Mr. Coal, I now realize that you must have taken a real liking to—if you'll pardon my expression—Blackie, but there's not another horse in this whole country that can match Blackie's speed, power, and endurance. I couldn't possibly part with him."

"Five."

"I'm sorry, Mr. Coal," Whitlock snapped with an air of finality.

Coal stared so hard and long at Whitlock, the man thought

Coal might possibly shoot him right there in front of witnesses. The thought did indeed cross Coal's mind, but he turned and stalked away. While standing there above the table, it had not escaped Coal's scrutiny that of all the chips piled atop the table, Whitlock's was second smallest.

Another idea then took shape as Coal remembered something else Solomon had tutored him in. Coal would wait and hope that Whitlock's luck stayed bad; then, if Whitlock still refused to sell the horse, he would just have to obtain it the best way he could.

Once outside of the saloon, Coal remained still for a minute or so, focusing his eyes to the darkness. Walking Indian light, he made his way into the wagon and went to sleep. He did not dare to look again upon the stallion for fear that he would simply steal it, and in Texas, horse thieves were relentlessly hunted down. Coal fell asleep with a smile on his face. Next morning, he awoke to the sound of Lars's hardworking hammer. "Mornin', Coal. Am I mistaken, or do I see a secret smile in your eyes?"

"Mornin', friend Lars. Ah guess what ya see is relief, now at this damn shoulder's done quit throbbin'," he lied.

After washing in cold water, Coal strapped on his piece, tied down, and went out into the streets of Stirrup. He bought his breakfast in a small but fairly clean eatery, ignoring the gawking stares from customers and pedestrians who passed the window where he sat eating and planning. When he was done with that, he headed for the general store. As Coal crossed the street, he detected something in the eyes of other black men who were not yet free, and it made him feel good inside. Into the store he sauntered, taking his time at finding exactly what he was looking for. Coal bought three flannel shirts and roughly hewn trousers. Then he purchased something that he had only seen white men wearing, a black suit with white shirt and black string tie, with hat and boots to match. Prior to exiting the store, he also bought a new deck of playing cards.

Later that same evening, as Lars was saying goodnight to him,

Coal beckoned, inviting the big man into his wagon. Lars seated himself across from Coal on Solomon's bunk, and Coal surprised him by dealing a hand of poker.

"Now tell me if Ah'm right, Lars. Ya got the queen of spades, hearts, and diamonds, along with the five of clubs and the deuce of hearts, right?"

"B-but how di . . . ?!" Lars stared open-mouthed.

"Never you mind, friend Lars. It's a li'l somethin' else ol' Pinkney schooled me in. Now watch my hands, Lars, like ya never watched anythin' else in ya life. Ah'm cheatin' ya, but Ah wants ya to tell me if ya kin honestly see me doin' it."

They played draw poker. He dealt Lars two more cards, knowing Lars then held four queens. Without turning his cards over, he gave all five to Lars. "Now tell me if Ah'm right, Lars. Ah got all four aces and the nine of clubs, right?"

"B-but I was watching you! How could you have?"

"Friend Lars, if you didn' see me even after Ah told ya Ah was cheatin', it's a damn good bet that that snotty-assed Whitlock won't. Mistuh Pinkney told me once, when he was teachin' me what Ah jes' showed ya, that the hand is faster'n the eye. Tonight, Ah'm gonna bust Whitlock clean!"

"Is it because of the way he looked at you last evening, Coal?"

"Ya saw that, huh? Jes' like Ah was shit! Not only his money, Lars, but that fine stallion, too. Ah'm gonna own that horse, Lars. Ah jes' gotta."

Going home with Lars that evening, Coal took all of his money with him. Withholding $2,000, he put the rest in the safe-keeping of Mrs. Munsen until he asked for it.

Chapter 7

While enjoying dinner with the Munsens, Coal held them spellbound with tales of his five years with the Kwahadi Comanches. After dining, he bathed and shaved with hot water prepared by the kind old lady. So unaccustomed to fine clothing was he, Coal stared at the suit of the white man for a long time before starting to get dressed. Lars entered Coal's room to find him standing in the middle of it, in his drawers.

First he donned the shirt, and Lars tied his string tie for him. Cautiously Coal stepped into his creased new trousers prior to putting his feet into the gleaming black boots. Standing over by the window, Lars held a look upon his face which might have been centered on a son, had he possessed one. Finally, Coal slipped into the long suit coat, but he hesitated at going in front of the mirror until Lars practically pushed him there. Coal was severely startled then by what he saw.

As he stared at his sparkling, immaculate image, a strange happening occurred. Coal's eyes suddenly filled and spilled over. Deeply moved with understanding of what he was observing, Lars went and wrapped a huge arm around him.

"Coal, son, I'm not certain, but I think I know how you must be feeling at this moment. Yes, Coal, the mirror is not lying to you. You also are a man, just like any other. Now if you don't dry up, you'll soil your fine new shirt," he poked, making Coal grin.

Lars left him there to compose himself and went downstairs to sit with his wife. He didn't say anything to her; he simply waited. Upstairs, Coal completed his dressing by strapping on his six-gun. He then placed the black hat upon his head at the very same cocky angle to which he witnessed other men of confidence wearing theirs. Once again he viewed the mirror, and a new feeling gripped him. Call it vanity.

"Ah'll be goddamn if Ah ain't a fine figure of a man!" he admired out loud. "Just as sure as horses fuck horses, Ah am!" Coal laughed, turning one way, then the other.

The room suddenly rang with his laughter, and he strolled out, closing the door behind him. When Lars heard him coming down, he interrupted Mrs. Munsen's needlework. "Mother," he whispered, "look at our Coal."

Handsome and bright-eyed, Coal stood at the foot of the stairway. What Mrs. Munsen's eyes beheld sat her bolt upright as her sewing fell to the floor. "Coal," she murmured, wiping at her eyes. "My, my, look at Coal."

Crying, she went and motherly held him in her arms. "This town won't ever recover from the shock of you, son. If I wasn't a lady, I'd go over to that saloon with you both this very evening." She beamed, laughing.

Grinning as they had never seen him do before, Coal asked Lars if he was ready, and they left. On their way to the saloon, townsfolk gawked at something they had never seen, a well-dressed black. Had it not been for their conglomerate fear of his six-gun, Coal would surely have been tarred and feathered, just for being so spotlessly attired.

And Coal strutted, putting the capital *S* in strut. Lars, in his Sunday-go-to-meeting suit, walked proudly beside him. About a hundred feet from the saloon, Coal imperceptibly flicked his right wrist, easing his coat behind and to the inside of his gun handle. If suddenly he had to get to it, he didn't want any damn coat hampering him.

Again, as on the preceding night, Coal paused at the entrance prior to entering. This time going in, he pushed the doors wide and held them there. As though by some invisible signal, every eye in the joint turned his way, and more than one cowboy choked on his drink that evening.

"Well, Ah'll be double-goddamn!" they heard someone say.

No longer was Coal smiling, but cold-blooded serious. Spying Whitlock at the same table, Coal made a beeline for him, his eyes holding those of the gambler's.

Well, I'll be a sonofabitch if this doesn't beat all, Whitlock mused, observing the decked-out Coal striding with form. Men grumbled their distaste, while many of the resident whores entertained secret, silent inclinations. One of them whispered to a colleague, "That nigger Coal ain't only bad, he's kinda handsome, too. Ain't he, Holly?"

"Ah hope to tell ya," Holly agreed, her tongue suggestively slithering over her lower lip.

Coal halted in front of Whitlock's table. "What's the name of the game?"

"We're playing a little draw, Mr. Coal. Care to sit in?" Whitlock greedily invited, sensing easy prey.

"That's what Ah come for," Coal grated through his teeth. "Table stakes?"

"No limit," Whitlock countered, surprised with Coal's apparent knowledge of the game.

Grabbing a chair, Coal sat with his back away from the patrons, having the entire establishment visible in front of him. Reaching into his inside coat pocket, he withdrew a wad of banknotes and placed them before him. Whores and clientele gathered closer. There and then, Coal made up his mind not to dilly-dally. Lose a few hands here and there to avoid suspicion, and then crush him at the earliest possible opportunity.

Two hours later, Coal was $5,600 to the good, and Whitlock was profusely sweating. One other man also remained in the game. Standing on the inner rim of the crowd was Sheriff Tucker, intensely watching. Coal appeared as fresh as when he had entered, his alert eyes taking in every move of the third gambler's fingers. He was dealt two tens, an ace, plus the nine and five of hearts. The dealer dealt himself nothing. Coal and Whitlock eyed each other.

"Your bet," said the dealer to Coal, who hesitated, making Whitlock surmise that he was uncertain of his hand. Whitlock went for it.

"Ah'll bet . . . five hundred," Coal announced. Whitlock rechecked his own cards and smiled.

"I'll meet your five hundred . . . and raise you two thousand," Whitlock smoothly challenged.

Coal knew he was taking a great risk betting so much without the deal being in his own hands, but he had a feeling, and he badly wanted that beautiful steed. The dealer eyed them both, having already decided he wanted no more of this private war. For the longest while, Coal simply stared at the pot before slowly placing $2,000 into it, making it $5,000.

"Cards?" asked the dealer.

"Three," Coal answered, causing a ripple to course through the onlookers.

Whitlock, suddenly aware that Coal only held a pair, laughed as he requested one card. As luck would have it, Whitlock drew the king of clubs to go along with the king he had kept along with his three sevens, giving him a full house. The gambler's whole being seemed to expand in his chair. Now he'd show this nigger in a white man's suit how to play the white man's game. Watching his eyes, Coal knew that Whitlock had something good. As of yet, Coal had not looked at his new cards.

Holding them close to the chest, he slowly separated the fresh three. Ten of spades, three of diamonds, ten of diamonds. Coal's dick almost stood up at the sight of those two new tens, which gave him four of a kind. His eyes lifted to find a sweating Lars standing next to a fascinated Holly, then shifted down to Whitlock.

"Well?" Whitlock teased, knowing he finally had this nigger by the balls.

"Whitlock, how much ya got there in front?" Coal asked.

Hurriedly the gambler counted his cash, finding it to be $3,700, which he eagerly stated.

"Ah'll bet thirty-seven hundred." Coal shocked everyone.

Whitlock did not believe he could lose with such a hand and quickly shoved his bank to the center of the table. Coal deliberately let the drama of that moment fill his frame as he reveled in it.

"Well, now, I think your luck has just run out, Mr. Coal. I have here a lovely full house for you to blink at," he gloated, reaching for the money.

Whitlock was suspended over the pot with his arms encircled to rake it in, when Coal's voice stopped him.

"Raise up ya paws, goddamnit, 'cause that money ain't yours to handle," he informed the gambler, and very, very slowly spread all four tens for everyone to see.

Lars then let out a triumphant roar. Jake Whitlock appeared as though his asshole had suddenly fallen out. Red-faced, he glared at Coal, hating him. Instead of immediately reaching for the money, Coal observed Whitlock's eyes.

Badly shaken, the gambler desperately wanted to try Coal, but the memory of what he had witnessed the previous night restrained him. Instantly his mind went to his horse. "Last night, you offered me five thousand for Blackie. Is that same offer still good?"

Coal studied the man. Aware that he now had him by the balls, he squeezed hard.

"That was last night, gambler man. Tonight ain't the same."

"Explain what you mean, Mr. Coal?" Whitlock hissed, livid with rage.

"What Ah means is this. You is now broke, goddamnit! Stone-flat-fuckin'-busted, 'cause Ah done kicked yo no-gamblin' ass!" Coal dug at him, remembering how scornfully he had been looked upon by this man. "And a gambler with no money is jes' like an old ass what's hole ain't workin' no more," he twisted the knife. "Ah've been without all my life, so Ah knows how ya feels. So, Ah'm gonna bet ya one thousand against the stallion. Take it, or go fuck ya self!" Coal cussed him.

His last statement almost provoked Whitlock into going for iron, which Coal was secretly hoping he would. That way he would get the stallion for no more than the mere cost of a bullet.

"You've got a bet," Whitlock agreed, feeling degraded and ashamed.

Only then did Coal begin to stuff his winnings into his pockets. Whitlock anxiously retrieved the cards to resume play, but again Coal's voice restrained him. "There's gonna be a slight change, Mr. Whitlock," he said, bringing silence to the saloon hall. "This time we jes' cut for high card, winner take all."

Whitlock nodded, and Coal shuffled the deck prior to flattening them out in a straight line.

"Whenever ya ready, Whitlock, ya kin pull," he softly declared with double meaning.

The gambler pulled a six, and Coal ten.

"Now, Whitlock, Sheriff Tucker standin' here kin vouch that Ah got my horse fair and square."

Coal then took a piece of paper from Lars and wrote something on it. "Whitlock, if ya jes' jot ya name on the bottom, that'll make it all legal-like. Right, Sheriff Tucker?"

Whitlock complied, and the smiling Coal tucked his receipt into his pants pocket. "Whitlock, jes' so's ya won't go hungry," Coal softened, "here's a hundred to stake ya. But there's one thing Ah wants ya to know, gambler man. If'n Ah catches ya anywhere near my new horse, y'all be dead before God gits the news."

Lars rejoined Coal as he moved away from the table and through the crowd. "Tell me, Coal," he urged, "am I imagining things, or did you actually play the game fair?"

"Friend Lars, he thought Ah was so stupid, Ah didn't have to cheat 'm. He beat his own fool self. Ah wouldn' lie to you, Lars." Coal looked up into his eyes.

"I believe you, Coal. Perhaps that stallion was meant to be yours, after all."

"Soon's Ah saw him, Lars, Ah knowed it." Coal smiled. "C'mon Lars, let's git some suds water."

This time, the barkeep gave him smiling service, but only one of the bawdy girls was brazen enough to approach them. She was a full-bosomed blonde, and her name was Holly. Coal was totally unfamiliar with the customary byplay between men and women, and it never crossed his mind that Holly was as taken with him as she seemed to be. He figured she was after some of that money she had seen him win. He also remembered the strange way she kept staring at him just after he smoked Bad Frank Stitch.

Holly invited him up to her room, but Coal begged off, making arrangements for later when she promised to meet him after midnight in his wagon at the livery stable. Coal had something else he was aching to do. Finishing their beers, they headed for Lars's house. Donning a fresh shirt and trousers, Coal grabbed his old hat and six-gun and raced to the livery. In the far end stall, Coal spied that magnificent head with the white diamond between its eyes.

"Hey, Big Black," he said, grinning, "Ah told ya Ah'd come back for ya, didn't Ah tell ya?"

The great steed whinnied and reared up on its hind legs. Perhaps it was his scent, but it was clear to Coal that the animal recognized him instantly. Prior to placing a saddle upon its back, its new master rendered it a lump of sugar. Leading him from the stall, Coal mounted. It seemed as though that was precisely what the horse had been waiting for. It started to prance, and Coal gave it a gentle spur.

With a sudden burst of speed, the Morgan thoroughbred almost shot from under him as it took off. They literally flew from the stable at a full gallop on out into the corral, hurtling a six-foot fence. Coal urged him on, and the fine stallion gave him an exhibition he was never to forget. In less than three minutes, Stirrup was far behind them.

To Coal, the experience was more like riding a giant eagle, as the steed appeared to wing low along the ground's surface. There in the moonlight, man and horse blended into one gigantic black shadow, and Coal could feel the wind singing in his ears. Sensing Big Black still had not shown him all that he could really do, Coal spoke softly into its ear. Magically it responded to his voice and daintily commenced galloping at high speed. Racing hooves began to beat such a rapid staccato upon the earth, Coal yelled with glee.

"Do it, ya big, black show-off. Do it for me!" he laughed, and the stallion did its thing.

Raising its tail up high, Big Black showed his asshole to the world. He flew. Presently Coal reined him in and dismounted. To his admiring surprise, the powerful animal wasn't even winded yet.

"Ah'll be damned! Ah'll sho-nuff be damned!" Coal laughed aloud under the stars. "Big Black, if our lives ever depends on ya speed and my six-gun, shit, we ain't never gonna die!" He grinned, hugging that satin-like, muscular neck. "Tell ya what, Big Black, we gonna make a deal, you'n me. Ah takes care of you, and you takes care of me. How's that?"

Again the animal whinnied, making Coal's teeth flash in the darkness. "Damn if ya can't all but talk! Everything Whitlock said 'bout ya is true, but he musta plumb forgit to mention somethin' else. You pretty smart, too!" He swelled with pride, marveling at the beast he loved on sight.

At a trot with a brilliant moon above, Coal headed back to town. Dismounting inside the livery, he unsaddled his new pride and joy. He then began to rub the animal down, all the while talking to it. Other than his six-gun, that stallion was the only thing Coal had ever owned, and he loved it as though it were human. Completing the rubdown and feeding, Coal was just preparing to leave when his ears caught a faint sound behind him. Crouching, he whirled, and was an eye-wink from firing when she screamed.

"No, Coal, don't!!"

Recognizing Holly the whore, Coal replaced his six-gun almost as fast. "Oh my God!" she gasped, clutching beneath one breast. "Ah thought Ah was dead for sure."

"Ya never come closer. Sorry Ah scared ya, ma'am, but ya should never ease up behind a man that way."

"Ah'm sorry too, Coal. Ah been standin' there listenin' to ya talk so sweet to your pretty horse. Ah swear!" Holly stamped her foot. "Ah ain't never had nobody talk ta me like that in my whole life. Maybe Ah shoulda been a pretty horse." She giggled, making Coal smile at her silliness.

It is a rare occurrence in the life of any professional whore when she is sexually stirred beyond her perpetual quest for money. But Holly was for Coal, and she told him as much, prompting him to glance strangely at her. It soon became evident to Holly that Coal was unaware of his appeal to women, especially so to women such as herself.

Ah'll soon change that, thought Holly. *Ah'm gonna give him some trim like he never even dreamed of!*

A seductive Holly began the interplay, enjoying and experiencing what was also, for her, a first. Presently they were naked there in the wagon, all except for Coal's strapped-down six-gun, which he absolutely refused to remove.

"Coal, how many times ya been with a woman?"

"You make three," he honestly replied, remembering the slave girl Solomon brought to him one night in Fort Sills and the Arapaho Indian girl they found in northwest Texas.

"And you're how old?"

"Almost nineteen."

"Jes' three, huh? Lordy! Ah bet you've still got your cherry," Holly teased, raising him to his good elbow.

"My what?" he asked, prior to understanding. "Practically," he agreed, experiencing a softness previously unknown to him as he fondled her plump, pliant rump. Holly's fingers roamed over his body.

"Coal, w-was any of the other two . . . white?"

"No ma'am."

"Ah'm glad, 'cause you'll be my first nig . . . Ah mean, my first black man, too. Lordy! Coal, you is purely endowed in some places," she impishly giggled.

Holding his staff, Holly slid down the length of him. Never having head rendered to him before, Coal discovered the sensation to be maddening. Holly's mind raced back to the previous night and the expression upon Coal's face when he gunned down Bad Frank Stitch. Her recollection evoked Holly to busting her cookies once, twice, and then again in rapid succession. His alien blackness, the lethal dangerousness of him, compounded by the orgasm-inducing contrast of their bodies, all served to elevate Holly to unprecedented erotic heights.

In dumbstruck awe, Coal observed her actions, which made him squirm deliciously. Lifting her head, Holly gazed up at him, with her eyes weirdly glazed, as when a woman is come-drunk. She moaned aloud.

Unable to withstand it anymore, Coal raised Holly up and onto her back as pain ripped through his shoulder. Ignoring it, Coal clumsily rammed himself into her, making the whore holler. Having observed animals fucking more than he had himself, that was how Coal mounted her; from the tip of his joint to his nuts, he thrust into her. Again and again, Holly hollered, squeezing his body to her own.

"Coal, oh God, Coal! Ah can't stand it! Oh my Lord, sweet Jesus!" she ranted, making Coal wonder crazily whether she had come to fuck or pray.

"Coal, if ya makes me scream like that, someone'll come," Holly groaned, spreading herself wider to him.

"If a sonofabitch sticks his head inside this here wagon, it'll be the last damn thing he'll ever see," Coal assured her.

"Gracious peace alive!" she cried, bringing her knees back to her jawbone, exposing all of the cunt she possessed.

As he had seen horses and bulls do, Coal pumped, pumped, and pumped some more as juices spurted down into Holly's butt crack. It seemed to Coal that the more he fucked her, all the more he wanted to dick-punish her plump, hot hole. His rod brick-hard, he slashed through her like a rapier. All of a sudden, he began to feel that unfamiliar shattering churning inside his loins, exploding into her. Raising from her, his eyes found a quivering Holly with one forearm held against her head.

"Goddamn!! Coal, honey, you positively sure you had some pussy before . . . anywhere?" Holly gasped.

"Right now, Ah ain't too sure. It wasn't like this," he admitted.

Soon they had another go at it, and it was near dawn when Coal gave her a twenty-dollar gold piece and told her to go.

"Coal, will Ah see ya again?"

"Ah don' think so, Miss Holly. Ah'm leavin' soon."

"That's too bad, 'cause you're nice, and Ah likes ya a lot. Coal, last evenin' Ah saw Deputy Colter talkin' to that man you won your pretty horse from. Maybe it ain't nothin', but if Ah was you, Ah'd sleep kinda light-like. Ya understandin' my meanin'?"

"Sure do, Miss Holly, and Ah thanks ya kindly."

"Do ya have to leave so soon, Coal?"

"Yes ma'am, Ah give the sheriff my word."

"Ah only jes' met ya, Coal, but Ah'll miss ya, and Ah'll think about ya too, sometimes," she sadly told him.

"And Ah'll surely remember ya too, Miss Holly. Ah thanks ya again for what ya told me."

"Think nothin' of it, Coal. Bye now, and you take care, you hear? Bye, Coal."

Chapter 8

Coal slept until a little past noon before rising, and the first thing he did was see to the care of his horse. Then, taking two sets of saddlebags from Lars's racks, he filled them with the things he would take along. Lars came into the rear where Coal was preparing, his face etched with sadness.

"Mother and I will sorely miss you, Coal. Will you ever come back this way?"

"Ah don' think so, friend Lars, 'cause Ah jes' can't stand this part of the world no more."

"When and if you can, will you write to us?" The old Swede was near to tears.

"Ah'll write, Ah promise."

"Coal, I told Mother that she must not cry when you leave. She promised not to, but I know she will." Coal made no reply.

"Any idea where you'll be heading, son?"

"After Ah go and see Running Wolf, Ah'll be headin' for Mexico probably, somewhere 'round Sonora. A while back at Fort Arbuckle, a man told me'n Solomon about some fine range country down there. Now, since Ah gots me more money'n Ah ever dreamed of, Ah kin git me as fine a spread as a man could want. Besides, if'n Ah stayed here, Lars, Ah'd be havin' to smoke me a different redneck every day, and Ah don't wanna live my new life that way. Lars, if a man was to keep on killin' and killin', he might jes' one day lose hisself in that very same killin'.' "

Lars nodded at the wisdom in Coal's statement. "Come, Coal, Mother has prepared a special dinner just for you, sort of in your honor."

"In a minute, Lars. First, Ah got somethin' Ah wants to say to ya. Ah wants ya should have this wagon and all of Solomon's guns 'n wares."

The blacksmith started to protest, but Coal held up his right palm. "Lars, you and Mrs. Munsen is the only pure friends Ah ever had in this here world. Ah wants ya to have 'em. Call it a trade if ya likes, for the saddle and saddlebags. Besides"—he grinned fondly—"ain't ya heard that it ain't healthy to rile me?"

"Heaven forbid!" Lars laughed, and they journeyed to the house.

Upon entering, they removed their hats. In silence, the lady of the house pecked them both on the cheek, feeling very emotional at that moment. They shared the silence until she spoke. "Coal, what time are you leaving?"

"A few hours before sundown, ma'am, 'round three. Ah wanna git in a few miles of travelin' while it's still light. Besides, Ah don't wanna be hunted for killin' a sheriff and three deputies sportin' shotguns."

"Then we'd best sit down to dinner now," she said. "It's after two already. My, how time sure does fly when you don't want it to."

At the table, Coal again told her how much he loved her cooking. The old couple never took their eyes away from him during the meal, openly displaying their true love for Coal. When dinner ended, everyone returned to the living room. Unable to control her emotions any longer, Mrs. Munsen sat on the sofa next to Coal and cried when he wrapped his arm around her shoulders.

"Will we ever see you again, Coal?"

"Yes ma'am," he lied, "ya sure will," and Lars nodded his approval of that lie.

"Coal, son, if you settle anywhere, take an old woman's advice and get yourself a wife. A man needs a woman to do things for him which only women can do."

In reality, the thought had never occurred to Coal. "Yes ma'am, Ah surely will, If Ah sees one who makes me wanna do jes' that."

"And Coal, dear," she continued, "ride safe, for there's all sorts of danger out there in that world."

"Ah will, Mrs. Munsen," he promised.

"Don't forget this what you gave me to hold," she said, reaching into her apron.

"Folks, both of ya have cared about me, ever since Ah was a li'l fella. Showed me the only real affection Ah kin clearly remember, so Ah wants ya both to accept this from me."

He handed her $5,000, figuring that with them both being in their sixties, Lars wouldn't be able to work hard much longer. And with a nest egg, they could live out the remainder of their lives in peace and comfort. His eyes cautioned Lars not to argue with him.

At the hitching post outside their home, Coal hugged them both farewell, and his eyes blurred when a tearful Lars bearhugged him in return. Moving closer, Mrs. Munsen held his face in her hands. "Write to us, Coal, write to us often, and God bless you, Coal, for the son-like gesture you just did for two old people. We'll pray for you every night and day, son, together we will," she sobbed.

Climbing onto Big Black, Coal peered down at them. "Ah loves ya both," he said, surprising himself.

Gently spurring his stallion, Coal rode away. At the very edge of town, he turned in the saddle for one final look at them, waving farewell for what he thought would be forever.

Learning from Deputy Colter approximately when Coal would be leaving town, Jake Whitlock waited three miles out of town, alone in the surrounding mountains. He had a long-range rifle and a heart full of hate. Ambush!

Coal, riding easy on the high-spirited, high-stepping animal, sat in his saddle, wondering what the rest of life held for him. Never in his wildest dreams had he imagined that one day he would possess the fortune that now was his. He had to force himself to keep his imagination in check, for the sensation of his newfound freedom in conjunction with the treasure could have very easily become too heady a wine.

High up in the rocks ahead of him, about a hundred yards away, something flashed from the reflection of the sun. In one fluid movement, Coal pitched himself forward and out of the saddle while simultaneously grabbing his rifle, landing heavily on his wounded shoulder. Pain shot to his brain, momentarily clouding his vision as bits of shale sprang up all around him. Whitlock, seeing Coal's action from his lofty perch, blew his cool and fired too rapidly, spoiling his aim.

"Ah'll bet my black ass it's that goddamn gambler man," Coal cursed, scurrying behind a fallen tree trunk.

The log afforded him instant cover while he checked the terrain. A resentment long kept in abeyance began to creep from Coal's pores. He could taste it. Patiently he waited for Whitlock to fire again; then he dashed up from his position and advanced. "Ah'm gonna sho-nuff kill his rotten ass for this, the bushwackin' bastard!"

Bullets ricocheted from the rocks around him, the shales stinging his face. Once more, he hastened forward, arriving in the same rock bed as Whitlock, yelling to him. "Whitlock, Ah'm gonna do somethin' bad to ya, ya sonofabitch!" Coal promised.

Then, for no obvious reason, Coal suddenly laughed aloud, the sound of it racing through Whitlock's bones like a cold, Arctic wind. Quickly raising his rifle, Coal got off five rapid-fire shots, pinning his would-be killer down. While Whitlock shielded his head, Coal raced around to the far side in order to come up behind him.

Not being able to see any signs of Coal after lifting his head again, the gambler panicked. Fleeing his position to go to another, he ran smack into Coal, who fired on sight, striking the gambler man in his groin.

"Oh my God!!! Look what you've done to me!" Whitlock screamed, still standing slouched against a large boulder with his rifle at his feet, his hands shielding what he no longer possessed.

"Ah gived ya my money jes' so's ya could eat, and ya tries to sneak-kill me. Ya think that was somethin'?" Coal grinned. "Watch this!"

Squeezing his trigger, Coal planted a bullet into Whitlock's nose bridge, precisely where his eyes met. The dead man slid down the boulder, leaving a red smear of blood from the open hole in back of his skull where the bullet had exited. Going over to the body, Coal roughly searched it and found what was left of his cash, taking it back. His first inclination was to bury Whitlock.

"Fuck that!" he decided. "Let the buzzards have some eatin' of another buzzard."

Working his way down out of the rocks, he found Big Black. "Big fella, Ah'm gonna have to learn ya how to git outta the way when there's shootin' goin' on. It ain't healthy to jes' stand around watchin' like ya did. It could mean that ya is bright when ya watch that way, and it could mean that ya heart is big and ya don' scare easy. All that is jes' fine." Coal grinned, stroking its muzzle. "But then it could be that ya jes' don' know no better. So, Ah'll jes' have to learn ya the right way, jes' like Ah'm gonna learn ya a lot o' things."

During those following weeks, while on his way to Comanche country, Coal completely isolated himself from so-called civilization, living off the land and abundant wildlife surrounding him. Knee-length blades of grass were there for Big Black to graze upon, and they survived in fine style. Daily, Coal would spend hours on end with his magnificent stallion, teaching it to halt on a twig, only to take off and go at full tilt. Throughout their jour-

ney, Coal displayed a patience with the beast he was totally unaware of possessing, and was handsomely rewarded.

Those bright, alert eyes of the Morgan were no surface illusion. Big Black intelligently responded to Coal's teachings like a
young child. At times, Coal would pretend men were standing in
front of them; then they would practice backing away while Coal
sat in the saddle with his guns drawn. Sudden gunfire from atop
its back, which at first greatly disturbed the sensitive beast, no
longer registered. Sometimes Coal would hide from it and whis-
tle, only to have the stallion instantly seek him out. With each
success, there was a reward of a lump of sugar, a wild apple, or
simply gentle words and a loving pat. But always, something.

The most difficult feat Coal accomplished was teaching his
animal to lie on the ground and remain absolutely still for an
extended period of time. Horses rarely recline upon the ground
in the presence of man or other animals, because in that position, they are vulnerable and utterly defenseless. In time, Coal
gained the steed's trust, the maneuver was mastered, and Coal's
heart swelled with pride in accomplishment.

When he was not preoccupied with schooling Big Black, Coal
sought total mastery of his other love, the six-gun. Solomon
Pinkney had taught him most of what he knew in the art of gunistry, but alone there on the plains, Coal augmented those teachings. Daily practicing with his left hand for five to six hours until
his fingers bled raw soon had him uncertain as to which hand was
the faster, and he adapted to the added weight of Solomon's
matching six-gun.

As he leisurely rode to his destination, Coal saw the string of
new forts, which then stretched throughout east-central Texas.
After Texas became a part of the United States in 1845, those forts
were quickly erected to combat the Comanches, Kiowas, Chey-
ennes, and the Arapahos. But those same forts were still unmanned
by the calvary troops, whom the Texans expected in abundance.

This situation was soon to change drastically by a twist of fate.

Gold was discovered at Sutter's Mill in California, and hordes of settlers, prospectors, and plain gunmen flooded through Indian land. With them, they brought disease. More specifically, cholera, and Coal himself almost died while living with the Comanches in 1849.

There were many moments during his sickness when Coal came close to wishing for death. Copious diarrhea and vomiting carried Coal beyond misery. He became dehydrated with a burning thirst for water, most of which was contaminated, and his jet-black skin grew cold and clammy, turning bluish in the early stages of the dreaded cholera epidemic. Severe abdominal pains and muscle cramps almost drove him insane as his breathing went to a shallow, rapid, gasping. And he was not at all alone in his suffering. Many hundreds of Comanches and their brother tribes could be seen careening in staggering torment all over the Texas plains, and they died by the thousands.

Running Wolf, Una, and most of the young men whom Coal shared his teens with were among the victims of this terrible and vicious malady.

Coal somehow survived, and he thought it was a miracle. When he recovered, he remained among the Comanches, with whom he shared a mutual affection, helping to administer aid to the sick who were still dying all around him. After the epidemic ran its course, more than half of the Indian population and thousands of whites had fallen victims to it. It wasn't until the summer of '55 that Coal decided to leave and find another life for himself.

Chapter 9

Bidding farewell to them forever, he departed from Comanche country and traveled south to the Republic of Mexico. Crossing the Rio Grande, he rode up into the High Sierras, where he remained alone for several weeks.

One morning, Coal awoke with the profound desire to see and be around other humans. Whistling for his four-legged companion, Coal saddled up and rode down from the mountains. Upon leaving the highlands, the thicker, hotter air of the plateau made him sweat in his Indian buckskin shirt, and he changed into another one of lighter material. Just after midday, Coal came upon a signpost of bold, red lettering: CATALINA DEL REY.

In this year of 1855, the appearance of a black man in all but a few places in Mexico was unprecedented. Unaware of this, Coal wondered at the stares directed at him as he entered the town. Women with baskets atop their heads and children gazed in utter amazement at the negrito with his two pistols astride a giant black steed. Small children ran and skipped in pace with his horse, pointing up at Coal. Having a real fondness for the little ones, he simply returned their smiles. However, being in a strange place, Coal's eyes and ears stayed keyed for unexpected danger.

The excited chatter of children soon brought men out of the shaded and cool cantinas. Coal studied their apparel, the high-domed sombreros and the guns they wore. He could sense and clearly see that some of them were mean men.

Won't be no trouble, long's they leave me be, thought Coal.

They in turn observed the way he sat upon his horse, such a horse as they had never seen. Eyes beheld his guns, most of all the guns, and his ebony skin.

Coal was indeed a strange man to them. None of them smiled, but a few nodded a silent "Howdy." Sighting a large cantina with a good-sized water trough out front, he guided Big Black to a halt there.

Slowly removing his skin-tight gloves and tucking them into his belt, Coal melted from his saddle, easy-like. After letting his horse drink, he led it over to a hitching post, which stood in the shade of the cantina. Curious onlookers stood a respectable distance away, covertly commenting about the hombre negrito.

Patting the animal's neck as he spoke to it, Coal then turned and walked up the steps on into the cantina. Big Black's eyes remained on Coal's back and then the swinging doors after his master disappeared inside. There were at least fifteen obvious Mexican putas congregated inside and almost as many men. Some of them were gambling, which Coal wanted no part of, and others were either talking to or fondling the putas. As it always seemed to be in his case, all chatter immediately ceased.

Coal, his spurs hardly making a jingle, walked Indian light up to the far end of the bar. Several men there were white fugitives from American justice, who by hook or crook lived by the gun. Outlaws!

They sized Coal up, quickly assuming that he was probably a runaway slave on the lam, just as they were. But one thing confused them, and that was the way in which Coal sported those guns, hung low, the handles at his hip bones. One gunman leaned over to whisper to a companion. "Ain't no slave Ah ever seen had a way with six-guns. This nigger wears 'em like it's the most natural thing in the world to him."

Rotund and sweating, the barkeep asked Coal his choice in Spanish. Coal pointed to the beer keg.

"Cerveza?"

"If that's what ya calls it."

He had a powerful thirst and drained his first mugful, handing it back for another. Sensing a presence at his right side, Coal slowly swiveled his head. To his pleasant surprise, there stood a smiling woman in a low-cut yellow blouse.

"Buenos días, mi amigo. Cómo esta usted?" she inquired, and Coal gave her a creased brow, instantly letting her see that he did not understand the lingo. She then addressed him in thickly accented English.

"I said, good day, my friend, and how are you?" she repeated.

"Oh, Ah'm fine, ma'am, and a good day to you, too," he politely answered in his natural soft tone.

"My name is Inez Moraldo. Cómo se llama? I mean, what is your name?"

"Mine's Coal, ma'am."

She moved closer to him. "You have only one name, Señor?"

"Ah'm only one man, ma'am," he countered, evoking a genuine smile from her. She eyed him.

"Hmmmm, I like you, negrito lindo. You have the gentle voice, and you do not smell of sour horse sweat as most do who enter here. You will buy Inez a drink, sí?"

Coal looked down at the pretty puta. "If ya wish, ma'am," he consented, a smile flirting at the left corner of his mouth.

Inez ordered tequila with salt and lemon, seemingly very much taken with him.

"You are a pistolero, Señor Coal?"

"No ma'am, jes' a man searchin' for somethin' or someplace," he softly told her.

"But you wear the guns of the pistoleros," Inez persisted.

"Ah'm wearin' boots too, ma'am, but Ah ain't walkin'." Coal smiled.

Inez's sudden outburst of laughter filled the cantina. Coal instantly liked this woman with her carefree manner, tinkling laughter, and seasoned roundness of body that caressed his eyes.

"Coal, do you like me?"

He was in the process of answering her when they were interrupted by the furious snorting of Big Black. In a flash, Coal was out through the swinging doors. A gaunt, scar-faced man was trying to mount its back, and Big Black was having none of it. Two agitating cohorts stood by, laughing at his futile attempts, just as Coal appeared on the top step of the cantina. The man with the scar was then raising his hand to strike Big Black into obedience, and Coal's entire bloodstream turned to ice.

"Hit my horse, redneck, and won't nothin' save your stinkin' ass!"

Big Black's tormentor did not immediately turn to confront the voice, but Coal noticed that the man's back went ramrod stiff. Very slowly the man wheeled to face up at him. Coal almost prayed for the scarface to pull his iron as their eyes intangibly clutched.

Scar Flint was a notorious gunhawk, and killing was his favorite game. "You talkin' to me like that, you nigger sonofabitch?"

"Ah ain't talkin' to that dog-assed bitch who ya call ya momma!" Coal made him crazy.

With lightning speed, Scar Flint drew, and three simultaneous shots reverberated. Flint's bullet creased Coal's face from left cheekbone to ear, drawing blood. Single bullets from each of Coal's six-guns struck Flint's Adam's apple, lifting him off his feet and slamming him backward into the piles of horseshit, then decorating the middle of the street, blood spurting from Flint's throat, eyes, ears, and mouth. He was a dead man in midair.

"Lord God A'mighty!!" someone yelled. "Did ya see that?"

"I think I did," came a reply.

"Flint's brother is gonna go plumb crazy over that," another remarked.

"Shit!" came a response. "Roscoe Flint had better think twice, and after he's done thunk on it a few times, he better leave that there niggah alone!" the voice warned.

Coal stood there, his eyes blazing from the wine of killing still riveted upon the gunfighter he had just put away. Through sheer will, he had remained standing on his feet after bullet force sent his senses reeling. For minutes, he hung rooted to that spot until a Mexican spoke at his side.

"Señor, beware, Señor, for his brother will most certainly come seeking vengeance when he returns this evening," he warned.

"Ah hope his daddy is with 'im, then this town'll see a three-dog funeral," Coal heard himself say.

Forcing his eyes away from the killer sprawled in horseshit, he focused on Inez standing in front of him with her eyes glowing in a way he could not fathom.

"Coal, por favor, come up to my room and I shall attend to your face, it is bleeding."

He allowed himself to be led, only to turn when he reached the swinging doors. Walking away from Inez, he gathered up his saddlebags.

"Anybody else goes near my stallion there, and Ah'll have his balls hangin' from my saddle horn!"

Not one man there doubted that he meant exactly what he said. Inez then ushered him upstairs into a sparse but clean room. Displaying smooth, full limbs as she raised her skirts, Inez ripped two white strips from her slip.

Quickly going to her washstand, she poured fresh water into a basin and proceeded to wipe the blood away from his cheek and neck where it had dripped to. All during the time Inez was cleansing his wound, he sat staring straight ahead. *How strange he is*, she deduced in silent scrutiny.

"Aiiyee chihuahua!" she suddenly exclaimed. "What I have seen this day is still tingling within me. Coal, do you know that you are hombre mucho? Magnífico!"

His mind was then on the bullet that had almost taken his life, and big brother Flint, so he offered no reply to her appraisal. He'd be damned if he was going to hightail it. He intended to stay right there until big brother arrived, and to hell with it. "Ya finished with what ya doin'?" Coal harshly inquired.

"S-sí, sí, Coal. I only wanted to wash it all from your neck."

"Ah'm sorry, Inez, ain't no reason Ah should bite at'cha that way. Ah'm much obliged to ya for cleanin' me up'n all, an Ah thanks ya kindly," he said, reaching into his pocket and extracting a twenty-dollar gold piece, which he extended to her.

Glancing down at the money, her dark eyes flashed up at him and then saddened. "A puta I am, Señor Coal, but please do not insult me with your dineros."

Coal gazed deep into those black, long-lashed eyes, finding her meaning.

"As Ah was ridin' into town, Ah noticed there ain't no law in sight. How come?" he changed the subject.

"The man you just killed, he did the same thing to our law last week. We have no law here."

"Inez, tell me what ya know 'bout that man's brother."

"Roscoe Flint? He is the older brother of that pig now laying in the road out there. Older and meaner."

"That ol' man downstairs, he seem to feel that Flint'd be comin' here this evenin'."

"He comes in every evening around eight, after he completes his duties as foreman for the Triple Circle Ranch, which is just four miles out of town."

"Every evenin', ya say?"

"Sí, almost without fail."

"Ah think the news of his brother might jes' bring'm in sooner."

"I think not, Señor Coal. No one here would dare take him such news, for fear of what he might do to them. He is truly vicious. I have seen him castrate a man upon the blackjack table in this very cantina."

"That nasty, huh?" he softly queried, his big eyes narrowing.

"Your face, Coal, does it hurt very much?"

"No. It burns."

"Inez thinks it shall leave you with a scar." She marked her own face.

"If that's the worst thing ta happen to me in life, Ah'll live a good life."

"You must be hungry, sí? Wait here for me, Coal. Inez will bring you something to eat." She smiled and left the room.

Shortly thereafter, she returned with a large bowl of chili, a platter of enchiladas, and a pitcher of beer. Placing the food upon the table, Inez poured his beer into a glass and invited him to sit and enjoy it. Instinctively trusting her, Coal sat down to the different but good-tasting meal. While he dined, Inez sat sipping tequila and smoking a weird-smelling, crudely-rolled cigarette, intensely observing him in silence.

"Tell me, Inez, ain't ya gittin' on the wrong side of folks here by helpin' me?"

"They, mi negrito lindo, can bésame culo!" she cursed.

"Do what?"

"Kiss my beautiful ass! Not to the left or to the right, but exactly in the middle," she translated, making Coal grin at her sassiness. "Coal, Inez Moraldo does not belong to any man. Until this very day, I had yet to see the man who Inez desired above all others."

His eyes searched hers, finding only sincerity there.

"Meanin' me?"

"Sí, mi negrito lindo," Inez replied, holding his eyes with her own.

"That makes three times ya called me that. What does it mean, Inez?"

"It means 'beautiful black man.' Coal, you do not like Inez to call you so?"

"Ah likes it alright, Ah guess," he shyly responded.

"Coal, you never answered the question Inez was asking you just before you ran out of the cantina." She smiled warmly.

Coal's mind raced back, and he showed her perfect white teeth, causing her heart to skip. "Yeh, li'l Inez, Ah likes ya very much," he confessed. "The food, too."

Raising herself, Inez went and placed a tall chair under the doorknob, jamming it. Returning, she stood directly above and in front of him.

"Then why have you not kissed Inez?" she asked, and he studied her for a long moment.

"Ah guess it's 'cause Ah don't know how," Coal informed her, causing her head to cutely tilt to one side. "Ah've had only three women in bed in my life, and Ah never tried to kiss 'em, 'cause like Ah jes' said, Ah don't know how."

Coal's honest revelation only served to augment the flame that his physical nearness had already created inside her, fanning it to blazing. Inez eased onto his lap. "Here, Coal, Inez shall teach you the correct way," she whispered, her breath coming fast. "Open your mouth, mi corazón. No, Coal, not wide open, open as though you were about to speak."

"Like thi..." he began to say, and she planted her full lips upon his own.

In unison, their bloodstreams ignited. Coal, discovering that he liked this quaking thing called kissing, did so again and again. Then suddenly Inez pushed him away from her and backed against the brass railing at the foot of her bed, her sparkling eyes appearing somewhat dazed. The sight of her soft, round breasts heaving and falling stimulated his whole frame.

From the instant Coal had entered the cantina below, Inez became intrigued by his uniqueness, physically wanting him. But this all-encompassing ecstatic madness now gripping her was emotionally overwhelming to her spirit, causing her to push away, only to stand there and stare at Coal like a wild, frightened thing.

Rising from his chair to move to her, Coal was met halfway as she threw her arms around his neck, filling his mouth with her searching, curious tongue.

"Coal, when one kisses correctly, one must also be dressed for the occasion," Inez whispered.

Following her lead, his eyes surveyed her flawless body as he undressed. Having less to remove, she finished first and helped Coal out of his boots. As they got into bed together, Coal laid his six-guns on the pillow next to his head. Rolling onto her side, Inez began kissing him again. "Aiiyee, how Inez loves your virgin mouth," she murmured, finding it with soft regularity.

Overanxious, Coal painfully entered her. "No, no, Coal, not like a burro. Here, let me show you. Move your body as I am moving mine. Ahh, sí, gently Coal, with feeling," she tutored.

Sliding farther under him, Inez situated herself perfectly and proceeded to grind in rhythm. Coal found her groove in short order, and thereupon set fire to her ass. Having abstained from sex throughout most of his prior existence, and living outdoors while eating only enough to sustain himself, Coal's lean, muscular body served him well.

Inez, spreading her legs wider than wide, wrapped them around Coal's torso and introduced him to south of the border pussy. For an interminable length of time, they fucked splendidly, with Inez crying out a stream of endearments. Whenever she sensed that Coal was nearing his pitch, she would softly speak in English while slackening the pace, prolonging the climax. In the meantime, she was experiencing a come fit. Finally Inez poured it on, making him erupt deep inside of her.

Lifting his cheek from next to hers, Coal looked into her eyes. To his surprise, tears were overflowing down the sides of her face.

"Coal"—she wiped her eyes free—"look once more into my eyes, for Inez has something to give to you which she has given to no one in her life. No, no, don't move, stay inside of me as you are." He waited, wondering.

"Querido, I have known many men, but none of them have known Inez. For you see, a woman must first love her man with her entire soul before he can possibly know her. That is what Inez wants to give to you, Coal, for that is the way I love you."

Slowly slipping from his embrace, she gathered water and towels prior to washing both their bodies. All of this being new to Coal, he laid there watching her do her thing; then they dressed.

"Ahh Coal, our lovemaking was muy bueno," a flushed Inez prettily acclaimed. "Good, good, good, sí? I am still feeling beautiful inside myself."

"Ah been standin' here by this window, searchin my no-schoolin' brain for the right words to tell ya jes' how good it really was, Inez," he softly agreed.

"Oh, mi corazón, but you have just told me in those very words, and I feel pretty in a way I have never known. Would you like more beer, Coal?"

"Yeh, Ah'd like that jes' fine, ma'am."

"Then un momento, mi negrito lindo." She laughed. "Inez shall get it for you right away and hurry back."

Chapter 10

Inez had been wrong in her assumption when she told Coal that no one would dare go and tell Roscoe Flint of his brother's death. The two cronies who had been laughing at Scar Flint's attempts to mount Big Black subsequently made straight for the Triple Circle with the bad news. They were reining up beside Big Black just as Inez was leaving her room to get beer for Coal.

"Is this that nigger's horse?" Flint asked them, drawing his iron and pointing it at the animal's left eye.

But the stallion's beauty caught his eye, making him desire it for himself. "I'll jes' kill this nigger and take his horse for myself," he decided, dismounting.

Flint slammed through the swinging doors, six-gun in hand. Inez was then in the process of picking up the pitcher of beer when she saw them. The informers quickly pointed her out as the whore who had taken the nigger up to her room to fix his face. "You there! Yeah you, ya nigger come-suckin' spic-slut! Where is that nigger ya took up to ya room to fuck on?"

Attempting to ignore him, Inez turned away from the bar with the pitcher in her hands, meaning to go and warn Coal.

"Jes' one more step, spic bitch, and I'll shoot out your cunt!" he menaced her.

Instantly every Mexican man inside the joint curtailed his activities. One chivalrous young vaquero had to be forcibly restrained by his older companions, who knew that he was no match for Roscoe Flint.

The mean man walked up to her. Then snatching Inez by the thin blouse she wore, Flint ripped it straight down the front, exposing her breasts. As she sought to cover herself, Flint grabbed her by the roots of her hair. Still no one attempted to intervene, seeing no point in dying for a puta.

"I asked ya a question, bitch!" Flint evilly grinned, striking Inez with a backhand blow across her mouth, knocking out teeth.

Reeling with blood coursing down her naked bosom, she grabbed the bar rail to keep from falling. Flint continued his advance, asking her again, and those beautiful dark eyes flashed hate at him from above her bloodied mouth.

"Kiss my ass, dog!" Inez cursed, spitting blood and chipped teeth into Flint's face.

Right there at close range, Flint gut-shot Inez. The bullet, entering her stomach and exiting from her slender back just under the right shoulder blade, sent Inez sprawling with a grapefruit-sized hole yawning from her back.

Hearing the gunshot, Coal instantly surmised that it was big brother on the prowl. Raising the window of Inez's room, Coal jumped the one flight, landing catlike on the balls of his feet. Drawing one of his six-guns, he swiftly made his way around to the front of the building. Squinting through the dirty windows, he spied Flint standing over the blood-splattered form of Inez Moraldo.

Rage. Pure black rage gripped Coal's bowels and squeezed his brain. Mexican townspeople, then peeping under and over the swinging doors of the cantina, sighted Coal coming and scattered. Like something possessed by a demon, Coal catapulted through the doors.

"Flint!"

The mean man turned at the sound of Coal's voice, only to

meet the bark of Coal's six-gun as a bullet shattered the knuckles of Flint's hand, which held his gun. Crouched like a panther preparing to leap, Coal fired again, completely demolishing the hand that had shot Inez. Flint, his knees suddenly turning to liquid, crumpled to a kneeling position.

With eyes aflame, his face a death mask, Coal straightened up and moved toward Flint. Then, with great deliberation, he fired a third time, and Flint screamed like a close-built bitch losing her cherry to ravage, as Coal shot off most of his right ear. Coal did not want to kill him only once, but over and over again. Like nothing Flint had ever experienced, fear grabbed him down low, and he pissed himself.

While standing over the near-dead Inez, Coal noticed that all of the vaqueros had drawn their guns and were facing the American fugitives who had done nothing to halt Flint's vicious woman killing. A kneeling Coal raised Inez's head to his chest, and her blood soaked his shirtsleeves. His vision clouded when she lifted a limp hand to his cheek.

"C-C-Coal, I-I-I tried to w-warn y-y-you . . ." Inez gasped, then died there in his arms.

Gently laying her head to the floor, Coal raised his hate mask to Flint. Mean Man stumbled to his feet and began backing away, leaving a trail of piss and blood. "Nooooo!!" Flint begged. "Don't shoot me again! Pleeease!!!"

"Flint," Coal said, grimacing, "Ah ain't gonna do no such thing to ya."

Reaching into his gun belt, Coal inserted his hands into those black skin-tight riding gloves. Walking to where Flint stood, Coal swung from his heels, catching the killer deep up under his heart with a digging left hook and knocking him backward over a table. Before Flint could move, Coal was on top of him like a cat and pulling him to his feet. A pain-inducing right-handed punch plunged into Flint's groin just prior to a whistling left hook, which splattered Flint's nose flat to his face. Still another left landed to

Flint's head, raising a walnut-sized lump to his right eye. A straight right then struck Flint at center throat, followed by a short, crisp left hook to the gut, which resounded like a bass drum when Coal connected.

The woman killer lay unmoving, out cold. Without a word, Coal strode to the bar and got a pail of water, which he doused into Flint's face, reviving him. Then standing Flint up against the far wall of the cantina, a coldly enraged Coal proceeded to beat Roscoe Flint to death.

A road staccato of rights and lefts to Flint's head echoed like pistol shots. Flint tried to talk for his life, but Coal would have none of it, unleashing another volley of lefts and rights to Flint's mouth, sending teeth flying. Flint tried to fall, but Coal hauled him over to the rail banister posts and started in again. Coal's gloves transformed into a sticky, messy crimson as he pounded away.

With tears in his eyes, Coal pleaded to the half-dead killer while grasping the now-misshapen head between two blood-soaked gloves. "Tell me where yo daddy and the rest o' yo fam'ly is!"

Getting no response from the unconscious Flint only served to infuriate Coal all the more. Bringing his knee up hard, he crushed Flint's balls flat, making the dying man vomit. And still Coal kept at him, pounding Flint's body and head until thick, red blood poured from his ears.

Coal, gone insane, whipped Flint's eyes completely out of his skull. He even tried to reach into his mouth and pull out his tongue, so loathsomely filled with contempt was Coal for Flint. Veteran whores and hardened outlaws grew ill as they witnessed mayhem.

The mean man hung there, his locked arms the only things keeping him upright. Horizontally kicking, Coal ran his spurs deep across Flint's stomach. Then standing there before the corpse, Coal panted, spat upon it, cursed it, and then fell into wailing away at it again.

"Señor! Señor, Señor," an elderly Mexican pleaded. "Por favor, señor, it is enough, for he is as dead as any man shall ever be."

Coal shoved him away. "That scum hangin' there, he didn't have to kill a pretty li'l helpless woman jes' 'cause she done me a kindness. She mighta been a whore to y'all, but not to me! And even if she was, this sonofabitch didn't have to kill her, god-damnit! He didn't have to do that, the scurvy sonofabitch! Aghhh!!!" Coal screamed, gone out of his head.

Making eyes pop, his hands instantly filled with his six guns and he emptied them, firing twelve shots and bowing Flint's head away from its neck. Whores passed out when their minds could no longer tolerate the blatant exposure to raw, naked chaos. Almost as quickly as it came, it vanished. Coal appeared to be somewhat dazed and surprised at his bloodied pistol handles held in his gloved hands. He raised his eyes, and people backed away. Retracing his steps to the lifeless Inez, he lifted her body to carry her up to her bed, which they had just shared. On the way up to her room, he had to pass what used to be Roscoe Flint, still draped over the banister. While holding in his arms the dead whore who loved him, Coal kicked the cadaver loose to the floor.

Although he could not then define what it was that he had felt for the lovable, laughing Inez, the loss of it had transformed him into an avenging, raging demon. Upstairs, he washed her deci-mated body, recalling how she had washed his own less than an hour ago. Opening her closet where a few dresses hung, Coal chose what to him was her prettiest and covered her naked, de-stroyed torso.

Leaving Inez alone upon her bed, Coal went to check on Big Black. After getting a stall and feed for his animal, he walked back through the main floor of the cantina. On his way upstairs, three Mexicans approached him.

"Señor, we wish to help you bury your friend or do anything we can to help you prepare her for burial," one stated, and Coal glared at him.

"Where in the fuck was ya help when she was all alone down here with that crazy man, huh? She was one of ya own people. At least somebody coulda yelled for me. Ah could easily kill all a ya for lettin' her git murdered that way, but 'cause Ah feels that she wouldn't like it, is the only reason Ah ain't doin' jes' that," he told them.

"Señor, we are very much ashamed, señor, but we are not gunmen. Perhaps a coffin, sí, Señor? She will need the coffin to be buried in," a white-haired man suggested.

Coal stared hard into the old eyes and then nodded his consent before striding away. Throughout that night, Coal isolated himself with the young woman who had befriended him and subsequently died for it. No tears fell from his eyes, but his heart ached terribly. As he touched her lifeless hand, the iciness of death made him shiver, but he held onto that hand until dawn peeped over the rim of the mountains.

Townsmen and women arrived with a coffin and laid Inez into it. Each pounding of the hammer closing the lid was a blow to Coal's inner depths. At the burial, Coal stood alone and away from those in attendance, holding the reins of his horse. Silently he bade farewell to the woman he would have taken away from that life, had she lived. That day was not an easy one for him to live through, but then neither were any of the others in Coal's first twenty-five years. The previous day, he had felt the need for human company; now, he hated everyone and everything except the animal he rode upon.

"Well, big fella, it's jes' you'n me again. Let's move!" He spurred him, and Coal left Inez Moraldo there, cold and alone in the ground.

With the speed of the wind, Big Black galloped away from his master's pain. At the top of a rise in the land, Coal reined him in for one last look at the far-off gravesite of Inez. Gently spurring again, the stallion responded with another burst of speed. The farther away they traveled, his hurt seemed to lessen. All morning, Coal rode, on into late evening. Purposely avoiding the towns various signposts indicated, he rode up high into the Sierra Madre mountains of Mexico.

Around about twilight, Coal camped near a mountain stream. Far into the night, he laid gazing up at the stars, which seemed near enough to reach out and touch, before finally falling asleep.

In this particular area of the Sierra Madre where Coal chose to pitch camp, the ever-dangerous Nedni Apaches roamed. The Nedni Apaches were the famed Geronimo's people, and extremely warlike. They were also blood enemies of every living and dead Mexican. The Mexicans of this era, in turn, hated and despised the very mention of the word *Apache*.

In the year of 1837, the state of Chihuahua had issued a standing bounty on the scalps of all Apaches. One hundred pesos for a grown male scalp. Fifty pesos for a grown female scalp. Twenty-five for the scalps of Apache children.

Knowing of the existence of the bounty did not tend to make the Apaches sociable, and every stranger who was not an Apache was indeed held suspect.

Long after the sun was up, the snorting of Big Black awakened him. Coal laid still, slowly cracking his lids. Then springing to his feet as if snake-bit, he found no danger. That is, none that he could see. Studying Big Black, he saw that the steed's head faced south, his great nostrils dilating as his ears twitched this way and that. Coal casually strolled to his horse, his muscles coiled to create havoc with his six-guns. Apache Indian eyes secretly observed him, uncertain how to react toward one with skin such as they had never seen before.

"There is somethin' botherin' ya, ain't it, big fella?" Coal whispered. "Ya smells somethin' ah can't see, don't ya? Okay, Ah'll take yo' word for it. Jes' a few seconds and Ah'll have this saddle on ya back, then we gonna git the hell outta here!"

Coal still did not see them, but by then, he could damn well feel them. No sooner had he tightened the under cinch that secured his saddle and leaped into it, did a deadly Apache arrow whiz past his nose.

"Oh shit! Pick 'em up 'n lay 'em down, big fella. Move!!" Coal yelled, sparking his horse.

As if cannonized, the stallion shot away. Vaulting over a five-foot hedgebrush like nothing, Big Black half-slid, half-ran down a steep embankment with ruthless, warrior Apaches in hot pursuit. One of them suddenly appeared out of nowhere, pulling back on his bowstring, and never knew what hit him as Coal shot two holes in his head while passing by.

"Show 'em yo asshole, Big Black!" he commanded, and the powerful steed all but flew with his tail raised high.

For about a quarter of a mile or so, the Indians and their speedy ponies stayed on Coal's ass, but they didn't know what real speed was all about.

As though tired of lingering, Big Black began to skip, steadily widening the gap with each sure-footed step. With his jet-black mane sticking out on the wind in full gallop, the Morgan thoroughbred covered ground like a blanket.

Coal discovered something about himself that morning, something he wasn't at all certain he liked. He found that he enjoyed the excitement generated by the presence of danger with death hovering near. Glancing back over his shoulder, Coal pulled up. Laughing with the thrill of challenge coursing through his veins, he turned and faced into the direction of the cursing, angered Apaches in the distance. Coal raised a mocking fist at them, yelling and daring them to come on again, cursing back and laughing.

"Uh-oh, Big Black, here they come again!" He grinned and took off from there.

This time, he raced harder and faster, the excitement of that dangerous game sending his pulse racing. After outdistancing the small band of warriors, Coal saw that they were not easily discouraged. Although they had ceased chasing him, they were still tracking him. Steering Big Black to higher ground so that he could see for miles into the direction he had just traveled, Coal spotted eight of them approximately two miles away, steadily following his tracks.

"Alright, goddamnit, now that's enough of this here bullshit!" he cursed aloud.

Dismounting, he pulled his long-ranged Pinkney rifle from its scabbard and patiently waited for them to get closer. The Apaches could not see Coal lying in wait, but he saw them pretty good. Once they moved into sure-hitting range, Coal gave them a braid-raising exhibition in marksmanship. Drawing a bead on the leader, Coal fired, dropping him. He could see them looking in all directions, frantically seeking to find out where his shots came from. Quickly Coal pumped off four more rounds, dropping two more braves. And as he figured it would, they changed their minds pretty fast, outrunning themselves getting away from that deadly Pinkney rifle.

Even though he knew they had given up tracking him, Coal nevertheless slept all night with one eye open, and Big Black's saddle remained right where it was, on his back.

Chapter 11

A few days after his confrontation with the Apaches, Coal awakened with a start, wondering what it was. One glance at Big Black told him the animal had also heard it. Then from somewhere in the distance, the gonging of church bells again reached his ears. After eating the last of his rations, Coal mounted and rode off into the direction of those sounds. Almost two hours later, he came upon a monastery at the foot of a lush valley. From Coal's mountaintop position, he leisurely feasted his eyes on the quiet, picturesque scene. Never had he seen anything quite like it.

Rolling hills blanketed with rich, green grass formed a backdrop that settled like a crest of jewelry above the monastery. The unfamiliar architecture was truly magnificent to Coal's eyes. With the early morning's sun caressing its walls with a luminous lustre, it was indeed a tranquil sanctuary concealed within nature's confines, reaching out to touch him. And each time those bells resounded, white doves would swirl and arc in a winged dance above the belfry.

Coal rode down to it, drawn by the compelling structure and its existence. As he drew nearer, his eyes caught sight of something that made him wonder. He observed what he took to be men walking in pairs, in groups of ten or twelve. What kind of men were these? Coal studied their reddish robes with hoods and the ropelike sashes around their waists. His mind instantly went to his guns when he noticed how those robed men kept their hands concealed within the sleeves of their getups. He rode closer, his eyes glued upon those very weird men. About fifty feet in front of what Coal thought were the tallest doors on Earth, he halted. This procession of walking men seemed endless, making him wonder if perhaps they were simply passing through one door and out of the other in a circle, since they all looked alike to him.

"Buenos días, my son," he suddenly heard from behind.

Whirling in his saddle with his right hand filled with instant iron, and the hammer a hair's breadth away from slamming home, Coal stared at the man in a dress and a hood. "Mistuh, Ah don't think my daddy looked anything like ya," Coal curtly replied in a voice soft yet cold, his eyes watching those sleeves hiding the priest's hands.

"In the eyes of God, my son, everyone is his children," voiced the Padre, his brown eyes gentle.

"Ya tryin' to tell me that's who you are?"

Below the gentle eyes, a cherubic mouth smiled. "No, my son, far be it for me to even assume such omnipotence," he said, noticing that Coal's eyes never once left the spot where the priest's hands lay clasped and hidden in the folds of his sleeve. The Padre revealed them, and Coal's six-gun was instantly holstered.

"My name is Padre Dominic, and yours?" he inquired, reaching up and offering his hand to Coal, who took it.

"Mine's Coal."

"Only one name, my son? How strange. Every man I have had God's honor to meet had at least two," he remarked, evoking Coal to ponder his statement.

Padre Dominic's eyes were then studying Coal's face in a concentrated manner, and Coal asked him about that.

"You, my son, are the first Africano I have had the pleasure to see, Coal."

"First what?"

"Africano, my son. You are black, so undoubtedly you are Africano," he clarified, and Coal frowned.

"You mean you did not know this? Hmmmm, stranger yet," he musingly deduced. "Come down from your fine stallion and come into the monastery with me. I shall see what I can do to mend your face. That wound you have there should have been treated before now. How long have you suffered it, my son?"

"A few days or so, Ah guess."

"Enter with me, my son. We have healing salves, which I shall apply to your wound. You can also leave those pistolas you are wearing on the saddle horn of your saddle."

"Mistuh, Ah goes nowhere and does nuthin' without my guns."

"My son, there will be no need for them inside the house of God."

"So ya say, but it'd be a damn sight better for me to git caught with 'em than without 'em," Coal persisted.

The priest examined Coal's manner and his eyes as he spoke about his six-guns, then shrugged. "It is of no consequence. Come, we shall see to your face," he urged, and Coal glanced back at his horse.

"Your handsome steed will be safe here, too; there are no thieves in the house of God."

"He ain't inside, he's out here."

"No matter, my son, here he is secure."

Reluctantly, Coal took him at his word and followed him inside. As they entered the inner sanctum, the pungent odor of incense permeated his nostrils, and liking it, Coal inquired about it, and the Padre told him what it was. The interior of the monastery was cool, as in a cave. Conducting Coal through a maze of corridors, Padre Dominic came to a freshly painted door and entered.

"Coal, my son, sit over there by the window in the light, and I shall gather the ointments."

The holy man returned with three articles. One was a jar. The other a bowl containing greenish-looking water. Last was a flat box with white powder in it. Twisting a piece of clean cloth between his fingers, he dabbed it into the green liquid and gently washed the surface of the wound free of crusted blood. When the antiseptic dried, he sprinkled a thin film of powder along the length of the scar. Over that, he smeared on the salve, which smelled like buffalo fat.

Immediately after his treatment, Coal rushed to the window. Big Black was exactly where he had left him, swaying his raven silk tail. Coal turned to the priest.

"Ah'm much obliged to ya for what ya jes' done for me, Mr. Dominic, and Ah'd like to pay ya for it."

"Pay me? My son, has no one ever done you a courtesy without seeking tribute?" His question instantly brought Inez to Coal's mind.

"A ol' man and his wife did. Then a woman did"—Coal frowned—"and she got kilt for it," he concluded, momentarily shutting his eyelids.

"Forgive me, my son, for I can see that it has left you with pain inside your heart."

"Ain't nuthin'," Coal muttered, wanting to kill Roscoe Flint all over again.

"Coal, I am seldom, if ever, curious, but you make me so. I can feel—for want of a better word—feel a goodness emanating from you. It is there in your loving concern for that beautiful animal outside, and in your eyes. Yet I can also sense an element of danger surrounding you. Tools of violence encircle your waist, but your voice and eyes tell yet another tale. If it is not an imposition on my part, let us talk, you and me."

In no time at all, those extremely different men found themselves deeply engrossed in meaningful conversation. Coal discovered that he divulged to the priest matters concerning himself that only he knew. Even about his mother and Becky.

It was almost evening and time for Padre Dominic's prayers when they terminated their conversation. The priest invited

Coal to attend the rituals, but he begged off, and his host did not persist. Before departing, he inquired as to Coal's destination, learning he had none.

The man with the gentle brown eyes then invited Coal to use a cabin located atop the hill overlooking the monastery, and he accepted. When he left, Coal remained, thinking. Always one to examine his own feelings, Coal realized that he had sorely needed to talk to another human being who in turn acknowledged him as one and the same. He was glad he had ridden to and found that valley monastery. Before darkness settled, Coal left to take a look at the cabin. Riding to the top of the hill, he dismounted and ventured inside. Lighting a match, he found a candle and then surveyed his new abode.

There was a cot, a table and two chairs, a picture supposedly of Christ, and an entire wall of dusty books upon shelves. Silently Coal read names and titles of books he never knew existed, whereupon a deep inner craving for knowledge enveloped his being. Although he could read, the only literature previously accessible to him were the few books that were owned by Mrs. Munsen. After unsaddling his mount and turning him loose to graze, Coal chose a work depicting the history of the Greek Empire. He fell asleep reading it.

Early that next morning, when hunger jerked Coal from sleep, he went hunting and bagged a young deer. After skinning and eating, the sun was well up in the sky. With the book, Coal went outside the cabin to sit against a tree and read in the shade. Padre Dominic found him there late that afternoon. Pleasantly surprised to discover Coal could read, he immediately bestowed piles upon piles of musty-smelling old books on him.

"Padre, Ah got some pretty good'n sweet deer meat hangin' out in back the cabin. You'n your friends kin have most of it if ya likes."

"Gracias, my son. Seldom do we indulge in such luxuries, Coal, for we are not hunters."

* * *

In the following months, Coal grew obsessed with learning, and his uncluttered mind eagerly devoured every accessible piece of knowledge. Many nights, as the good priest prepared for bed, he would gaze upward from his window and see a light burning in Coal's quarters. Subjects that initially were incomprehensible to Coal would be patiently explained to him by the priest. But the one subject Coal shied away from was religion.

To Coal's way of thinking, no one could convince him that a white man somewhere up in the sky gave one good damn about his black ass down here on Earth. He told the priest as much, and the priest avoided ever attempting to convert Coal. But he did render Coal many religious works to study and read, which one day led Coal to make an inquiry that baffled the holy man.

"Padre Dominic, if Christ did come from the tribe of Judah, which your Bible says was and is the blackest tribe in Israel, and Christ was a black Jew, how come all the pictures Ah ever seen had him lookin' like a white man?"

His query drew the priest to his feet, only to pace about the grass in front of Coal's cabin. For long moments afterward, he made no reply, seemingly wrapped in deep thought.

"Coal, I must admit that your question warrants an answer which I cannot supply you with. It is also an intriguingly interesting one. Undoubtedly Christ has obviously been portrayed according to the artist's conception. You see, in the Scriptures, it states that God made man in His own image. So, perhaps each artist who subsequently painted and identified with Him did so with the mental conception of Christ being like himself."

"Hummph!" Coal grunted. "Seems like a lie with no beginnin' and no end. If a man is born black, don't seem right that history should lie and make him somethin' he never was."

Padre Dominic did not let on, but Coal's question deeply troubled him. "I'm inclined to agree with you, Coal, because Christ definitely was a black Jew. Coal, have you ever thought about God in one way or another?"

"A few times Ah have. Times when Ah'd see a Bible-totin' preacher, or hear folks talkin' 'bout religion."

"Do you believe there is a God?"

"Can't rightfully say if there's a God or not. But if there is, Ah know Ah could never be one o' his followers."

"But why, Coal?"

"'Cause if there's a God, Ah knows he don't like'n don't give a damn 'bout black folks like me!"

"Madre de Dios!" the priest exclaimed, crossing himself. "But Coal, my son, no, that is not true!"

"It ain't, huh? Padre Dominic, Ah'm gonna tell ya somethin'. Ah'm the only black man Ah ever seen who didn't have the flesh-colored scar of shackles on his arms, legs, or neck. Where Ah comes from, it's rare for a black man to even git water from a white man to take a bath! Whole fam'lies git separated, and black folks can't do nuthin' 'bout it. If ya thinks Ah'm lyin' to ya, visit Texas an' see for ya self. And ya wanna know somethin' else, Padre? Preachers say the same thing in Texas, sayin' we's all God's children . . . every Sunday."

Coal's twenty-sixth birthday came and went with him still in residence at the hilltop cabin, and with each passing day, the bond between pupil and tutor grew ever stronger. Father Dominic of the Bible and Coal of the gun. A peculiar character blending, for sure, but these two men thoroughly enjoyed their friendship and absolute mutual trust. In spite of intermittent attempts by Coal to give him money in reciprocation for his lodgings and daily education, the priest would never accept it. But whenever Coal returned from his frequent trips into the mountains to hunt, Father Dominic would graciously receive the meats rendered by him. Other than the daily amenities, Coal seldom conversed with the other priests, and they did not impose themselves upon him.

Father Dominic, recognizing an innate intelligence in his eager pupil, soon began to teach Coal the language of the land he then rode upon. By the time Coal reached his twenty-seventh year of age, he could speak Spanish fluently, and his English was no longer punctuated by idiomatic utterances.

Seasons expired into seasons, only to return again. Three years passed while the matured Coal broadened his literary scope of the world and its knowledge therein. Now his mind possessed such things as philosophy, history, geography, language, religions and their origins. Whenever he conversed with the Padre, they did so in Spanish, as they were doing on the evening of Coal's twenty-eighth birthday, May 17th, 1858.

"Coal, forgive me, but I have been boasting about you to my fellow Brothers in Christ." Padre Dominic fondly smiled. "But it is true, you are a truly fine scholar and an even finer person. And now, if only you would discard those guns of yours, everything would be perfect."

"Father Dominic," Coal said, laughing, "you are the most determined man in creation! You just never quit tryin', do you?"

"I would not be your friend if I did quit," he wisely countered.

Coal sat there warmly appraising his dear friend, who had presented him with something he had never dreamed of attaining, an education. For several weeks prior, Coal had been harboring an itch to move on and see what life held in store for him. He dreaded having to say goodbye, but the urge was strong within him. Coal decided to wait until his moment of departure, and that way, he could make it short and quick.

Next morning, when he opened his eyes, it was with the feeling of utmost sadness. He lay wondering which direction he would take. Coal knew he did not ever intend journeying north again, for as far as he was concerned, if he never again saw the despised land of his birth and enslavement, that would be too soon. After packing his saddlebags, he rode Big Black down from the cabin to bid farewell to his everlasting friend and teacher.

Tending his garden, Father Dominic observed Coal slowly approaching on his high-stepping stallion. He studied Coal's eyes when he halted there beside him, sighing resignedly.

"For many days now, I have known that this moment was coming. Coal, my son, must you leave?" inquired the holy man with deeply saddened eyes.

"Sí, Padre Dominic, for I feel I must find that something . . . or someplace."

"Then I shall pray for you to find that which you seek. And also, Coal, it is my profound wish that somewhere one day, you will also find God."

"If I do"—Coal smiled downward—"I'll be sure to tell him that the good Padre Dominic is in line for a promotion, because you're the best man he's got in his whole army."

"Madre de Dios!" He crossed himself again.

Coal then dismounted and silently embraced with the Padre. His tutor took hold of the horse's reins, his eyes holding those of Coal's.

"Coal, my son, in the three years you have been here, I have truly felt inside my heart that you are the son I never had or will have in this life. So, take these words of advice to your bosom. Many men in your young life have died from those things strapped to your thighs. That is enough to account for when once you meet your maker."

"Padre, I can't promise you that even more won't do so, for I cannot predict the future. But I shall honestly try to avoid it. Farewell, good Padre Dominic." Coal hugged him again before fluidly springing back into his saddle.

"Farewell, my dear son, and may God ride with you always," he said, and watched Coal spur his stallion away.

For three weeks, Coal rode, happy to be in the saddle again. Out of the State of Chihuahua on into the State of Sonora he journeyed, pleasantly recalling those unforgettable three years. It had been good, all of it. His raw confidence of his pre-monastery days was now enhanced and fortified by the knowledge acquired during his stay there. He was now an educated man, and Coal felt inside his heart that he was more of a man amongst men now that the stifling cloak of ignorance had been discarded completely and forever.

Like wild geese finding their way without the aid of maps, Coal rode, letting his instincts lead him all the way.

Chapter 12

One day in his third month away from the monastery, Coal was riding southward and again preoccupied with fond thoughts of Father Dominic. His left hand went up to the same side of his face, fingering his scar. Perfectly it had healed skin-level and not lumpy, due to the expert and excellent doctoring by the holy man. His thoughts of the man made him smile as he guided Big Black up an icy stream, cooling the animal's hooves. Suddenly their ears caught the gut-screams of a man in agony, making the horse halt in its tracks.

Standing high in his stirrups, Coal scanned the area ahead, but his eyes detected nothing. Quietly guiding his mount out of the stream, he dismounted. "Stay," he whispered, and the stallion froze where it stood.

Crouching low, Coal cautiously advanced forward toward a ravine he spotted. As of yet, he could see nothing to associate with the terrible screams he had heard. Once more it re-sounded, even louder. Crawling Comanche-fashion to a hedge, Coal peered through and sighted something he instantly wished he had not, for his first inclination was to turn away. It was none of his business.

Standing upright in a buckboard with tears of frustrated anger spilling down his young face was a good-looking Mexican in bonds with a rope tied around his neck. But what restrained Coal from turning away was the heinous act being perpetrated by four men, two white and two Mexican. They stood encircling an object at their feet. That object was another boy. Squinting, Coal saw that there was some kind of sticky substance smeared from the lad's throat to his hairline. Running amok all over his head were an army of large red ants, entering up into his nostrils, his ears, mouth, and eyes, soon to devour his very brain.

RAGE! Unbeckoned, unchained, fury gripped Coal, and he stood up, feeling his blood turn ice-cold.

"Stand away from that boy, you low-life sons of bitches!" Coal bellowed.

Three of the four men wheeled, snatching for iron. Lightning isn't fast. Cobras aren't fast. COAL was how one spelled fast that day in the sunlight. Coiled like a spring wound tight, with his fingers curled tentacles, Coal deliberately waited until the torturers had turned his way with the barrels of their six-guns coming up fast; then he drew and fired both six-guns three times, inserting two bullets apiece into the skulls of three different men.

With smoking six-guns in his mitts, Coal stalkingly advanced on the fourth scoundrel, a fancy-dressed Mexican in a wide sombrero. "Go on scum, pull! Pull, you motherless snake! Pull!" Coal stalked him, his eyes aglow.

"No!!!" he refused. "No-no-no, Señor, not against what I have just seen!" he cried, and Coal put all of his 175 pounds into a flat-arched swing.

The top side of his left six-gun landed with devastating force upon the lips of fancy man, driving his front teeth down his throat. He sank to the ground like a fancy wet rag. Swiftly Coal leaped onto the wagon and untied the crying youngster's hands.

Together they dug the other fellow out of the ground, hastily wiping away what ants and honey they could from his face. Lifting the heavy body like a child, Coal threw him over his shoulder and raced to the stream with him. Still in awed shock from the actions of the hombre negrito and his pistolas, the youngster could only watch, clenching and unclenching his fists in anger.

Coal worked feverishly, repeatedly submerging the fellow's head under the water, sensing that this procedure would float the ants out of his nose and ears. The young man was still alive but nothing on him moved, even after Coal continuously placed his head under the water. More ants swam from his head, but Coal knew many more remained inside the skull. For fear of drowning him, Coal had to halt momentarily. A brief interval transpired, and he then commenced with the same procedure. Just as Coal thought, more ants appeared upon the water's surface.

"You speak English?" he asked the youngster, for some reason concealing the fact that he spoke Spanish.

"Sí, Señor."

"How fast can we get him to a doctor?"

"Doctor Ramirez has been the houseguest of my father for quite some time, señor. He is there this very moment."

"Let's be on our way then," Coal urged.

He whistled for Big Black, and the stallion came running. Carrying the stricken man in his arms, Coal gently placed him inside the buckboard. "Toothless" was only then regaining consciousness.

"Who is this bastard in the fancy duds, ahh, what's your name?"

"Francisco Santos, Señor. The one you saved is my brother Miguel. This one," he snarled, kicking the bloodied man in his ass, "is Carlos Tomasino. His father is the archenemy of my father."

"No man should be allowed to live after doing what he just did to your brother," said Coal, his lips curling with scorn.

Strolling over to where the bloody-faced man was just stirring and drawing one of his six-guns, Coal fired twice, shattering both knee-caps and crippling Carlos Tomasino for life. Then, dragging the unconscious Tomasino by the back of his coat collar, Coal picked him up and threw him onto the wagon next to the stilled form of the tortured young man. Stunned, young Francisco could only gape wide-eyed.

Racing away from the scene, he instructed the boy to lead the way to his home. Presently Coal saw many vaqueros tending cattle feeding upon lush grassland. The beef on the hoof looked good enough to eat on the hoof. Sighting the speeding buckboard heading toward the main house, several Mexican cowboys left the herd to ride alongside the buckboard all the way to its destination, their eyes staying upon the black hombre who drove.

From the porch of the spacious house, sharp old eyes scrutinized the wagon's approach, examining the kind of man he had previously only heard and read of. Don Humberto Santos, Mexican cattle king, stepped from his veranda. No sooner had the wagon come to a dust-flying halt, did the youngster leap from it, running to his father. Francisco then rattled off a rapid stream of Spanish as the men who had ridden behind them listened in rapt attention. Once, during his highly animated discourse, Francisco placed both hands at his sides and then quickly pulled them up in the manner of a man drawing two guns. Then he held up six fingers and pointed at the ground, saying: "Uno, dos, tres!"

Vaqueros rushed the stricken Miguel into the house, and Francisco completed his tale by pointing into the direction from which they came. Cat-like, Coal swung his body back over the driver's seat, standing upright in the buckboard. Reaching down, he grasped Carlos Tomasino by his suit jacket lapels and hurled him into the dust at the feet of the cotton-maned cattle baron.

"Just in case your son dies from all those ants inside his head, you might want to take ahold of this sonofabitch," Coal stated through clenched teeth.

The range lord, whose eyes had not overlooked a single movement of Coal's from his moment of entry into the front yard, walked up close to Coal and stared into his eyes.

"Señor, my youngest son tells me that you have killed one of the sons of my worst and oldest enemy, and permanently crippled the other while also saving the lives of two of my own. Señor Negrito . . ."

"The name is Coal," he softly corrected the Don.

"Señor Coal, it is indeed my pleasure to make your acquaintance. I am Don Humberto Santos, who owns all of the land your eyes can see east, west, and south of here," he declared, and then raised his voice a few notches higher. "And I now say to all who bear witness this day. Hear and know this to be! I hereby declare that all I own or shall ever possess is yours to share, Señor Coal, with me and the family Santos for so long as you shall live. Nothing, Señor Coal, and I mean nothing shall be refused you upon the land of Santos. I am in your debt for as long as life lasts within my heart, for had it not been for you, I would be burying two sons on the morrow."

His unwavering eyes told Coal that he indeed meant every word of his declaration. "You owe me nothing, Don Santos. I had no choice other than to do what I did."

"Be that as it may, I and all of my sons would face death in your defense, Coal. From this day and forevermore, you are also a son of Don Humberto Santos. And now Coal, step into our home while I see to your brother, who you have rescued and returned home to us."

The Don started inside, but Coal did not move. Turning in his tracks, he faced Coal for a wordless minute or more, their eyes locked in a silent something which only they understood. Then Coal suddenly smiled to him, showing his teeth in a fashion he seldom did. Retracing his steps, the Don wrapped an arm around Coal's shoulders and he let himself be led into the house.

Upon entering the grand home, Coal was struck, optically struck by the tasteful grandeur of it all. Never had he seen such splendor or even conceived that such beauty could be enclosed with the framework of a house. Although it could not be detected by looking at him, Coal was awed, captivated, overwhelmed. He followed the Don up a mahogany-banistered, red-carpeted, winding stairway, to a door of polished mahogany.

Inside, the family of Miguel Santos hovered together while awaiting the doctor's prognosis. Standing nearest to the bed was Francisco. Coal discovered three other young men, whom he instantly discerned as sons of the Don. Also present were two women and a very young girl. He observed in silence.

Doña Luz Santos, with raven black hair streaked with gray at her temples, anxiously watched her unmoving son. Holding on to her arms were two of the three Santos daughters. The distinguished Dr. Ramirez straightened up from the prostrate form, his visage dour.

"Miguel will live," he announced, causing Luz Santos to clutch her breasts, "but I'm afraid he shall always remain as he is this very moment," he sadly concluded.

Every eye went to the powerfully built Miguel, staring, and forever to remain in the limbo state of catatonic shock.

"Muchas gracias, Don Ramirez," they heard the trembling voice of Don Santos say. "And now, amigo, if you will be so kind as to attend to the son of my enemy, I wish to be alone with my family."

"As you wish," he obliged, heading for the door. Coal also moved as though to exit.

"Stay, Coal!" the patriarch's voice held him. "You, too, are family!"

A room full of Santos eyes then fell upon the jet-black man with his two walnut-handled six-shooters strapped to his thighs. Coal stayed, and his large dark optics met their gazes. Never had any of them ever seen a black man in the flesh, only in their textbooks, which displayed drawings of Coal's people who inhabited the dark continent of Africa, a proud heritage as old as time itself.

They found him to be strangely unique. Yet in that same strangeness, they all felt the compelling strength of him, which seeped from his very pores. Not a single eye was hostile. To the contrary, those eyes of the family Santos welcomed him. Emotionally, the lips of Doña Santos trembled in a silent *thank you*, and Coal experienced the newness of humility.

"Luz, my only," said the Don, "today, with the eyes of God looking on, Coal saved the lives of our Miguel and Francisco. I have brought him into our home as my son. Therefore, he is also yours. Coal, go and say hello to your new mother."

Coal, his eyes abright with the feeling of that moment which they all were sharing, fully faced the matriarch, the regal, stately, mother of clan Santos. She advanced to Coal, a grateful queen whose tears were close to spilling, and placed her slender jeweled hands against his cheeks. Then raising on tiptoe, she kissed him.

"Bienvenido, Coal, son of mine. Welcome for life. You are now ours, as we are yours. Ours is a closely knit clan, my son, closer than close. Love us as your own, and we most assuredly shall love you in return."

Filled to the top with feeling, Coal could only nod in reply to her words and then gently embrace her. He did not trust his voice to speak just then.

"And now," resumed the Don, "meet your brothers and sisters. Coal, do you know when you were born?"

Clearing his throat free of emotion, Coal turned back to him. "Yes, sir. It was on the seventeenth of May, 1830, on a plantation in Charleston, South Carolina."

"Coal, this is Escobar, the oldest son until you. Born November sixth, 1830."

Warmly smiling, Escobar strode up to Coal and hugged him. "Gracias, mi hermano," he told Coal.

"And next"—the Don smiled—"is my reckless Antonio."

The outrageously handsome Antonio ventured forth and gripped forearms with Coal, for they were of the same mold. Then in accordance to their ages came Raoul, followed by Francisco with hero worship canvassing his face. He alone had seen Coal venting his wrath upon the wicked, and nothing on Earth could possibly have been more impressionable to a fifteen-year-old.

Walking to where the girls stood close to their mother, the

Don wrapped his arms about them and brought the girls to Coal. "My son, this is my first, oldest, and gentlest. Sonia."

She, too, embraced Coal, softly saying, "Gracias, Coal, gracias, mi hermano."

Esmeralda, twelve years old, a combination of shy and sassy, giggled, hesitated, and then flew laughing into his arms, her child's heart already captured by her new brother. A grinning Coal scooped her up and held her there in his arms.

"Miguel," Don Santos continued, "as you know, lays there before us. Alita! Where on earth is Alita?" he barked.

Alita, the twin of Antonio, was the apple of her father's eye and the flower of their family. She was more like her father than any of the others; some even said that she should have been a boy. She was truly the daughter of a king, an enchanting princess. At twenty-three, she was lithe, not quite lean, yet ample-bodied. Alita's head adorned an almost too long neck, but it was her head that immediately commanded one's attention. From constantly being outdoors with her brothers and riding the rangeland under the protective eyes of the more than a thousand vaqueros who all worshipped her father, Alita was as brown as a mountain berry at that very special time of year called autumn. Although her mouth was a wee bit large, the contours of her lips made one forget all else. Her small, exquisitely shaped nose was the exact duplicate of her mother's, accentuating the doelike slant of her eyes, which illuminated and enhanced it all. Alita Alesandria Santos was devastatingly lovely, an enchantress.

While standing there at his window, Don Santos caught sight of her and another rider he recognized to be Don Ricardo Santiago, the son of a dear old friend and the fiancé of Alita.

As certain as every strand of hair upon his head was white, the Don mused, he could foretell to the world what Alita's reaction would be the instant she cast her eyes upon the pitch-black handsomeness of Coal. Just as he wanted Coal for his son, he knew in his heart that Alita would also want him—for herself.

And to the wise Don, it was God's will. *Ricardo Santiago*, thought the Don, *young man, you are in trouble.*

He observed as his favorite child galloped up to the crowd of vaqueros then lingering in the front yard of the hacienda, and he witnessed them informing her of the fate that had befallen her favorite brother. She disappeared from his vision as she raced into the house and up the stairs with Don Ricardo in her wake.

The door to Miguel's room flew open, Alita halted in her tracks, and Coal's heart stood still; it was not that she had forgotten her brother as she stood frozen there, but more so the fact that she had become instantly and irrevocably captivated.

So, this is he whom our vaqueros spoke of, Alita silently appraised Coal, feeling her breath catch within her bosom and her heart turn over, and over, and over. Before a single word passed between them, their souls locked. Suddenly to both of them, there was no one else in the room . . . the world.

Everyone felt it as their vibrations reached out to touch one and all. Coal and Alita did not know what the future held in store for them, but whatever it unveiled, it was for damn sure they knew they would see it together. Ever so slowly, she approached Coal.

"I am Alita." She met his eyes, standing regal, strong-willed, and untamed.

"My name is Coal," he softly replied, wanting more than anything to tame her without breaking what his eyes then thrilled upon.

They remained standing close, searching the mirrors of their souls. Don Santos broke the trance. "Coal, my son, this is Don Ricardo Santiago, Alita's fiancé."

"Howdy," Coal said, never once removing his eyes from hers. Finally Alita backed away to go to Miguel's bedside.

For long seconds, she stood above her brother; then reaching down, she gently touched his face, eyes blank upon the ceiling. When finally she did raise her eyes, Alita found the two men who loved her in optical combat. Don Ricardo was glaring raw hate at Coal. And what the family was then witnessing in Coal's eyes was the prelude to what young Francisco had seen only a couple of hours earlier. Coal knew exactly what to do with all of that hate he saw. The room acquired a sudden chill.

"Francisco!" his father called. "Show your new brother where to stable his horse," he ordered, wanting to put distance between Santiago and Coal.

"Un momento, Cisco," Alita intervened. "Come, Coal, I will show you."

Ricardo stepped slightly into her path. "Alita, my dearest, I don't think . . ."

"You are correct, Ricardo, don't think!" she interrupted him. "In particular—and I am saying this to you in front of my family— do not think of me as your betrothed, from this moment on!" she declared, making Ricardo appear stunned. "Coal, come," she urged once more, extending her outstretched hand to him.

Hand in hand, they passed the seething Ricardo as if he no longer existed. Down the winding stairway, they ran. Once outside, Alita released his hand and effortlessly mounted her horse. Springing atop Big Black, Coal turned his animal, and they left the yard at a gallop. From Miguel's window, her parents watched as Coal and Alita disappeared over a rise, racing with the wind. Sitting easy-like in his saddle, Coal glanced to his right and discovered her eyes upon him as they rode. Then the voice of dead Inez came to him from out of nowhere.

"You are a pistolero, Señor Coal?"

"No ma'am, jes' a man searchin' for somethin' or someplace."

With shattering lucidity, Coal suddenly realized that it had been neither. His subconscious searching had been for someone. A few miles later, they came to a mountain clearing of sterling beauty, where Alita reined her palomino and dismounted. When she removed her flat-crowned riding hat, long, thick waves of raven black tresses cascaded down to the base of her spine. Her eyes sparkled as she gazed upon the still-mounted Coal, who breathlessly observed her. His eyes drinking in—what was to him— the most adorable and desirable woman on Earth. No sooner did he dismount than a rapturous Alita was instantly in his arms.

Tightly Coal wrapped strong arms around her tender young body and crushed Alita to him, making her groan deliciously. Their hands touched and explored in very much the same manner as Coal breathed in the flowery scent of her, his hands rising from her body only to fill with her hair. With her head encased within the strength of his fingers, Alita's glowing eyes sought his own.

"Coal, from the moment of my birth, I have not known the feeling of a man inside of me. I pray my innocence shall not turn you away," she whispered, and for the first time in their lives, he kissed her. Again and again, he lovingly kissed her breath away.

"Alita, I love you. I mean really love you. Without knowing it, I've been searching all of my life, for you. Do you believe and understand that?"

"Oh sí, sí, my Coal. Sí, my beautiful negrito," she happily cried out. "As Alita loves you, mi corazón, from the instant I entered poor Miguel's room. Coal, now, if not today, then tomorrow. Marry me, Coal, be Alita's husband!" she implored.

"Alita, it's about time you asked me." He laughed aloud, and she loved the sound of that first laugh from him.

Then his smile disappeared, and he gently held her lovely face between his hands. To her, his eyes seemed overflowing with love for her. "Alita, I do want you for my wife. To live with, love and laugh with you, grow old and die . . . with you. And in between all of that, I want you to mother every child I shall ever father. Would you be happy with that for us, my love?"

"Sí, sí, my Coal," Alita radiantly accepted his proposal, her heart singing. "Oh, my dearest love, how I do love you, Coal."

There, on an isolated mountain plateau with the snow-capped peaks of the Sierras to the left of them, the green valleys below, and a dazzling blue sky above, Coal and Alita pledged together to each other forever—their young lives.

"It is only fitting that I ask your father and mother for you,

Alita," Coal whispered. "I hope they won't think you and me are moving too fast."

"Oh, they will consent, my Coal." Alita laughed. "They also were in that room when our love was born."

"Yes," he softly agreed, "they were for a fact." He smiled down into loving eyes. Then they mounted and rode back to the Santos hacienda.

Chapter 13

Minutes after Coal and Alita had ridden off to be with themselves, ten men from the small army of Don Humberto Santos rode out to gather up the two slain gunmen and the dead oldest son of Don Raphael Tomasino. One vaquero drove the same buckboard Coal had driven earlier. Also inside with the bodies was the crippled remains of the evil Don Carlos Tomasino. Many of the Santos vaqueros opined that Coal had made a grave mistake in sparing Carlos's life.

Retrieving the three bodies, they proceeded to deliver their grisly cargo onto the rangeland of Don Raphael Tomasino. Encountering five of the Don's men immediately upon approaching his acreage, they handed over the remains. Instant gunplay most certainly would have erupted had they not been outnumbered two-to-one. Don Humberto's hawk-faced foreman then informed them of the ghastly deed Carlos had perpetrated prior to getting maimed. Then he told the five to haul Carlos's cursing, screaming, mangled ass on home to his daddy.

At the sight of what remained of his only sons, the countenance of Don Tomasino turned grape-purple with rage. When they finally were able to calm down the hysterical Carlos, he rendered his version of what had transpired earlier that day.

"Padre, that black devil is the angel of death! Madre de Dios!

We were only teaching the sons of your enemy a lesson, when that black demon appeared as if out of the depths of the very earth, bellowing at the four of us. Going for our guns, we all drew on him together. Mi padre, you will never believe this! Crenshaw and Argus, men of vaunted speed, our dead Manuel and me, we never even got off one shot before that black hand of Satan fired six times sounding as one! He shot my brother, then Argus and Crenshaw through their skulls with two bullets each! And padre, none of the bullets are more than mere inches apart. Go on, examine them and see for yourself, if you think I am exaggerating."

Don Raphael and his men did just that, finding the wounds precisely as Carlos had described.

"I want his balls!" Carlos ranted on. "I want his hands sliced off while I watch it, and his tongue slowly pulled out of his head! Do you men understand?!" The deranged cripple screamed at them.

"Carlos," his father softly interjected, danger in his tone, "how is it that you also attempted to draw your weapon and yet did not also perish at the side of your brother?"

Ashamed, he could not meet his father's scrutiny, and the Don guessed why.

"Only that black devil can tell you that, mi padre."

"Hmmmm, perhaps so. But, Carlos, my son, if you have shamed us, I will kill you."

Don Raphael turned away, pondering, and walked over to his fireplace. *I wonder, could this be that same devil black who demolished the existence of the Flint brothers in Catalina del Rey?* His mind raced back through three years prior, to the salesman who had spent the night at his hacienda and how he had described the black Angel of Death. He recalled how the man had raved on and on about "El Diablo Negrito con las manos mágicas" (the black devil with the hands of magic), telling of how Coal had killed one lightning-fast gunman while receiving a face wound, then waiting for and beating to death with his fists, the oldest brother, finally concluding with a highly graphic description of Coal shooting away the entire head of Roscoe Flint. It must be him, thought he. In that instant, he decided to send for the brothers Vasquez.

Throughout all of Mexico, the Vasquez brothers were infamously reputable. Only weeks earlier, in a bordertown gunfight, the three of them had killed ten professional American gunmen in a face-up, stand-up, shoot-out. Yes, he would offer them $3,000 each for the head of el diablo negrito. Summoning a few of his men, Don Raphael dispatched them on a solicitous journey, seeking the trio of death merchants.

"On the day after tomorrow, after I have settled my oldest son into the ground, I shall go and get the head of the one called Coal," he announced to the growing numbers of men gathering in his front yard. "And I shall return with it!"

Arriving on the wind, Alita and her Coal reined their mounts to a halt in front of the veranda. Don Humberto was there sitting alone, watching the sunset, with his forearms upon the railing. His eyes studied the radiant glow that was his daughter's face, silently appraising her.

This evening, she seems more beautiful than ever. Always she has been the light of my life, and now she brightens the life of the man of her choice. So be it, it is good.

Francisco, running onto the veranda, then off, stood smiling up at Coal. "Coal, I'll take your saddlebags up to your room if you want me to."

"Thanks, pardner." Coal winked at him. "I'm much obliged."

Dismounting, Coal whispered something to Francisco, who nodded and then disappeared into the house again.

"Don Santos, if you'll be free later this evening, sir, I'd appreciate it if I could speak with you and Doña Santos?"

The Don's eyes met those very serious ones of Coal. "Mother and me will be free, Coal," he consented, as Alita studied them both.

"Thank you, sir. And now if you and Alita will excuse me, I'll bed down my horse."

"Coal"—Alita frowned slightly—"we have servants to attend to such matters."

He turned back to her, apparently studying the ground between them for a moment or more.

"Alita, just to avoid ever speaking on this again, know this to be a fact. Nobody, and I mean nobody, takes care of Big Black except me. Ya see, he doesn't take too kindly to other people's hands, and I like that about him, because it's the way I've trained him," Coal enlightened her, his eyes beaming with pride in his stallion. "Big Black and me, we're like family, and believe it or not, he's even saved my life once. I'm selfish about him, and I really love him, Alita."

Intensely observing his daughter's face as she listened to Coal's voice, the Don noticed her eyes never left Coal's face as he spoke to her.

"Then it shall be as you wish," Alita complied, still atop her horse.

"I respect you even more for understanding that," he strangely replied, making her wonder.

Walking away with his horse, Coal addressed her over his shoulder in that soft way of his: "See ya, pretty lady."

In her saddle, she watched him stroll away, and she grinned, secretly elated. Getting down, she ran around the veranda and perched herself on her father's lap. As he had always done since her infancy, he placed an arm around her waist and snuggled her.

"Ha, ha, ha!" Don Humberto laughed. "Already I see that Coal will not let you dictate to him as you so boldly take advantage of me, my spoiled lovely."

"So far, Papá, that is the one thing I love most about him. I find it difficult to associate my Coal with the man who killed one brother and then beat the other to death over the shooting of a whore. Those actions do not fit the man I am finding him to be, Papá."

"So, you have already decided that Coal is the same man who that salesman talked about for hours?"

"Am I wrong, Papá? Do you not also think Coal is indeed that very same man? He still carries the mark from that bullet upon his left cheek. But Papá, he is so tender with me. I do not believe that lying salesman. Hummph, the devil reincarnate indeed!"

"And you probably never will believe it, until you witness that which you have only heard of. Alita, my dearest child, do you want him?"

"Sí, Papá, more than life."

"Then hold on to that strong will of yours. My new son is not the kind of man one can break or mold to their own liking. Any attempt to do so would result in only one thing being broken, and that would be you, my child."

"Papá, do you know this because you see something of yourself in him?"

"Precisely." He smiled.

"So do I, Papá," she quietly agreed.

"Come"—he lifted his favorite offspring—"let us prepare ourselves for Coal's first dinner in his new home."

A while later, Coal left the stables with young Francisco, who had been watching and talking to him as he tended to Big Black.

"Do you think the woman has finished those clothes of mine that you took to her?"

"Sí, Coal. I will get them for you and bring them upstairs to your room. One of the servants will show you where."

Entering the house, Coal encountered the Don and Alita's twin conversing in the foyer. "Coal, Antonio informs me that the son of my dear friend—whose heart was so ruthlessly broken by that daughter of mine—has been drinking heavily and brooding. My son, Ricardo is not a coward." The Don paused, groping for the right words. "What I mean is, it is my wish that you do not kill him if he challenges you. He also loves Alita, and at this moment, he is not rational, to say the least."

"I won't kill him, unless he shows me he's acquired a sudden hate for livin'."

"Ricardo has been telling our vaqueros that he does not believe what they are saying about you. He keeps repeating himself as if trying to convince himself, my brother. He shall bear watching," Antonio advised Coal.

"Well, I hope he doesn't convince himself, for his father's sake. Okay, Don Santos, I'll stay away from him, providing he keeps his hands away from that pistol he's wearin' as if he knows what it's for," Coal promised.

"That is all I ask, my son, that you show restraint. Antonio, show your brother to his room."

They walked talking up the stairs, and Antonio opened the door for Coal to enter. The bedroom was tastefully furnished in thick dark mahogany, with window drapes of a rich, cloud-like blue material and matching carpeting. Coal was quite taken with it.

"Coal, I told Father not to ask of you what he did. Showing restraint to a jealous fool with a gun could be fatal."

"I don't see Ricardo as a problem, Antonio. By the way, I'm glad you came upstairs with me, because I'm anxious to know the twin of the woman I love."

"Coal, mi hermano, I pray in my heart that you are truly the man for the person who was with me even before I was born. Alita is high-spirited, and of a breed which only a special kind of man could handle. Do not take my words lightly, Coal. You will have to handle her, really do so, to help her grow into the woman she has yet to become. Am I making sense, Coal?"

"To me you are."

"Then I am glad. My whole family is still talking about what initially transpired between you and Alita. It was a beautiful thing to witness."

"Yeah." Coal smiled. "I thought my heart stopped the second I saw her. I can still feel it."

"Coal, we have not discussed it, but have you thought of what is to come? I assure you, Don Raphael will come for revenge. He and my father have been archenemies since before Alita and me were born. You see, both he and my father sought the hand of the same woman, and my father won her, my mother."

"Oh? Something like the way it is now, between Ricardo and myself."

"Exactly, Coal."

Turning that bit of information around inside his head, Coal reached an instant conclusion. "I have no intention of havin' an enemy hangin' around my neck for more than twenty years. Not even twenty hours. Ricardo had better beware that his heart doesn't put his ass in water too deep to swim out of."

Antonio guffawed at Coal's statement. "Very aptly put, Coal." He slapped his thigh.

"About your question, though, Antonio, yes, I have thought about what my new enemy will think to do in retaliation. I suppose he'll bury his sons and then come for me. I'll just have to handle it the same way he brings it."

"Coal, without seeming the braggard, I am considered by many to be faster than most," he proudly stated, his handsome face smiling.

Stepping into a hot tub prepared by one of the servants, Coal glanced over at him. "That does not surprise me, Antonio, you have the look of a fine gun. I can tell."

"My brother, whenever the Tomasinos do arrive, I shall be to the right of wherever you are."

With only his head showing above the water line, Coal studied Antonio. "As it should be, brother," he said, grinning. "You are kindly welcome."

They were both laughing when Francisco entered, carrying Coal's freshly done clothing. His old black suit, which he'd only worn that one time, was looking as good as new. Ever alert, Antonio noticed that his kid brother was then walking very much so in the same manner of which Coal did, holding his head just like him. When Antonio remarked about it, Francisco's face turned a deep red hue.

"That's alright, Tony, I don't care if you make fun of me. I only hope that one day I shall be able to use the pistolas one tenth as well as our brother Coal. Coal, will you teach me? I have a brand-new six-gun, which father gave me on my last birthday. Will you?"

"If Don Santos says it's okay, I'd be glad to, little brother."

"He's already pretty good, Coal; I have been teaching him. Seriously, he's good."

Coal dried himself without replying and began donning his clothes.

"Sí, Coal, Antonio has been teaching me. But Tony, what Coal does is more than simply drawing fast." The youngster seemed stumped while trying to explain.

"What is he trying to say, Coal? More than drawing fast?" Antonio asked.

"I can't rightfully say, Antonio, he's tellin' it." Coal grinned.

"Never mind, I know what I mean! Tony, when Coal gets his guns, it's like his hands don't actually move. More so like the flicking of his wrists, Tony. Right, Coal?"

The lad did indeed have sharp eyesight, thought Coal.

"Show him, Coal. We're brothers, so you can show Tony," he urged.

To Coal, those two guns of his were not playthings. But as the kid said, they were brothers.

"Okay, little brother, as soon as I'm done dressing, I'll show you."

"Ayiiee! Now you shall see, Tony, you'll see and you still will not believe. Watch."

Carefully dressing so as to make a good impression at dinner, Coal decided it was far too hot for that suit coat. Reaching for his double-holstered gun belt, he carefully tied them down over his freshly creased trousers. Then he turned to face Tony. Daily, Antonio won money by gambling on his speed with his father's vaqueros.

Coal stood waiting, and Francisco wondered why he only watched Antonio's face instead of his hands. Actually, Coal was watching Antonio's eyes, for there would be where the danger signal would come from. Antonio braced himself with a wide-legged stance. Coal, a bit more closed stance. The handsome son of the Don suddenly went for his iron and never cleared leather. Coal's wrist flicked, and Antonio found himself staring into the barrels of twin six-guns on an exact level with his eyeballs. "Ai-iyee caramba!" Antonio yelled, putting away his half-drawn pistol. "If Ricardo were only here to see what I just saw! Madre de Dios! He would quickly forget the madness he is now contemplating. Coal, my brother, you did not seem to even move!" he exclaimed.

"Ha! That was nothing!" Francisco corrected him. "You should see our brother when he is doing it for real, instead of a game like now."

In his long-sleeved white shirt and black trousers with shiny black boots, Coal, along with Antonio and Francisco, entered the living room where the rest of the family waited. Ricardo Santiago and the Castilian Dr. Ramirez stood near the fireplace. Coal inwardly laughed as a humorous thought crossed his mind. He was thinking that Ricardo was indeed standing next to the right man. The dejected former fiancé of Alita Santos held an almost empty brandy glass in his hand, and he was very high.

Coal's eyes then fell upon his beloved Alita, and she literally took his breath away in a laced Spanish gown of blue. Her mass of wavy tresses hung loose about her shoulders. Everyone observed as Alita moved to meet her chosen one and kiss him full upon his lips in front of her parents. In that day and time, Alita's aggressive act would most certainly have been frowned upon by other aristocratic Mexican families, considering it in bad taste. But the clan Santos were an uninhibited lot, and Alita, most of all, could do no wrong in the eyes of the immensely rich and powerful Don Humberto Santos. Ricardo was fuming.

"Now that we all are here," the Don said, smiling to Coal, "let us proceed to our table and dine. Coal, my son, you will have no need for your guns while at the dinner table with your family."

Coal's first impulse was to refuse, but he felt the eyes of Alita upon him. He gazed into them, and silently she spoke to him. Reluctantly he unfastened his belt and handed his six-guns over to Don Humberto. His eyes never left her face during that interval, for she was his only reason for complying.

Throughout the elaborate dinner, Ricardo menacingly stared at Coal, who seemingly ignored him as he had promised. But without looking directly at Ricardo, Coal watched his every move. Seated next to Coal, Alita whispered, "When are you going to ask them, Coal?"

"In time, my love. But it's real good to know that you are impatient." He grinned at her.

Under the dinner table, Alita's hand mischievously fondled Coal's thigh until he mean-eyed her; then she laughed aloud, making everyone wonder what their private joke was all about. Dinner was as fine as any Coal had ever sat down to. Being the first ones finished, the couple excused themselves, quickly going out onto the veranda and into the yard.

They were embracing when Coal felt strong fingers steel-gripping his shoulder and spinning around. Without warning, Ricardo, who outweighed Coal by about forty pounds, crashed home a terrific left hand to Coal's face, laying him flat on his ass in the grass. Having seen Ricardo rush from the house, the entire family then stood on the veranda, watching that scene.

"It had to come, Papá." Antonio angrily gritted his teeth. "Let it be settled now, once and for all. Coal has promised you not to kill Ricardo, and they have no weapons."

Coal, his senses lopsided from the impact of that punch, felt himself being pulled to his feet by the front of his shirt and severely tagged again. By then, the men of the family and many vaqueros stood nearby. From somewhere in the distance, Coal could hear Ricardo fat-mouthing.

"Ha! You are not so much the hombre when you do not have your guns, are you, perro?"

Swerving unsteadily, Coal regained his feet with blood leaking from the corner of his mouth. Alita was aghast with seething anger at Ricardo, fearing that Coal would be injured or worse by the bigger man. Ricardo's mistake was in not taking full advantage instead of strutting around the yard making derisive slurs about Coal. He was still top-dogging it when Coal's senses cleared and his eyes found him.

"You have punched me twice, once with my back turned, you bastard," Coal cursed, as his blood drenched his shirtfront. "Hit me or even look at me again, and I'll send ya home to your daddy in a sack!"

"Talk! You, señor, are nothing but talk!" cried Ricardo, once again advancing on Coal.

From behind him, Coal heard the voice of Don Santos. "You are free from your promise, my son, do as you will."

Bracing himself, Ricardo cut loose with a haymaker of a right hand, and Coal deftly stepped inside the arc of that roundhouse swing, viciously plunging his left fist wrist-deep into the pit of Ricardo's gut, making Alita's eyes glow. And before Ricardo could fathom what had been done to him, he was instantly banged dizzy with that same hand just behind his right ear, quickly followed by a crisp, hard-knuckled, right hand, which crushed Ricardo's nose flat.

Coal felt that nose bone give under his fist, and Ricardo's blood rained. Still game, Ricardo landed another left to Coal's head. But now with his brain attuned to combat, Coal retaliated with zealous savagery. A crunching left hook connected again upon that badly broken nose, crossing Ricardo's eyes as it was trailed by a thunderous, digging, right hand under his heart. Ricardo groaned from that one, and Coal sensed that he had him going, and immediately opened up with a barrage. A series of left and rights to Ricardo's head closed one eye.

The aristocrat was fighting back, but the sting had left his fists, making Coal disregard him as he poured it on, driving his adversary to the grass. Bloodied and ripped, Ricardo stumbled to his feet and charged, making Coal want to kill him. He tried to do just that.

As Ricardo charged, Coal pivoted while digging a pain-inducing, pulverizing, right hand to the kidneys, causing Ricardo to bend and fart out loud. A whistling uppercut straightened him up, emptying his mouth of front teeth. Now Ricardo was in pain, bad pain, but still he came at Coal. Deliberately, Coal banged shut the other eye, blinding him. Slicing into Ricardo's skin with knuckles hardened from years of labor, Coal tore into the bigger man again, driving him to the ground. Whereupon Coal leaped on top of him just as restraining hands sought to pull him away with voices pleading.

He had not touched this man, Coal thought frenziedly. Why should this sonofabitch have attacked him from behind? The thought made him crazy, and he tried to bite into Ricardo's throat.

"Coal! Please, mi corazón," Alita pleaded, "it is over! Please, Coal, you will kill him if you do not cease! Don't! Coal, please for my sake, please!"

"Okay, goddamnit! I'll stop!" he heard himself say to what seemed like a thousand hands holding him.

Coal stepped back, trying to focus; then his eyes found Alita, gone pale under her deep tan. All of the family and their vaqueros also filled the yard. His flashing black eyes then fell to the beaten-to-a-pulp Ricardo Santiago. Coal walked toward him again, and the brothers and the Don moved to once more intervene.

"No need, I won't touch him again today," Coal panted, standing over and staring down into a face with eyes shut punch-tight. "But Santiago, I swear on my life, if you ever even come within my sight again, I'll take your back-stabbin' life!" he vowed.

He wheeled then and strode up to his room to be alone. Slamming the door behind him, Coal went to a mirror and examined the inner wall of his mouth. That first left hand from Ricardo had ripped the inside of it. The condition of his beautiful shirt, all spattered with bloodstains, did not serve to calm him any, either. He was in the process of tearing it from his body when Alita entered, carrying a basin of hot water with fresh towels hanging from her right arm. Naked to the waist, a glaring Coal turned to her.

"Coal, mi cariño, I have brought these things to wash away the blood."

"Leave them, I'll do it myself!" he snapped, not angry with her in particular, but just sizzling mad at Ricardo.

Alita did not leave them, and she did not go. Placing the objects upon the dresser, she lifted a towel and dipped part of it into the basin. Coming to where Coal stood, Alita moved closer, looking into his face. He avoided her eyes.

"Coal, you are angry with your Alita?"

"No!"

"Then allow me to do what is for me to do."

With tender loving care, she wiped the corner of his mouth and chin. Soaking the cloth again, she added soap, and from his neck and chest Alita removed the mixture of blood belonging to the men who loved her.

"The inside of your mouth, Coal, it is painful?"

"Ain't nuthin'," he muttered.

"You are angry with me. Coal," she murmured softly. "I think I should wish to die if you have changed your mind about us. Do you really think I wanted you hurt by him?"

Tears then welled in her eyes. "If that is what you think, I shall prove to you how wrong you are. I will go and get one of your pistolas and kill Ricardo Santiago for hurting you. Will you then believe your Alita loves and wants only you?"

Seeing her tears fall drained all of the anger from Coal. "No, my love, don't even think of doing such a thing. Coal shall never change his mind about you, Alita," he soothed. Then he kissed her deeply, and Alita tasted his blood.

They were still kissing when a knock sounded. They turned, and into the room marched the clan minus their parents. Smiling, Escobar presented Coal with a silk white shirt, which was similar to his ruined one. Thanking him, Coal slipped it on. "It is my favorite of all the ones I own, Coal, I want you to have it, my brother."

"It's beautiful." Coal smiled, and they all smiled with him. They were not at all certain as to what his mood would be.

Esmeralda, inching closer, was dangerously near to tears, and Coal put his arm around her shoulders, hugging her to him.

"Oh, Coal, I thought you would not fight him after he struck you. I would simply have perished from the sheer hurt of it all," she dramatically stated.

"I had no such feelings," chirped a jubilant Francisco. "I knew you would tear him apart, and you did."

"Coal, are you seriously injured?" inquired the gentle Sonia.

"No, Sonia. It was only a fight."

"And what a fight!" Antonio remarked. "Coal, that right hand you landed to his kidneys took all of the fight out of him. We heard him fart from that one." He laughed.

Doña Santos then entered, holding a glass containing a misty-looking substance. "Coal, my son, this is rock salt and hot water. It will rapidly heal the cut in your mouth if you rinse with it. After you have taken care of that, my husband and I will be in the downstairs parlor." She winked at him. "I understand that you wish to speak with us concerning a matter of great importance."

"Yes, Doña Santos"—he winked back, smiling—"mighty important."

"Come, children," she said, beckoning at the doorway. "Alita will see to the rest of his needs."

They filed past her and out, leaving the couple alone. "Alita, you're not supposed to be with me when I ask your parents for your hand, are you?"

"You do not wish for me to be?"

"No, I do not. This is the one time in a man's life when he should be on his own."

"Then I shall wait along with my brothers and sisters. Coal, please tell me again," she softly requested.

"I love you, pretty Alita."

When she departed, Coal rinsed his mouth with the solution rendered by Luz Santos.

Sitting down on the side of his bed, he collected his thoughts. Coal had more than $12,000 then, with which he intended to build a fine ranch. With Big Black, Coal knew he had the nucleus of a dynamic herd. His was of a mind that, together with the thoroughbred riding mounts, he would also buy some cattle and raise the kind of beef he encountered upon first entering onto that land.

In America, $12,000 would have been plenty. Here, it was more than enough. Already Coal had seen the area he wanted for his animals and the site upon which he wanted to build a new home. Sensing that where Alita had first taken him to was her favorite spot on Santos land, Coal decided to build right there. He recalled the emotion that had consumed him there at the site. He had felt within himself the very same thing he then envisioned in her lovely eyes. There, and only there, would they live and raise their own family. In Coal's mind, he could see the house as it would be.

When he stood up from the bed, another thought blossomed that evoked a grin, and he made a mental note to implement it immediately after completing his audience with Alita's parents. Leaving his room to go downstairs, he almost stumbled over his brothers. They all wished him good luck, making it clear to Coal that there were no secrets in that family. He thanked them and then entered the parlor.

Standing before this king and queen of an empire, Coal spoke with his very soul projecting from his eyes. "Today when I came to this land, I was searching," Coal said in fluent Castilian Spanish, shocking them.

His every word up until then had been in English, and even Alita was unaware that he could speak her native tongue. Don and Doña Santos beamed at the pleasant revelation, and Coal continued:

"And then when I saw Alita, I instantly knew what I was seeking. You see, I am a man who never once told a woman that I loved her. In less than an hour after meeting my Alita, I told her so. And I do love her truly and forever. Folks, I never meant anything more in my life."

Coal's eyes began to fill then, and he did not fight the feeling as they overflowed. "I have asked her to be my wife for all time, and she has consented. But to me, it just wouldn't be fitting without the blessings from the two people who raised her to be the woman I love. I promise that I shall take care of her in the manner of which she is accustomed, and I will never break her heart. We wish to be married as soon as possible," Coal entreated, as the feelings of his heart poured from his eyes.

"My son, you have stated—and even a blind man could see—that you and our Alita are in love. But Coal," said the Don, lovingly glancing at his own wife of thirty-seven years, "you and I both know there is something else of even greater importance."

Coal searched the older man's eyes for some clue of what he was alluding to.

"Do you want her, Coal? Do you desire her above all others, my son?"

"Yes, Don Santos, more than life."

The patriarch smiled to himself. "Coal, I'll tell you something. Today, after you so neatly put her in her place concerning your beautiful stallion, she came and sat upon my lap as she has done since infancy. Alita told me your exact words in reply to that very same question. When mother and I saw what happened when you both saw each other for the first time, we knew this moment to be inevitable. That is as it should be. Coal, my son . . ."

He was interrupted by the door opening and Alita rushing into the parlor. "Papá, Mamacita, I could wait no longer," she sighed, her face radiant. "Tell us, Papá," she implored him.

Then taking Coal's arm as she moved to his side, Alita saw the wetness upon his cheeks. With her dark eyes flashing fire, she wheeled on her parents, ready and willing to defy even them, for her Coal.

"As I was saying, Coal, my son, take her for life. Alita is yours. Sí, Mamá?" He smiled.

Wiping at her eyes, Doña Santos nodded yes, and Alita smothered Coal's face with ecstatically happy kisses.

"I thought they had gone mad, Coal, and refused us permission. Oh Coal, I'm so very, very happy." Alita laughed. "B-but those tears . . . your face. Why?"

"It was you, Alita, you that you saw on my face. I was telling your folks about this thing I have in my heart for you, and the water just came from nowhere. I didn't call for it," he explained, grinning, "it just came."

"Aliyee cariño!" She squeezed him to her. "Coal, Coal, my Coal, this is madness! I love you so much, so fast, until I joyously ache from it," Alita whispered, sensuously finding his lips with her eager mouth.

As if by magic, they were suddenly surrounded by the whole family, with everyone kissing everyone. In their heightened exuberance, the brothers almost tore Coal's arm off with their congratulations.

Standing among their offspring but sharing a private thing of their own, the Don embraced his Luz. To them and for them, this was indeed the finest moment in their rich and full life together.

Onto the veranda ran the brothers, repeatedly firing their six-guns up into the night. When vaqueros came in search of trouble, they were told the grand news, and festivities instantly commenced. From out of nowhere, wine, food, and more wine appeared. Young Francisco brought Coal his guns and observed him strap them on. Then, strolling out into the midst of the celebration, Coal drank wine and also fired into the air along with the laughing Brothers Santos.

Chapter 14

The sun was almost to mid-sky when the grand house of Santos awakened. Coal of the one name lay there listening to sounds inside and out. Hours after everyone had gone to bed, Coal had lain on his own by the open window, staring off into the moonlit night. That night of his betrothal had been crystal clear, with the multi-scented odor of nature everywhere. From his bed, Coal gazed at those snow-capped domes of the Sierra Madre standing majestically off in the distance. The moon-swathed mountains formed a protective shield against the winds from the north, for the tender, softer valleys stretching endlessly below.

Viewing all of that, Coal felt at peace with the world for the first time in his turmoil-filled life. His mind drifted to the conversation he had held with the Don and his wife after receiving their blessings. With Alita at his side, Coal refused a gift of land, informing the Don that he only wanted the assistance of the many laborers then inhabiting the Don's domain.

Coal insisted that he must purchase the land from the Don on which he would build his home. His prospective father-in-law argued that if it were one of his other sons, it would only be natural for them to receive those bestowments. But Coal was adamant in his belief that only this way would he feel in his heart that what he owned was his. Don Santos vehemently persisted, but to no avail. Their women did not intervene, simply watching and enjoying the display of wills between the men they loved.

Finally Coal had his way, but only after yielding to one concession. He agreed to accept the family gift of one thousand head of prime beef to graze upon his land, his to own. After agreeing on the price of the land Coal would buy, the Don reluctantly told Coal that he would accept his money in the morning after breakfast. It was also understood that the dowry brought into their union by Alita was not a gift, but hers by birthright. When that was settled, Coal drew the Don off to one side and whispered to him. What he whispered was the same thought that had made Coal grin prior to coming downstairs. Don Santos immediately dispatched fifteen riders to fulfill Coal's request of him.

Coal was thinking of those series of events when he saw his door quickly open and Alita slip inside. Among Mexican aristocrats, this brazen act on her part was unprecedented. Observing her enter the sunlit bedroom, Coal thrilled at the sight of her. "Coal!"—Alita laughed infectiously—"it is almost noon, and my family and I have so much to show you. Today you shall see the land and our people of this land. They also wish to look upon you, for undoubtedly word has already spread throughout the valleys and hamlets. Arise, my negrito lindo, arise and enjoy this very special day," she laughingly urged, falling on top of Coal and kissing him.

"Good mornin' to you, too." He grinned. "But I don't see how I can get up right now, being that I'm as naked as a rattlesnake."

"And why not? We are to be married soon, are we not?" she teased, her eyes twinkling.

"Out! Out of here right now, before I tan your backside," he menaced, still grinning.

Alita backed away from him, running for the door. Once there, she halted. "Coal," she said, with her hands upon her hips and a strange something in her eyes. "If you felt it necessary, would you?"

"Would I what?"

"Would you resort to tanning my backside?"

Removing the bedsheets, Coal stood upright, exposing his naked body to her. "Quick, Alita. Quick like yesterday," he assured her.

Her eyes scanned his body, all of it, and Coal noticed Alita's blouse begin to rapidly rise and fall with her breathing.

"I would fight. Alita would fight you like the tiger cat!" she vowed, her moist lips parting.

"Matters not," Coal softly declared, his eyes full of love and steel. "I would still tan your beautiful rump, and tan it damn good. Make no mistake about that, young lady. Now get!" He jumped at her, and she screamed. Laughing, Alita flew out of the room.

After washing, Coal donned his clothing and six-guns. Counting off the money he would pay to the Don, he grabbed his hat and left the room.

In the foyer below, Coal spied a lean, rawhide of a man standing there. He also wore two six-guns. His sombrero in hand exposed iron-gray hair and a matching moustache that hung to the lower extremities of his chin. His skin was almost brown-black from constant exposure to the torrid Mexican sun. He was fifty-eight years old, fit, fearless, and he sported those two guns for good reason. For years he had been and still was the formidable enforcer for Don Humberto Santos. He was the legendary Gavilán Santanna.

When Coal reached the foot of the stairway, the man who had watched him all the way down smiled. "Buenos días y felicadades, Señor Coal. I am Gavilán Santanna."

"Howdy, Señor Santanna, and buenos días to you, too."

As warriors do, they measured each other, liking what they saw.

"So, it is you who has lassoed the flower of clan Santos."

"I reckon you could safely say so," Coal softly answered.

Santanna's eyes roamed the length of the negrito before him, and again he smiled. "It is good, and I am glad, for I would not have liked facing those things on your hips there, amigo."

"Nobody ever has who did so," Coal countered, and suddenly they both rocked with genuine laughter.

Don Santos found them that way. "Ah, there you are, Coal. It does my old heart good to see my new son and my strong right hand joined in laughter. Coal, the family is holding breakfast for you. I must first converse with Santanna, then I shall join everyone."

Almost bumping into Doña Santos as he entered the dining room, Coal held still when she kissed his left cheek, her eyes searching for any signs of that previous night's violent fight. Apparently pleased, she motioned him to the table.

"Coal, be seated there between Alita and Essie. Essie has forbidden us to seat you anywhere other than beside her," she said, and laughed. Coal went and sat.

Then, catching her completely off guard, Coal gave little Essie a quick peck on her cheek, and the twelve-year-old instantly turned beet red. She was greatly teased by her family as the servants entered with breakfast. Arriving late, Don Santos seated himself at the head of his table.

"My son," he announced, "I have given permission for Don Raphael Tomasino and whomever he brings with him to enter onto my land tomorrow. He has sent word that he wishes to converse with me here. He will arrive at noon."

Eating with his head down, Coal looked up and placed his fork on his plate. "Don Santos, ain't nuthin' enemies hate worse than talkin' to one another. It's me he's after, I can feel him already."

"No one comes onto Santos land to do harm to a son of mine, Coal."

"That may be, but I just became your son, and I doubt if he knows that yet. Sir, if he does what I know he will do, I'm gonna put an end to the feud once and for all."

"Not even the bold Tomasino would bring violence among my loved ones. Forget that, Coal. I think he is of a mind to call it off for good. He has no more sons, except for the half one who was sent back to him," the Don reasoned.

"That is why he is coming for me. Mark my words, Don Santos."

"Then if he comes seeking vengeance," Antonio broke in, "he'll encounter something he never dreamed existed. We shall not let our Coal fight alone!"

With ease, Coal drifted into effortless Spanish as he sought total comprehension, shocking the rest of them, who had not heard him do so. Alita went wide-eyed with loving admiration.

"With all due respect, sir, I think what you have just expressed is more so your wish than it is a fact," Coal stated. Don Santos studied him, then nodded for him to continue.

"Family, I have seen men who have been hurt way down in the gut where they live at, and I know that they can only be stopped in one way. Antonio told me the whole story yesterday, sir—now bear with me, please. Here is a man who many years ago lost out to you in a battle of the heart. Not only that, sir, but during all of those years of him mourning his loss, that very same woman he lost has borne you eight children. Five of them stout-hearted sons. He has hated you more each time one of them yelled out his first hello to this world.

"And now, after all of his suffering, more pain comes to him from the same direction as it originally did, and he is left with nothing but hate for you and yours. Don Santos, nothing known to man can make that kind of pain disappear, and it won't stop with mere words. If Raphael Tomasino lives much longer, it will be you who dies, and no one here wants to see that happen. Now what that adds up to is this. Don Raphael Tomasino must die," Coal pointedly stressed.

"B-but Coal, my son, how can you be so certain?"

"I'm certain because I'm the one who gave him no other choice than to die. I broke up and crippled the last of his family tree."

Escobar, the introverted one who seldom spoke but was highly respected by his father for his fine sense of reasoning, got their attention.

"My father, Coal is right. I did not realize it until listening just then, as we all did. Don Tomasino is coming here to die tomorrow."

Don Humberto rose from his chair, consternation clouding his demeanor. "How can I kill a man who has come to talk? Can anyone tell me how?"

"As long as talking is all he does, he will live," Coal answered him. "But when he does what I know he will do, you will not have to kill him, for I shall have already done so."

The dining room grew hushed. Reaching under the table, Alita gripped the hand of her husband-to-be. Luz Santos, sitting and listening to Coal, knew that his words were true. More than anyone present, she alone knew the inner character of Don Tomasino. Yes, he would come, and he was coming to die. To die where she was.

"Enough of this talk of death!" spoke Doña Santos. "Today is a day of great happiness, for only last evening, we gave our Alita to the man of her choice. Let us now rejoice and give thanks to God for all the love which surrounds us."

"My very own sentiments, Mamacita," added Sonia.

"Father, I am curious," Antonio persisted. "Have you spoken to Santanna about this?"

"Yes, my reckless son, just prior to sitting down to breakfast."

"And what did he say?" prompted Antonio, sensing his reply.

"What did he say? Why, he said exactly what Coal just stated."

"There, Father, do you see?" said Escobar. "Our Coal is right, no?"

"Yes, Escobar, he is. Although I wish he were not, he is. Don Tomasino is coming to die, and suddenly I know why. The only remaining weapon he possesses with which to punish your mother for choosing me instead of him is to let her see him killed before her very eyes, here where she lives."

Luz Santos felt as though her husband had inserted his hand into her skull, removed her brain, and examined its contents prior to replacing it.

"One more thing before we go riding," Coal softly held them. "There is something I wish to say to all of you. I have lived practically all of my life in the land where earth's most violent men dwell in abundance, and I have also learned many things about violence and violent men. I know there is but one way to handle such men as those who are coming to visit tomorrow. They must be shown a greater force than their own, for force is the only power they respect. And I ask that you all do not judge me too harshly after the sun goes down."

Sonia Santos left her chair and went to the side of her sister's betrothed, gently touching Coal's face. "Coal, mi hermano, if Papá did not make it clear enough to you yesterday, then permit me to do so now. We—and that includes you, Coal—are one! Coal, I am a person who visibly trembles at the mere mentioning of violence, truly I do. But hear me, Coal. Anyone who comes here after you, comes for and will find us all! Whatever is done by you will not be judged by us. It will be sanctioned!"

Antonio leaped from his chair, smiling wide. "Father, did you not hear our Sonia? No one, but no one could have better expressed our feelings," he said, and laughed. "Come here, my beautiful sister, I want to kiss you." And he did.

"Now," voiced Escobar, "let us show our brother the land of Santos."

Outside, Coal took one look at Esmeralda's pony and called to her. "Essie, after I saddle Big Black, it would be my pleasure if you rode up with me. Because ain't no way that little fella is gonna keep up the pace."

Visibly elated by his invitation, she blushed adoringly. "I would be honored, sir." She curtsied while the family beamed on.

Coal then took her by the hand. "C'mon, little lady, you can help me saddle him up," he said, grinning down at the sparkling child.

Observing them walk off toward the stable, the others mounted and waited.

"I was watching Coal with our baby girl just then. I think he will make a fine father for your children, Alita," Sonia whispered.

"Hummph!" Alita feigned annoyance. "There will never be any children if all of you keep hanging around us."

"B-b-but Alita!" Sonia gasped, lifting one hand to her breasts. "Surely you would not indulge in sex prior to your wedding bed, would you?"

"You can wager your maidenhead I would. All Coal has to do is say that he wants me now." She shocked Sonia, and that time, she was not pretending.

"Coal would not do that, would he?"

"No, I don't think he would, but we were speaking about me, dear sister."

Esmeralda and Coal emerged from the stable without his stallion.

"Coal, where is your horse?" asked Francisco.

"Silencio, Frankie!" Esmeralda hushed him. "Go ahead, Coal, do it for me, please."

As the Don and his wife looked upon that happy scene, everyone wondered what she wanted of him. Coal placed his fingers to his lips and whistled. Bolting from the stable, with his eyes searching for Coal, came Big Black. Finding him, the stallion trotted up to his master and nudged Coal's chest with his great head. Little Esmeralda jumped with glee.

"Let's ride!" Coal grinned, springing into his saddle. Then extending his arm down to her, he hoisted the family baby up in front of him.

"Make him go, Coal, make him fly as you said he could," Esmeralda urged.

The eight of them galloped from the yard. Raoul's high-stepping steed pulled at the bit, wanting to run. With all of the Santos horses being thoroughbreds, they kept pace.

"Race him, Coal. Raoul thinks his horse is the fastest in all of Mexico," said Esmeralda.

Riding just to the left of them, Raoul heard his sister's request and took off. "Coal, oh Coal!" Esmeralda cried. "He's too far away now, we'll never catch him."

"Oh yeah? Watch our smoke, little sister. Pick 'em up and lay 'em down, big fella!" he commanded.

Coal had to laugh out loud at Big Black's reaction. The Morgan took off after Raoul's mount as if it had stolen the last bale of hay. Raoul had almost a quarter of a mile lead when Big Black started to open up his stride, seeming to dance over the surface as he raced.

With his tail raised high, his long black mane stretching out on the wind stung the face of Esmeralda as she screamed with excitement. Closer and closer, they gained on Raoul. Turning his head, Raoul saw them gaining and began to really push his own fine animal.

"Run, Big Black, fly, fly, fly!" screeched Esmeralda.

Big Black accelerated, his strong hooves tattooing the ground beneath them.

"He does fly, Coal!" she laughed. "He does, he does!"

By then they were approximately fifty yards behind Raoul's steed. "Watch him now, Essie, watch him now. Move, big fella, move!"

As though resenting having tasted dust from the other horse's hooves, Big Black extended himself. Coal had not seen him do that since the morning of the Apaches. The giant stallion closed the gap to even. Then seeming to linger momentarily, Big Black kept pace alongside the other animal, looking him over, then left him behind. Coal's well-muscled mount shot away, showing Raoul's horse its asshole in a cloud of galloping dust.

After passing him for keeps, Coal reined in and waited. Shortly, Raoul drew reins next to them, him and his horse sweating. Raoul simply stared in awe at Big Black. "My brother, you are absolutely positive he is only horse? Perhaps maybe horse and eagle?"

Coal had to laugh at his expression. "The first time I saw him do that, it amazed me, too, Raoul. He's mine, and I still don't believe him yet."

Minutes later, the family joined them, praising the big stallion, which then pranced as though it knew it was the center of attraction. Following the race, the family Santos and Coal set off on an eastern course. Along the way, Coal saw and met many people who lived upon the land of Don Humberto Santos, people of the earth who toiled that same earth. They all loved the children of their sainted Don, and Alita was their pride, just as she was her father's. Coal experienced a dreamlike effect from it all, as if it were unreal. In the eyes of those people, Coal saw what he interpreted as love, whereas in the past, most eyes he observed either held hate or scorn. He wondered where the line of separation became evident.

Coal saw no visible signs of law, but he felt it. These people laughed, laughed with their eyes, the place where deceit cannot be concealed if one is discerning. Coal, who was always attuned to and for danger, detected none. While he was observing them, they in turn scrutinized this new son of the Don Humberto. They did not miss what intermittently transpired between Coal and Alita whenever their eyes would meet, which was most of the time. Seeing how her lips would part and his chest would heave during those moments.

Those native inhabitants knew the gut feeling of love as it came from the earth, and here was something to match love from wherever it came. Also, in the eyes of the family, the natives could clearly see how they also felt about Coal.

A few hours before sundown, they turned toward home at a gallop. Alita, with her long hair resting upon the wind, showed her Coal that not only the men of the family Santos could ride. She sailed over ditches in the terrain, guiding her palomino as though they were one entity. With her body sitting light in the saddle, hers was a picture to implant itself forever into the mind of anyone who observed. The children of Humberto and Luz Santos galloped together like a line of calvary in its stage of charge.

Sonia rode like a man, giving Coal the impression that she had been taught by a man. The brothers held no superiority in the saddle. Little Esmeralda, her head moving from left to right as she watched those on both sides of her, tilted her pretty head backward and peered upside down at Coal.

"Coal, I love you, and shall love you always," she vowed.

"As I love you, too, little sister."

Later that evening, when Coal looked out his bedroom window, he was taken by surprise. Strangers he had not seen before moved about. There was an atmosphere of gaiety in the air and in their animations. He heard the strumming of Spanish guitars and the singing of men and women.

Freshly attired, the brothers came into the room. They proceeded to explain that the people of their father's kingdom wanted to show their newfound affection for him, and the joy in their hearts for the coming marriage between their own Alita and the gentle-voiced negrito. While they were conversing, a knock sounded. One of the servants entered, carrying a new Spanish-made suit of black, with a blue-white shirt sewn in the fashion of the Castilian aristocracy. Coal was informed that the suit was a gift from Doña Santos. Getting out of his tub, Coal detected a weird odor he remembered from somewhere. Inez! That's the kind of cigarillo she was smoking that day. He then saw that it was Antonio who was smoking it.

Antonio told Coal that every man on the land of Santos also smoked the special tobacco, then gave him one to try. After smoking it, Coal found that it took him an hour to get into his new clothing. When later he saw his Alita downstairs at dinner, she appeared more than beautiful to him; she was exquisitely unreal.

The evening sparkled with joy running rampant as the engagement festivities commenced. People were dancing all around them, and during one dance sequence, Alita invited Coal to give it a try. His attempts were awkward at first, until he got the hang of it from observing the other men. He was soon doing a contrived distortion of his own. Coal even danced with Doña Santos, instantly capturing the hearts of her people.

As he spotted Santanna riding in from the range, a familiar bell rang inside Coal's head. Excusing himself when the dance ended, he strolled over to where the ominous foreman was dismounting.

"Señor Santanna, I'm not often curious, but I am now. Tell me, was it you who taught Sonia how to sit a horse?"

The hawk-demeanored Santanna's respect instantly soared for the one called El Diablo Negrito.

"Sí, mi amigo, it was I who first placed her upon a horse. It was I who taught her everything . . . about horses."

His eyes as he spoke of Sonia told the discerning Coal what was better left unspoken.

"I kinda figured as much." Coal smiled. "I kinda figured."

"Señor Coal, mi amigo, would you care to join me in a talk, a drink, and a smoke?"

"It's time we did. Lead on."

They walked away from the festivities to a cabin where Santanna lived. After they closed the door, subdued tones filtered back from the celebration.

"I am not one to hedge, Señor Coal . . ."

"Just Coal will do, Santanna."

"Sí, Coal, my pleasure. Tell me, what do you plan to do tomorrow?" he asked, and Coal gauged the man sitting across from him.

"I intend to give him whatever his hand calls for, Santanna," he answered, almost in a whisper.

"I, then, shall be to the left of you, amigo. Bueno?" Santanna smiled, almost evilly.

"Muy bueno. Santanna, my man, that's pure cheatin', you and me!" He laughed aloud.

"Ha, ha. Sí, Coal, it is true what you say. El Diablo himself could not survive what shall be awaiting the Don Tomasino. If what we both assume is correct, and he truly wants to die, then he will have come to the right place to depart from this earth."

Chapter 15

Day half-broke over the Valley La Nevada. A heavy gray mist hung low over the land. As it is in one family, so it was in the currents which then coursed through the mainstream of Don Santos's domain. Existing there was an ominous, almost tangible something lurking. One could taste it in the air, reach out and touch it.

Gavilán Santanna awoke giving thanks to Lucifer for having granted him one more day of existence. Long ago he had ceased pondering as to why his Don even allowed that scum of a family to exist at all, or to even be remembered. Had it been his to will, he would have erased the memory of them forever. Santanna liked Coal, this compelling new son of his Don. He was greatly anticipating seeing Coal's heralded hands in action, to see if indeed he was faster than the legendary Santanna, who had killed sixty-seven men in his fifty-eight years.

Escobar and Antonio had not yet acquired the wisdom to examine the real reasons for the anticipation on their part, pertaining to the coming confrontation. Aside from the fact they each had confidence in their own abilities was the inner feeling of invincibility subconsciously attained with the knowledge that Coal and Santanna would also be there; and regardless of whatever occurred that afternoon, there would be no way harm could befall them.

Don and Luz Santos emphatically forbade the eighteen-year-old Raoul and the fifteen-year-old Francisco to set foot outside that morning, for anything whatsoever. To disobey at that particular time would be to feel the sting of their father's wrath. However reluctantly, they obeyed their parents.

Don Raphael Tomasino did not have to awaken that morning, for he had not slept a wink since what remained of his sons was returned to him. The premonition of doom that then hovered over him, strangely enough, did not affect him. If anything at all, he found the foreboding comforting. On this day, he would kill the father of that Santos clan, and the dreaded El Diablo Negrito. Either that or let the eyes of his beloved Luz witness a scene that she would possess to her grave.

Pasqual, Flacko, and Pepe Vasquez. Their names instilled naked fear into the hearts of all but a few men in the whole of Mexico. Their father, killed in a gunfight not three years prior, had taken each son at the age of nine and drilled him in the skills of gunfighting until the pistol fell from small, tired fingers. Lupo Vasquez daily schooled his sons for hours, ten straight years, until he felt they had reached his desired plateau of skillfulness. And now aged twenty-six, twenty-seven, and twenty-nine, they were three finely-honed assassins. Human killing machines.

Of the trio, the middle son, the razor-thin Flacko, was by far the deadliest, a gunistry genius. These brothers awoke smiling at one another, for they were the only people they loved. During the border gunfight, which had prompted the mind of Don Tomasino to solicit them, Flacko had drawn iron and instantly wiped out three of the ten Americans they killed, before either of his brothers had fired a single shot.

"My brothers, what do you say to the suggestion that after we kill this negrito swine today, we sit upon his dead chest and drink wine?" Flacko laughingly inquired.

"I like the idea fine, but I also remember what was told to us before we took this job, about El Diablo Negrito. It would not be wise to make light of his gift," cautioned Pasqual, the oldest.

"Bah! There is no one on earth who can kill me while looking into my face!" Flacko declared, believing it.

"Nevertheless, concentrate on him!"

Quietly sitting in Coal's bedroom, Alita watched a metamorphosis take place before her very eyes. Although she was aware of the impending crisis, she was not prepared for the change in Coal. His eyes, when he did turn them her way, were void of anything even remotely resembling love or compassion. He appeared cold and distant, not at all like the laughing, smiling Coal, whom she loved.

Since dawn, she had been sitting there in total silence. It was her presence that awakened him. Coal did not speak or motion her to him, and she did not move his way. They touched without touching. After lying still and peering at the mist floating outside his window for more than two hours, Coal arose. Before donning a stitch of clothing, he began the ritual of cleaning his six-guns.

Alita observed as he almost tenderly caressed those two iron extensions of himself. When he was positive that the nomenclature of each was as Solomon Pinkney had designed them to be, he slid both into holsters on the bed beside him. Coal then dressed with utter deliberation, indicating to her that his mind was on what was to come and nothing else.

Orders from the Don to his men went like this: "I want all of you men away from the main house, for I wish to extend to our visitors the feeling of good will, even to Don Tomasino. I will personally remove the hand of any man who fires on them without first having been fired upon. But, if you do hear gunfire, then permit no one to leave my land unescorted and alive."

All morning the women of clan Santos prayed to their Madonna. The men simply waited idly until just before noon, when they heard the rumblings of oncoming hoofbeats. "Wait here, woman I love. I'll be back," Coal softly told her. He did not kiss or so much as touch Alita bodily.

"Yes, Coal, come back to your Alita," was all she said.

Santanna waited below, looking up the stairway. When he sighted Coal heading down, he was being followed by Escobar and Antonio. Together they awaited the Don's appearance and were not surprised in the least to discover that he was unarmed. He was unwilling to assist Don Tomasino in committing suicide at the expense of Doña Luz's peace of mind. Hoofbeats halted, and Don Humberto walked onto his veranda. He found his enemy with a face distorted by spiritual pain endured beyond the breaking point.

"Where is that bastard called El Diablo Negrito?"

"My son is the one you speak of," answered Don Humberto. "His name is Coal!"

"I said where . . ."

His query was answered in silence as Coal, moving like a black panther stalking, came onto the veranda, followed by Santanna, with the brothers close behind. Santanna wore no hat upon his hawk-like head; his iron-gray mane flowed to his shoulders, and his eyes were two red pools of fire. He and Coal took positions on both sides of the Don as Antonio went to Coal's right and Escobar to Santanna's left.

Flacko Vasquez slithered from his saddle, followed by his own brothers. Three more villains who completed the funeral entourage also dismounted, leaving only Don Tomasino in the saddle. Instinctively Coal picked out his target. Flacko. *He will be the first one to kill,* thought Coal. He could taste the danger of Flacko from forty-five feet away. Flacko did likewise with Coal.

"You are the swine who murdered and maimed my sons?!" Don Tomasino bellowed.

Imperceptibly Coal moved, covering his side of Don Humberto with the left side of his own body. Coal knew how to get that show on the road.

"Yes, I am. I'm only sorry that their mother wasn't there to get her share, scum!"

Don Raphael screamed in outraged fury, and fingers grabbed gun handles all over that front yard. Crouching as was his natural move, Coal simultaneously cleared leather with Flacko and fired, making his two and Flacko's one sound like one and the same. Coal felt hell-hot flames penetrate his left thigh at the precise instant two holes spurted blood from the forehead and heart of Flacko Vasquez. In that same split second, Santanna's guns shattered the faces and liquidated the rest of the family Vasquez, as the yard went aflame, soaked red with blood.

Coal saw Escobar wheel crazily, grabbing his stomach after shooting and killing one of the three remaining gunmen still standing. Firing from the hip, Coal and Antonio blew away the chests of the last two. Something happened to Don Tomasino as he witnessed the bloody carnage from his perch atop his mount, and it froze his hands. He merely sat there with his face gone chalk white.

Santanna and Coal, without any visible signal between them, calmly reloaded while Antonio kept his pistol trained on the right eye of Don Tomasino.

"Wait! Don't kill hi . . ." Don Santos began.

"The time for talk is over!" Coal snapped. "Pity just died! C'mon, Santanna!"

Like two merciless angels of death, Coal, limping and bleeding, with Santanna went to stand directly in front of Don Tomasino. Together they pulled back on the hammers of their six-guns, and the entire head of Don Tomasino erupted and disappeared in a hail of bullets, tearing him from his saddle and leaving his left foot caught in the stirrup of his rig.

His headless neck crimson-painted the green grass beneath it, as the men of clan Santos looked on in shocked silence. And then with frigid deliberation, Coal and Santanna stepped over the decapitated Don Tomasino. Straddling the bodies of those who had come to kill, they systematically administered the coup de grâce by dispensing single shots into the back of each skull. One, by one, by one.

As suddenly as the outburst of gunfire died, life-giving rays of sunlight pierced the mist hanging over the Valley La Nevada. There would be peace in that valley for years to come.

Chapter 16

Abody-strewn front yard in the Empire of Don Humberto Santos told a grim story. The depiction of the culmination of years of jealousy, hate, envy, and distrust. Don Raphael Tomasino had entered the land of Santos with murder in his heart. In sequence, his targets had been the man he thought had stolen the woman he loved and married her, and Coal, who had decimated the last male strain of the Tomasino clan, leaving him an ugly cripple for life.

With Don Tomasino gone forever from this earth, the people of Valley La Nevada believed that the prolonged enmity had finally ceased for all time. That is, all except Coal and Santanna. Those two men were of a mind to ride onto the land now owned by Don Carlos Tomasino and burn him. They agreed that that procedure was the only way of insuring themselves against future uprisings, the total eradication of the last member of the Tomasinos. But Don Santos's word was law, and he absolutely forbade it. Members of the Santos family knew that Santanna would never disobey his Don, but they were not at all certain of what Coal would do after he recovered from his wound.

Escobar Santos had been kissed by Lady Luck. When Coal saw him clutch his gut and fall, he knew Escobar was hit in a vital spot. The bullet entered just to the right of his navel, exiting from the rear of his right hip. Had it remained lodged in his intestines, he undoubtedly would have perished. After patching him up, Dr. Ramirez diagnosed that he would be up and around in a few weeks.

While the doctor was attending to the more seriously wounded Escobar, it was Alita who painfully removed the bullet from deep inside the thigh of her man. Coal cursed a blue streak while this was going on, and Santanna good-naturedly supervised Alita's task. Coal cursed him, too, and Santanna laughed until his tears rolled. Alita thought them both insane as she tediously dug through flesh, sinew, and blood. Stretched out behind her as she knelt before Coal on the veranda were the cadavers of seven men who had come to kill but died instead.

While awaiting Coal's return up in his bedroom, Alita had screamed with the initial burst of gunfire. Then the following thunderous volley drove her to the door and down the stairway. Coal and Santanna were grimly administering their coup de grâce when she haltingly approached the veranda. What she then witnessed completely drained the color from her face. The headless torso of Don Raphael was still spouting blood and hanging from that one stirrup.

The other bodies, which were grotesquely distorted in the grip of death, lay twisted and destroyed before her eyes. Seeing her man and Santanna fire their final shots while alternately straddling those still forms, Alita had to grab hold of the railing to keep from swooning. At that moment, she was still unaware of Coal being wounded.

When finally they turned her way, Alita's heart jumped inside her bosom, and she raced to meet him, thinking he was injured far worse than he actually was. The sight of Coal with blood streaming from the hole in his thigh stung her into action. She screamed orders to their servants, who had seen it all, and was rendering aid to Coal by the time her wounded brother was carried into the house.

Don Humberto was still standing where he had originally halted, transfixed by the actions of Coal and Santanna. They seemed to have silently communicated prior to committing that final dual act. Their utterly cold-blooded detachment made him shudder.

Along with her youngest sons and two daughters, Luz Santos had witnessed the entire gun battle from behind the shutters overlooking the veranda. Moving swiftly down the stairs, Doña Luz found her husband slowly shaking his head from side to side. Then, gently wrapping her arm around his shoulders, she guided him into the house.

There was no celebration that evening. The atmosphere then surrounding the hacienda was more like the calm after some disastrous event, as in the aftermath of a tornado. Having limped up to Escobar's bedroom, Coal, Antonio, and Santanna sat around his bedside. Oddly enough, they did not extensively rehash that bloody clash. They mostly enjoyed that unique bond created between men who have faced death together and subsequently survived together.

When Coal began moving around again with his normal dexterity, he busied himself with the task of building his future. Don Santos supplied him with a workforce of 230 men and women. In Coal's mind, there existed a grand picture. He often wondered how it had ever manifested itself there in the first place, but it had, and he could mentally envision it with great lucidity. One day, he verbally tried to show it to his dear Alita.

"Lita, close your eyes and try to imagine what I see. It's there in your favorite place where we first rode to. Remember that spot where you dismounted while I sat on Big Black, just filling my eyes with you? Well, when I got down and wrapped my arms around you, I got my first peep at those pretty mountain peaks with the snow on top. Okay now, you're looking down from there to where all those young pines are growing."

Alita began to smile with her eyelids shut.

"Sweetheart, in your mind, remove those pines. Now, with

those same pines, which smell so sweet to me, I'm gonna build us our home. Yeah! Our front door will be about a hundred yards from that clear, shallow river. The house I see in my mind is three-tiered, with our bedroom facing east. We'll have an extra-large window so that we can see from the mountains to the right, to the heavy pine country on the left, with the river running past our house on down through the valley. Lita, honey, imagine the whole thing done up in pine logs. Love, would you like that?"

"Oh, sí, mi cariño. I envisioned it all as you spoke. Coal, it's beautiful!"

"And Lita, honey, between the house and the high range where we first stood, take a proud look at all of those fine stallions sired by Big Black, with mares ready to foal. Roaming nearby is the cattle your father has given to us. How do you like that?" Coal grinned.

"My dearest," Alita quietly whispered, "I can hardly wait. I know it will be exactly as you just pictured it for me. Coal, the strangest thing just occurred to me. I don't know what your last name is or what mine shall be."

"That makes us even, because I don't know it, either."

"Do you mean that your parents were not married?"

Coal eyed her for a long second, then, "Does it make a difference, Alita?"

"No, my Coal, it does not."

"Lita, it's impossible for me to say whether my folks were hitched or not, the way slave trading was conducted. I never knew my father."

"But then what will be my last name, Coal?"

"Exactly. Coal. It shall be Alita Alesandria Coal. This thing of two names is a European and Asian custom. When I was living with the hard-fightin' Comanches, most of my friends there had but one name."

"Y-you lived with the Comanches, Coal?"

"For a fact, pretty lady." He smiled at her expression of amazement.

"How long did you live with them? Madre de Dios!" She crossed herself.

"Oh, I don't know exactly, for many years."

"D-did you know many Comanche squaws?"

"Yes."

"Did you bed them?"

"I see where you're headin', but before you do, know this to be. No woman I've known or will ever know means one damn thing compared to you! Next to you, they all look like cowboys to me. That answer your question?"

"Yes, my darling, I just wanted to hear you say it," she said, and blushed.

"Now gettin' back to what I was saying about that one name business. In some of the books I had the good fortune to read and study during my stay at the monastery . . ."

"The what?!!!" Alita exclaimed, wide-eyed, with one hand held against her breasts. "No Coal, no!" She laughed. "Not you, querido, not you in a monastery!" She cried with hysterical laughter.

With feigned indignance, he cocked his head to one side. "You mean to tell me that you didn't know I spent three years in a monastery?" Coal inquired, evoking pure screams of mirth. "I'll have to tell you about that sometime. Anyway, some of the books my dear friend Padre Dominic gave me to read told of men of my race and of the Indians, who all had but one name. Seriously, I can't for the life of me see any reason for having more than one. Coal is all the name I'll need, and the only one I'm ever gonna have."

"As you wish, mi corazón," Alita said, kissing him. "Dearest, who named you Coal?"

"My lovin' momma did. Like I remember her sayin' to make me and Becky laugh, I was and still am black as coal." He smiled.

"It is perfect, because I adore your name. It fits you in more ways than one. First, of course, is your color. Then second, you are like the coal, which once having been placed into the fiery furnace, seems to burn forever. As when you are angry. And also, you are hard like the coal, and soft like the coal. Alita would have been oh so proud to have known your mamacita."

"Lita, if she were alive today, there would be no man on earth who could keep her in chains the way she was when last I saw her. But she's gone now, sweetheart, and I don't really like to talk about Momma and my sister Becky."

"Coal, when shall we be married?" Alita changed the subject.

"Six weeks from today, love. The trees are all down now, and the workers start on our house tomorrow. We'll get hitched in our new home and there we shall remain, absolutely alone for one whole month. And then after that, we'll open the house to everyone, the way your people seem to like to do."

"This waiting is unbearable. Coal, why do you love me?"

"Why? Sorry, but I've never asked myself that question, for to me there doesn't have to be any why. I find loving you is the most natural and easiest thing in the world for me to do. Irregardless of why. Lita, honey, I will love you even after I'm dead."

"You are a strange man, my negrito lindo."

"Not really, just been leadin' a damn strange life." He grinned at her. "Since we're askin' questions today, why do you love me, Alita?"

With demure shyness, she blushed again, glancing up at him through her lashes. "If I tell you, you will not think your Alita is brazen?"

"No, sweetheart."

"Each day I am finding many things which I love about you, but these are predominantly inside of me. Coal, whether you know it or not, you possess the ability to make me feel wild, like an Apache squaw. You also make me think of my virginity as useless. And then"—she smiled endearingly—"there is the strength of your presence. I could fear nothing in your presence. Mamacita says there is nothing more captivating or appealing to a woman than is the pure and gentle strength of a real man."

"I do all that, huh?"

"Sí, and much, much more," Alita said, snuggling against him on the veranda. "Coal, do you know that there will be hundreds of people attending our wedding?"

He squeezed her closer. "There's only one person who I'm particular about attending, and that's the beautiful young wench who is sittin' out here with me on her father's porch."

"Tell me, Coal, be serious now. Do you really think I'm a wench?"

"With me you are."

"Do you love me more or less when I'm that way with you?"

"That's when I love you most of all, Alita," he answered, kissing her.

"Querido, why then haven't you taken me by now? You can, you know, anytime you wish."

"There'll be plenty of time for taking you, as you say. Ha! You're gonna get taken so much, you'll wish you never saw me or my taking tool!" He laughed aloud.

"Ahh cariño, but I did see you, and you are mine, mine, mine!"

Chapter 17

Rising with the sun on that following day, the people of Valley La Nevada zealously took to their tasks. Theirs were chores motivated through the love and loyalty they held for the clan Santos. Scores of burros pulled and strained while uprooting tree stumps, leveling the foundation for Coal's homesite. Singing could be heard as the first logs were settled into place.

Coal was no architect, but he definitely knew what he wanted. He had only to define his wishes to those skilled craftsmen supplied by Don Santos, and they artfully satisfied him. Within three weeks, his home was partially constructed. On most days, Coal would be right there among the workers, supervising his dream house. Not only was the house made of pine, but likewise was the furniture, corral, and the surrounding fences. Eight days prior to their wedding, Coal's dream was realized.

Riding Big Black up to the crest of the high range, he viewed it all with a chest full of emotion. All alone, he sat admiring his ranch, and suddenly he startled the big stallion by yelling at the top of his lungs. Coal knew what had evoked that outburst. It was motivated by the profound feeling of pride in accomplishment and the joy of fulfillment.

"There's our own place in this world, big fella," he said, grinning. "Now you can get fat and sassy and have all the mares you can mount. How's that?" he asked it, stroking its satin-like neck.

Their new home was located among the remaining pines, giving the illusion that through some sheer twist of magic, the logs had collapsed into an orderly, systematic heap. Coal himself had not yet inspected the completed interior, and decided to do so along with the rest of his new family when he brought them to it after dinner that evening.

Mexico had its own share of violence and injustices, but Coal knew he could not have owned such a ranch in the land of his birth. The house with its three tiers was just perfect, and Coal had found and made a niche for himself in the Valley La Nevada.

"C'mon, Big Black, let's go and tell pretty Lita all about it," Coal laughed.

While assembled at dinner, the family heard the rolling rumble of horses' hooves. Leaving the table to investigate those sounds, the Santos family was pleasantly surprised at what they encountered, especially so the wide-smiling Coal.

On the night of his and Alita's betrothal, Coal had requested his prospective father-in-law to dispatch fifteen men on a very special mission. The object of that mission was then smiling and striding toward Coal with outstretched arms. The women viewed that scene from the veranda.

"Hello, my everlasting friend." Coal emotionally beamed, embracing him hard.

"Hello, my son, hello, Coal." Padre Dominic hugged him back, smiling broadly and on the verge of tears upon once again seeing his beloved pupil. "I came as soon as I received your message, my son. Coal, you are well?"

"Just as well as you look," Coal said, grinning. "And you are more than welcome here, Padre. Padre Dominic, allow me to introduce my new family and future wife," Coal proudly stated, introducing him to each member.

"This is indeed a great moment for me, my son. Daily I have prayed for you to find true happiness, and it appears that my prayers have been answered."

"And now, Padre, here is the living reason why my life has

changed. Alita, say hello to the good Padre Dominic"—Coal paused, grinning—"from the monastery," he concluded, as Alita curtsied low.

"Padre"—Alita smiled with mischief dancing in her eyes—"tell me, por favor. Has my Coal truly lived among the holy men of the cloth such as you?"

"Yes, that he did, my child. For three fine years he did so, and has been sorely missed since his departure," he answered, smiling at their obvious mental attempts at placing Coal in a monastery.

"Padre Dominic, I have summoned you here to conduct our marriage ceremony one week from tomorrow, if you will?"

"Need you ask? But of course, my son. How could I possibly refuse the two of you with all of this love I am seeing before my eyes?"

"Padre, come into our home and dine with us," Don Santos invited.

He was ushered to the seat directly across the table from Coal, his gentle brown eyes missing nothing as occasionally he would smile.

"Coal, if my old eyes do not deceive me, it appears there are two ladies here who are in love with you," he smiled, his eyes resting upon little Esmeralda.

"Alright Padre, now you leave my little sweetheart be," Coal laughed, as Esmeralda blushingly hid her face behind Coal's back.

After dining, Coal invited all of them to see their new home. He guided them along a course where one minute they were riding, then the next instant, his house suddenly appeared as though from out of the mass of pine trees. Coal had purposely kept them all, including Alita, away from that area until his home was completed. Alita's joyful eyes brilliantly expressed her utter satisfaction.

"I'm glad that our new home does those pretty things to your eyes, love."

"Oh cariño, your Alita could live here for the rest of her life and then some. I love you, Coal." She dazzled him with her elation.

"This is what I was trying to make you see, that day up on the high range. Lita, love, here we shall have all that there is," Coal promised her, with a heart full of love.

The family roamed throughout the premises, inspecting and admiring everything. Coal dearly loved the smell of pines and simply paraded about his dream, sniffing, sniffing, sniffing.

Eight days later, in the Valley La Nevada, Don Humberto Santos tearfully gave his favorite child in marriage to the man named Coal.

Adorned in high-crowned Spanish veils and a gown consisting of delicately made white satin and lace, Alita Alesandria Santos emanated a glow from under those sheer veils. She was positively radiant as her father led her along the path to Padre Dominic and her Coal. Then releasing her at the side of Coal, the Don rendered the priest a tearful nod and stepped backward. On the opposite side of Coal stood Gavilán Santanna. In spite of the more than three decades of difference in their ages, they had grown tighter than wet rawhide. Santanna was Coal's best man.

In front of the structure of pines and farther along Coal's right were the Brothers Santos. On Alita's left were Sonia, Esmeralda, and childhood friends of the bride. From the instant Alita stepped from their new home out into the sun, her beautiful eyes never left the face or figure of her Coal. While she held onto her father's arm, warm, ecstatic tears threatened to blind her as she thrilled upon the emotions within her bosom. Never in her sweetest dreams had she imagined it being this way. How ravishingly handsome did Coal appear to her.

Immaculately attired in a blue ruffled shirt, Coal covered it with a sky-blue velvet suit designed in the fashion of the gentlemen of Mexico. The jacket was short-waisted with wide lapels, and his boots sparkled in the noonday sun. Observing his Lita-love as she came toward him, Coal felt that no other was ever more enchantingly beautiful.

While conducting the ritual of vows, Padre Dominic was momentarily thrown off balance by a devilish Coal, who suddenly winked at him as he repeated his vows. Alita wondered at the Padre's expression and his mercurial change of hue. Quickly glancing up at Coal, she found the epitome of innocence. Shortly thereafter, it was done. Coal and his Alita were one.

Then came time for their acceptance of wedding gifts; and they received everything from jewelry to a goat.

Each Santos offspring, upon the day of her or his marriage, would automatically receive $50,000 in Spanish gold. Alita's wedding chest contained twice that amount in the form of her dowry. Don Santos sensed that Coal would not have accepted it otherwise. After graciously accepting their gifts, Alita went into one of the rooms with her bridesmaids and friends, and Coal enjoyed a wedding toast with his brothers, Don Santos, and Santanna. Don Santos then beckoned to all of them, and they went upstairs into the bedroom of the newlyweds.

Raising his drink aloft, the Don pivoted in a small circle to all. "On this day, which truly fills my heart," he emotionally began, "I, my sons, and Santanna, who knows me better than any other, will drink and smoke to the first marriage among the children Santos."

Reaching into his vest pocket, he withdrew the smoke of the earth people. Seven small, crudely rolled cigarillos were then passed around. A knock sounded, and a smiling servant entered, carrying a magnum of potent Castilian wine. The men raised their goblets to Coal, toasted, and drank.

As his smoke was ignited, Coal's mind once again drifted to his initial exposure to the pungent-sweet smell of marijuana. Getting high, they laughed and swore, drank and smoked, for as long as propriety would permit. When they emerged from the bedroom, Coal felt as if he floated all the way downstairs to his bride.

Having been searching for him, Alita peered closely into his eyes and instantly surmised what he had been doing. She laughed.

"Cariño, I have a confession to make," she whispered.

"Make it, my love." He grinned down to her.

"My sisters, along with my friends and me, we have been doing the same thing you just did."

"Little Essie, too?"

"Sí, my Coal, Essie also. It is my wedding day!" Alita happily cried. "Oh Coal, look at her."

Singing her little heart out, Esmeralda moved about the throng accompanied by six men with guitars. And sing she did, as her liltingly rich soprano voice brought joyful tears to the eyes of almost everyone. Enjoying life as he never had, Coal stood behind Alita with his hands clasped around her middle, warmly smiling, watching, and listening to the adorable Esmeralda.

He discovered something else about himself during the celebrations. He wholeheartedly disliked wine. It had the tendency to make him feel unbalanced, which instinctively he frowned on. Soon after the sun receded over the mountains rimmed in white, Coal and his bride changed clothing and then rode up to their spot to gaze down upon their home. From there, they observed the silhouettes of their guests against the many patterns of numerous lanterns. By prearrangement, Santanna and the family herded the countless people on their collective ways.

The couple watched them file away and over a swell in the land. Seconds after he sighted the last of their guests disappear, Coal stood up to leave.

"Coal, mi esposo, your Alita has a problem. My mother has given me a beautiful nightdress to wear to our bed," she informed him, shyly glancing. "But Vera Sánchez of the village, who is like a second mother, she says that I should wear nothing at all, and my naked body would then inflame you forever with desire for me. What do you think?"

"Lita-love, I seriously doubt that your question is for the reason you've just explained to me." He laughed at her. "I think you just want to hear it from me, to hear me sanction what you have already made up your own mind to do anyway."

"Ayiiee, cariño! Coal, it thrills me when you do that. When you read your Alita so crystal clear. If sex is better than the sensation your insight often gives me, let's ride!" She imitated one of his expressions.

Pulling up outside of their corral, Alita immediately vanished to the upstairs, and Coal unsaddled their horses. He led Big Black into his stall and instantly out again, as if changing his mind.

"Big Black," Coal said, lighting another one of those dynamite smokes left him by his father-in-law for his pleasure, "you and me, we have done just about everything together. But not tonight. Tonight is one time I'll have to be strictly on my own." He spoke to his animal friend, feeling very, very good. "Now I haven't forgotten our pact, not ever. I look after you and you look after me, right? Right! Well, now, my reason for bringin' you back out of your stall is so that tonight you can get married, too. Coal's gonna turn your big black ass loose. Right out here among these plump-rumped lady horses, Big Black. I want you to show 'em that you can do something else besides trot around with that two-gunned black fella on your back all the time. Deal? Deal."

Coal then released him into the corral with four thoroughbred mares, which he had purchased for that specific purpose. What then occurred made Coal laugh until his belly ached. Big Black trotted over to the mares, sniffing and also letting them get a whiff of his scent, lingering next to each one for what seemed the same length of time. Then with his head held high—what appeared to Coal as abnormally high—the powerful stallion pranced on feathered feet and took itself away to the far side of the corral, where it whinnied loudly up into the night. *Playing hard-to-get*, thought a laughing Coal.

High and mellow, he was still laughing when he entered the house. Coal noticed that Alita's personal servants had cleaned away every remnant of the wedding celebration. He had laid down the law, that absolutely no one was to be within one mile of their place after the reception. Prior to going upstairs to Alita, Coal lit one more of those potent Mexican hand-rolls and got bombed just right. After blowing out the lanterns below, he climbed the stairs to his bride.

Moon glare ricocheted from those luminous Sierra mountain peaks and into their bedroom. Coal entered and closed the door behind, wondering why, since there was no one else around. Unmoving, he stood just inside the doorway. Alita, with her knee nearest to Coal slightly raised, reclined with her arms somewhat close to her sides, and he could clearly detect the rise and fall of her breasts as she breathed. Slowly removing his clothing while she observed him, he then moved to their wedding bed, only to stand just above her and to her left.

In total contrast to the way she stood out in the semi-darkness, Coal appeared almost ghostlike. His body was a shadow to her eyes exploring the length of him. Like fire was that initial contact of their bodies when he settled his frame next to hers. Alita emitted a whimper as his right hand ran the course of her, and she found his lips with her own. Soft, wet, hot lips seeking beyond that which had previously only been spoken of.

"Oh how I do love you, my husband," she whispered, arching her pelvis as his long fingers explored between her legs.

Without attempting to enter her, Coal gently rolled on top of Alita, while kissing every inch of her face. With a suddenness, she parted her legs, and ever so softly, Coal pressed it to her, instantly transforming Alita into a wild thing set free. Trembling with desire and exquisite pain, her body alternately came to and then withdrew from his in an intriguing gyration as Alita began to murmur in her native tongue.

Coal was not talking then, but slowly commencing to fuck her with deeper penetration, situating her tender body under him until they were a perfect fit. Then finding the real groove, he brought her into it.

The surrounding hills echoed as a delirious Alita began to

scream for dear life, death, joy, and yes, her mamacita, too. More than once, Coal made his loving bride holler for her momma.

"Lita-love, ain't nuthin' or nobody in this world can help you now," he spoke into her ear while grinding her pussy to a frazzle. "Not Momma or Daddy. Nobody but Coal can help you now, precious. C'mon now, give Coal what you've been wanting me to be taking, like you say."

His voice only tended to quicken her gyrations as Alita whipped it to him, giving up what she didn't even know she had. By then, her torso was vigorously rippling, like a flag caught in a driving, relentless wind, her body juices giving off stimulating sounds of wetness.

"Ayiiee, Coal, mi cariño! Oohh!! Nothing should be as this." She gasped for air. "Coal, I try for words, but I cannot think. Ayieee!!!" Alita ecstatically cried out.

"Don't even try to think, Lita-love. Tell me with your sweet body."

Those were somehow just the right words to say to her. Alita's pelvis rose and fell to meet his own, with the lips of her cunt clinging and yet lubricant. Coal felt her quiver just prior to squeezing him with surprising strength, instantly followed by a sound from deep within her, from the place where only women live. It was a half groan, half outcry, as Alita experienced orgasm for the first time in her life. The overwhelming force of that sensation made her want to run from it.

"Coal!!! Querido!! What did you just do? How? What? Coal . . ." Alita started to say, when riding the crest of that initial shattering orgasm came another, of even greater magnitude.

Alita could not catch her breath, it seemed, and again she felt that awesomely good, all-consuming ecstasy. She trembled, screamed, and then succumbed to that devastating inner explosion. They came together that last time, clinging to each other.

Throughout the entire night, they searched for and found it all. The more they discovered, all the more they sought, as daylight came and went. Early that next evening, Alita prepared the first meal of their marriage.

"Cariño," she said, smiling, "let's eat our food upstairs. It's easier that way."

"What's easier?" Coal teased her, suddenly realizing that he smiled and grinned at her more than anyone in his life.

"You know." Alita blushed.

"I'm all for it," he agreed, hugging and kissing her until her knees sagged. "I'm a man who hasn't been hangin' around beds too much, and I've got a lot of catchin' up to do."

Immediately after eating, they made more love. Then they talked, planned, and loved, loved, loved. Next morning, they awakened only to laugh hysterically at the fact that they were both as hungry as lobo wolves.

Chapter 18

Coal and Alita's month swiftly passed in glorious, isolated splendor, and Alita became pregnant during their honeymoon. One night in the fall of 1859, the clan Santos came visiting. It subsequently turned out to be a night for rejoicing.

While Coal and Santanna smoked and paced with the Don and his sons, Coal became the proud father of a beautiful, healthy baby girl. As Coal frantically paced and wore out the grass in front of his house of pines, new Grandmamá Santos brought him the grand news. Racing up to his bedroom, Coal was so happy, he was lightheaded. But to Coal's complete surprise, his beloved Alita appeared saddened.

"Lita-love, are you alright?" he asked her, his smile vanishing. "What's the matter?"

"Sí, cariño, I am well. Nothing is the matter, my Coal."

"Then why are there sad tears in your eyes, sweetheart?"

She avoided his eyes while holding their new infant in her arms. "I-I-I did not bear you a son, Coal. Forgive me."

Coal gazed down upon her as if she had lost her mind. "Are you plum crazy? Lita, how could any man on earth not be happy to have a child as lovely as my new daughter?"

Reaching down, a beaming Coal gently picked up his only child. Then walking over to the light of a lantern, he peered at the tiny bundle held in his outstretched hands. Suddenly Coal broke into joyous, tearful laughter, bringing his daughter close to his chest. Alita studied him hard, then slowly she began to laugh with him, and tears of happiness fell.

"Coal, my dearest, you are not showing a display of happiness just to keep your Alita from feeling shame, are you?"

"Shame?!! Hey, lady, do you remember what I said that mornin' about tannin' your rump? Well, if I ever again find you being ashamed of anything of ours, I'll do just that!"

"Coal, you did not wish for a man-child? Look at me," she implored him, and he did, straight into her loving eyes.

"Honestly? Well, I suppose I did. But from my heart and soul, Lita-love, I swear a boy would not have made me any happier. And I love you now even more, sweetheart, because of our little girl here. That's a fact! Lita, honey, look at her. Why, she's even prettier than you are, and that's impossible!!" Coal laughed with his heart in his eyes.

"Then I too am happy, my love, truly I am," Alita cried.

Coal named her Autumn, for that was his favorite time of any year.

Well be it that their infant was a girl, because Coal was adamant in his refusal to even consider naming a son of his Humberto.

"Not on your life!" he would crack to Alita, making her scream mirthfully while holding her swollen stomach. "I hope you noticed that your daddy did not name one of his own sons any such thing as Humberto! Can you imagine hangin' a handle like Humberto on a poor defenseless kid? Humberto?!!! Now that's what a body would do to someone they wanted to get even with, not your own kid! C'mon now, Pa Santos," Coal would good-naturedly tease his father-in-law, "you know I love you like a father, but tell Lita that it ain't near fair to do such a thing to an innocent baby."

During moments such as those, clan Santos saw a Coal never

before seen by anyone. This joking, laughing man was new, even to Coal himself.

In no time at all, ten months to be exact, Coal got caught flat-footed. It was early morning, in late summer of 1860, a few hours before dawn, when little Coal made his unexpected, solo appearance.

Alone with his wife, Coal singlehandedly delivered his son while broken out in a cold sweat. He later confessed that throughout the entire episode, he was frightened for the first time in his life.

When the elated Santos family arrived that morning, Coal met them at his front door while holding his image in his arms. Doña Luz immediately reached out for her first grandson. Many times, Don Humberto was overheard to say that Luz's grandson was more greatly loved by her than even he was. Little Coal was her Coalito.

Coal took to fatherhood much in the same manner he had taken to his six-guns. He loved it. During those first three years of their marriage—in spite of the fact that he was busily building his herds of thoroughbred mounts and choice beef—Coal always found time for his wife and children. He was adored by his children, and he loved them excessively so. No sooner than the youngsters were able to keep their food down without having to be burped, their doting father had them up in the saddle, riding the range with him.

By the time little Coal was two years old, everyone was remarking how much like his father he was. Not just in looks, but in character. His little heart was as big as a lion's, and he left no doubt in anyone's mind that he had a mind of his own. Many were the mornings when Coal had important matters to attend to, the little man would insist on his father taking him along. Coal would simply hoist him up, place him between himself and his saddle horn, and ride off with him.

Being exposed to range language used by his father and those in his employ, the little fellow could curse pretty good, too, by the time he reached the age of four. When he could sit a saddle, Don Santos presented his grandson with a pinto pony. With a saddle made to accommodate his little legs, he then rode after his father without asking permission, causing his mother and grandmother no little consternation.

By 1864, Coal's original herd of cattle initially given to him by his father-in-law had tripled in size, and Mexican beef sold for top money. Coal sold much of it to the Mexican Army, which was constantly fighting revolutionaries. Not that he was partial to the Army, because he was not. But he was a businessman.

One day while Coal was on his own range supervising, Confederate officers representing the Confederacy in America visited the hacienda of Don Humberto Santos. They offered the Don more than the normal price for his beef, because they were in bad need of it to supply waning strength of those fighting to preserve slavery and the South.

Since the Don and his only son-in-law always did their business in concert, the Don informed those officers that he would first speak with Coal, for half of the beef sold would be his.

What he did not inform them of was that Coal, his son-in-law, was black. That evening, when Coal arrived with his wife, children, and Santanna to dine with his in-laws, the Don met them outside.

"Coal, my son, we have visitors from your native country who wish to buy some of our fine stock. They must truly be in dire need of good beef, because they are offering us rather exorbitant prices."

"That's okay by me, Pa Santos. I'll be inside after I stall Big Black. Alita, you and the kids go on inside, I'll be there shortly." He smiled, being followed to the stables by Santanna.

"Daddy," said Coalito, "I want to go with you."

"C'mon then, son, you can give Big Black his oats."

When Alita and Autumn entered, her father introduced her

and his granddaughter to the Southerners. With Autumn being almost the color of her mother, the officers did not detect anything amiss.

"Ah'm charmed to meet ya, ma'am," they told her, smiling and instantly charmed by the beauty of them both. "You folks surely have a fine spread here," the senior officer, who was a Colonel, stated.

"Thank you, sirs," Alita replied in English. "Father, where is Mamacita?"

"She and Sonia are up in Essie's room, Alita my dear."

"If you gentlemen will excuse me," said Alita, "I'll go up and sit with my mother and sisters, and leave the affairs of business to the men of our family."

After Alita had gone upstairs, a captain who had been smitten by Alita's loveliness addressed Don Santos. "That daughter of yours is a raving beauty, Don Santos. Makes a man wish she were not married."

"Thank you, Captain. Oh, here's her husband coming now," the Don remarked, seeing Coal approach the veranda from the window where he stood.

Coal halted outside to converse with Antonio and Raoul, and remained there for several minutes. Inside, the conversation continued.

"I'm told that the war in your country is a terrible one," said Don Santos. "As all wars are. The North is winning, yes?"

"At the moment they are, Ah'm sorry to say," answered the Colonel. "But this supply of your choice beef will help us immensely, for well-fed soldiers have a tendency to fight better," he concluded, sipping the aged brandy rendered by the Don.

With Santanna at his back, Coal then entered, holding the hand of his young son. The four officers almost choked on the drinks, the Colonel actually sputtering. They visibly reddened upon sight of the two-gunned Coal.

"Gentlemen!" announced the Don, "my beloved son-in-law,

Don Coal, the husband of Alita, whom you've just met. The little one is my grandson, the other my foreman, Santanna."

They stood in unison, hands on sabers and at rigid attention. The Colonel's eyes narrowed.

"How do you do," he said through clenched teeth, and the Don instantly sensed something awry.

"Howdy," an unsmiling Coal returned.

"He is married to your daughter?" snapped the tactless captain.

"Why does that create such a reaction in you, Captain?" queried Don Santos.

"I'll answer that," said Coal. "These bastards are all slave owners, Pa Santos, and my black face brings out the bigot in their mangy hides. Isn't that right, rats?"

"Now you look here, boy!" said the Colonel, and Coal backhanded spit and blood from his mouth all over Doña Santos's carpet.

They went to draw their sabers and pistols, only to find themselves facing four cocked six-guns.

"Upstairs, little Coal," snapped his father, but the little one did not move. He was staring with big eyes at the crackers. His fierce expression was not that of a mere boy.

"If I was as big as my daddy, I'd beat on your ass!" he told the Colonel.

"Santanna, get his little ass upstairs!" Santanna scooped him up and returned in a matter of seconds.

"Pa Santos, if I'd known these were crackers wantin' to buy our beef, I would've given you my answer outside. Not only won't I sell them one cow, I wouldn't even sell them cow shit!" barked Coal.

"We no longer wish to buy, Don Santos," the Colonel said, and glared at Coal. "But you, Don Coal, there is something I want from you! Satisfaction!"

"I don't think you are aware of what you are requesting," the Don cautioned him.

"I am fully aware, sir!" he bellowed, as the womenfolk appeared wide-eyed in the living room doorway, Alita with a firm grip on her son.

"You say you want satisfaction, huh?" Coal almost whispered. "To get it, all you have to do is step outside the home of my in-laws," El Diablo invited.

"That will suit me just fine!" he replied, and they headed for the front door.

"No, Coal," voiced Santanna, "let me have him."

"Not on your life, Hawk. I owe something to him and his kind."

With the family watching from the window, Coal and the Colonel faced off, while Santanna kept his guns on the other three. The Colonel got out of his long coat of the Confederate uniform. Alita had to practically mug little Coal to keep him inside. Coal waited for him to pull, and when he did, Coal shot him seven times before he hit the ground.

"Which one of you sonsabitches is next?" Coal challenged the other officers standing shocked by what they saw him do with those six-guns. Not a word.

The Brothers Santos came running with vaqueros close behind. "What's going on, Coal?" Antonio wanted to know.

"Just a little housecleanin', Tony. Now you scum, wipe up his ass and get on back to that shithole you call home."

Thirty vaqueros escorted them from the land of Santos. Later, Coal sat alone with his Alita.

"Lita-love, I'm sorry you and the children had to see me croak that pig."

"It is of no consequence, my Coal," she surprised him. "But there is something else you do not know of. Your son. Before we came downstairs, I had to take father's pistola from him."

"Well, I'll be damned! Li'l Coal!" he yelled. "Get your butt in here!"

"Yes, Daddy." He appeared, guessing why he was so loudly summoned.

"Your mamá told me what happened upstairs. What were you intending to do with your grandfather's pistol?"

"The same thing you did," he answered his father. "I saw him try to pull that long knife of his and cut you, Daddy!"

"Ya didn't like that, huh?"

"Not one damn bit!" the almost-five-year-old cursed, and exited from the room.

While Coal, Alita, and their children enjoyed their full lives together, Escobar and Antonio brought lovely wives into the Santos clan, and happiness reigned supreme. On that night of Autumn's birth, her proud father had not spoken words lacking truth. She was almost too beautiful. Coal's Autumn was a miniature dream in bronze, moving her godfather Santanna to remark, "Coal, my closest friend, Santanna thinks that by the time she reaches her mid-teens, we shall have to, I think, kill a few heart-stricken caballeros for what they most assuredly shall be thinking of doing to her."

Coal would only smile and gaze in wonder at his daughter of seven. Autumn had long, curly ringlets of jet-black hair, with her mother's eyes and nose, and the gentle disposition of Sonia.

Little Coal was the image of his father, except for his hair that was thick, black, and curly. His skin was a shade or two lighter than Coal's, which still made him very dark indeed. At the age of six, he was already taller than his sister. Members of the clan would often remark to Coal about his son's brassiness. Known to possess an unbreakable will like his father's, little Coal would tackle anything and anyone. The only person he did not give any static to was his daddy. They had arrived at an everlasting understanding on Coalito's fifth birthday.

At his fifth birthday party, in view of the clan and his father, the little fellow hauled off and struck his sister for not letting him have his way about something he wanted. Surprisingly, while angered by that act, Coal softly told him to apologize to Autumn. He angrily refused, and to the distress of his mother, grandmother, and sister, his father turned him over his knee and severely tanned his backside. Still he refused, and the punishment was repeated with the same results. Getting his little ass spanked only made him more adamant and stubborn. Slipping out of his father's grip, the little man-cub took off in flight, running far up onto the high range. Coal could have caught him, but decided to leave it alone until they both had calmed down.

Santanna came and stood at Coal's side. "Compadre, tell me, because I am curious. I have always known you to have mucho inteligencia, sí? Then tell Santanna how come you try to spank yourself out of your son, huh?"

In no mood then for riddles, Coal frowned, then suddenly smiled at his friend. "You wise old buzzard." Coal grinned. "You're right. I could have torn the hide off of his rump, and it still wouldn't have made one damn bit of difference to him. Hawk, I think that's probably why I didn't catch him and fan his little tail some more."

Never had Alita known Coal to punish or even raise his voice at either of their children until that day, and it disturbed her greatly to see Coal angry with his son. It had always been she who disciplined them. From where Alita sat with her family, they all could see Coalito, far up the grassy hillside, observing them. Autumn had forgotten being struck by then, and her only concern was that her baby brother was probably injured by that sound spanking administered by her father.

"Daddy," she said, with tears in her eyes, "please go and get him. He didn't hurt me."

"Tummy"—he used his pet name for her—"if our little tiger decides to spend the night up there, Daddy'll go and bring him down. Don't worry your pretty little head about it."

Don Santos, who had said nothing until then, spoke quietly to his son-in-law. "Coal, don't look up, but I think my stubborn grandson is returning from his hour of self-inflicted exile."

Without seeming to, Coal had kept watchful eyes upon his only son all during the time he sat alone up there. "I see him comin', Pa Santos, been watchin' him closely. But what I'm aimin' to see when he gets here is what kind of guts he's got. Lita-love, good or bad, you're gonna find something out about your son in a few minutes," Coal predicted.

The Don, Santanna, and the brothers all nodded their heads in understanding of Coal's prediction.

Little Coal arrived and halted at the perimeter of the family gathering, not at all certain that his father would not spring on him. Coal merely watched the youngster's eyes as his cub stared right back at him across the distance, eyeball to eyeball. Clan Santos grew silent, observing this thing transpiring between father and son. Then walking past his father without a word, young Coal strode up to Autumn and gently kissed his sister's cheek where he'd hit her.

"I'm sorry, Tummy, I didn't mean it," he apologized.

His back remained turned to his father for minutes. Coal noticed his wife dab at her eyes with a handkerchief. Turning, little Coal resumed staring at his father, looking more like Coal than ever. That scene prompted Don Santos to recall his first encounter with Coal in front of the main house when he had asked him to come inside, and he smiled to himself. *Like father, like son,* he mused.

This miniature of Coal searched his father's eyes and then went to stand directly in front of him. "Daddy, I know I should not have hit my sister. I will never do it again," he promised.

Santanna saw a quick something flicker in the eyes of Coalito's father. Coal, his gaze fixed upon the lad, suddenly reached for him, and Doña Luz jumped in her seat. But little Coal never so much as flinched. Gripping those small arms in both hands, Coal raised his son to his chest, hugging him close.

Turning away from the rest of them, Coal strolled away with his son in his arms, kissing one side of the little one's face. Coalito's arms suddenly wound about his dad's neck, and he let himself be carried.

"Oh how proud I am of my men," Alita said to no one in particular.

"Me, too," Autumn echoed.

Never again in life was he spanked by his father, for there was no necessity for it. They had reached a lifetime understanding.

"Santanna, did you really see what happened there? My old heart sings with pride," the Don declared, his voice strangely hushed.

"Sí, Patrón, Santanna saw everything, even the words, which were not spoken. The little one may perhaps someday be even more man than his father is."

"And his grandfather also," Don Santos answered, with something suddenly in his eyes as he wiped them.

Walking easy, Coal carried his little man, and they talked with each other.

"Daddy, you still mad?" he asked into the ear of Coal.

"No, son. Does your bottom still sting ya some?"

"Yeah!" Coalito snapped, then drew silent for a moment. "Daddy, wanna know a secret?"

"Sure, Coal, tell it to me."

"Earlier, when you hit me, I wanted to fight you back, I did."

"Why didn't you, Coal?"

"'Cause I was wrong, that's why."

Big Coal grinned to himself. The little fellow mentioned nothing about being afraid to do so.

"Daddy, I never before saw you get angry at me, like that."

"Your daddy wasn't really angry, son. I can't get that way with someone I love. But I was purely riled at you for being so shitty to your sister. Coal, son, I'm gonna tell you something about your dad. I would get riled at God, for hurtin' one of us. Can you understand that, or is it difficult?"

"I understand, Daddy." Then, as an afterthought, "When I grow up, I'm gonna feel that way too, right?"

"No need to wait, little man, you can start right now."

"Okay. Daddy, why was mamá and grandmamá wiping at their eyes back there?" He surprised Coal, who was unaware of the lad witnessing it. He thought his son had only been watching him.

"I think it's because they were proud of the way you acted when you returned, and realized that they love you even more than they knew. You apologize to them, too, when we get back there, you hear?"

"Okay, Daddy. Things like that make big people cry? I mean, women cry?"

"Not only women, little Coal, sometimes men, too. You see, son, it doesn't make a man a sissy if he cries. Sometimes the water's just got to come out, and nothin' can stop it."

"Even you, Daddy?"

"Even me, son."

"I love you, Daddy," he voiced out of the blue.

"As your daddy loves you, little Coal. More than anything else in this world."

"Even more than Momma and Tummy?!" he wanted to know.

"Not more than them, son, but different. You see, little Coal, they are ours, yours and mine. We are a family, and we belong to them, too, make no mistake about that.

"But Coal, son, you are me, and ain't nothin' in this world any closer than that is!" he explained.

"And that is why you love me more than anything in the whole world, Daddy?"

"Yes, my only son," Coal whispered.

"I love you like that, too, Daddy, now since you told me about it," he replied, wondering why his father suddenly turned to observe the top of the mountains.

Chapter 19

Don Ricardo Valspeda Santiago, who almost eight years prior had fled to Spain after his near-fatal beating at the hands of Coal, once again returned to Mexico. He brought with him an eight-year hate for every living member of the Santos family, especially Coal. Never, in fact, had he forgotten that ass-whipping. Even after all the years of his exile, he still had trouble breathing, due to Coal having caved in his ribs with pulverizing body blows and crushing his aristocratic nose.

Miles away from Santos land, at the hacienda of Don Carlos Tomasino, the cripple sat contemplating total destruction of the tranquility then existing in Valley La Nevada. Together, the Dons Santiago and Tomasino pooled their mutual hate of Coal, planning his and his family's demise. From his wheelchair, Don Carlos toasted to the death of El Diablo Negrito.

No longer sporting the nose of the Spanish aristocrat of which he was once so proud, Don Ricardo's nose was then only a boneless piece of flesh, which sagged between his eyes. As he steadily drank wine at Don Carlos's fire, Ricardo's mind drifted to a recent day after his arrival from Madrid. While shopping with one of his many sluts in the city of Sonora, he envisioned something which convulsed him with fury.

Stepping from a stylish carriage was none other than Don

Humberto himself. In his arms, he proudly held a cocoa-pigmented boy with a crop of curly black hair. That handsome child was the duplicate of the man who had damn near crippled him in a vicious fistfight. Doña Santos was holding the hand of a tiny girl who appeared to be near the same age as the lad.

Ricardo recalled how he maneuvered closer in order to see them more clearly. As he did so, the beautiful girl-child had turned her face into his direction, smiling the smile of Alita. How he still despised that face of a mere babe. He imagined Coal in bed with Alita and moaned aloud, bringing his host to scrutinize him oddly.

Not one child, but two! He silently raged. He would see to it that Coal died the death of a dog, and he also vowed to ravage Alita. How dare she? How dare she dismiss their two-year engagement for that . . . that nigger gunman? No more than a slave, a nigger.

He visibly cringed, thinking of Alita in the arms of Coal. *Have fun while it lasts,* thought Ricardo, *for soon all four of you shall be gone from this earth.*

"These gringos, who I have personally chosen to do what we are paying them exceedingly well to do," said Don Carlos, "are the worst mercenaries money can buy. They enjoy inflicting the worst upon their victims. As it is, they cannot now return to their own country because of their infamous and foul deeds. I have ordered them to wreak havoc upon the entire Santos clan! You, Santiago, you only lost your sweetheart and your pride! But I have lost my brother, father, and the use of my limbs! I swear to you here and now, that I shall erase Coal and the Santos blood line forever!"

"Olé!" Don Ricardo yelled. "I only want the head of Coal on a stick, to mount it upon the gateposts of my hacienda, and then to feel Alita under me! After I have satisfied myself with her, I shall give her to the mercenaries, and then kill her and her children!"

"Bueno, Don Santiago!" Carlos laughed. "Tomorrow when the

sadistic gringos arrive, we shall finally have our revenge! Drink, drink, Ricardo, to the deaths of them all!"

Beautiful Estralita Santos, the wife of Antonio, was a delightful chatterbox, and that was precisely what she was doing one evening before death ran rampant. The family was dining at the Santos hacienda.

"And do you know what else? Essie pointed out to Loretta and me the man who Coal once ruined in a fistfight over Ali . . ." Antonio's knee knocking beneath the table came too late.

Seated between his wife and Esmeralda, Coal looked up from his dinner, and his eyes took on a frightful change. Slowly he turned his head to the right, and Esmeralda would not meet his gaze. Santanna quietly observed Coal, as did the others. His sworn oath that he would kill Santiago if he ever saw him again rang in their memories. Those same words had made Ricardo flee to Madrid almost eight years ago. And now he was back.

So filled with loathing did he instantly become, Coal had to control his hateful anger at the table. He addressed Esmeralda in a chilling whisper. "Essie, you have seen Ricardo Santiago? That scum has returned?"

"S-sí, Coal. He was strolling with a painted woman in the streets of Sonora," she said, still not meeting his eyes.

Coal silently seethed for long moments, and then, "Pa Santos, do you remember that morning of my first breakfast at this table, when I predicted what Don Raphael would do? Well, sir, I just got another feelin', gut deep! That pig who I should have and would have killed had his father not been so close to you, that same pig is now about to do somethin' to get himself wasted. By me! Damn! I even hate myself when I get these kinda feelings about a man. Mark my words, Pa Santos, he's gonna make me kill him in a way ain't no man been killed before!"

His venomous distaste of Santiago was so severe, Coal had to remove himself from the table and storm out onto the veranda.

Santanna followed him and found Coal cursing to himself in two languages. Coal turned to find his companion at his side.

"Hawk, that was the first time in my life when I felt a premonition which warned me and scared me both at the same time. Warning, yes, but never the other."

"It is best to heed such warnings, friend Coal. Now that Don Gaspar Santiago is dead, what do you say, Coal, about riding immediately to his son's ranch, walk in, and dispose of him? You are correct in your feelings; he brings trouble. Santanna can smell it, too."

"You both will do no such thing," came the voice of Don Humberto from behind them. "As long as he does not attempt to harm us, we shall let him live in peace."

"Do you really believe that, Pa Santos?"

"My son, it is not a matter of belief. We here have enjoyed nothing but peace ever since that day of days. Now we have small children around us, and life could not be better for any of us," he reasoned.

Coal stared hard at his father-in-law, his eyes black pools of ice. "Okay, Pa Santos, I'm gonna do as you say, because I feel in my heart for you, I truly do. But hear me, Pa Santos. If your permitting that scum to live on brings harm to my wife and children. . . ." Coal was interrupted by his brothers trooping outside. "If any hurt touches them in the slightest way, Coal will not be responsible for what he does to anyone!!" Coal warned.

"Ahh, Coal," frowned the Don, patting the side of Coal's face. "Coal, such words. Never, but never should there be such words between you and me, huh? You are my son, who I love as deeply as those who came from my loins. Would I knowingly subject any member of my family to harm? Would I?"

"Understand me," Coal whispered yet roared, "this has nothin' to do with what you and me feel for each other. It's what I feel about that sonofabitch! He's come back for vengeance, and he'll strike at the weakest ones of us, the ones who can't fight back!

Goddamnit! If that bastard knew what I was thinkin' about his ass right now, he'd swim back to Spain."

"Coal," Doña Santos called from the veranda window, "you'll leave the children here with me tonight, sí?"

"Ya see!" Coal pointed. "She feels it, too! No, Mamá Santos. Tomorrow when we come here for dinner, I will bring them with me," he said, and she withdrew herself.

"Patrón," Santanna addressed his Don, walking directly up to him. "Por favor, Patrón. All through the many years we have been together, Santanna has never spoken one word in contradiction of you. But now, Santanna must do so. Coal is right! I remember once before he warned you, and you did not heed. Don Santiago should not be allowed to live any longer. Neither he nor the cripple! For as long as they breathe, we would be foolish to sleep, even lightly! Santanna has spoken."

"Padre, they are both right," Antonio agreed.

"And too, you would not wish what would be the consequences to be on your conscience," Escobar cautioned.

"So then, we should simply ride down on them and shoot them like dogs?" asked the Don.

"Exactly," declared the twenty-two-year-old Francisco.

"Sí, Padre, that will do, unless we can think of a better way," Raoul joined in.

"Madre de Dios! What have I bred in this house of mine, assassins?! Poor Miguel up in his room, does he also agree?"

"Ah, if only Miguel were fit and healthy," Santanna spoke up for the stricken Miguel, "we would have rid ourselves of them long ago."

"What is it, Santanna," inquired the exasperated Don Santos, "have I grown old and soft? Or have my sons grown anxious to usurp my authority?" Santanna did not reply.

"It is unlike you to think such a thing of us," Escobar faced up to him.

"Personally," said Coal, "I respect you too much to lie in your face. Yes, you have grown old and soft. You now have peace that you wish to be uninterrupted. Fine. But have you forgotten what it took to secure and bring about that very same peace?"

Inside, just off the veranda, the Santos women drew nearer the open window. Coal was surprised to find his own son standing at his side and intensely listening.

"Pa Santos, we all love you, and in the final rundown, your word shall be the last one. There is no one here or anyplace else who shall challenge your authority, so long as I live," continued Coal. "But the issue is not you or the power you possess. Santiago and Tomasino are the problems we speak of. The swines. I know you will take the wait-and-see attitude; it is your nature. Okay then, we'll wait and see," he concluded, not wanting to see the dejection in the old one's face.

"Padre, in the event that harm does come to one of us, will Coal and me as your oldest sons have your personal sanction to retaliate as we see fit?" queried Escobar.

"Yes, my son, and from then on. Do not think I have misunderstood what those who love me have said, for there was a time when I could and did eat fire, too. As Coal so honestly stated, the good life has pulled my fangs, I admit. But let it be known that there is no one here who has the ice which flows through my veins—if one digs deep enough to find it. Coal, son, I want more protection placed on my grandchildren, especially when you are not with them. Also, Santanna, you will assign more men to work closer to the perimeter of the main house, thereby putting greater security around our women. Now, my young liquidators"—he smiled—"let us reenter the dining room and try to erase the anxiety we undoubtedly have created."

Santanna and Coal remained where they were as the brothers followed their father inside.

"Coal, mi amigo, he has done all he can do for the moment."

"Yeah, Hawk, but those two fuckin' problems are still walkin' around," Coal cursed again.

"Perhaps underneath"—Santanna nudged him with an elbow—
"you and me, we are just feeling the need to use our six-guns
again, huh, Coal? Maybe we jump at shadows?"

"Yeah." Coal eyed him with a who-are-you-kidding look.
"And maybe shit don't stink!"

Long after his wife and children were asleep, a deeply troubled Coal lay watching the stars from his bed, recalling events
which would have frozen the blood of most men, but had never
seemed to have fazed him too much. But that was before, when
there was no one to even consider other than himself. Now, with
his treasured family under the threat of unseen forces, Coal was
initiated to what fear and uncertainty was all about. To him, the
mere thought of life without any member of his little family was
unbearable. "What I should do is go right now and blow off the
top of his goddamned head!" he said aloud, startling Alita from
sleep. She found him sitting upright.

"W-what is it? Coal, is something wrong?"

"Ain't nothin', Lita-love, just talkin' in my sleep," he lied.

Except for his nullifying fear of leaving them alone in the night
without him, Coal would have gone that very instant, alone, and
implemented what he was then thinking. That night, his slum-
ber was a fitful one.

Morning ushered in bright and crystal clear, and the day remained beautiful throughout. At dinner that evening, laughter
filled the house of Santos. The then-nineteen-year-old Esmeralda sat in the seat she had kept from the moment Coal joined
her family. "Coal, I am sorry about last evening, for I can see that
it is still on your mind," she told him.

"Oh yeah? How come you can see so much, little lady?" he
teased.

"Your moods I can see, even when they escape others," Esmeralda opined, to which Coal said nothing, silently resuming
his assault on a steak.

Seated beside Sonia, Santanna sensed something still gnawing at Coal. From long experience, he well knew that in that day in time, not even witches had keener premonitions than did gunfighters. He only wondered when and where it would happen. Coal, to chase away the uneasiness incessantly squeezing at his vitals, occupied himself by playing with his children. Later he returned to his ranch with his family.

Next morning, Coal arose with the sun. Not wanting to disturb his sleeping Alita, he quietly dressed and left their bedroom. He was eating breakfast prepared by their Yaqui Indian cook when Alita appeared, yawning.

"Ha! You look like a fish that just got hooked." Coal grinned at his love.

"I guess I woke up as soon as I felt you were gone," she said and smiled, bending to kiss him.

"Lita-love, why don't you come along with me and get a look at your father's face when he sees the splendid results of Big Black's stable mischief? Those four-year-olds your brothers are riding are fine, but these three-year-olds are something special. I'd bet that in two years, they'll be matching Big Black for speed."

"Querido, how old is Big Black?"

"I don't really know. He was about three or so when I got him. Big Black's got at least eight more real good years left in him. Why?"

"No special reason, except that I cannot imagine you riding any other animal than Big Beauty." She smiled. Then, suddenly laughing: "Tummy and me, we call him that."

"Oh yeah? Well, his name ain't nothin' like what you just said. It's Big Black!" Coal feigned offense.

"Oh dear me!" Alita laughed infectiously. "How sorry I am, Señor. Never would I think of such sacrilege."

Rising from the table, Coal passionately kissed his teasing wife. "There, that ought to keep you quiet for a while," he laughed.

"Lita-love, an escort will bring you and the children to your father's house. I'll meet you all there later, okay?"

"Sí, cariño . . . Coal," she called, and he turned back to her. "Do that again," Alita softly requested, and he did.

"One more of those," Coal said, grinning, "and we'll end up back upstairs."

A heavy-lidded Alita locked her arms around his neck, again kissing her husband and stirring him to his soul. "Do not spend too much energy today, my love, for your Alita has something special in store for you tonight."

"Ma'am, I surely will take that into consideration." Coal squeezed her bottom. "See ya later," he said, pinched it, and left laughing from their home.

Outside he encountered his foreman of two years, a formidable fellow faithful to Coal and his family. His name was Nunio, and Coal thought enough of him to have made him a gift of one of Big Black's sons. Although Nunio Pele worked for Coal for a living, he was also pretty nifty with his own six-gun. To work for Don Coal, it was mandatory.

"All set, Nunio?"

"Sí, patrón, only the ones which you chose. Seven altogether. Patrón, I have also stationed two extra men to assist the remaining five in escorting Doña Coal and your children to the Santos hacienda."

"How come?" Coal asked, feeling something strange which creased his brow.

"I don't know, patrón. Perhaps it is this feeling I get from you these past days, perhaps not. Anyway, it is better safe than sorry, sí?"

"Sí, mi amigo. Good thinking, Nunio. Muchas gracias." Coal smiled.

"Por nada, patrón, es mi trabajo."

"Let's ride," said Coal, and they galloped off.

There have always been maniacs. Woven into each turn of man's evolutionary process, maniacs were always evident and sometimes prominent. More so in some periods than in others, but existing in all.

Chadwick Yepper was most definitely one of this demented breed. A maniac. In conjunction with his dementia, Yepper also possessed a death-quick six-gun. This nut held under his command others who also were immersed in varied stages of utter insanity. These sick and sadistic characters were the mercenaries hired by the cripple. Prior to sunup that same morning, they embarked on their grim and dastardly mission.

Splitting up into two separate groups, they alternately headed for the outskirts of Santos land in one direction, and in the other to Coal's house of pines. This latter group was led by Yepper. Along with him and his men was Don Ricardo Santiago.

Precisely one hour after Coal departed for his meeting with the Don, he arrived at the Santos estate in time to see Sonia, Esmeralda, Loretta, and Estralita Santos leaving on an all-day shopping trip to Sonora. Accompanying them was an armed escort of six trusted vaqueros.

Coal waved to a laughing Esmeralda, who threw him a good-bye kiss. After scrutinizing the outriders to his personal satisfaction, he went to the corral, where many vaqueros congregated with Don Santos, viewing the new thoroughbred mounts.

From the westernmost section of Santos land, the four escorted young women exited for their trip to the city. One handsome young vaquero, who was riding inside the carriage in order to do the driving, was making big eyes at an aloof Esmeralda when suddenly she saw the top of his head disintegrate, sloshing blood over them all. The youngster had been rifle-shot between the ear and his right eye. Instantly thereafter, a fusillade of rifle fire then emptied the saddles of six horses that galloped alongside.

Shoving the dead young man out of her way, Esmeralda succeeded in turning the wagon around and homeward. But by then, home was the same distance away as Sonora. The yelling women did not see the killers when they fired from ambush, but they soon did, and gutsy Esmeralda began putting the whip to the asses of two flying horses that pulled the carriage. While the other women screamed, Esmeralda was steadily cursing and driving. To them, it appeared as though an army was in pursuit. In truth, it was nine degenerates sired by Satan.

Cursing herself for not having taken the dead youngster's pistol, Esmeralda soon had the horse team flying on air. She actually was putting daylight between them and their pursuers, when the carriage wheel twisted and broke in a hole in the road. The last thing Esmeralda remembered was hurtling through the air, then darkness.

She landed head first into a rocky ravine, wickedly striking her cranium against a huge rock. The sound of that impact was hard and wet, badly fracturing her skull. To their subsequent misfortune, Sonia and her sisters-in-law were only badly bruised and shaken up when the carriage overturned. In seconds, the mercenaries drew reins upon that scene, licking their chops.

"Hey y'all, this bitch in the ditch musta busted her head open when she landed—she's dead!" one yelled.

"Well, these pretty young fillies over here sure ain't dead, by Gawd!" another leered. "Who's gonna fuck 'em first a'fore we kill 'em?"

A tall, freckled, red-necked gunman, who appeared to be the leader, strolled to a half-conscious Sonia, who was trying to get to her feet. She vainly attempted to fight him off as he ripped the clothing from her body. After drooling at her nakedness, he lowered his grimy trousers, displaying filthy, unwashed long drawers, crusted with shit in the rear.

"This is the one I want, sho ain't wearin' no weddin' ring like them others." He laughed and viciously banged his fist against Sonia's jaw to make her submissive.

Ramming his hardness into Sonia, he yelled to his cronies then raping the wives of Antonio and Escobar.

"I'll be goddamn!! This fuckin' bitch ain't no goddamn virgin. This whore's been diddled before, fucked good 'n plenty, too!" he cursed and laughed.

Those madmen repeatedly took turns ravaging and sodomizing the young Santos women. When finally they had their fill, they methodically disemboweled, then sliced the throats of them all. And laughing, they rode away.

Chapter 20

Approximately three hours after waving goodbye to a happy Esmeralda, Coal sat perched atop the high corral fence, awaiting the arrivals of Alita and his children. Squinting against the bright sunlight, Coal spied a riderless horse in the distance. Instantly he sensed that either Santiago or Tomasino was somehow involved with that solitary horse. Those sonsabitches! he silently swore.

"Hey Hawk, I see trouble comin'."

They leaped from the fence on the run, followed by the Don and his vaqueros. "Coal!" shouted Francisco. "That is Cortez's horse! He was one of the men riding escort for my sisters!"

Both Coal and Santanna were already into their saddles. Down a rise, they raced at a flying gallop, as the others quickly mounted to follow. Not bothering to dismount and open the big gate at the outskirts of the range, Coal and Hawk drove their mounts up and over. Frantic with concern over Esmeralda, Coal tried not to think of what they might find. Not that Sonia and the others did not matter to him, but at that moment, Coal's only thoughts were of his favorite relative.

From a galloping half mile away, Coal sighted dark spots of debris from the wrecked carriage. In a cloud of dust, they skidded to a halt, and hardened men vomited upon that decimated scene of slaughter their eyes beheld.

Raped raw and mutilated were Sonia, Estralita, and Loretta Santos. Antonio immediately went berserk, having to be physically held to the ground by five vaqueros. Not only had the young women been ravaged in every hole they possessed prior to getting their throats cut from ear to ear, but the fiends had deliberately slit each one of them straight up the middle, from pussy to collarbone. Giant sand flies and ants were already feasting upon their still-warm intestines.

Santanna quickly dismounted beside his destroyed Sonia and howled like a lobo wolf. Then turning with his eyes blazing, he charged at Don Humberto. It took six strong men including Coal to hold him back. Removing himself from the chest of Santanna when others took hold, Coal raced along both sides of the road, searching for Esmeralda. Coal was seething.

"Coal, we can't find any signs of Essie!" Francisco yelled, only to be quieted by the upturned palm of Coal.

"Shhhh, Cisco," he said, slightly cocking his head to one side. Again Coal's sharp ears caught an almost inaudible sound.

With his ears leading him, Coal half-dove, half-ran into a nearby ravine, finding her.

"Essie's alive! Essie's alive! You men get the goddamn buggy into workin' shape right now! We can't put her on a horse, her head is damn-near split wide open!"

No sooner had the vaqueros gotten Antonio and Santanna under control did the Don begin to run on foot toward Tomasino land. Tracks made by the departing killers pointed in that direction.

"Cisco!" Coal hollered. "Go catch your daddy, I think he just snapped!"

Running him down, his youngest son and three vaqueros had to scuffle with him before they dragged him back. Santanna only glared at him, killing-mean. They placed him onto the wagon with Esmeralda and Coal, who held her cracked skull in his lap. On Coal's orders, vaqueros buried the corpses of the women, which had lain for hours under the scorching sun and had already begun to decompose.

"Don't shake this goddamn buggy any more than you have to," Coal cursed to the driver.

Painstakingly they made their way back to the hacienda, as Coal's thoughts dwelled on his own little family. Knowing they were under armed escort and probably inside the main house by then, he threw it from his mind. It left for a second, then came right back. They finally arrived at the main house; Doña Santos was informed of the murders, and instant wailing commenced. Seizing his mother-in-law by her shoulders, Coal shook her.

"Mamá Santos! Where's Alita and the kids? I don't see them anywhere!" His question immediately brought the wailing to an abrupt halt. She stared at him, open-mouthed.

"Alita? The chil . . . Coal!!!" she screamed. "They never came!! Oh, mother of god!"

Coal was again vaulting onto Big Black, momentarily surprised to see the Don already mounted and armed to the teeth. Coal and Santanna raced by him and away toward his house of pines. Watching them go, Don Humberto barked these orders to his vaqueros:

"Twenty-five of you men, over here! Ride into every section of Santos land and gather all of my vaqueros. All!!! Tell them to be here when I return. I must now go to my daughter and grandchildren." By then, Coal and Santanna were nowhere in sight.

At about the same time when that carnage was being implemented on the road to Sonora, Alita was home, laughing with her children and helping them dress for the ride to their grandparents. From her wide-view bedroom window, she could see the corral. What she suddenly observed there drove Alita to the window, only to quickly withdraw and nestle her little ones to her bosom, frightened. She had seen a strange gringo sneaking up behind one of her vaqueros and slicing his throat. Accompanying that man was Don Ricardo Santiago.

Without panicking, she herded her children upstairs, to where Coal had built a dummy inlet into the wall situated behind a heavy stand-up chest. There, she struggled with the chest so that she could hide her children behind it, but it would not budge. Using an ax handle, she finally managed to move it forward. From downstairs, Alita could hear the agonizing screams of her cook, his wife the maid, and their own children, followed by laughter and gunshots.

"Now children, Mommy wants you both to stay here. And you, Coalito, I mean it! Wicked men are in our house, and they wish to hurt you! Children, you must not leave this spot until your daddy comes home. You must hear him call out your names first. His voice. Autumn, mi linda, make Daddy call to you more than once so you can be absolutely positive it is he. Regardless of what you both will hear, my children, you must not make a sound. Is that clear? Coal? Alright. Autumn, little Coal, your mother loves you both with all of her heart and soul," Alita whispered, kissing them.

With strength she was unaware of possessing, Alita shoved the chest tightly into place. Then flying downstairs, instinctively steering harm away from her offspring, the protective Alita barely reached her bedroom when they found her. That brave woman showed them no fear, charging into the killers with the ax handle she still held in her hands. Whereupon they proceeded to beat her beautiful face into ugliness. Halting the attack, Don Ricardo ordered them out of Coal's bedroom and commenced with defiling Alita Coal.

After raping and beating her, Don Ricardo masturbated into her once-lovely face. When he was gone, he gave her to the other degenerates and then went on a child hunt. "Here, children," he evilly cooed, "no one's going to harm you, children. I have candy. Come out, come out, wherever you are."

They are here somewhere, thought he, as he roamed throughout the premises. *I'm going to find them and slice their little nigger throats.* "Sonofabitch!" a frustrated Don Ricardo cursed.

By this time, the mercenaries had Alita buck naked and almost out of her mind with agony. Punch-puffed to sausage size from the terrible slugging she had suffered, Alita's lips were bloodied and her left eye swollen shut. Filthy, odorous sperm was smeared the length of her body, and every major entry into her anatomy had been ravagingly and incessantly attacked with mind-breaking continuity.

"Pleease, no more," Alita pleaded, "my husband, this will kill him!! Pleeease!!! No more!! No mooooore!!!!" she begged them.

"Shut up, you nigger-lovin' bitch!" Chad Yepper cursed her, coldly breaking Alita's nose with his fist and then laughing. "Hey, Sam! Lemme see ya fuck her in the ass one more time, Sam!" He guffawed, and Sam fucked her in her ass again as Don Ricardo looked on from the bedroom doorway with a satisfied smile upon his face.

"Señor Yepper, I have changed my mind," said Ricardo. "Don't kill her now; she'll probably die anyway, from the looks of her. Leave her as she is, so that nigger of hers can see this bitch that way. Tie her arms down, so she can't kill herself before he arrives."

Reaching down, he caught Alita's nipples between his fingers and crushed them until they bled, grinning while she screamed. Then Ricardo lowered his face to only inches from hers. "I know you, bitch! You would kill yourself to avoid seeing in his eyes what I know you shall see when he finds you this way! But no, I want you to see it! I only wish I could remain here and witness the memorable occasion."

After tying her down to the bed, they all pissed on her from head to foot, and Don Ricardo deliberately shoved the ax handle as far as it would go up into her vagina, leaving her for the man named Coal.

A hard-riding, frantic Coal expected to see some signs of trouble from a distance, and when he did not, his optimism grew. It was short-lived. About fifty yards from his fence, Coal spotted one of his vaqueros with a sliced throat. "Take caution, amigo," Santanna warned from his side.

Spurring Big Black, Coal hurdled the pine fence at full tilt and was off his mount before it halted. With both six-guns drawn, Coal threw his body against the solid pine front door. Having been left slightly ajar, it offered no resistance, and he plunged in, sprawling. Straddling the doorway behind him, Santanna yelled, "Upstairs, Coal!"

Throwing caution to the winds, Coal scaled the stairs three at a time and slammed on his brakes at the entrance to his room.

"Ohhhhh," was the only sound he made, heart-shaken to his bowels.

Transfixed, with his blood ringing inside his ears, Coal stared in horror at his Lita-love. *This can't be real,* thought he. Alita Coal lay spread-eagled with more than half of the wooden ax handle shoved up her body. Slime and urine covered her face, anatomy, and their bed linen. Coal froze, paralyzed.

"C-C-Coal, p-please, cariño, d-don't l-l-look at m-me. K-kill me, darling. If y-you love m-me, Coal, mi corazón, kill m-me, please, kill me, Coal!! PLEEEEEASE!!!" Alita begged her husband for death.

"N-no Lita-love, no, sweetheart," he choked, untying the ropes that bound her. "Don't ask that of me, I cannot," Coal cried, tears of anger and pain streaming.

From down below came the thunder of oncoming hoofbeats. Dismounting and running like a man thirty years younger, Don Humberto Santos reached their bedroom and saw his flower as they had left her, before Coal could undo all of the knots. Something exploded inside the Don's chest then, and his heart stopped as his body keeled over. Falling straight down, his face crashed against the floor. When he saw what had happened to his

Alita, the benevolent old man's heart ceased to beat forever. Don Humberto Santos died instantly.

Momentarily halting what he was doing in order to catch his falling father-in-law, Coal glanced back over his shoulder and screamed from the depths of his soul. "Noooooo!!"

In the confusion of the rapidly occurring sequences, Coal had laid his six-guns upon their bed as he untied those ropes. With one of her hands then freed, Alita cocked one of Coal's pistols and pointed it at her temple. "Alita loves you forever, my husband," she said, and then shot her brains into Coal's face as he leaped to restrain her. He was in midair when his six-gun discharged with a roar.

That very instant, a dreadful metamorphosis occurred inside of Coal, leaving Arctic ice where his soul once was. His head shook this way and that. Classic Alita, who loved her Coal more than life, died twitching before his very eyes, defiled by the filth of maniacs who in the throes of their conglomerate degeneracy had sodomized and brutalized her, driving Alita Coal to suicide. Coal's face was then a truly frightening visage to see.

"H-Hawk, look at what those scurvy sonofabitchin' bastards did to my Lita!!" Coal raged.

Santanna grimaced with loathing. "Even I could not have conceived such an act."

Then, as if suddenly stung out of his initial shock, Coal bolted from his bedroom. "Children!! Babies!!" he bellowed, fear-stricken with what he knew he would find.

Streaking downstairs, Coal discovered the headless torso of their cook, father of the small family who served them. Alongside him lay his wife and children, all of whom had been mutilated in the worst ways. Their ten-year-old daughter and seven-year-old son had both been sexually assaulted prior to being shot in the back of their skulls. Coal vomited upon the kitchen floor.

Backing away and stumbling from the rear door of his home, Coal was by then beside himself with fear that his own beloved children had also fallen victim to that ghoulish, fiendish slaughter.

"Autumn!!! Coal!!!" he screamed to them. Silence.

"Damnit, Autumn! I heard my daddy!! I'm gettin' the hell out of here!"

"No you did not, Coalito, because I did not." She held on to him, with huge tears cascading down her cheeks.

"Autumn, you're making me mad now!" little Coal warned his sister, fighting to free himself from her frantic clutching. "I heard my daddy, goddamnit, and don't you tell me I didn't. Daddy!! Daddy!!!" he bellowed at the top of his little lungs, but his father was too far away to hear him.

His uncles and fifty vaqueros were then searching everywhere, except the attic. In Coal's panic, he had completely forgotten his secret hiding place he had built in the event of trouble. While racing and screaming through the stables for them, he suddenly remembered. Catapulting through his back door again, he leaped over the bodies and took to the stairs.

"Have you found them?" Santanna barked, as Coal barreled past him and the brothers standing outside his bedroom.

"No!" Coal snapped, streaking for the attic. "Coal!! Tummy!!! Babies, please answer me!! It's Daddy, goddamnit!!!"

"I told you so! Daddy!! Daddy, we're in here, behind this damn thing!" little Coal cursed.

At the sound of his son's voice, Coal's heart almost leaped from his chest. Hurling the furniture aside like nothing, Coal filled both arms with his children, kissing their faces and squeezing them until they ached from it. Then, holding them away at arm's length, he quickly examined both with his eyes before drawing them to his chest again. Chattering loudly, they hugged their father for dear life, wetting his face with their kisses.

"Oh, Daddy, we heard Mommy screaming such terrible screams!" a sobbing Autumn told him as she clung tightly, still frightened. "And she kept on screaming, Daddy! I had to wrap my arms around Coalito to keep him from going and trying to help Mommy, because Mommy said we were to wait here until you called out to us."

"They was hurtin' my momma! We gonna hurt 'em back, Daddy?" young Coal wanted to know.

From the moment Coal threw that chest of drawers away from the wall, Santanna and his brothers had viewed this scene born of tragedy. In spite of what had happened downstairs, love still reigned in the attic.

"H-Hawk, I-I don't want them . . . the children to see," Coal murmured, seemingly unable to stem the flow of hurt that then poured from his eyes.

"Say no more, Santanna shall attend to it," he said, and the brothers went to assist.

"Daddy, where's Mommy?!" Autumn inquired. "I want to see her. They hurt Mommy, Daddy, and we heard it all," she cried. Coal wanted to scream.

But he also wanted something else. Coal wanted his eyes to fall upon the animals who had wrecked his world and decimated his Lita-love.

Coal's got somethin' unreal for your asses, he silently vowed.

"Daddy! I asked you, are we gonna hurt them back?!" his son demanded.

"Yes, son," he softly replied. "That, I promise," he added, wondering why those damned tears would not stop.

"Oh, Daddy," said Autumn, "I've never seen you cry. Why, Daddy? Is it because they hurt Mommy?"

"It don't make a man a sissy 'cause he cries," Coalito informed his sister.

"I didn't say that. Daddy, please don't cry, it hurts me so," Autumn pleaded.

Those two little ones tried to comfort their father with gentle pats upon his back and the soft utterings of children, evoking an even heavier flow of tears from the man named Coal. If not for the fact that his daughter was rapidly approaching the level of hysteria, Coal just might have cried forever, for the pain was that deep. Yes, it was.

"I'm gonna go and see what they did to my momma!" declared the little fighter, heading for the doorway.

"No, son."

"I said I'm gonna . . ."

"I said no, Coal. Come away from the door like a good fella. Children, Tummy . . . Coal, son, I . . . your momma . . . your momma is dead."

"Ohhh noooo, Daddy!!!" Autumn's flesh-raising scream echoed. "Say no!! Say no, Daddy! Please!!" she sobbed. "Not my mommy, no Daddy, not my mommy!!!" she wailed, breaking Coal's heart.

He wrapped his arms tightly around his gentle girl as she clung to him, trying to get inside of her father to hide from the heart-wrenching, terrible sorrow.

Son Coal went stone silent, his large black eyes projecting something far transcending pain. Recognizing what he envisioned there, Coal pulled his lad to him so that he would not see the ugly distortion of his man-cub's features.

As Coal quietly attempted to console his children, the initial shock of seeing what had happened to his wife began to recede. In its vacancy, an ultraviolet hate storm commenced to brew, and tears no longer fell from his eyes. All of a sudden, they were clear and bone dry.

Coal's comin', and ain't nothin' in this world can save every one of your asses from Coal. You scums have killed and defiled my only, so you have also killed my compassion and my heart. As I find each one of you bastards, don't ask for no goddamn mercy.

"Mercy just died!" he heard himself say aloud.

"What, Daddy?" Autumn asked.

"Ain't nothin', Tummy, sweetheart. Coal, Tummy baby, I want both of you to wipe your eyes now. We're gonna go downstairs and then ride out to your grandmamá's and . . . and bury your mamá. Then Daddy's gonna be gone away for a spell. While I'm away, I'll be expecting you both to behave like your pretty mamá and me have taught you to do. Will you both do that for us? Fine. And always remember that your pretty mamá purely loved us all, she did. More than life."

Coal did not have the heart or desire to mention the fate of their grandfather, who they dearly loved.

"Must you leave us, Daddy?" queried his daughter.

"Yes, sweetheart, but Daddy'll be back, never fear. Won't nothin' stop that."

"I'm going with you, and help you kill those mean men who killed my momma, Daddy! You're gonna have to whip me, Daddy, to make me stay here!" stated the little man.

"Coal, son, for the first time since I helped deliver you into this world, your daddy's feelin' pure mean. You wouldn't make me light up your backside when I'm feelin' mean, would you, son?" Coal softly questioned him.

"I . . . guess not," he hesitantly replied, sighting something in his father's eyes that was totally new to him. "I guess not, but you gotta promise to kill 'em, Daddy, just like they did my mamá!"

Gazing down into his son's face, Coal remembered feeling exactly that way long ago, in a ramshackle barn when last he felt the warmth of his mother's arms. "I promise you that, my son. Daddy's gonna kill 'em as many times as he can."

"They had no right to kill my mamá!" he angrily persisted. "The no-good bastards!"

"What's that you said, Coal?" His father scowled at him.

"I said, the bastards!!" young Coal repeated, unblinkingly meeting his father's eyes.

"Then I guess you meant that, didn't you, son?" Coal conceded.

"That's right!" the six-year-old confirmed.

Reappearing in the doorway, Santanna indicated to Coal that the slaughter had at last been cleared away. Lifting Autumn into his arms, Coal handed her to Santanna. Then, carrying his son downstairs and putting him atop Big Black, Coal reentered his once-sublime house of pines for the last time. Vaqueros waited with Santanna and the children. Minutes later, flames stretched their fiery tentacles outward from the bedroom window of Coal and Alita.

Autumn screamed, and her godfather drew her to his chest, calming her. Exiting from there without a backward glance, Coal mounted his stallion. With his son between himself and the saddle horn, Coal rode away.

A short while later, a distraught Doña Santos sighted them coming from far away and went running to her grandchildren. Pulling up in front of the main house, they saw many vaqueros armed and ready. Hundreds of them. They all knew of Coal's reputation, and everyone wondered what then coursed through the brain of El Diablo Negrito.

As the children were taken inside by Raoul, a distressed but calm Luz Santos came to Coal. "My oldest son"—she touched his cheek—"when you ride for blood, miss no one. Coal, you must get them all! Most of all, get Tomasino and then bring him to me!"

"Yes, ma'am, you're entitled to the last of him," he coldly agreed, and they walked into the house.

There in her living room, where only yesterday happiness reigned supreme, Doña Luz studied the silent, heartbroken man she truly loved as her own son. Still badly shaken by the sight of an ashen and dead Don Santos, Doña Luz was smoldering with unquenched hate. In one day, death had taken away her two oldest daughters, leaving her youngest more dead than alive, and her beloved Don Humberto also gone forever.

Thank God for her sons and her grandchildren, thought she, and *thank God for Coal being there.* Her sons did not possess the cold ruthlessness which the present situation demanded. But Coal did, and Doña Luz wanted vengeance from the depths of her anguished spirit. She wanted an irrevocable peace established forevermore, and to her way of thinking, there was only one way of accomplishing her desire with certainty. Coal.

"Mamá Santos, if I'm correct about the kind of vermin who killed on us today, I may have to be away for a long time. You see, it ain't just Santiago and the cripple now, and I'll never be able to look myself in the face again until I get every last one of them. The way gittin' was meant to be," Coal chillingly informed her.

Doña Luz wrapped herself with her arms against the ice of him. "Coal, my son, your children, my grandchildren, will never suffer harm during your absence. I swear it."

"I have no doubt they will be safe with you, Mamá Santos; I know you love them. I think I'll go up and see how Essie is, then afterward, I'm gonna soak this ground for miles around in somethin' red," he quietly announced.

The doctor was still at Esmeralda's bedside when Coal silently entered. He stood off and to the side, watching and listening.

"Esmeralda, can you feel any sensation in your fingers?"

"S-sí, doctor," came her weak response.

"That is good. Your Santos skull took the greater damage while protecting your brain. I have done all that I can do," he said, and raised up. "Now you must fight to hold on to your life. Fight, Esmeralda, as you have never fought before. Coal"—the doctor addressed him—"only a very few minutes, she must preserve her strength."

Coal approached the bedside and gently took hold of her limp hand. She opened her eyes.

"H-have they b-been caught yet, C-Coal?"

"No, little Essie, but I will catch them."

"C-Coal, am I g-going to die?"

"No, Essie, not if you want to live badly enough. I want you to live."

"One o-of our s-servants t-told me w-what happened to Alita, C-Coal. W-when you have finished w-w-what you must do, c-come back, Coal. P-p-please come b-back."

"I will, Esmeralda; my children are here. This is my home. I promise," he told her, then he gently kissed her cheek and went away.

Chapter 21

Darkness found close to a thousand angry men with torches, encircling the graves of Don Humberto Luis Santos and Alita Alesandria Coal, as the piercing shrill of Doña Luz's voice filled the night. There, above the coffins of her husband and daughter, she cried out for vengeance in blood. Reminding them all that it had been he, who then lay dead at their feet, who unfailingly saw that none of his people ever suffered from need, hunger, or thirst. And en masse, she made her vaqueros swear an oath to wreak total destruction upon their hated enemies.

Later, when the hordes of mourners had drifted away from there, three sorrowful figures remained. Coal, Autumn, and little Coal.

"Lita-love," he said, just above a whisper while holding his children at his sides, "I don't want you to worry none about us, sweetheart. We'll make it somehow, but we'll miss you somethin' awful. And the children and me, we'll always love you, pretty Lita. Say goodbye to your mamá, children."

With that, Coal turned away from the gravesite of his beloved Alita. At the corral, he surprised everyone when he told them to get some sleep, making the vaqueros whisper among themselves.

"At dawn, I want every man of you here. Be here! On second thought, camp here. I also want one hundred men on guard, in a circle around the hacienda. Take turns so everyone will be well-rested come mornin'," Coal ordered, and then guided his children into the house.

He was not the least bit surprised to find Santanna almost walking on his heels. "Santanna does not believe that you are not going to make a move against them now, mi amigo, tonight!" the Hawk growled.

"That's because you know me. Get Nunio and my brothers, Hawk; we won't need the others until mornin' when we ride down on the cripple. For Ricardo, and what I have in mind for his ass, we're enough."

"Sí, patrón, sí, Coal." Santanna suddenly smiled, looking like Lucifer personified. "Ha! I knew my friend Coal would not sleep one night with this thing yet unavenged. It is good!"

On the banker's estate of the late Don Gaspar Santiago, bloodthirsty villains were laughing and enjoying the putas in their company. They bragged and joked about the events that occurred earlier, and predicted the evil they were yet to commit. Outlaws stood guard outside the main house of Santiago, away from the building and encircling it.

Stalking those men were seven unseen avengers with a blood thirst of their own. Coal's thing had always been the six-gun, but almost twelve years living with the Comanches had taught him something about knives, too. Stealthily inching forward like the panther cat of his color, Coal and the Hawk drew closer to their prey.

"There, Coal," Hawk whispered, "in front of you about thirty feet. See him?"

"Yeah, I see him."

As quiet as death, Coal covered the mouth of the man and sliced his throat from ear to ear, real easy-like. Instantly his eyes searched for another. Hawk and he found two more close together, but in the act of sneaking up on them, a twig cracked. The mercenaries stood up at the sound, only to encounter two human flying projectiles.

Leaping knife-first, they plunged those knives deep, again

and again. At that precise moment, Chadwick Yepper was just sitting his ass down in the outhouse, which was not too far away from the Santiago residence. A few seconds after his ass touched wood, he heard the gurgling sounds of a man choking on his own blood, and he immediately sprang upright, hoisting his pants up over shit and all.

Through a crack in the outhouse wall, Yepper peeped into the moonlight, sighting swiftly moving shadows. He could not tell how many they were, and he was not about to go out and investigate. Yepper froze absolutely still as they passed by him, never once thinking to look inside the outhouse where he stank. After killing all of the guards, the avengers headed for the main house.

"Where's Nunio?" Coal asked.

"The man he came upon, they killed each other, my brother," Francisco informed him.

Yepper coolly examined his predicament. If he yelled to his men inside, it would mean revealing his own position. And with as much hell as they were raising inside, chances were they wouldn't hear him, and then his ass would really be up a tree. So he waited.

The men who had just lost their wives, sisters, and father stood listening outside the main door to what was being said inside the home of Don Ricardo Santiago. "Hey, Sam! Show that bitch in your lap how you fucked that nigger-lovin' spic in her asshole this morni . . ."

Flying free from its hinges, the front door crashed in, and the man named Coal entered with a bloodied Indian knife in one hand and his six-gun in the other. "Who is Sam?!!" Coal belched flame, grabbing one man by his throat. The others froze where they were, being covered by Santanna and the Brothers Santos. "Who is Sam, you mangy sonofabitch?!"

The fellow pointed to a tall, bearded creep who was naked to the waist. Coal then shot the informer point-blank into his mouth and threw him away. Slowly he strode over to Sad Sam Bunker.

"So, my wife was a nigger-lovin' spic, huh, Sam? Well, you know what you and your gang has got on their asses now?! A cold-blooded nigger-Comanche!"

For openers, Coal kicked Sam's balls flat. Making Sad Sam scream was then Coal's only dream. He knelt down over the writhing rapist, digging his fingers in and lifting Sam by his throat.

"Sam, if you want to live, you'd better tell me who all was at my pine house today, and who did what." Coal whispered, slamming his gun butt against Sam's lips.

Sad Sam told everything on everybody. Sam even told it over again. *Anything,* he thought, *anything to get away from this crazy-eyed nigger.*

"What of the carriage, and the women in it?" Santanna roared. "Who was there?!"

"Th-th-that wasn't our bunch," sputtered Sam. "We was with the boss at that pine house. F-Fletcher was leadin' the other group," he squealed.

Having heard Coal's voice from his rear bedroom, Don Ricardo had his ass halfway out of his window when a searching Francisco found him. "Por favor, Francisco, we have known each other since before he came to this land. Don't give me to him! Kill me, but I beg of you, don't give me to him!!"

"Hey, Coal!" Francisco yelled, "look what I found!"

"Hawk, hold onto Sam here for a second," Coal said, racing to the rear of the house.

No sooner than Coal laid eyes on Ricardo than he leaped, battering him to the floor. Half-conscious, Ricardo felt his trousers being ripped away from his ass, and he screamed. When he tried to forestall what Coal was doing, Santiago was brutally kicked in his chest by a cold-eyed Francisco. Coal finished ripping his pants off of him. Then, dragging the cringing, begging Santiago into the front room, Coal halted in the middle of the floor. Going over to Sam, Coal again dug his fingers into that scrawny throat, pulling him to his feet.

"Sam, these eight fellas here, are they all of the ones who went to my house?"

"Yessuh, all exceptin' Chad Yepper, Mistuh Coal. A-a-and it was Yepper who stole that big red stallion from yore corral, too!"

"When did Yepper leave here?" Coal asked, and Sam swiveled his eyes around the room.

"H-he was here a few minutes ago," Sam informed Coal, trying to preserve his life.

"Raoul! Escobar! Search outside for his ass!"

Then, striding back to the half-naked Don Ricardo, Coal withdrew his knife from its sheath.

"Get up, snake," Coal whispered.

"No!! Oh God, no!!" Santiago blubbered, and Alita's mutilated remains flashed vividly inside Coal's head, bringing tears to his eyes.

Viciously he kicked Ricardo's mouth, sending blood and teeth splashing over everything nearby. Too groggy to maneuver or protest, Ricardo watched as Coal knelt down beside him.

"Scum! You took my wife and ravaged her; now Coal's gonna fix ya real good," he said, grinning at the mesmerized aristocrat.

Without further ado, an unfeeling Coal castrated him. Not only his balls, but the whole damn thing, Comanche-fashion, so that he wouldn't die, just bleed real bad. Seeing what Coal had just done, Sad Sam developed a fear stroke. His eyes began to roll inside their sockets, and thick, white slobber oozed from the side of his mouth.

"C'mere, Sam," Coal hissed, driving him over to the fireplace with a painful boot in his ass.

Removing a heavy iron poker from its rack, Coal laid it into the blazing fire. While it was heating, he turned and walked to the eight ghouls standing against the wall, death-slow, as if he had all the time in the world.

"Sam there"—Coal thumbed back over his shoulder—"he told me the whole story about what you crackers did to the mother of my children, my only wife. He told me how she begged you bastards for mercy, then was punched, kicked, and funned with. How you all emptied your filth all . . ."

Without warning, Coal drew his six-gun in a blur and blew away the brains of one, then another. ". . . over her!" he continued, as if nothing had happened. "Then you tied her down, like that pig over there said you did. Ya tied her down so she couldn't kill herself like she begged me to do. So she would be alive when I got home, didn't you?!"

Grabbing another by his hair, Coal looked into the man's eyes. "My Lita-love was the one woman you should've never touched," Coal told him, and then stabbed his wide-bladed Comanche-knife deep into the man's ear and twisted it around inside his head. "You should have passed her by," he softly concluded.

By then, the poker lying in the fireplace was white-hot. To test its intensity, Coal applied it to Sad Sam's thick beard. In one split second, Sam's face and head went bald-clean. Sad Sam then begged for mercy.

"Didn't you hear my wife when she begged for mercy, Sam?! Is this how you did it to her, Sam?! Hawk! Antonio! Grab ahold of this bastard for me," Coal said, and they held him face down to the floor.

Taking the white-hot poker, Coal separated Sam's ass cheeks wide, and slowly rammed that sizzling steel right up Sam's virgin asshole on into his stomach to halt inside of his chest. The sodomizer's body convulsed, went rigid, and died.

"Olé!! It is good!" Santanna declared, lifting himself from atop Sad Sam's shoulders and walking over to the remaining defilers. "You are not nice men. I think Santanna will make you sorry, no?"

With his long-bladed skinning knife, Santanna collared one of the five, driving his blade up from groin to jawbone. Then, as though previously dilled at the procedure, the Brothers Santos placed their pistols behind the ears of the last four baby fuckers and fired twice each. The half-dozen putas who then were piled into one corner of the room feared they would be next.

"Get me some barbed wire!" Coal ordered. "And get those whores the hell out of here!"

Again lifting the still-hot poker, Coal smilingly cauterized Don Ricardo's castration. Ricardo hollered for his daddy when the hot steel hissed against his groin cavity. Coal did not want him to die just then, for his was to be a slow Comanche death. Dragging him outside, Coal stuck Ricardo's head deep into the horse trough, reviving him. Afterward, every inflammable possession of Don Ricardo's was put to the torch.

As Ricardo regained consciousness, he began to beg for death, only to have Coal take the barbed wire and gift-wrap his ass into it. From eyeball to ankle, Ricardo was wrapped. His agonizing howls echoed through the mountains. Unravelling his lariat, Coal tied it to the barbed wire and mounted Big Black.

"Let's ride!"

At a trot, they departed from the inferno that was once the hacienda of clan Santiago. With his body encased in those thorn-like prongs, Ricardo screamed for death to embrace him. Coal bounced him all the way to the slender feet of Doña Luz Santos.

"Ma Santos, this is the scavenger who killed Alita. This is Santiago, who you fed at your table and treated like a son. What do you think should be done with the rest of his filthy life left in him?"

"First, por favor, one of you men revive him for me."

Water was then thrown into the face of the near-dead Don Ricardo, and he stirred, opening his bloodied, half-blind eyes. As he did so, Luz Santos, squatting in a very unladylike fashion, spat into his bleeding countenance.

"Ricardo, bastardo. I want you to know that I am praying for your soul to rot in hell! Sí,"—her voice lowered to a whisper into his face—"you, you who courted my loveliest child. You pig who would defile a happily married woman and mother. Your obvious suffering makes me rejoice!!" she cried, again spitting into his wire-sliced face.

Pieces of torn flesh hung from his body, indicating the stabs from the wire, which tore into him at every bump. Coal knew this to be one of the slowest ways on earth for a man to die.

"Coal, mi niño, I think you should ride him around some more until your mount tires!" she said, glaring.

"Yes, ma'am, that's exactly what I was thinkin'. Change mounts with me, Antonio."

Saving Big Black's stamina for the coming morning, Coal remounted and then dragged Ricardo's ass back and forth over Alita's fresh grave and then on out to the range for hours. During that grim interval, Coal occasionally heard from the man who approvingly rode at his side.

"It is good! It is good!"

Much later, Coal and Santanna returned on sweating mounts. All that remained in Don Ricardo's barbed wire coffin were the bones of his chest.

Chapter 22

Native inhabitants of any land inherently possess a grapevine of communications systems which rivals telegraphy. In the realm of tragedy, such news travels with even greater rapidity. So it was that the natives of Valley La Nevada learned of the heinous crimes perpetrated by the mercenaries. Scores of husbands and sons of those natives also worked for Don Carlos Tomasino, and they wanted no part of the hell and fury that would inevitably be his.

Many of them deserted their patrón during the night, refusing to die in defense of what they felt in their hearts was wrong in the eyes of God. Under the cover of darkness, more than two-thirds of them returned to their own homes.

The six whores, who had not been molested while the murderers of Alita were executed before their eyes, told of the terrible wrath of El Diablo Negrito. They trembled as they told their families of the sequence with the sizzling poker being shoved up the gringo's culo until it disappeared. They also spoke in hushed tones of the Brothers Santos, saying that Don Humberto's sons had all looked on without an inkling of mercy in their eyes, indicating that each son of their sainted Don was of one and the same mind.

Terrified, those putas had observed the faces of the Santos

men when the husband of Alita coldly wrapped Don Santiago into the feared barbed wire. The brothers smiled, they informed those listening in rapt attention. After listening, the people of that land settled down to await word of the demise of Don Carlos Tomasino, for with positive convictions, they knew with certainty that he was already a dead man who still sat in his wheelchair. Most assuredly, they agreed, he would not live through another day.

Not long after Coal and Santanna returned with the chest bones of Don Santiago, strong and angry men who had lived their entire lives under the benevolent rule of Don Santos made ready to avenge the deaths of their Don and his daughters. In the silence that followed dawn, Doña Santos observed her sons as they mounted, inwardly preparing herself for the possibility that even more of her beloved family would die.

"Coal, mi niño, do not forget what I have requested of you. I await your deliverance of that miserable cripple to me. I have prepared a very special death, which I have in store for him!" the matriarch declared.

While Doña Santos stood upon her veranda, Coal separated their vaqueros into three groups. His strategy was to attack the Tomasino hacienda from three different sides, killing anyone who obstructed their paths in defense of the cripple. Escobar and Raoul each led one group, while Francisco and Antonio chose to ride at the head of the third contingent led by Coal and the Hawk.

"If at all possible, no one must kill the man called Fletcher," Santanna ordered, thinking of Sonia. "He is mine, he belongs to Santanna!"

"Let's ride!" Coal commanded.

Turning their mounts into the direction of Tomasino land with the rising sun at their backs, close to a thousand men took off at a churning gallop.

Immediately after seeing them put the torch to Santiago's hacienda prior to leaving, Yepper returned atop the red stallion to watch the fire. In him was the feeling of good fortune. Now, with half of his men dead, he could keep their shares of the Tomasino money after paying off the others. His keen instinct for self-preservation was urging him to hurry and collect his cash, and then haul ass back to the States. In his maniacal mind, as he sat observing the fire, Yepper actually heard the chilling nonexistent screams of the dead men inside that burning house. Although he thoroughly enjoyed those sounds of his dementia, he realized that their deaths had subsequently deprived him of gun power.

Skirting eastward, he drove the speedy stallion hard. When he arrived at the Tomasino home, his men informed him that their mission had come off without a hitch. The one named Fletcher met Yepper coming through the doorway. Fletcher was ripped on tequila.

"Hey there, Yepp. Man, did we have a ball! Them good-pussy Mex bitches was sure a treat! Here, have a drink," he said, and offered the bottle. "Say, whar's Sam and the others?"

"Dead!!" Yepper replied, brushing Fletcher and his bottle aside. His eyes found Don Tomasino.

"What'cha mean, dead? All of 'em?"

"Every fuckin' one of 'em. That nigger dog and some spics caught 'em cold and made 'em pay. Alright, Tomasino, fork over the rest of my money. We done what'cha asked for, what we was paid to do," Yepper demanded.

"But of course. Only tell me, why are you in such haste? There still is the matter of killing El Diablo Negrito."

"It ain't our fault we didn't find the nigger at home. At least we killed his wife and kids," Yepper lied, evoking a glow in Don Carlos's eyes.

"The children, too?" He smiled. "And his precious Alita?"

"Goddamn right! When I'm paid to do a job, by God, I do it right! Now pay up! As for that nigger, you got more'n enough men to handle that. I'm sure all you Mex's kin kill one nigger," he cleverly dug at Don Carlos. "We're wanted men, and it don't pay for us to linger too long in one place," he concluded, making Fletcher eye him.

"Bueno. I shall give you your money, since you are afraid to stay," Carlos sneered.

"Cripple!" Yepper's eyes grew wild. "If you ever again even hint that I'm afraid of some nigger or anything else, I'll make ya git up out o' that wheelchair and run!! Now am I gonna git my money?" he menaced, not giving a damn about the seven vaqueros then mixed inside that enclosure with his own men.

"Here is your dinero," said Carlos, pulling the money from his desk where he sat. "Por favor, Señor Yepper, be reasonable. What you possess now is nothing. After you have paid your men, you won't have much left. I'm now offering you one thousand more, to each of your men and to you, if you stay until the black one makes his move of revenge," he tempted Yepper.

"Bullshit!" Yepper countered. "What with my share and the shares of my dead men, I'll be alright."

"Who in hell said that you kin take all their shares?" Fletcher challenged him. "It seems ta me like the rest of us should split up them shares, too!"

"Tell ya what, Fletcher. If you feel that way about it, take it! Now!" Yepper snarled, his right hand startlingly filled with instant iron. He was fast.

"Shit, Yepp, you knows I ain't nowheres as fast as you are." Fletcher backed down, and Yepper smashed him across his mouth, drawing blood.

"Then shut up, you stinkin' sonofabitch!" he cursed him. "Is there any other white man in here who's got anything to bitch to me about? Just any fuckin' thing at all?" he twanged. Not a word. "Now then, after I give you coyotes what I promised y'all, anybody who wants to kin stay, with no hard feelin's from me. I'm leavin'!"

"We're stayin'! We ain't got a lot of money like you," said Fletcher, with hate-filled eyes.

"Fair enough," Yepper readily agreed. He could move much faster and far less conspicuously, alone.

After dispensing their shares, Yepper, gunman that he was, slowly backed out of the door. Not one of them who saw him go for his six-gun on Fletcher even thought about chasing him. Those outside and unaware of what had occurred simply watched him ride north toward the Texas border.

Yepper was a maniac, that was true, but he was by no means crazy. Possessing a clever mind enhanced by keen instinct, he followed that instinct, which warned him that to linger was to die.

At that period in time, it had not been long since the Civil War in the States had ended, and Yepper just knew that no nigger was gonna ride across the American border looking for a white man to kill, even if that man was on the most wanted list of every sheriff in Texas. His live instinct did indeed save his life that morning. Coal missed his ass by two hours.

Thunder reverberated from the Earth's surface as the men of Santos came. With the blinding brightness of the new day sun at their backs, they swept down upon what remained of Don Tomasino's vaqueros. More than five hundred of them had stayed to fight, simply because they were men with a loving thirst for combat. And fight they did.

Sighting the charging Santos riders coming, and not wanting to be swept under by the sheer force of numbers, they themselves charged head on to meet the onslaught: People of Valley La Nevada were to speak of this battle far into the twentieth century.

Flashing steel glittered in the morning sun, only to be quickly dulled by the stain of man's blood. Screams, curses, gunfire, and sizzling knives intermingled and sang a choral symphony of death. Men fell upon one another, toppling from their saddles, and dead horses crushed riders beneath them as they collapsed. Close combat was the only combat.

From the window of his home, a completely horrified Carlos

Tomasino witnessed that bloody battle to the death. Nine hired gunmen also observed it and instantly regretted their foolhardiness at having remained. They now wanted to run, but there was no place to run, except through that shit outside. So they stayed.

Two hours after it commenced, the hectic battle still waged on, but odds inevitably took their toll, and they valiantly perished while protecting the cripple. Approximately half of the Santos vaqueros died along with them, but not one Tomasino rider was left alive.

Swerving high above, vultures circled in drooling anticipation. Knowing that the men inside Tomasino's house were the only ones left, Coal ordered a dismount to attend the wounded, count the dead, and send their remains back to Valley La Nevada. Those with minor wounds or none at all stayed for the finale. Counted amongst the dead was another of the Santos clan. Raoul.

Smeared with the blood of the vanquished, they remounted, and at a walk steered their horses toward the house of the cripple. With steep mountains located behind the house, the trapped mercenaries were approached from all three sides. At the sight of those bloodied warriors slowly advancing, raw fear gripped the bowels of degenerates who had killed for the mere love of killing.

"You fuckin' no-legged cripple spic bastard!" Fletcher swore. "If ya think we're gonna die for your greasy ass, by Gawd, ya got another think comin'!"

"But you men are the only ones left!" Don Carlos sweated and cringed, vividly recalling his initial encounter with El Diablo Negrito. "I'll give all of you men five times the amount I promised. Kill him, and they will not fight any further!" he yelled.

"Ya dumb som'bitch!" Fletcher hollered. "Are ya blind, too? Can't ya see what looks like a goddamn army still comin'? Fellers," he said to his men, "maybe we kin still talk our way out of this here shit. Fuck you, Mex!"

"Fool!" Don Carlos raged. "Don't you have enough sense to realize they must have made your confederates inform on all of you! They know what each of you did to their women! They will kill you all!" he tried to reason.

"Maybe, but we still might talk our way out. You're on your own, spic!"

Seventy feet away, the men of Santos halted, and Coal scanned the scene before him, yelling to the men inside.

"If one shot is fired from that house, not a livin' ass will survive! In another minute, it's gonna get pretty goddamn hot inside there. My men are on your roof right now, settin' fire to it. Come out, and bring the cripple with you!"

Inside, footsteps could be heard upon the roof.

"Amos, grab this fuckin' cripple!" Fletcher ordered.

Wishing for his legs, Don Carlos begged the mercenaries to kill him. The maniacs lifted him and his chair, and with one of them carrying a white flag, they slowly sifted outside. Carlos saw no one coming at them except Coal, and had he a gun at that moment, he would have killed himself.

Coal, Santanna, and the Brothers Santos advanced to stand in front of the burning structure.

"Unbuckle those gun belts," Coal whispered through his teeth.

"Look Mistuh, ya got us all wro . . ."

"Now!"

Panic and uncertainty prompted the talkative one to go for his gun, and before even Santanna could react, Coal blasted the killer's heart from his chest with four rapid shots from two six-guns. They did not have to be told again, as gun belts quickly fell into the dust.

The cripple's bowels broke on him, and he flung himself out of the wheelchair, groveling like something from under a rock. He began to frantically crawl back into the flaming building.

"Tony," Coal said, "get his stinkin' ass back over here. Strip!" he barked at the others.

Another of the hirelings tried to con his way out of doom, and Santanna shot daylight through his skull. Grinning, yet not grinning.

"Which one of you is Fletcher?" the Hawk bellowed. Stumbling and falling while trying to get out of their pants, six men pointed straight at Fletcher.

"Come to me, maricón," Santanna beckoned. "The Hawk has something especially for you. Coal, make these other scum watch this."

Santanna then hog-tied the freckled Fletcher and made everyone back away. Vaulting back into his saddle, he guided his stallion until it pranced next to Fletcher's head. "That young woman with no wedding band? She was the world to me, and now Santanna will take your filthy life!" He smiled.

Spurring his mount while simultaneously pulling back on the reins, Hawk made the stallion rear up on its hind legs, only to descend upon the sniveling, naked degenerate. First he aimed the pounding hooves at the body of Fletcher, breaking his bones. Then Santanna rode circles around the stomped, bleeding mess, all the while talking to him. Again he raised the animal up, and this time, he came down on Fletcher's skull, smashing it. For thirty minutes, Santanna's animal rose and fell until nothing but pulp remained. The maniacs vomited their conglomerate fears as unsmiling vaqueros staked them out with their backs to the ground, spread-eagling their naked torsos in the dust.

Far off in the distance where the earlier battle was waged, buzzards could be seen and heard fighting over the delicious flesh meat of men. More could be seen in the bright blue sky, hurrying from every direction to the breakfast call. Stretched out with their faces to the sky, the murderers of helpless women and babies laid with their arms and legs wide open.

"Cut off their balls, so the buzzards can smell the scent of their fresh blood!" Antonio ordered his riders. "Watch me, I will show you how it is done."

Bending, Antonio grabbed himself a random handful of genitals. "Pig! This is for my Estralita." He then drew his skinning knife and began to slice.

Due to the agonizing screams alarming them, the flock of buzzards momentarily took flight, only to immediately return.

"Leave them alive!" Santanna ordered. "Let them see the vultures pluck out their eyes as they lay here helpless."

The cripple was then convulsed with fear by the terrifying retribution his eyes beheld. Coal picked him up from the ground and flung him into his wheelchair. Then, with one six-gun, he commenced to pistol-whip his head until he went cross-eyed. "The greatest mistake of my life was to let you live after that first time, but I did, and from your mouth you ordered the death of my wife! You filthy pig of a man." Coal grimaced with scorn.

Holstering his six-gun, he put an arm lock on the cripple's head. "Open your goddamn mouth, you sonofabitch!"

Forcing Don Carlos's lips and teeth apart with his Comanche knife, Coal sliced out the tongue from his head.

"Olé!" Santanna applauded. "Now Coal, mi amigo, let's put him in the wagon and let him see his family home burn to the ground!"

The blazing inferno that once was his family home crackled and fumed in the sun until it fell into a smoldering heap.

"Now I'll take you to Doña Santos," Coal informed the last of the treacherous Tomasino clan. "She's got a present for you."

It was mid-afternoon when they left there amidst howling pleas from the mercenaries.

"Pleeeease! Don't leave us for them buzzards!"

"For God's sake, kill us first!"

"It ain't human that you folks kin do this to another man. Kill us, goddamnit!" they heard as they departed for home. Not even one man turned to give them a backward glance.

Doña Luz was found seated in the exact spot where they had left her. In her arms, she held a large, red vase. Her dead Raoul lay cold in the front parlor. At the foot of Sierra Madre, men could be seen digging fresh graves for the newly dead.

"Here he is, Ma Santos, the cause of it all."

"Gracias, mi niño. And now, Coal, have our men dig a hole to put this sperm-of-a-dog into it. Up to his filthy neck!" Her orders were quickly carried out.

In order to keep him upright on his useless limbs, vaqueros lowered his tongueless hide into the hole by ropes. Whereupon they filled in the space around him with dirt to hold him secure. The matriarch of clan Santos glowered as soil was poured in until it covered his shoulders, and then three native women knelt around his skull with its roving eyes, to smear thick, sweet, molasses onto it.

"Perro! Do you remember what you did to my strongest and bravest son, my Miguel? You made him lose his mind forever! Ahh," she said, smiling, "your eyes tell me that you do. It is good. And now, it is your turn, Don Carlos Tomasino, and I shall sit and watch until I see the white of your bones!" she vowed.

Bending in front of his nose, she removed the lid, and giant red ants scurried over the rim. With cold, seething deliberation, she emptied its contents onto the head of Don Carlos Tomasino.

In spite of the loss of his tongue, Don Carlos damn near talked when those ants began to march inside his cranium. And there Doña Luz remained, until the skull of Don Carlos Tomasino gleamed brightly in the night. The carnivorous ants kept right on past the ground's surface where his chin was, eating down, down, down.

Chapter 23

That night, the man named Coal rested himself and his mount. Going into the room where his children were asleep, he lifted each one and carried them into the bedroom given to him long ago. Getting in between them, Coal held them at his sides as his mind held on to that last grim vision of his dear wife. Merciful sleep finally embraced him, and Coal closed his eyes, which were filled with tears for lost Alita. The last thing he remembered prior to drifting off was the name Chad Yepper.

He awoke to find his image perched atop his chest. Usually when the lad did this particular act, there was always a smile on his handsome face. Young Coal was not smiling this morning, just staring at his father.

"Howdy, son." He smiled, and still the boy stared. "Something on your mind, Coal?"

"Yeah, Daddy."

"Want to tell me about it?"

"I just want to know, did you get the men who killed my momma?" he asked, stern of face.

"Yeh, son, all except one."

"How come?"

"He ran, son, so your dad will just have to go and find him."

"Do you know where he went, Daddy?"

"No, Coal, not exactly, but I've got a pretty good idea."

"If I was bigger, I'd get him. I'd ride his coward-ass down, and get him good."

"Coal, son, lately I've noticed you cussin' quite a bit. I want you to put a stop to it."

"I only do it when I'm angry, Daddy, like you do."

"Oh yeah? Well, there's only one catch to that, son. No one is gonna wash my mouth out with soap like I'll do to you if you don't put a halt to it. I mean that, Coal. Hell, pretty soon you'll have your sister doin' it."

"No, Daddy, she won't ever cuss like you and me. She's a lady . . . like Momma."

"Where is your sister?"

"Grandma's braiding her curls." He laughed. "Girls, ughh!"

Coal washed and dressed with little Coal observing him, mimicking his actions. Finally Coal strapped on his six-guns.

"Daddy, when will I be allowed to wear a gun on my hip?"

"When I feel you can handle one correctly."

"And you don't know when that will be, right?"

"Oh, maybe six, seven years from now or so."

"I'll be thirteen then. How old were you when you got your first gun?"

"Thirteen."

"Okay," he agreed, satisfied.

Going to his chest of drawers, Coal extracted a bundle of money and shoved it into his saddlebags. *With money, it will be much easier to catch Chad Yepper,* thought Coal. He turned to his son and raised him up to his chest.

"Little Coal, after breakfast, I'll be leaving you and Tummy for a while. Take care of yourself and behave like the little man you are, and always look after your sister. I don't know when I'll be back, but whenever I am, I want to hear good things about you, okay, son?"

"Okay, Daddy. Daddy, if something happens to you, what do I do with Autumn and myself then?"

Big Coal had to smile at the grown-up question presented with the utmost seriousness. "In that case, your Grandma, Essie, and your uncles will tell you what to do then, son, and you must obey them. But Coal, son, nothin' will keep your daddy from returning to you and your sister. C'mon now, let's eat."

The native housemaid who served breakfast was placing Coal's food in front of him when Autumn's voice stopped her.

"No, that's not the way. My mommy always gives Daddy his coffee first, and again when he is done. The food comes in between," she corrected.

"Sí, Señorita Autumn," the maid replied, warmly smiling.

That is the second time this morning, Coal recalled. *They both still speak of their Mamá as if she were still alive. Maybe it's good that they should do so, but it eats right through me. Perhaps by the time I get back, they will have accepted the fact that our Lita-love is gone.*

Finishing his breakfast, Coal left the table and stepped onto the veranda. Mounted and waiting in front of the house were the Brothers Santos and Santanna. Coal frowned and squatted in front of his children. "Little Coal, don't forget what we spoke of upstairs," he reminded, kissing him. Then he tenderly hugged a tearful Autumn, softly whispering to and kissing her face.

"My brother, we are ready when you are," Escobar announced. Coal intensely studied them.

"Escobar, am I still the oldest son?" he asked, unaware that Doña Luz then stood behind him with her grandchildren.

"Sí, mi hermano, that has long since been established."

"Then you, Antonio, Francisco, and Santanna are to remain here with Mamá Santos. Enough of us are gone as it is. Wait, Antonio, before you say anything, because I'm not in the mood to argue with anyone. I'm goin' after one man. One! All I need is me. You fellas will be needed here to protect your properties and mine. Put my herds with yours and make them one like we are.

I'm dependin' on you fellas to keep the family and my children safe. Now those faces I'm lookin' at ain't necessary. I'm much obliged that all of you wish to come along, but I'm goin' alone. See ya when I get back home."

Doña Luz moved toward Coal, and he turned. She kept her voice low so that the others on horseback could not overhear. "Coal, mi niño, they would not listen to me, for out of love, they were determined to accompany you. Gracias, Coal. Take care, and do not worry about your children. I shall pray for you. Coal, dear Coal, we love you, and we want you to come back to us," she cried, emotions distorting her delicate features.

She then wrapped her arms around him, and Coal hugged her tightly. "Vaya con Dios, mi niño," she uttered. When he kissed his children farewell, little Autumn's arms had to be pried from around his neck as she sobbed.

"Daddy must go now. I love you both more than life."

Each of his brothers then dismounted to embrace him and render their words of parting. Santanna remained in his saddle, and Coal eyed him hard.

"Amigo, if you are about to say to me what you have just stated to them, Santanna suggests that you forget it. In the first place, I am Santanna, not one of your younger brothers. In the second place, you will need Santanna, I think."

"Dammit! Hawk, I . . ."

"Patrón, do you wish to fight Santanna? If so, then we fight and get it over with, and I shall still go with you," he declared, matter-of-factly.

For a tension-filled moment, their eyes locked; then a slow grin crept into Coal's face. Springing into his saddle, he turned Big Black. "Children, mind your elders. I'll see ya. Santanna, let's ride!"

That day was crystal clear when they rode away, and every eye of the clan Santos stayed upon them until they drifted out of sight.

"Grandma," cried Autumn, "if I pray every night and day for my daddy, will God surely bring him back to us?"

"Sí, manita, God shall not let him perish. Now we go inside and pray for su padre, sí?"

"Sí, Grandmamá." She nodded.

Little Coal walked away, mumbling to himself and already missing his father. "Sí-sí-sí!" he mimicked. "I'm gonna see about my pony!" he informed them all, and raced off to the stables.

Just after the torrid sun hit mid-sky, Coal picked up the trail of Chadwick Yepper. By the spaces between the tracks of his stolen red stallion, Coal knew that Yepper was traveling fast.

"Coal, he is setting a rapid pace. I think he will be hard to catch."

"Ain't nothin'. Even ridin' my red stallion, he'll have to rest sometime. He's got a full day's start on us, Hawk, but in time, we'll shorten it. Right now, I'm content to keep on ridin' steady, savin' our mounts for when we need 'em."

Yepper did not really think that Coal would pursue him, but just in case, his idea was to put as much ground between himself and any pursuers as he possibly could. Yepper knew horse flesh and was delighted with that mountain of muscular speed he then rode upon. He was not about to run the red stallion into the ground.

At that moment, he was resting inside a cantina about seventy miles ahead of his prospective executioners. Yepper had heard about Coal's reputation, but it did not perturb him. He figured that if Coal was stupid enough to catch up with him, why, then, he would just have to kill him, that's all. His main concern lay in avoiding the law on the other side of the border. He knew places where he could hide out alone, and he had lots of money. What Yepper wanted most of all was to rid himself of that ominous feeling that still haunted him.

Coal was also thinking. Knowing from the information given to him by Sad Sam that Yepper was a wanted man, Coal figured it was only a matter of time before he got to Yepper's bad ass. His hope was that no sheriff would apprehend the bastard before he did. There were many other pitfalls, any of which could deprive Coal of his one desire, such as other gunmen, Indians, etc. The sickening thought occurred to him that he might very well find Yepper dead somewhere. *If so*, thought Coal, *then I shall raise his rotten bones from the grave and grind them to dust under my boot heels.*

Santanna and Coal did very little conversing as they rode, each man intensely observing Yepper's tracks. Occasionally they would increase their pace, only to halt intermittently. During the following days, they came upon Mexicans who had seen the gringo on the red horse, and they would point into the direction he had taken.

Coal, who years prior had ridden out of Texas into Mexico, was not the same Coal who then was returning. This Coal, although still gifted beyond words with his six-gun, was now a man of means. Older, thirty-six, and far wiser, this matured man had experienced life, love, fatherhood, and severe emotional loss, and he was a damn lot angrier from the pain inside his broken heart. He was not all that had changed.

After the Union victory in the War Between the States, Texas itself had undergone drastic changes. It was poor, hungry, and defeated. Desperate men constantly murdered one another for less than nothing. Now under Union military governing, once proud Texans rebelled with regularity, only to be harshly punished by those Yankees in power. Hundreds were hung by their necks until dead.

Many former slaves, freed by Lincoln's Emancipation Proclamation and the South's subsequent surrender, had turned outlaw to survive. Yet there were still others who chose to live amongst the Indians, who were a lot better off. While tracking Yepper, Coal saw many black men wearing sidearms. They were free, or so they thought.

He and the Hawk drew unblinking attention to themselves wherever they went. The Mex and the Nigger (as they were covertly described) were indeed the odd couple to South Texas eyes. Many scroungers and hold-up men were sorely tempted to try and relieve them of their clean apparel and fine stallions, but there was something in their style, a quiet, stoic confidence, which made dangerous men ponder the outcome of such a venture.

One evening, as they were dining at a saloon in Huntsville, Texas, they were put to the test, and word of the unholy duo rushed through Southeast Texas like a prairie brush fire. While sitting at a table where he could situate his back against the wall, Coal instantly smelled trouble when he spied three unwashed men heading toward them. He addressed Santanna in Spanish.

"Hawk, I think we're about to have some unwanted visitors."

Turning his head slightly to the right, Santanna ran his eyes over them, grinning that pure evil grin of his. "They are not so much, compadre. But in truth, I would like to eat and complete my dinner before I have to kill someone."

"Just sit easy and see what they're up to. If we have to talk to each other, keep it en Español."

"Sí, patrón."

The trio had a reputation, and it was all bad. They were takers.

"You! Nigger!" one of them spat. "A white man jes' tol' me that that thar' big black stallion outside is yorn. Now that ain't true, is it, nigger?" The saloon went tomb-still.

Coal did not even look at him or make an immediate reply; he simply kept on eating. But Santanna stopped, staring hard.

"Ah'm talkin' to ya, nigger! If'n ya don't know how ta answer me, by Gawd Ah knows how ta larn ya," he pushed.

Not seeming to watch his antagonist who spoke, Coal slowly pushed his plate away and stood up. The Hawk followed suit.

"Hawk," Coal snapped in Spanish, "if we have to pull, I'll take the two nearest to me."

In shock from hearing foreign words coming out of Coal's black face, the takers stared wide-eyed. What kind of nigger was this who didn't speak English? Stupidly they glanced from one to another. Coal eyed the leader.

"You speakin' to me?" he asked from between his teeth.

"Yore the onlyest nigger in here that Ah kin see, and that's pretty hard ta do," he cracked, laughing at his own sick humor.

"The name is Coal."

"Ah said, nigger!"

"Señor, un momento, por favor," Santanna intruded, displaying a smile he did not mean. "I do you a favor, yes? I am telling you, Señor, this man who you harass is no man to do that to. Señor, he will kill you. Queek!"

"Ah ain't asked you a goddamn thing, greaser! Ain't no nigger who ever was born kin do nothin' ta me!" he bragged aloud.

"If I have to tell you my name again, you got big trouble, mister," Coal softly warned him.

"No nigger threatens me, by Gawd!" the fool yelled, advancing to within arm's length of Coal.

Dipping his shoulder in the opposite direction, Coal wheeled, brutally backhanding the cracker across his mouth. The resounding *whack* propelled him reeling into some tables and onto his ass. Two other crackers, who did not seem to have liked what they had just witnessed, helped him up and joined the threesome. Coal raised his left palm to them.

"Don't come any further unless you want to die."

"Ain't no nigger kin hit me and live!" the fool hollered, and went for his six-gun, as his friends did likewise.

Coal and the Hawk came up with iron so fast, eyes bulged in their sockets. As one, firing from their hips, they wasted all five where they stood. When the smoke cleared away, five men laid stone dead in filthy sawdust. The curious thing about it all was that each had been killed with bullets through their hearts. Only one of them got off a shot, and it went into his own foot.

"Somebody git the sheriff or the provost marshal!" a southern voice twanged.

"Patrón, I think we should get out of here. Now," Santanna urged.

His eyes still upon the dead men, Coal did not reply, and Santanna repeated his statement.

"No, Hawk. We came here to do somethin'. If we become fugitives, we'll never catch Yepper."

The Hawk didn't like it, but he went along with Coal's decision.

Within minutes, the provost marshal appeared, a captain in the Union Army. He was accompanied by eight soldiers with their rifles at the ready. Three of the soldiers were black. The captain scrutinized each corpse, his eyes taking in the way they laid sprawled, their guns and their fatal wounds. Coal could tell from the man's eyes that he was more than a little curious. The officer questioned bystanders, and everyone appeared to have seen something different, but the opinion was that it had been a fair fight.

"The two of you did all of this, did you?" he addressed them.

"We played it the way it came," Coal replied, intensely watching him.

"I am Captain Andrew Dewey, the provost marshal. I would appreciate it if you both would follow me over to my office and sign a statement."

"Are we under any form of arrest?" Coal wanted to know.

"No, you are not. It has already been ascertained that it was a fair fight."

"Then lead on, Captain," said Coal, grabbing his saddlebags and throwing them over his left shoulder.

As they were leaving, the sheriff arrived. Upon seeing what they had just done, he, out of plain curiosity, followed the party to the provost marshal's office. "First off"—the captain smiled—"I'd like to know your names and where you both come from."

"This man is Gavilán Santanna. My name is Coal."

Captain Dewey studied him. "How come just the one name, Mr. Coal?"

"It's all the name I have to give you, Captain. We come from the Valley La Nevada in the State of Sonora, Mexico. I raise thorough-bred Morgan mounts and prime cattle there."

Coal unshouldered his saddlebags and withdrew papers verifying his stature. Now the captain was highly impressed and more than curious. He returned the documents to Coal. "It appears that what you have told me is true. But how is it that you speak as I do?"

"I was born in this country. I left here a long time ago and settled in what is now my home."

"Was ya a free man when ya left here?" The sheriff spoke for the first time.

Coal surveyed his person, instinctively disliking the man. "If you can read, all you have to do is examine those papers of mine."

"It makes no difference if you were or not, Mr. Coal. Our Army has abolished slavery and slave ownership," declared Captain Dewey. "Mr. Coal, if I'm not being too personal, what brings you back to America?"

"I'm lookin' for a rat. You might be able to help me, if you will. I think he's a wanted man here."

"If he is, Mr. Coal, I'd be more than glad to assist you. What is his name?"

"Chad Yepper."

"That one! You are not the only person looking for his hide; he's a bad one. Yepper's wanted all over the states of Texas, Kansas, Colorado, and New Mexico. Our reports on him say that he's not just an outlaw per se, but a clever, dangerous lunatic. He has committed the most sinful crimes against men, women, and children."

"What information do you have concerning his haunts, places

where he's been known to lay around in? His trail led us here to Huntsville, then we lost him a few weeks back."

"It appears that you want him pretty bad, Mr. Coal. I do intend to help you, but now you've aroused my curiosity. Mind telling me what he's done to you?" Dewey pried.

"He killed my wife, and other members of my family."

Captain Dewey sympathetically shook his head, then went behind his desk. "Here is the picture of the man you want, right?"

He did not know Coal had never seen Yepper when he handed him the photo with Yepper's name printed under it. There was also a $5,000 price on his head.

"That's the rat." Coal's voice lowered as he peered into the eyes of the photo.

"I'm sorry we don't have any of his cohorts under lock and key for you to interrogate."

"He left all of his men in Mexico, Captain. Dead. He's the only one who got away."

"Now y'all jes' lissen here!" the sheriff intervened. "Ah wants ya to understand somethin', Coal. We in America here, ain't about to put up wit' no runnin' feuds comin' out o' anotha country!"

Santanna, realizing right from the get-go that Coal did not like the man, spoke up. "Tell me, Señor Sheriff, this maricón who we search for, he is wanted, no?" The sheriff nodded.

"Then do not look upon this situation as a feud. When we catch up with this bastardo, just call me and my compadre 'bounty hunters,' " he said, grinning satanically.

"We don't take lightly ta the likes a them, either!" he sneered at Santanna.

"Perhaps you like baby killers and molesters of women a bit better, sí?" Hawk fumed. He also did not like the sheriff too much.

The lawman glared but said nothing. He didn't care for greasers any more than niggers. Sensing impending trouble, Captain Dewey resumed. "As for the information you wanted, Mr. Coal, it appears that Yepper prefers to stay away from interior habitats, frequenting mostly the border towns. It affords him a way out, in the event he has to run. He knows that most sheriffs will not pursue fugitives beyond their legal jurisdictions. But take care, Mr. Coal, the man you trail is lethal. Word is that he has challenged twenty or more men and killed them, face-up," he informed Coal, before suddenly remembering that scene of destruction across the street. "But then you're not too much worried about that, are you?"

"I'll be even less worried soon's I lay eyes on him, Captain. Thank you, sir, for your help. I thank you for me and my family. If ever you get down my way, we'd be more than glad to have you sit awhile," Coal invited.

"If ever I am, I most certainly shall," he responded sincerely.

"Hummph! Y'all best wait until ya meet up with Chad Yepper, a'fore ya go handin' out invites," said the sheriff, making the captain frown with open distaste.

Coal trained eyes on him. "Perhaps you might just see that pig shit before I do, Sheriff. If so, tell him I slept with his mother out on the trail, would you?" Coal dug at his bigotry. "Even shared her with my horse!"

"Now jes' what in hell was that suppose ta mean?"

Ignoring his query, Coal was striding toward the door when it suddenly flew open. A miniature, toothless, grizzled old man stood there, showing his gums. "By crackey! Ah know'd it was you, no sooner'n Ah heard talk 'bout them hands of yorn. Hot damn, hot damn!" the wiry little fellow cackled, approaching Coal with his left hand extended.

Coal accepted it only because there was something familiar about the Oldtimer. "Ah'm pow'ful miffed thet ya don't remember me, young'n. Don'tcha recall thet night in Stirrup when ya blowed out both a Bad Frank Stitch's lights?"

Instantly Coal broke into a wide smile, warmly gripping the gnarled hand inside both of his own, and remembering that it was this old stranger who had spoken on his behalf. "Forgive me. Of course I remember you backing me up. How are you, old man?"

"Oh, fair-to-middlin', for a man of ninety-one. Hot damn! A black cat sure as hell must a gone and shitted in my hat! Ahh, no offense thar', young'n," he apologized to an openly smiling Coal.

"No offense taken. I'd sure like to buy you a drink, Oldtimer, if you have the time. I never thanked you properly for what you did fo' me that night."

"Young'n, ya sure knows what ta say outta yore mouth. Lead on!" he cackled.

Leaving there, Coal saw both stallions exactly where they had left them. Walking back into the same saloon, they took the same table. Coal had more up his sleeve than just a social drink. He and Hawk drank beer with the Oldtimer after ordering him a fifth of bourbon.

"I hope that will partially make up for my not instantly re-membering you," smiled Coal.

"Quite aright, young'n. Ah'm old enough ta understand jes' 'bout anythin', jes' 'bout. But Ah am glad ta see yore still alive, though. Ah had a feelin' ya would be, what wit' them mercury hands of yorn." He again showed his gums. "Whar' ya been, Coal?"

Briefly Coal told him most of what had transpired over the past years. "Oldtimer, I don't know your real name," said Coal.

"Why, it's Travis, young'n. Travis Bowens. Ain't used it fer so long, almost plumb forgit it myself. Ah been answerin' ta Old-timer since Ah was sixty-five or so."

"Travis, this man with me here is my closest friend on Earth. Meet Gavilán Santanna."

"The hell you say!" He peered at Hawk, shaking his hand. "He's sho-nuff a mean-lookin' cuss, ain't he, Coal?"

"That he is, but not a better man lives. Travis, tell me some-thing. If I were to give you one hundred dollars, would you help me find a certain man?"

Travis sputtered and coughed, choking on his whisky. "Young'n, fer that much, Ah'd find Julius Caesar!"

"No, Oldtimer," Coal said and grinned, "this man is very much alive. Three months ago, he and his gang-raped and murdered my wife. I want him, somethin' bad."

"And rightly ya should. Ah'd be plumb tickled ta find'm for ya, if'n Ah kin. Thar' ain't too many people in these parts who Ah don't know, since Ah was born jes' 'bout before everybody. What's the som'bitch's name?"

"Chad Yepper."

"Jesus Christ on a tin can!" he exclaimed. "Young'n, you are huntin' a mean 'un! I heard tell of him doin' things even Lucifer would blush at. Is he supposed ta be in Texas?"

"He is. We trailed him this far, then we lost his tracks."

"From what Ah done heard here and thar', young'n, he seldom comes this far inland. He'd be more likely ta show up in Stirrup than here. Ah ain't guarantee'n nothin', but Ah knows some fellars thet might be able ta git a line on 'm."

"You do that, Oldtimer, and I'll certainly show you my appreciation," Coal promised.

"Young'n, Ah ain't nevah been one ta mix in on things like this, but Ah kin swear thet in all my years, Ah ain't nevah harmed neither woman nor child. And Ah purely hates them thet does. Coal, young'n, Ah'll search 'm out fer ya fer nothin', if ya wants."

"That won't be necessary, Travis. Tell ya what. If I find him through you, you'll never have to go prospecting again for the rest of your life."

"Thank ya kindly, young'n, but it's thet what keeps these ol' bones o' mine from fallin' apart! And thet's the truth." He laughed. "Coal, if'n Ah was ta ketch up with 'm or larns whar' he be, how does a party git in touch wit' ya?"

"Since like you said, he'd be likely to show up in Stirrup and other border towns, I suppose I'll stay in that area, around Stirrup. That way, you won't have too far to travel to reach me. Say, Oldtimer, is Lars Munsen still the blacksmith in Stirrup?"

"Ya mean yore frien' what tried ta talk ta Bad Frank Stitch a'fore ya blinded him dead, right?"

Coal was silently amazed at the old one's memory. "He's the one."

"He was, when last Ah was in town there."

"If you can't locate me immediately, leave word with him."

"Fine, young'n, thet way ya stands a better chance ketchin' up wit' thet snake."

Coal reached into his leather vest pocket. "You might need to buy some information, so here's money. If you need more, let me know. I want him, Oldtimer."

"Ya don't have ta tell me, Ah kin see it in yore eyes. Heh-heh," he cackled, "Ah gonna do my damndest ta find 'm, jes' so's Ah kin see them hands o' yorn in action one more time! It'll purely add twenty years back on ta my life."

"Oldtimer, was my friend the blacksmith in good health when last you saw him?"

"Don't see no reason why he shouldn' be, he don' carry no gun. Might be somethin' to thet, now thet Ah thinks 'bout it, heh-heh. Ya gonna look in on 'm?"

"I think I will. While I'm here, I'll have a talk with Pace Tucker, if he's still alive."

"He's thar. Too ornery ta die, Pace is. Got shot through, he did, awhile back. But them gunslingers had best find anoth'a way ta kill Pace Tucker. He's got more bullets in 'm than he's got teeth. And kilt ev'ry one of 'em thet put a bullet in 'm too, by crackey!"

"On my way to Stirrup, I'll be doin' some searching to see what I can find. Remember, Oldtimer, any word of Yepper, and you get to me as fast as you can, and I'll see that you get those added twenty years you spoke of."

"Sure will, young'n," he promised, covertly eyeing the Hawk. "Say, Coal, don't Sanny-Anny here say nothin' at all, no time?"

Coal guffawed, laughing so hard his eyes filled with water. Santanna merely stared at the gutsy little old man.

"Santanna talks with these, Señor Oldtimer." Hawk patted his six-guns, pretending to be offended. "You wish to talk with Santanna?"

"Not on yore life, young'n. Not me! Jes' makin' sure ya warn't no dummy!" he cracked.

Even Santanna was a young'n to Travis Bowens.

Chapter 24

During the next few weeks on the way to Stirrup, Coal searched Laredo, Parker's Fort, Fort Concho, El Paso, and others as he hunted for the killer of his Lita-love, but with no luck. Inwardly, it mattered little to Coal how long it took, just so long as he found Yepper alive.

Around two months later, about nine o'clock on a Friday night, they hitched their horses in front of the Munsen home.

"Coal, mi amigo, is something troubling you? You have spoken but little these past few days."

"Yeah, Hawk, there sure is, but for the life of me, I can't put it into words. For more than three days now, somethin's been eatin' at me, and I can't recognize it."

"Be patient, my friend, it will soon identify itself. Do not force it, Coal."

Striding up to the front door, Coal knocked. It was Mrs. Munsen who opened it, and for a split second, Coal experienced a moment of dread. The kind old lady clutched her bosom. "Oh my God! Lars! Lars!" she screamed.

With joyful tears streaming, she hugged her Coal, kissing his face and yelling for her husband. They could hear Lars bumbling and stumbling down the stairs.

"Lars, our Coal is back. He's come home, Lars, he's come back home," she cried.

Lars Munsen halted at the foot of the stairway, his eyes taking in the mustachioed Coal and his fearsome-looking companion. He blinked his eyes, not believing it. "Coal, Coal. Hello son, hello Coal," he whispered, managing to run the short distance with his trousers half on.

As Lars embraced him, Coal could feel the wet upon his own cheek. For a long moment, Lars just held him, and Coal understood. No sooner did Lars turn him loose, than Mrs. Munsen rushed back into the arms of her Coal.

"Oh son, we thought we'd die before ever seeing you again. My, my, but you do look fine, Coal. Fine, fine, fine! And a moustache and all!" She half-cried, half-laughed. "Coal, son, we prayed and prayed for you to come back just once more so that we could see you again. And here you are!"

Fighting to control his own emotions, Coal sported a mile-wide grin. "Words can't say how glad I am to see you both. You look just the same to me."

"Come in, come in and close the door," she urged, getting her first good gander at Hawk.

"Mr. and Mrs. Munsen, this fierce-lookin' fella here is my right arm, my compadre, and no man could be closer to me. I want you both to meet Señor Gavilán Santanna."

"Señora y Señor, it is my great pleasure to meet those who love my patrón as much as I do," said the Hawk, sweeping his sombrero across his body in a wide arc. Then taking the small hand of Benta Munsen's in his own, he bowed low and kissed it with all the Latin charm of a gay caballero. Coal blinked twice, and Lars's wife blushed red.

"The two of you, go into the sitting room and have a sit while I fix something for you to eat. Now, Coal, I don't want to hear anything to the contrary. Just sit, and I'll have it ready in a bit," she ordered.

"Darn if it ain't Coal!" Lars beamed when they were seated. "You could have knocked me over with a feather when I saw you standin' there in the doorway. Like Mother just said, son, we prayed every single night since you've been gone. Those four letters we received from you have been read a hundred times, son. What with the war and all, it's a miracle we got any at all. Coal, Mother even took a drink of hard whisky when we got word of your marriage. Bragged for a month, saying that you did take her last words of advice to you." Lars laughed, noticing a sudden hardness creep into Coal's features at the mentioning of his marriage.

Bewildered, Lars stopped talking. Mrs. Munsen reentered then, informing them that their food would soon be hot and ready. She sat close to Coal upon the couch, touching his hand.

"What's the matter, son, didn't it work out?" Lars inquired. "Your last letter was so glowing about your Alita and your children, we just took it for granted that all was well. But just from looking at you now, I can see that something's gone haywire."

Mrs. Munsen looked into his eyes. "Son, if it's not too personal, tell us, Coal?"

"Ain't nothin' I can't speak about to you two," he softly said, wanting to kill Yepper more than ever.

Coal told them about his cholera and the Comanches, his subsequent years at the monastery, and his initial meeting with Francisco and his father-in-law. "Then I met the person who filled my life all the way up to the brim. We fell in love from the very first second we saw one another. Folks, I can't begin to describe how perfect our world was then. As you already know, we got married. No bride was ever lovelier than my pretty Alita, and we thought we couldn't be happier. But we did become so.

"Sweet Autumn and my little tiger, little Coal. They really completed it for us, they put the finishing touches on our whole thing, and for the first time in my life, the sun stayed bright. I had a home built for us made of nothing but pine, and Big Black was busy making me a herd of horses second to none. Our cattle was better beef than any man could hope for. I had a family, a whole completely beautiful family, and the best wife in this world. My Alita wasn't only beautiful to see, but even more so inside. And she loved me and our children, more than life."

They observed him then, those three people who loved him. Seeing his eyes grow hard and his features distort from the raw pain inside his heart. "I-it stayed that way until about five months or so ago; then our whole world fell apart. Men from here, this den of puke . . . they came, they came and destroyed it all. Hired by an enemy of my father-in-law's and mine, they came while I was at the ranch of my in-laws. And they ravaged, tortured, and raped my Lita-love to suicide. Seeing her that way, my adopted father died on his feet. Standin' up!

"While that was happening to her, more of that same band of scum were killing by butchery three other women of my family. They must have thought my youngest sister-in-law was dead in the ditch where we found her, or she would have suffered the same fate."

The Munsens sat shocked, and the old lady wept softly.

"B-b-but didn't you go after them, Coal?" Lars stood up, his face beet red.

"Yes. We found them and killed them all, except one. Their leader. He is my reason for now being here in Texas."

Mrs. Munsen gripped his arm. "But the children, surely they did not harm your babies, too?"

"The only damn reason they didn't is because they couldn't find them. Their lovin' momma had tucked them safely away before all of them attacked her. My children heard the whole damn thing happening to their mother."

"My God! Those dirty, filthy sonsofbitches!" Lars uncharacteristically swore, startling his wife and Coal, for swearing was something he never did. "I could wrap my fingers around their throats and squeeze them to shit. And I would, too! How could anyone do what you've described to other human beings?"

"They lived long enough to deeply regret their deeds," Santanna sneered. "But how little that means, when the ones whom you love have perished."

"Poor Coal," Mrs. Munsen cried, "how you must have suffered in your heart and still be suffering even now."

"Coal, son, will you be able to find this bastard? Do you have any idea where he is now?"

"No, Lars, I don't know exactly where he is, but he's near me," Coal suddenly whispered, his eyes aglow. "Hawk, I can actually feel him," Coal revealed, making Santanna inch forward in his chair.

"Patrón, this is the feeling we spoke of outside this house?"

"Yeah, Hawk, he's close by. I know it."

"In these past years, I have learned to adhere to your hunches, amigo. You think maybe we hunt some more now?"

"No, Hawk, we'll wait for him. Being the kind of man he is inside his head, it just might rankle him to hear that a black man is huntin' for him and talkin' about his ma." Coal smiled. "If it makes him mad enough, he might come lookin' for me, I hope. Then, there is the Oldtimer. We should be hearin' somethin' from him pretty soon now."

"Come, Coal, Mr. Santanna, dinner is ready," said the lady of the house.

Just as on the day he left them, the old folks sat and watched Coal dine while they sipped coffee. Santanna could plainly see in their faces what they felt in their hearts for Coal, and it made him feel good to envision it there. In his heart, he hoped that Coal's premonition was a true one.

"Coal," Mrs. Munsen said, smiling across the table at him, wanting to get the hardness out of his face, "the children, how are they? Lars and I would surely like to hear about them."

His facial transformation was instant, as his features softened and he smiled. "They're just fine. I could sit here all night tellin' you about them, because they're the best. Autumn—we call her Tummy—is all girl, prettier than any flower. Kinda bronze-like in color, with long, curly hair, and the sweetest disposition, like a girl child was meant to be.

"Little Coal? Now he's another bundle altogether. He's not easy to handle, but aside from naturally loving him, I like what I see in him, too. He's kinda strong-willed. If he's wrong, he'll own up to it. But if he thinks he's right"—Coal grinned—"ain't no changin' his mind. That goes for me or anyone else. He looks like me, only he's kinda brown in color, with a hatful of dark hair. His grandma thinks the sun rises and sets on him. Oh, there's one small detail I forgot. My little Coal, he cusses a little bit, and it's my fault, I think. You see, he follows me everywhere on that pony of his, and I guess he hears it from his daddy." Coal grinned.

"Señora, Señor Lars, Santanna shall also tell you. I was Coal's best man at their wedding, and I'm also the godfather of them both. Autumn? Ayiee! She is more than merely pretty, she is muy linda, even more so than her lovely mother. Coal, here, shall soon have big trouble with the young caballeros, because Autumn's face shall surely drive them mad. His son, Coalito, as we call him, has the heart of el toro. You know well his father's character, sí? Then you already know Coalito, for they are the same as one. Sí, one and the same." He laughed.

"Oh, they sound delightful," Mrs. Munsen sighed. "I purely wish I could see them someday, I'd spoil them no end."

"Perhaps you both shall see them. I'd like that just fine. I'd also like to wash and get this trail dust off my hide, if I may?"

"Of course, son. Wait here, and I'll get two hot tubs ready," she said, and smiled over her shoulder. Turning, she came back and touched Coal's face.

"It does a body good, purely good, to see you alive and well. You and Mr. Santanna are to stay here for as long as you're in Texas. I don't want to even hear anything different, and that is final!" She laid down the law. Lars laughed out loud.

"Fellers, I wouldn't argue with Mother, because there's no winning with her."

"Oh, shush, Lars." She waved a hand at him. "Coal, there's an extra room upstairs for Mr. Santanna, and yours is still as it was. It'll be pure pleasure looking after both of you. I do declare, the Lord is good. He sent you back to us, for a little while, anyway, and we're as happy as can be."

"Coal, son, Mother cried for a solid week when you left before. Wondering and worrying about you being on your own for the first time in this world. There was so much water in this house, I almost had to swim upstairs and down!" Lars whooped, slapping his knee.

"This is real nice of you folks, putting us up like this. I want to thank you both," said Coal.

"Thanks be hanged!" she remarked at the foot of the stairs. "Coal, you're the only family we've got, and that's the pure truth. Now let me get upstairs."

When she had gone, the men drifted into the parlor. Lars pointed to the added six-gun. "I see you're wearing two now, Coal, like Mr. Santanna here."

"Yeah, Lars, been wearin' them for quite a while now."

"Any preference for one over the other?"

"Can't say that I honestly have. When I get them, I sorta get 'em both at the same time, you might say."

"Aiiyee caramba, does he get them! Señor Lars, he, Coal, is the only man I have ever known to be faster than Gavilán Santanna. That, my friend, is also the truth. Sí, in my country, they still do not believe his hands." Hawk grinned, slapping Coal on his back.

"Tell me, Lars, does Pace Tucker still run things around here?"

"He's still the boss and does the supervising. But Colter, the one who almost made you kill him, he does the circulating since Pace got shot in the ribs about three years ago."

"I'd best go see him later and find out what he knows about Chad Yepper."

Lars almost leaped from his chair. "He is the man you're after?"

"That's him, Lars," Coal replied, instantly on the alert.

"You were right, son, he is near."

Coal stood upright, coiled spring-tight. "Where, Lars?"

"I can't rightfully say, but he's around. He's got a bawdy girl who works in that saloon where you killed Bad Frank Stitch. And Coal, here's something everyone doesn't know. First Deputy Colter is Yepper's first cousin, and they're real chummy when he comes into town. You see, since Pace was hit in the right side, he ain't nearly as fast as he used to be. Consequently, more gun-slingers come traipsing through town now. They don't respect him anymore. But Colter, though, he seems to get along real good with all of them, because the only difference between them and himself is that badge he wears."

"I knew it!" Coal's eyes gleamed. "He is near, almost close enough to touch. Hawk, I suddenly know a way to make Yepper come to me. It won't be too difficult for me to provoke Colter into making me kill him. From what Lars just told us, I think Pace Tucker would consider it a favor if I did. Some of that money I brought along will definitely get his girl's attention. Lars, how is the military situation here?"

"There's no provost marshal here, if that's what you mean. The only soldiers who come through here are the ones on furlough from the nearby forts, Coal."

"What name does Yepper's bawdy girl go by?"

"Holly," Lars answered.

"Well, I'll be damned!" Coal smiled as the pieces began to fit into place. *Yepper*, thought Coal, *get ready. Coal's comin'*.

"Qué pasa, amigo? I see you are smiling, but I do not see why."

"The night before I left here, Holly earned a twenty-dollar gold piece from me."

Standing there in the center of Lars's living room, Coal's mind was off and racing in cadence to the hoofbeats of a fast-moving stallion. *First things first,* he cautioned himself. *Talk with Pace Tucker first, get the gist of the current situation from him.*

"Your tubs are ready now!" yelled Mrs. Munsen.

"Fine, ma'am. C'mon, Hawk, let's scrub this dirt off, then I'm gonna' set a little trap for Chad Yepper." He grimaced, the scar upon his cheek appearing brighter than usual against his skin.

I'm comin', Yepper, he silently promised as he went upstairs. *I'm comin', you scurvy motherfucker. Coal's comin', you scum, and your ass belongs to me. So Colter is your cousin, huh? Well, the blood of mine for the blood of yours, sonofabitch!"*

Coal stripped and lowered his body into the tub. Reclined in the other, Santanna observed him. Hawk knew from experience that desire, too much of it, was apt to make a man careless. But it was of no consequence, for he was there to guard Coal's back. Front, too, if necessary. He was glad that Coal had not rushed out in anger like a fool, but lingered, to calmly arrange his plan inside his head. He could see Coal's mind hard at work, and he smiled. *No, my friend Yepper, you will not continue to prey upon the helpless for very much longer. Your executioners have arrived, and you have a date with Don Satan.*

"Wonder what the kids are doing?" Coal remarked, surprising Santanna. He would have wagered that Coal's mind was anywhere except on his children.

"They have long been asleep by this time." Hawk smiled. "What brings them to your mind?"

"Thinking of Yepper brought Alita to my mind. And in my thoughts, Hawk, Alita and our kids are always together. In my thoughts," he explained.

Chapter 25

Two men, four six-guns, one black, one Mexican together, would have caused mild spasms of consternation in any era. In Texas in the year of 1866, it was provocation enough for mild coronaries.

Leaving the Munsen home, Coal and the Hawk strode upon the wooden sidewalk on their way to the sheriff's office. The few people on the street at that time all stopped in their tracks upon sight of them. Coal opened the door and walked inside. Seated at his desk under the light from a lamp, Pace Tucker was going over some papers. Looking up into the inner darkness, he did not immediately recognize Coal. When he did, he bolted up, and a real smile broke through as he stretched out his hand.

"Howdy, Coal, howdy. Ah'll be damn if it ain't Coal, same as ever."

"Howdy, Sheriff Tucker." Coal returned the smile and handshake, his eyes appraising the fact that Pace was not the same as ever. Years of gunfighting had finally extracted its toll.

The sheriff invited Coal and what he thought was that ferocious-lookin' ol' Mex to have a seat. Subsequently, Coal discoursed what he had heard of the situation there in Stirrup, and observed a man of once great pride hang his head in shame. Pace went on to explain how it had taken him more than a year to regain any respectable speed with his six-gun. He grew visibly angry when telling Coal how Colter all but ran Stirrup.

"Sheriff Tucker, would you miss Colter very much if he was to die sudden-like, say from lead-poisonin'? You see, I'm huntin' Chad Yepper, and I mean to kill him as many times as I can. I also know that he and Colter are cousins, blood cousins, so I'm gonna take back part of his family for what he took of mine. Don't worry, Sheriff, I won't do it stupid-like. I'm gonna' make him pull on me."

"Coal, you knows Ah can't uphold murder. He's got to pull on you first."

"Good enough. Where is he?"

"Coal, young'n, Ah've known ya evah since ya was a boy, so Ah'm obligated ta tell ya this. What you got in mind is one thing, but Ah seen 'm git to his iron more'n once. Colter ain't no push-over, he's faster than Ah evah was!" Pace warned.

"He's a dead man," Coal whispered. "Where is he?"

"Right where he always is, in that same saloon where ya first showed yore speed."

Abruptly wheeling on his heels, Coal headed for the saloon, with Santanna at his back.

"Hawk, I don't want you to take part in this, understand?"

"Sí, patrón, I shall watch everyone except the man you are about to kill. It is why Santanna is here."

To Coal's way of thinking, he was not merely baiting a trap. He had stumbled upon a relative of the man who had led the attack on his Lita-love. Walking through the swinging doors, they went straight to the end of the bar rail. The barkeep was the same one of years ago. "Two glasses of suds water," Coal ordered in a louder than usual voice. Most of those in attendance stared.

Searching his memory, the barkeep remembered Coal's face and where he had first seen it. Coal's eyes roved about and spotted Colter sitting at a table with two men and three whores. The deputy was laughing until he spied Coal. One of the whores was none other than plump-butt Holly, and she instantly remembered him, smiling openly. Coal then drank half of his beer and strode over to where she sat.

"Hello there, Holly. Ain't seen you since that night we spent together. Damn, but you look good, Holly, real good. Makes a man remember." He smiled, knowing what his actions would do to Colter's bigoted mind.

"Git away from this table, nigger!" Colter growled, standing.

Like a sledgehammer, Coal backhanded blood and snot from Colter's nose, sending him spinning into sawdust. "The name is Coal, cracker! Holly, would you like to have a drink with me?" Coal asked, seemingly disregarding the dazed deputy. Taking her by the arm, he guided her toward the bar.

The men at Colter's table had no idea what the hell was going on, for it had happened so fast. Holly was scared to death by then, and Santanna was ready. Coal deliberately kept his back to Colter, knowing that Santanna would warn him in time. "He is getting up, patrón," Hawk warned. Still Coal did not turn; then, "Coal!" Hawk yelled, seeing Colter going for his piece.

Spinning, Coal's right wrist flicked, and his six-gun sparked orange flame, sending three bullets through the middle of Colter's throat. With a look of utter surprise, Colter stared at Coal in disbelief, then dropped dead. Whores screamed bloody murder, but no one moved as Coal walked to Colter's body and stared down into vacant eyes.

"Too bad your low-life, scum-suckin' cousin ain't here to go to hell with ya!" Coal said to the corpse for all to hear. "But then, Chad Yepper can only kill helpless women and babies!"

Alita's puffed and bloodied face suddenly loomed in his mind, and Coal viciously kicked two dents into the dead man's skull prior to strolling away to his place at the bar.

"What are you drinking, Holly?" He wickedly smiled, wrapping his arm around her waist, knowing that news of this display would surely get back to Yepper's ears. To make sure of it, he filled his hand with her fat ass a few times.

The trap was set; now all he had to do was wait. Sheriff Tucker and two deputies came storming into the saloon. "What happened here?" he asked with a straight face, and was told what by a dozen people.

Standing over the remains, Pace scanned the lifeless face and then walked to Coal. "They say you had your back to him when he drawed, Coal. How'd ya beat him to it?"

"My left hand was still achin' from bangin' him across the mouth, so I knew I had hit 'm too hard for him to be clear-headed. The rest was easy."

"If'n it's true what they say ya said to his dead body, ya kin expect a visit real soon."

"Glad to hear you say that, Sheriff. I'll be in town until he shows up."

If Coal had only known. The two men who were seated at Colter's table both knew exactly where Yepper was then holed up. After waiting to see what the old sheriff was going to do about it, they departed.

Once outside, they made a beeline for his hideout. Yepper had to know, because they were not about to take on that black gunslinger. No, not that one, they agreed, not after seeing him pull iron the way it was supposed to be done.

"Say Bart, do ya think Yepper kin take him?" one asked the other.

"Yeah! If'n he ketches him afta' he's been on a one-month-long drunk, with more whisky and pussy under his belt than any one man kin stand! No shit, that nigger is pure lightnin' in a bottle!"

After a hard ride in the saddle, the two arrived in the small town of Benbow, Texas. Pulling up in front of the town's only pussy house, they rushed inside. The madame who ran that joint was a washed-up old bitch who answered to the handle of Fannie Crump.

"What's yore pleasures, fellers? Ah jes' got in some fresh, new poontang," Fannie grinned, revealing a mouth full of empty teeth.

"We ain't here fer none o' yore frowsy cunts. We got business with Chad! Now don't stand thar lookin' as dumb as ya is, ya ol' bitch. We knows he's here 'cause he tol' us he would be. Now haul ass on back thar and git 'm quick afore we tear up yore cathouse!"

Scurrying to the rear of the building, she disappeared. They waited, gradually growing impatient. Suddenly the door through which they had entered sprang open, and a grinning, crazy-eyed Chad Yepper stood there with his hand full of iron.

"Didn't mean to spook you fellers' nerves, but I had to be sure. Howdy Bart, Soldier, how y'all been?" he asked, his green eyes shifting swiftly from one to the other.

"We been jes' fine, Chad, but you ain't gonna be when ya hears what we got fer ya," Bart informed him.

Bart proceeded to dispense the grim details of how Colter had died and what kind of man had sent him on his way. They also described how Coal had killed his cousin while the deputy was still bringing up his muzzle to fire. The instant he mentioned Coal and his draw, Yepper's mind went to the house of pines. They supplied the final touches to their tale by relaying what Coal said while standing above the dead man, and how he damn near kicked Colter's head away from its neck. Yepper's face went chalk-white with rage.

"That black nigger sonofabitch! He's as good as dead! I'm gonna do the same thing to him that I did to his wife!" Yepper swore.

"You goin' thar today?" Soldier inquired.

"No, I'm not goin' today. If he's done found out that Colter and me is cousins, then what he did and said was just so's I would come runnin' at him like a fool jackass. But I'm gonna lay and wait for his black ass, wait until he thinks I ran off somewhere else. Then I'm gonna teach that supposed-to-be-fast nigger a lesson. What did Pace Tucker do after he saw what happened to my cousin?"

"Him and the nigger talked. We couldn't hear what they was sayin'."

"Oh yeah? Well he's a dead man, too! And Holly, what was that bitch doin'?"

Bart and Soldier threw furtive glances at each other, fearing what his reaction might be.

"Speak up, goddamnit!"

"T-that nigger feller?" Bart stuttered to the lunatic. "Well, he had Holly with him at the bar with his black hand restin' on her big ass and squeezin' it, right thar in front of God and the rest of us white folks. He seem ta know her from a while back, even hinted that he jumped up and down in her pussy before."

"That cur nigger dog! You mean no white man in the whole place challenged him?"

"Chad, ain't nobody in his right mind gonna do that! You must be crazy!" said Soldier.

The second those words left his mouth, Soldier realized he had made a fatal mistake. Cold-blooded Yepper shot Soldier point-blank in the forehead, killing him instantly.

"Now then, what was he gonna say, Bart?" Yepper asked, his glaring eyes portraying his madness.

"H-how t-te s-s-shit do I k-know?" Bart blurted out, scared to death.

"Bart," Yepper menaced, "do you think I'm crazy?"

"Now Chad, you knows that I knows you ain't n-n-nowheres near no-no crazy." Bart lied for his life, and Yepper smiled.

"That's why I always liked you, Bart, 'cause you tells the truth. Was anybody else with that nigger?"

"Now that ya askin', thar was! A tall, wiry, ol' Mex was wit 'm. Kinda looked like a eagle! He was sportin' two six-guns, too, same as the nigger."

"That makes three I gotta kill, when I pick my time to do it. Bart, tell ya what I want ya to do. I want ya should ride back to Stirrup and watch everything he does. I wanna know where he's livin' at, and where he spends his time. Do that for me, and I'll make it worth your while. Don't do it, and I'll cut off your balls, understand?"

"I get'cha loud'n clear, Chad."

"Ya know what, Bart? Just yesterday, I killed a man almost a hundred years old!" He laughed. "Four different fellers told me the old critter's been all over the territory doin' nothin' but askin' about me. Folks hereabouts called him the Oldtimer. Now if I did that to a old man, can you imagine what I'd do to you? Now git! And don't come back here without that information I want."

"I'm gittin', Chad, I'm gittin'," Bart said, and flew.

Bart Benninger took off like his ass was on fire, cursing as he rode away. "That coo-coo som'bitch! I'm gonna fix his crazy ass fer good, fer killin' my bes' friend. Poor Soldier, he didn't do nothin' ta deserve dyin'. That lousy bastard!"

Later that day, Bart reentered the town of Stirrup. He did not know where to find Coal, and he did not want to attract attention to himself by inquiring. So he decided all he had to do was hang around, and Coal would eventually show up.

Around eight, as they were leaving the Munsen home, they were engrossed in conversation. "Hawk, you think maybe the Oldtimer ran into some trouble?" Coal asked, unaware that in minutes, he would know the whereabouts of his wife's killer.

"It could well be, if he was careless. Santanna hopes not, for I like Señor Oldtimer."

"Santanna, until I get to Yepper, watch everyone from here on in. We don't know who his friends are from who ain't, and in this den of bigots, they'll defend a rat like Chad Yepper before they'd give you or me a drink of spit on the desert!" Coal scowled.

"Patrón, Santanna would not like to live in a country such as this one. I find it insane to dislike any man because of his color or because he speaks another language. It also is difficult for me to imagine you staying here for twenty-five years. I, Gavilán Santanna, would have killed them until I could kill no more!" Hawk frowned with distaste.

"Blame it on ignorance, Hawk. For eighteen years, I was ignorant. One mornin' I woke up decidin' I was not gonna be ignorant any longer, then I smoked through his chest the man who wanted to keep me ignorant," Coal recalled.

"To that, Santanna says, olé!" He laughed, and they stepped into the saloon.

Now I'll fix Chad's crazy ass fer good, thought Bart, as he saw them enter. He did not rush over to them, but waited until curious eyes stopped staring. Gradually he eased over very close to Coal and ordered a drink. Instantly remembering him as one who sat at that table with Colter, Coal was primed to blow Bart away if he so much as farted. Out of the side of his mouth, Bart whispered: "Ah has some information to sell, if'n ya wants it."

Coal's lips curled, and he turned his head slightly to Bart. "What would scum like you have to say to me?"

Santanna listened without turning their way.

"It's about Chad Yepper, but Ah can't talk to ya in here."

"Then name a place of your own choosing," Coal told him, believing it to be a trick. "But if you're up to no good, it'll be the last thing you ever do."

"Ain't no trick, Ah'll meet ya in the liv'ry stable in five minutes, alright?"

"Five it is," Coal answered from between his teeth. Bart downed his drink and left.

"Hawk, did you get all of that?"

"Sí, patrón. We shall enter it from the front and the rear, bueno?"

"You bet, let's go."

Four hands filled with six-guns cautiously entered, and they were surprised to find him alone. With their pistols aimed at both sides of his skull, they approached him. "Where is the man you left the saloon with last night?" Coal shocked Bart.

"Ya mean Soldier? Chad Yepper killed him early this mornin'."

"That is why you wish to sell me information on Yepper?"

"Sure is."

"That don't stand up too well with me," Coal sneered, slapping him hard across the face with his gun barrel. "Appears to me that you went straight to Yepper after I killed his cousin."

"Alright! Alright! Ah did!" Bart screamed in fright. "But then Ah thought he was my friend."

Again Coal pistol-slapped him, opening his cheek to the bone. He found informers to be a despicable lot, and he wasn't about to give him one thin dime. "I'll tell ya what I'm gonna give you in return for Yepper's whereabouts. Your life, which I'm about to take right now."

"No! Look, Mistuh, ya don't have ta give me not one damn thing! Ah'll tell ya fer free! Only don't kill me."

"I wouldn't take your word for shit!" Coal collared him. "You're tellin' me nothin', pig, you're gonna take me to him."

"Ohh no, please no, Mistuh! Chad's a ravin' maniac! Ya shoulda seen the way he murdered Soldier fer nothin'! Why he even tol' me how he jes' kilt a ol' man yesterday fer doin' nothin' but askin' about him. Please Mistuh, don't make me go back thar'!"

"Go there, or die here," Santanna promised.

"Wait, Santanna! Which old man, pig? What did he look like?"

"Ah don't know, Mistuh. Ah think they called him the Old-timer."

Coal went numb with guilt, and Santanna spat out a wicked flow of Spanish cursing.

"Where is he?" Coal whispered.

"He's holed up in a ho house in Benbow, 'bout twenty miles from here."

"C'mon scum, which whorehouse?"

"Which? Thar ain't but one. Why the whole damn town ain't much bigger'n one o' them holes they sellin' in the ho house!" Bart cracked.

"You're gonna show us, if you want to live. Get our horses, Hawk."

While Coal stood guarding the informer, his pulsebeat raced.

Coal's comin', you bastard. I've finally got your scent, and I'm comin' for your ass.

"I'm comin', Yepper!" he yelled.

Bart looked at Coal and silently cursed himself for not having done what Yepper ordered him to do. *Two goddamn maniacs in one day.* He trembled.

Lars came back with Santanna and the horses, excitement spanning his face. "Coal, Mr. Santanna told me, and I want you to take me with you."

"Can't do that, Lars. Won't do it, is what I really mean. You're no gunman, friend Lars," he said, seeing dejection replace what was on his face.

"I suppose I understand, Coal son. But you get him for me and Mother, too, get him good and proper!"

"I will, Lars, or I'll die tryin'. Lars, I can't really talk much right now, because I'm in a hurry. If I catch Yepper, I may not be back this way. But if I send some of our vaqueros for you and Mrs. Munsen, will you both come down to live out your lives with me and my family?"

"Yes Coal, son, we'd come straight to you."

"Adios then, friend Lars, and thanks for everything. Gotta move. Santanna, let's ride!"

Chapter 26

And ride they did, making dust clouds all the way to Benbow, Texas. One hour before dawn, they sighted the tiny community. Instinct warned Coal not to ride through the main street. Silently observing the distant shadows of Benbow, Coal made a plan.

"Which house is it?"

"The fourth one on the left," Bart answered.

"Is that cathouse open all night?"

"It, and everything in it," Bart half-joked.

"Pig, you're goin' in there."

Trembling, Bart began to protest. Coal only stared at him, and whatever Bart detected in those eyes made him change his mind.

"I want you to go in there and tell him that I found out from Holly where he is. Tell him that you raced here ahead of me to let him know that I'm on my way. Think you can handle that?" Bart nodded his sweating head.

"You'd better. Now if you tell him exactly what I just said, he's gonna want to get out in a hurry. When he does, he'll run into me, and then I'll take care of the rest of it. Now move!"

They rode closely behind Bart, making as little noise as possible. Questioned by Coal the previous night, Holly emphatically insisted she did not know where Yepper was. Santanna spotted the red stallion hitched outside the whorehouse and his heart swelled. "Patrón, there is your horse he stole," Hawk said, grinning.

Coal nodded, his features set in rock. When they saw Bart enter the whorehouse, Santanna raced around to the back door, and Coal stood by the adjacent building with his back against the wall.

Fannie Crump aroused Yepper from sleep. Suspiciously eyeing Bart, Yepper noticed the fresh lacerations on his face. "What brings you back so soon, Bart?"

Profusely sweating, Bart wiped his brow. "Ah come ta warn ya, Yepper, 'cause we's friends. That nigger and his friend found out from Holly where you be, and they's on the way here now!"

Yepper smiled as though secretly amused. "They found out from Holly, you say?" he asked, slowly lifting his six-gun from its holster. "Now I would say that was kinda damn strange, Bart."

"Ain't nothin' strange about it, Chad. Ah come ta warn ya!"

"Bullshit you did! 'Cause Holly ain't got no fuckin' idea where I'm at, you sonofabitch!"

"But Chad, Ah seen'm comin' fer ya!" Bart raised his right hand." Ah swear!"

"If ya did, it's 'cause ya was ridin' with 'em!" Yepper snarled, pointing his pistol at Bart's head. Sobbing, Bart sank to his knees.

"They're outside, right here, ain't they, Bart? Ya got just one second to tell me."

"Oh, sweet Jesus God!" Bart cried, pissing himself in fright. "Yeah, Chad," he confessed, "they made me bring 'em!"

Chadwick Yepper promptly shot off half of Bart's head and hat. Hearing those two shots, both men guessed what must have happened. "Hawk!" Coal yelled. "Don't go inside! No tellin' where he's at in there. I'll get his ass out pretty goddamn quick!"

Kicking open the front door of the building he stood against, Coal found just what he needed. A lantern. Igniting it while frightened occupants looked on, Coal stepped back outside and heaved it against the sun-dried whorehouse. Almost instantly, a crackling blaze was underway.

Peeping down from an upstairs window, Yepper spied Coal and pegged a shot at him. When the bullet whizzed past his face, Coal replied with two quick shots of his own, sending splinters flying from where Yepper's head had been only a split second before. Coal then darted across the street for a better shooting angle, but Yepper was nowhere in sight.

"Hawk! Can you see him anywhere?"

"Not yet, amigo, but Satan's feathers will soon bring him to us!" The Hawk laughed aloud.

Still in their nightcaps, town citizens squinted with sleep-filled eyes from bedroom windows. Naked, scared, and hollering like hell, whores with half-singed asses came fleeing out of that instant inferno, and mammoth Fannie Crump was seen hurling her huge smoking ass into a convenient horse trough.

Yepper emerged with his left arm locked around the neck of a naked whore, whom he held in front of himself as a shield. Sighting Coal, he immediately fired, but the struggling girl caused him to miss, and Coal did not return fire because of that young whore. Hearing Yepper's shot, Santanna came sprinting and firing, instantly killing the whore, who then slumped inside Yepper's armlock. Cursing, he dropped her, and as she was falling, Coal unleashed a barrage from both barrels into Yepper's shins, knocking his legs from under him.

He raised his arm to fire back, and a fusillade from the Hawk blew three of Yepper's gun fingers and pistol away. The wanton killer's eyes then glowed from the madness within. A trio of Coal, Santanna, and Death went to stand over the maniac with his shattered hand and legs. Knowing he was about to die, Yepper sought to hasten it.

"Yeah, you nigger sonofabitch! Yeah, I fucked that good pussy spic bitch of yours, and she loved it!" he screeched. "We all fucked her! In her ass, mouth, everywhere! And I was the one who broke her pretty face with these hands!"

Coal still did not fire again. Instead he put his six-guns away. It, this death he had stored away for the killer of his Lita-love, was not to come easy to Yepper. Standing directly in front of him, Coal kicked Yepper's nose flat, making him bleed.

"Santanna," he whispered, "find me an axe."

"Sí, amigo." Hawk grinned, racing off to find one.

The sun slowly began to peek over the rim of an eastern hill, bathing that curdling death scene in its wondrous light. Coal of the one name, with the blood of his ancestors pulsatingly screaming through his veins and spurring his imagination, mercilessly awaited Santanna's return with an axe. Thus commenced one of the West's most classical displays of overkill.

Clutching Yepper by his throat, Coal dragged him away from the heat of that sizzling whorehouse. Chadwick Yepper screamed when the same area of his brain began to paint a picture of what he thought was coming. He cringed, begged, and shit on himself, yelling like a bitch.

"Is that the way my wife screamed while you drove her insane with pain? Is it!"

Removing his Comanche knife from its sheath, Coal sliced the shirt off him and squatted on Yepper's chest. Then with that razor-sharp blade he proceeded to peel away the skin from Yepper's skull. Call it scalping. Yepper writhed in agony, but Coal had one handful of his hair and was kneeling on his arms. Not wanting to kill him right away, Coal left a half-hanging scalp and stood up.

"You slimy motherfucker," Coal cursed him. "I'm gonna kill ya a thousand times!"

Townfolk now blotted the street, transfixed by wholesome mayhem. Santanna came running with the axe. After handing it to Coal, Santanna turned to face and address that town's citizenry.

"This is a private affair! I will gladly kill the first man or beast that moves! Coal, mi amigo, you now have the axe. Take your time, and do with it as you will!" he calmly stated.

Retracing his steps, Coal stood above Yepper. "Which hand was it that you used to smash my Alita's face?" Coal grinned down at him.

Half-conscious, Yepper felt Coal step heavily upon his right wrist. Coal then raised the sharp axe and hacked off that same arm at the elbow. Picking up the severed, twitching limb, he heaved it into the flaming debris of the whorehouse. Walking away, he returned with a torch. Upon every bleeding point on Yepper's anatomy, Coal applied that torch, thereby cauterizing the flow of blood and prolonging life.

For approximately thirty minutes thereafter, Coal waited while squatting Comanche-fashion atop Yepper's chest and staring into his unconscious face, waiting for him to regain consciousness. Yepper began to stir, and his eyes opened.

"You're gonna remember that old man who you killed yesterday as you die, scum. Him and every woman and baby-child you ever destroyed!"

Then, very slowly, Coal began to knife-peel the skin away from Yepper's hairy chest. Assembled in horrified silence, the crowd could actually hear Yepper's skin ripping off, as the man named Coal Indian-stripped the hide away from his wife's killer. Bare.

When Yepper was one piss away from death, Coal beckoned to a man who was watching with his eyes bulging, telling him to gather the three stallions. When that was done, Coal removed his lariat from the saddle. After slicing it in half, he tied the long strands of rope around Yepper's knees, blood-stopping tight. Then straddling the almost-dead Yepper, Coal howled from the depths of his heartfelt agony: "ALITAAAA!!!"

For minutes afterward, he simply stood staring down at Yepper. Then abruptly he turned and began tying the ropes. One to

Don Raphael's saddle horn, and the other to his own. When that was completed, he mounted Big Black.

"Santanna"—Coal pointed—"I want you to ride that way, as slowly as you can. I will go in the opposite direction." The scar upon his cheek then glowed like a flesh-pink streak against Coal's jet-black skin.

Repulsed by the scent of human blood, the stallions reacted, trying to bolt away. Strong hands held them to a slow walk.

"Yepper!" Coal yelled back over his shoulder, "Die now! You low-life sonofabitch!"

Moving east and west, they very, very slowly split the sniveling degenerate straight up the middle, spilling his guts out into the street. After splitting Yepper in two, Coal galloped back to Santanna with the half-body bouncing behind him. "Hawk, let's ride!"

Swiftly skipping for the Mexican border, they dragged those pieces of things in their wake until nothing remained in the ropes. Just nothing at all.

Chapter 27

Doña Luz Madiera Santos, her three sons, and Esmeralda sat upon their veranda, quietly talking about Coal and Santanna. In the matriarch's lap, she held a sleeping Autumn. Thirty feet away and sitting alone on the veranda railing perched little Coal, his large black eyes cast way off into the direction his father had ridden almost eight months prior.

"They should have returned by now," Antonio said, and frowned. "I am beginning to worry."

"They shall soon return, never fear," said Doña Luz. "Coal and Santanna together, more than assures me of this."

"Sí, Mamacita." Esmeralda smiled. "Coal is coming at this very moment; he is on his way home. I can feel it. Here." She touched under her left breast. "Coal is alive, for I would know it, were he not."

"Essie," Escobar quietly called to her, "does Coal know of your love for him?"

"I think he does. He merely has never acknowledged it. l have been in love with Coal since that first day up in Miguel's bedroom, when he lifted me up and held me in his arms. I was every bit of twelve years old. That next morning, when we all went riding and he sat me in front of him atop Big Black, I knew I had fallen in love forever. On our way home that evening, I remember leaning my head backwards and smiling up at him—'Coal, I love you, and shall love you always.'"

"But Essie," Escobar went on, "those words were only the endearments of a mere child!"

"That is what you think, mi hermano." She smiled again.

Doña Luz was pondering over the morality aspect of Coal and Esmeralda. "Esmeralda, my baby, tell me this. What did Coal then reply to your declaration of love, do you remember?"

"Oh sí, Mamacita, exactly!" She sparkled. "I can still hear the gentleness that his voice held. He said: 'As I love you, too, little sister,'" she disclosed, and Doña Luz smiled. "Mamá, never did either Coal or me commit an adulterous act in the eyes of God. I swear it."

"You need not have said that, my child, for I know you and also the purest of loves which Coal held and still holds for our beloved Alita."

"Then Mamá, it is not wrong that I should love him so?"

"No, my child. Coal is ours, as we are his."

Esmeralda's eyes then scanned those of each of her brothers. "Sí, Escobar, Tony, Cisco?"

"Sí, little sister," they chorused, smiling.

Weeks later and only miles away from reentering Santos land, Coal and Santanna were having morning coffee on the trail. "Hawk, we haven't spoken too much about that Yepper thing since puttin' an end to his stinkin' ass, but I want you to know that I'm forever grateful. That's from the heart, Hawk."

"Es nada, Coal, mi amigo. You are the only man in my life who I have known a complete harmony of character with. We have faced death together, and we have survived together. Within my spirit, Coal, I am grateful for having lived long enough to know you."

"Now damn, if that wasn't a helluva nice thing to say, Hawk!"

"It is the truth, friend Coal."

Without further ado, they broke camp and anxiously departed

for the Valley La Nevada. "Coal, I can smell home on the wind, can't you?"

"Yeah!" Coal grinned. "I thought it was only my imagination, but it can't be, not if you smell it, too."

"Patrón," said the Hawk, suddenly reining his mount to a halt. "I have known this to be since the first night I sat along with you and the family at dinner. And now Santanna shall see what you have to say on the matter."

Coal threw a quick glance at him. "On what matter, Hawk?"

"Esmeralda."

"What about her?"

"She has loved you from the moment you came into the lives of family Santos. Is it not true?"

"It's true."

"Then what are you going to do about it? Santanna is certain that if she has survived her head injury, she awaits your return at this moment."

Had it been anyone else, Coal believed he would have been greatly annoyed with this personal questioning.

"Hawk, I'm not of a mind to think too deep on that subject, and I'll tell you why. I suppose in time, Esmeralda and me will hook up. But right now, Santanna, me and Alita are still as close as we ever were. In my mind, I know that she's gone and never comin' back. But in my very soul, Hawk, Alita hasn't moved one bit. Everywhere we've traveled, you and me, Alita has been right there with me. Just like from the very first."

"I am not surprised by your reply, amigo; it is the man I know you to be." Hawk nodded.

"Santanna, don't get me wrong. I'm not goin' to mourn and brood over the loss of Lita, but I am gonna let her remain inside me where she is for as long as she does. Because, I want it that way. Can you understand that, Hawk?"

"Sí, amigo, Santanna can understand anything a man wishes

for himself, but now you have more than Coal to consider," he wisely reasoned.

"I get your meanin', Hawk, and you're right. If Essie has survived, she will understand."

"And if she has not survived?"

The mere thought gave Coal a body chill. It also rendered him another perspective. If just the thought of her dead held that much meaning to him, then if he found her alive, it was no more than their fate that he should fulfill the life he found waiting for him.

"She's alive, Hawk. If she were not, I believe I would somehow know it. Hey, Hawk, there lays our boundary line. We're home! Damned if this early mornin' sun don't make a man's insides feel good."

"Ahh yes, to feel and know that one has accomplished what one has set out to do, makes everything in a man feel good." Santanna laughed.

"Let's get a move on, Hawk!" yelled a grinning Coal.

Spurring their mounts into a full gallop, they covered the distance in between. Nearing the gravesite of his Lita-love, Coal drew reins. "You go on ahead, Hawk, I'll be along shortly," he quietly said.

Santanna nodded his understanding and kept straight on to the main house. Francisco was first to see him coming, but when he did not see Coal, it brought on a feeling of dread. Searching the eyes of Santanna, he soon realized that his fears were unwarranted.

"Wipe away the sadness from your eyes, Cisco, he has only stopped at the grave of your sister. Has there been peace here, is everyone well?"

"Sí, Santanna, but each day and night, the conversation has been the same—you and Coal."

Coal of the one name removed his hat and held it in front of him, his eyes upon the grave of his beloved. Fresh flowers put there by someone waved in a gentle breeze. The pain no longer ripped and gouged at him, but it was definitely still kicking his ass. For many minutes, he stood staring down in silence.

"Lita-love, I sent Yepper to Hell, so you won't have to worry none about seein' him again. I mean to remain here for the rest of my life, sweetheart, so rest easy. I'm nearby, near you. I don't know what life has in store for me and our little family. But I'll try and make it a happy one for them . . . and for me. I love you still, more than life. See ya, Lita-love."

Coal did not linger after that. Full of life and yearning to see his children and Esmeralda, Coal leaped back into his saddle. Urging Big Black on, he sped toward the house of Santos.

Ecstatic with pure joy, a tearful, happy Autumn came running to meet him with little Coal racing ahead of her. Jumping from the saddle, Coal swept his laughing son up into his arms and held on until Autumn smothered him. Crying, too, Coal kissed their faces again and again.

"Oh, Daddy, we were so worried," Autumn scolded. "We thought something happened to you, because you were gone so long."

"Well, there is no need to worry any further, Tummy sweetheart. Daddy's home to stay."

"They were worried, Daddy, not me," voiced young Coal. Then, "Did you get that bad man, Daddy?"

"Yes, son. Daddy got him good and proper. How's your Aunt Essie and your grandmamá and the others?"

"There she comes, Daddy, can't you see her running?" a bubbling Autumn cried.

"I knew my Daddy would get his no-good ass!" Coalito cursed.

His father glared fiercely at him, and then Coal suddenly roared with unbridled laughter, swinging his arms open wide for the onrushing, laughing Esmeralda.

Visit our website at
KensingtonBooks.com
to sign up for our newsletters, read
more from your favorite authors, see
books by series, view reading group
guides, and more!

Become a Part of Our
Between the Chapters Book Club
Community and Join the Conversation